LEGENDS OF BREENA

Guardians
of the
Queen

Ed,
Thank you and I hope
you enjoy it!
Best Wishes,

M. K. Anthony signature

M. K. Anthony

ISBN 978-1-64191-644-8 (paperback)
ISBN 978-1-64191-646-2 (hardcover)
ISBN 978-1-64191-645-5 (digital)

Christian Faith Publishing, Inc.
832 Park Avenue
Meadville, PA 16335
www.christianfaithpublishing.com

Printed in the United States of America

To my husband, TJ, for always encouraging
me to continue and to follow my dreams.
You helped make this book possible.

Prologue

A person can go through life and never understand the true meaning of it. At least not until they leave this world and face our Maker. I used to be one of those people. I lived my life the only way I knew how, and that was by fighting my way through, always feeling like I had to prove to others that I was strong enough.

Being raised with four older brothers, I learned to defend myself. Crying was never an option in our household, at least when it came to dealing with my brothers anyway. It was not until just recently that new emotion took hold of my life. That's what a great love could do to a woman, especially when that love is abruptly torn from her heart. God gives us trials throughout our lives to see if we handle them properly. We may never understand Him, so all we can do is live our lives to the best of our abilities.

A man has entered my world recently, turning everything I know in life upside down. At first, I despised the man and everything he represented, but I did learn to gradually accept him. Well, not entirely; the man knows exactly how to get under my skin. But he does, nonetheless, become an ally, a friend…well, sort of.

My name is Leelah Bayard, and this is my story of how I became aware of the powers I possess and the destiny that I had to follow.

Chapter 1

The Meeting of the Royal Guard

A soft knock came from my chamber door. With despair, I clamped my eyes shut, praying that the woman on the other side would leave. I knew she would not, and the latch from my unlocked door clicked. My eyes stayed tightly shut as the door quietly opened.

"Lee, wake up!" Mira screeched, and I listened as she stumped across the room. "You have overslept." She threw back the heavy burgundy curtains so that the intense morning sun filled the room. I moaned and dragged the blanket over my head. "Are you feeling all right, Leelah? This is not like you. You are usually awake at the crack of dawn."

"I am fine, Mira," I mumbled into my pillow. "Just did not sleep well last night." Mira remained quiet for a moment. She knew what weighed heavily on my mind, but she would not talk about it knowing that it might upset me.

"Well, I am sorry to hear that, but you have to get up. You have a busy morning." As she said that, she yanked the blankets off me, ruining my warm cocoon I made for myself. Once the cool air hit my skin, it sent a jolt of energy through me. The fire was only glowing embers now. That's one thing I discovered since moving here to the castle; once the fire in your chamber goes out, it cools down fairly quickly. I was sure the aggressive storm last night did not help matters.

"I have overslept this one time and you cannot give me any mercy?" I glared at her while tying on my robe.

Smiling, she simply replied, "Nope."

After dressing for the day, I sat at my vanity so Mira could do my hair. She wore her dark brunette hair in a tight bun at the base of her neck like always. Also, as usual, she wore her normal gray-and-white uniform that all the servants have to wear. She was my personal maid, but I saw her more as my best friend. Mira and I talked about everything from politics to handsome men we might have seen. There was something different about her though. It was like she was literally glowing, and the smile on her face never faded away. I was just about to inquire why she was so bubbly, but then she beat me to it.

"Kaidan asked me if I would have dinner with him tonight."

"I beg your pardon?" I yelled, snapping my head back to look at her. "He finally asked you?"

Mira brought her hands to her mouth and nodded. She looked like she was about to burst. Kaidan Kimball! He was King Bryce's main guard just as I was Queen Rosa's guard. No one knew that about me though. Only the king, the queen, the royal guard, and a handful of the servants knew of my true purpose here. Everyone else thought I was just the queen's lady.

"I am so nervous! What if he figures out that he really does not like me?" she asked nervously as she turned my head so she could finish up with my hair.

"What do you mean? The man is wild about you!" I started to jump around in my chair in excitement. She wrapped her arms around my shoulders and pressed her cheek to mine. We just stared at each other through the looking glass for a moment. She was the closest thing I had ever had to a sister. We could almost pass as siblings; we were the same height and had the same exact hair color. Finally, I stated, "It is about time anyway! I have been sending him hints practically every day!"

Mira straightened and smacked me on the arm. "You did not… did you?"

I laughed at her dumbfounding look. "Most definitely! It seems like it worked too. I am so happy for you, Mira." If I was not meant to have happiness, at least Mira should. We were interrupted when a knock came from my door.

"Just a moment," Mira called.

She pulled the two braids she had done away from my face and tied them together with a velvet ribbon. Mira took the brush to the rest of my hair to flatten it down some. She stood behind and examined me through the mirror. Mira flicked some hair over my shoulder and turned for the door.

She bowed gracefully and opened the door wider, "Good morning, Your Grace!"

"Good morning, Mira," replied the queen.

She was stunningly beautiful. Her light-strawberry hair was twisted up like always with a plain gold band on her head. Today, she wore an elegant aqua dress that just flowed straight down and long sleeves that belled out at the elbows. She walked in and sat on the corner of my bed like she was just my friend and not the queen of Altecia. Still looking downward, Mira came over to me, "I am finished with your hair, so I will leave you two alone." She leaned down and gave me another hug across the shoulders. "I will come back and clean later."

"Thank you, and have an enjoyable time tonight if I do not see you before then. You deserve it!" I smiled.

"I will," she said softly smiling and curtsied before the queen one last time before walking out.

I turned in my seat and faced the queen. "Good morning, Rosa."

When we were in private, she preferred that I call her by her first name. One of Rosa's greatest attributes was no matter who you were, once you met her, you were instantly comfortable with her presence. She would have a conversation with you like you had known each other for years.

"Good morning, Lee." She gestured toward the door. "May I ask what that was all about?"

"Kaidan finally asked Mira to have dinner with him."

Rosa brought her hands together to her chest. "Oh, how wonderful!" she chimed. "It's about time too!"

I threw my head back laughing. "I said the same thing!"

She patted the bed with her hand, signaling me to come and sit by her, which I did with no questions asked. "I need to tell you something because, well, I am too thrilled and have to tell someone." She was almost bursting at the seams now. What is it with everyone this morning? "But you have to promise that you will not tell a single soul!"

Now, I was really eager to know. "I promise." Quickly, I positioned myself on the bed so I was facing her directly. "What is it that got you so excited?"

She seized my hands and took in a deep breath. Her eyes were sparkling with excitement, and I noticed they matched the aqua of her dress perfectly. "I think I may be pregnant."

"Rosa, that's great!" I literally screamed with excitement as I jumped and enveloped her in a hug, "How's Bryce?"

She let out an angelic laugh at my reaction, "He's ecstatic! We told each other that we could each tell one person for now until we know for certain. I think he's telling Kaidan as we speak."

I pulled back and gave her the brightest smile that I could possibly give. "I'm so happy for you both. The two of you have been trying for so long now. What a joyous time!" Last year, she came to terms with being unable to get pregnant and lost all hope at ever being a mother. She always feared that Bryce would turn to other means to sire an heir.

"God has finally blessed us," Rosa said as she wiped the tears of joy from her cheeks. "Please keep us in your prayers that everything will go smoothly."

"Oh, I definitely will, my friend," I said, grinning as I took hold of her hand again.

This was going to be a wonderful day! I had not even left my room yet, and I knew of two joyous things. Yes, today was going to be a magnificent day! I was so deep in thought when someone hammered on my door it made me jump.

"Lee, are you in there?" Kaidan shouted from the other side.

Rolling my eyes, "Yes! Come on in," I announced with annoyance.

Since I arrived here three years ago, Kaidan had been like a brother to me. I could love him one minute and be furious at him the next. He walked in, and once he saw Rosa, his entire face lit up. He shut the door behind him. "I just talked to, Bryce. Congratulations!" he spoke in a hushed tone. Rosa stood up, walked over to him, and laid her hand on his cheek.

"Thank you, Kaidan. And congratulations to you too!" He gave her an odd look. Having no clue by what she meant, Rosa continued, "I heard about Mira, it's about time!" As she patted his cheek she looked back at me and winked, "All right you two, have fun meeting the new recruits. I heard there are a few dozens of them." I moaned as she slipped out the door. I looked at Kaidan, and his cheeks were still rosy from what the queen had said. Bouncing up, I quickly wrapped my arms around his neck, causing him to stumble back a step.

He started laughing. "What's this for?" Kaidan instinctively wrapped his arms around my lower back.

"I do not know, maybe for Mira and the baby," I replied joyfully as he gave me a tight squeeze.

"Well, are you ready?" he asked, pulling his face back so he could look at me. "I went to the kitchen earlier, and Varon said that you had not been down there yet."

"I kind of overslept this morning." I backed away from him and started to smooth down the front of my dress. "I got woken up with Mira screeching at me."

Kaidan chuckled at that. "Well, are you ready then?"

There was something I was forgetting, "No." I ran over opened my wardrobe and popped open the hidden compartment on the bottom. Inside I had a dozen or so knives and a sword. Throwing knives was my specialty. It was because of that that I have the job I have now. I could look at a target and usually hit it every time. Snatching two, I put one inside of each boot. All my boots were made special so I could wear the knives comfortably and no one would know the difference. I grabbed two more in sheaths that tied perfectly around each of my thighs. While walking over to my vanity, I signaled Kaidan to turn around for a moment. He rolled his eyes and turned his back to me. Putting my foot on the chair, I yanked up the heavy sage-color fabric of my dress. After I was sure both knives were secure, I tied the dark-sapphire cloak around my neck. "Now, I am ready."

He groaned. "It's about damn time!"

Kaidan was a good-looking man only a few inches taller than my five-foot-eight self. His beard was always short, well-manicured, and matched the color of his soft brown hair, which lightly touched his broad shoulders. He was dressed in his normal attire, which was the blue and gray uniform of the royal guard, showing the king's coat of arms. It's the head of a red stag with a crescent moon and stars nestled in between the antlers, which symbolizes the legendary moon goddess, Selene, who's filled with wisdom and power. The top stretched halfway down his thighs with a belt around his waist that held his sword down on his left hip. His trousers were dark. At first glance, you might think they were black; but in closer inspection, you could tell they were a dark blue. Last of all, he wore high black leather boots that traveled halfway up his shin. I could see how Mira had fallen for him. I could have fallen for him myself, if he did not remind me some much of my four older brothers.

After we left my room, we walked a little ways down the cool, lightly lit corridor. As we passed Kaidan's room, Mira was inside, changing his bedding. Our two rooms were side by side and were the closest rooms to the royal living quarters. So, if anything went awry during the night, we would be close by. I looked up at Kaidan to see him smiling in the direction of Mira. He gazed down at me still smiling and lightly punched my right arm. I was happy for him. They were both great people, and they deserved to be happy.

When we got to the main entrance, I could still look up in amazement at the mere size of the doors. They were at least three times the size of me, maybe four, and it took two men to open just one of the double doors. Once the guards saw us, they instinctively started opening the one door for us.

The cool morning air hit me. I walked out, tilting my head up, and took in a deep breath. With the smell of salt in the air from the ocean below and the aroma of fresh new flowers popping up…I loved spring! The sounds of birds singing. I could sit in the gardens all day and just listen.

Being carried away by the morning air and sounds, I was completely ignoring Ara. Ara, who was now nudging me, was my horse. She was a Hybrid, a giant girl and made of pure muscle and power. Her body was completely white, except for the long wavy hair on her mane, tail, feet and also the diamond on her forehead, which were tan. When I stood beside her, her back was still a good hand's length taller than my height. Even though Hybrids are monstrous horses, they were still built for speed. With their long massive legs, they could outrun any normal horse. I have had her since a foal, and I could never get rid of her. Ara was the finest and most intelligent horse I had ever owned.

"Good morning, girl!" I rubbed my hand up and down her head.

"She was anxious to see you this morning, Lady Leelah," said Miles, who was one of the stable hands that helped take care of her for me. "I think she needs to run."

"We will go running today. I promise." I assured her, "Just hold on for a little bit longer." She pressed her head against me like she understood. I knew she did. Even with a saddle on, it was still difficult to get my foot into the stirrup, so I trained her to bow when I needed to get on. Do not get me wrong, I could pull myself up if I had to, but it's easier to do it this way since I had to wear a bloody dress. Before I could command her to bow down, Miles was there with his hands weaved together in front of me. All I could do was smile. I lifted my foot, and he gave me a boost into the saddle. Reaching down, I ruffled his sandy hair and thanked him. He blushed and quickly bowed his head to hide his embarrassment.

Kaidan rolled his eyes, and as he pulled his hood up, he said, "We better get going. We are already slightly late." I just nodded and gave Ara a light kick and clicked my tongue to get her going.

As we started to leave, I lifted my hood up to cover my ears that were now cold due to the steady wind and to cover my face a little. We went through the main gates of Castle Burreck and entered Burreck City. It's the largest city in our country of Altecia. The cobblestoned streets were filled with people opening shops for the start of the new day. We were heading for the guards' barracks, which was all the way at the end of the main street at the east end of the city. The main headquarters was in the castle, but was closed at this time do to remodeling. So we had to settle to meet everyone and swear them in at the barracks. It was where most of the guards who were not married lived.

As we approached, I could see the long line of guards just outside of the building. All of them were wearing the colors of the royal guard, the blue-and-gray uniforms with the king's coat of arms on their chests. They all stood at attention with their backs facing the long wooden building. It was a two-story structure. You could not tell by the front of it, but the building stretched out back so that it resembled an enormous backward letter *L*. The complex could easily hold a thousand men.

When we got close enough, I did a quick count in my head. Fifty-three men! Well, it looked like it was going to be a long morning. I moaned at the sight. Kaidan added a moan to match mine, and with misery, he muttered, "That is more than just a couple dozen."

These things always took time. We had to meet everyone individually. They had to take an oath and swear to protect and serve our kingdom and not to talk about my true purpose. It was a long process.

As we began to pass the soon-to-be new guards, I always liked to get a good look at them before I actually met them. The first man who was at the end of the line looked…how could I put this? Terrifying! The monster of a man had to be six foot five at least, but I had a feeling he was definitely taller than that. There was a dreadful scar that started above his right eye and stretched down to the corner of his mouth. He had no beard, because all the new recruits had to be clean-shaven in the beginning, but you could tell he always had one. His face was expressionless, and he stared straight ahead. I could not take my eyes off his scar, which had to have been so painful. It caused a chill to go down my spine and gave me a twinge in the pit of my stomach. All of a sudden, the man locked eyes with me. Startled, I quickly looked away. With all my ability, I tried my best to shake the feeling of his eyes burning at the back of my head as we passed. The rest of them seemed to range in age from late teens to late twenties maybe. Besides the man at the end, they all looked fresh and ready to go.

We stopped by the porch and dismounted. After tying our horses to the hitching post, we walked inside. They rearranged the main gathering room. There was just a long wooden table in the kitchen with papers on it, which I assumed were the contracts. All the lounging chairs were pushed aside, leaving the middle of the room bare. There once was a time when I used to spend all my free time here. It's been over a year since I had stepped foot in this place. Trying to block out all the memories, I turned to the general while I hung up my cloak.

"Good morning, General!" we said in unison. General Ulric Wolfe looked up from the paper he was reading.

"It's about time you two got here. I was about to start without you," stated the general, who was trying to sound annoyed, but we knew better. I rolled my eyes and Kaidan laughed. The general had been serving in the royal guard for thirty years and had been general for seven of those years. Now pushing fifty, he'd just started to get streaks of gray in his beard and hair. I think it only made him look all the wiser.

"Today should not take as long as you think. We are having all the recruits stay here, so we do not have to worry about who is going to which post," said General Wolfe. We have posts all over the country with a good number of guards at each. We would have more papers for them to sign, and then we would have to give directions on how to get there. So, needless to say, I was happy to hear that. I walked around the table and took my seat while Kaidan sat in between the general and me. Looking at both of us, the general asked, "Should we get started then?"

"Let's get this over with," I responded, and Kaidan agreed.

"First we have Caine Templeton. He's a nineteen-year-old from Mastingham."

I nearly jumped out of my seat. "Really?" I asked, and the general gave me a soft smile and nodded slightly. I was born and raised in Mastingham. It's in the northern part of the country and a good six days' journey by carriage. The city was half the size of Burreck City, but just as active. The port there gave constant flow of fishermen and merchants from the country of the north. My family still lived there. His last name was familiar to me, but I could not remember any Caines. This day keeps getting better and better. Someone from my home town…how exciting!

"He does not have much training but shows a lot of determination," the general added.

"All right let's meet him," Kaidan said.

A guard at the door opened it and called Templeton in. He came in and stood at attention in the middle of the floor in front of us. I personally thought he seemed younger than nineteen, but that's just me. He still had that boyish-looking face, but you could tell he's molding himself into a man. He was not big built, kind of lanky, but that would change as he started training.

"Templeton, I would like you to meet the guards of the king and queen," said the general, and we stood up. "This is Sergeant Kaidan Kimball." Kaidan stuck his arm out, and Caine walked up. They both grabbed each other's right forearm in a firm quick shake.

"And this is Lady Leelah Bayard, who is also from Mastingham." Caine looked puzzled at first, so as always, I stuck my arm out just like Kaidan. The men always hesitated but then end up greeting me like they did Kaidan.

"Are you Blacksmith Randall Bayard's daughter, Lee?"

I smiled. "Yes that would be me. You know of my family?"

"I know your father and your brother Wade. I actually worked for him a short time before coming here to join the guard. He's a good man." He had an endearing smile on his lips.

"Yes, he is!" Matching his smile, I stretched my hand back out to shake his, but he did something no other guard had ever done. Templeton took my hand and brought it up to his lips. I could feel the heat rise up my cheeks as my jaw dropped.

"It is a pleasure to meet you, my lady." He let go of my hand and took a step back to stand at attention again. I found myself just gawking at him. He had completely caught me off guard, and I did not like it one bit. After a moment, Kaidan kicked me in the leg, causing me to snap out of it. Quickly, I sat down and turned my eyes upon Kaidan. He continued staring straight ahead and was trying not to smile. I could actually see the corner of his lips twitching like he was on the verge of laughing. I returned his kick and gazed back to Caine, who was now looking at General Wolfe. The general told him of his duties and gave him his schedule. Kaidan read him the oath and swore him in. Now it was my turn.

"Caine Templeton, I am Queen Rosa's guard." I spoke, looking up at him and had my fingertips lightly on the contract before me. "No one knows of my true purpose. Most think of me as just her lady-in-waiting. You now have to swear that you will not speak of this to anyone not even your family back home."

"I swear, my lady. I will not say a word." He bowed deeply before me.

"The reason we keep it a secret is because no one would expect her to defend the queen. The enemy would be caught off guard. So we would like to keep it that way. Do we have an understanding?" General Wolfe asked Templeton.

"Yes, General Ulric Wolfe!" Templeton responded in a quick manner.

"Please, just call me General. Everyone else does." He spoke calmly with a slight crooked smile.

"Yes, General," Templeton said slower and took in a deep breath.

"Good! Now come sign the paper in front of Lady Leelah." He walked up to me, and I gave him a soft smile. He beamed a bright smile back and looked down quickly at the paper and signed the document. As he was still bent down, he lifted his head so he was eye level with me. All of a sudden, his face did not look boyish any longer. His hazel eyes grew with intensity as he gazed at me. I used to love how such a small action could cause a man to get all flustered. Now he was doing it to me. Caine stood up and took a step back. The general rose, and Kaidan cupped my elbow so we could follow suit. Thank God for him because I probably would be still sitting and staring like an imbecile.

"Well, congratulations, Caine Templeton! You are now an official member of the royal guard," the general announced.

"Thank you!" he said grinning.

"You may go now and see the Frobisher. He will supply you with a sword and armor."

Caine, who was still smiling, bowed, taking one more look at me and walked out the door. Once the door was shut, Kaidan roared in laughter, collapsing down into his chair. Before I knew it, the general and the guard at the door joined him. I snapped, "If this is all because of me, then I do not appreciate it!" It felt like my cheeks and the tips of my ears were on fire.

"Oh, come on, Lee! That lad got you all flustered. I cannot remember you ever getting like that before." Kaidan wiped the tears from his eyes.

"Kaidan is right! It's usually the other way around. I am sorry, Lee." The general, who was still laughing with his hand over his belly, said, "All right let's try to get control of ourselves so we can continue."

Slouching in my chair with my arms hugging my chest, I stared at the opposite wall, and trying not to cry in embarrassment, I took in a deep breath. Kai was right, men never affected me the way Templeton did a moment ago; but then again, a new recruit never kissed my hand or gazed at me like he did either. Finally, the laughter stopped, and Kaidan patted my shoulders, "Sorry, Lee, for laughing, but you would have done the same if it was me." I giggled softly because it was true.

We situated ourselves with new documents, and the general called for the next guard to come in. Men came in and then left as royal guards. Most of them were close to my age of twenty-five, all young and ready to defend our kingdom. Luckily, all the other men got flustered with me and not the other way around. As one of the men walked out of the room, my stomach started to growl.

"Are we almost done because I am starting to get hungry?" I complained to the general. Normally, I would not say anything, but I had not eaten since last evening. Now my stomach was making a racket as it was midday.

"She's right, maybe we should take a break for lunch," Kaidan suggested. "I am starting to get hunger pains myself."

"This is our last one, so be patient," the general replied. "His name is Dogan Ramstien. He's thirty-five years old and is well trained in all weaponry."

"Holy hell! Thirty-five years old? He's up there in age to be joining, do you not think?" Kaidan asked the general.

"I know, but I am about fifty! Am I too old for this job?" he inquired. On average, our people will live to the age of one hundred and fifty. So, thirty-five is still considered young, even though we rarely get anyone over thirty joining for the first time.

"No, General, I guess not. It's just odd to see a man of his age joining the guard," Kaidan said.

"What's his story?" I asked. "How is he trained in all weaponry if he's never been a part of the guard?"

"I want you to meet him first." He gestured to the guard. "Let him in."

Dogan Ramstien was the first man I saw earlier this morning, the man with the long scar over his right eye. His wavy chestnut hair just brushed the bottom of his ears. Dogan came in and stood in the middle of the room like the others had done before him. The only difference was he looked like he had done this stance his whole life. His shoulders were perfectly square with hands folded behind his back, chest up, and he fixed his eyes straight ahead. It seemed to be a natural stance for him. Dogan Ramstien was a monster of a man, and I was right, he was definitely over six foot, five by a few inches. He did not look like he belonged in the royal guard. He reminded me more of our enemies to the north...the Salvatorians. The man was enormous like them. Even though I could not see through his clothing, I knew that his broad shoulders and immense chest were well formed. For the second time, not only did he send a chill down the length of my spine, but all the fine hairs on my arms stood on end, and the man had not even talked yet.

"Dogan Ramstien, I would like you to meet the guards of the king and queen." Now his emerald eyes started moving between Kaidan and me, staying a little longer then I had liked on myself.

General introduced Kaidan to him, and they grabbed each other's forearms in a shake. Dogan nodded to him and took a step back.

The general then said, "Now I would like you to meet Queen Rosa's guard, Lady Leelah Bayard." I stuck my hand out so we could greet, but instead he just stood there in front of me with squinted eyes. It felt like he was looking into my soul. His eyes were so intense that as much as I wanted to look away…I could not. Despite his massive form, he bowed gracefully before me. "Pleasure to meet ye, m'lady."

Dogan's accent sent a chill down my spine yet again. I jerked causing my chair to tip back. I whipped my head around to General Wolfe and yelled in a panic, "He's a Salvatorian!" Then I look up at him and asked, "You're from Salvatoria?"

"Aye, Lady Leelah, I'm!" he answered with a ring in his accent.

"General, you cannot be serious?" Kaidan asked urgently with his voice tight in anger.

"He's got the experience with the enemy and can teach us all a great deal."

"What kind of experience do you have? Are you familiar with their army?" Kaidan asked.

Dogan responded with, "I was once a lieutenant fer the Salvatorian Army."

"I beg your pardon?" Kaidan and I yelled in unison.

"General, did you think that maybe this is King Alistair's plan?" I jammed my finger in the monster's direction. "Have him get in and find out everything he can about us…like our weaknesses?" I practically screamed.

"Yes, Lady Leelah! He has been over to the mage, he has told the truth about everything." No one can lie when they see the mage. Azzan makes them speak the truth. All guards have to see him before they can join. I even had to go see the man when I first arrived here.

Kaidan added, "What if they found a way to get around that?"

General spoke calmly, "The mage is confident that he is good."

"Why here, Ramstien?" I questioned him while trying my best not to grit my teeth. "Why come and join the guard that was once your enemy?"

He was quiet for a moment then replied, "'Tis all I ken how to do…they're now m'enemy!"

This was not settling well with me. I needed to get the hell out of here and away from this man before I completely explode. He's the enemy, and I could not be a part of this!

"I am sorry, General, but I do not agree to this!" I found myself glaring at the monster and looked him up and down. "I need to leave! I am sure you can finish without my presence here."

"Everything is going to be all right, Lee, but if you have to leave, that's fine," he said.

I said thank-you, and as I was walking to the door, Ramstien remarked, "This is the reason why you should never allow a woman to do a man's job. They're too emotional, and she obviously cannot keep hers in check." He did not say it in our language but in his native tongue. Little did he know that I could speak fluent in his Salvie language. In my hometown to the north, we had a lot of Salvatorian's that came to our port for goods. My father taught me the language when I was a little girl.

As I come to a complete stop in my tracks, I heard someone suck in their breath. Slipping my hand through the small slit in my dress, I took hold of the knife on my right thigh. Repressing the lip that wanted to curl, I twirled around. For a split second, I calculated the distance between us as my blade left my fingertips. It was heartening for me to find him facing in my direction when the blade stuck to the floor right between his feet. Dogan's brows were arched as he gazed down at the knife, and I marched up to him, yanking the knife out of the floorboard. Swiftly, I brought it up against his throat; and as my hand brushed up against his neck, his eyes grew with intensity. He might be three times my size, but I did not care for the man, and I was fuming.

I suggested in Salvie, "I would watch what you say around me, Dogan Ramstien, and in any language at that!"

It appeared like he was trying not to smile, which infuriated me even more. I pressed the blade harder to his neck; a small stream of crimson started to run down his pale skin. He never took a step back. Dogan just stood there like he was a boulder that would not budge. Next thing I knew, Kaidan had his hand around my wrist.

"Calm down, Lee…just relax." He cautiously pulled my arm down and fixed his eyes on Dogan. "You might want to watch your tongue with this one. She's tougher than most women."

Dogan never responded to Kai, only narrowed his eyes down at me as he instinctively brought his hand up to the slightly broken skin of his throat. I yanked my wrist free of Kaidan's grip and headed for the door again.

Kaidan yelled after me, "Where are you going?"

"I am going for a run!" I yelled over my shoulder while yanking my cloak off the hanger by the door. "I will be back at the castle before long!"

Chapter 2

Shipwreck

The horses jumped a bit after I slammed the door behind me. I was going on so much adrenaline that I was able to climb into Ara's saddle without her bowing down. With the reins in my hands, I veered her toward the ocean, itching to feel the wind in my face. Yelling at the people to get the hell out of my way, the streets were packed as I raced Ara through the city and turned into small alleys if the streets became too crowded to pass. It took about a quarter of an hour, but once we arrived at the gates that led to the beach, I was already feeling a calmness fall over me. Giving the best smile I could muster to the guard, who was my friend Sterling, I took the ramp down to the beach in a moderate trot.

Once I had her hooves touching the pearly sand, I loosened her reins and gave her a solid kick. Off we went! The sun felt luxurious upon my face; it was considerably warmer than it was this morning. I peered up the cliff wall to see the castle high above as we ran by. I should do this more often…it's so relaxing! Closing my eyes to feel the wind against my face, I could hear the waves crashing onto the beach. There's nothing in the world better than that. After a long while, I finally opened my eyes to enjoy the scenery that went on forever of sapphire ocean and sandstone cliffs. Little did I know that my tranquility was about to end abruptly.

Farther up ahead, there was debris washing up on the beach. The closer I got, the more debris there was. Slowing Ara down to a trot, we approached what now I realized was wood, from a ship I figured. There were pieces ranging in size, some as small as my hand to as big as Ara herself. Up ahead there was an object, what looked to be a man lying facedown on the beach with the waves crashing down on him. Yanking back on the reins, I jumped off my horse and ran into the water after him.

The water was freezing; it felt like tiny blades cutting into my skin. My legs started to go numb almost instantly. There was a sudden urgent feeling of getting the man onto dry sand. My gut was telling me that he was already dead, but I had to check to make sure.

It was not easy, but I did manage to flip the man on to his back. Wrapping my arms under each of his, I started pulling him up to dry land. It took me some time, but after laying him back down, I knelt down by his head. Trying to catch the breath that burned my lungs, I leaned forward and pressed my ear against his chest. What I heard startled me…a heartbeat. Sitting straight up, I found me gawking down at him in disbelief. The man was still alive!

Looking up the beach, I could see what appeared to be another body. I needed to get help! Unhooking my cloak, I tucked it tightly around his body. The man's face and neck had a blue hue to them. He was probably close to my height and age. His dark hair was cut close. Laying my hand on his bare cheek, I brought my mouth to his ear. "I am getting help. I will be back…I promise."

Standing up, I called Ara over. Pulling me into her saddle again, we raced back down the beach to the city, never realizing how far we ran, for it seemed to take forever to get back. The beach curved a little, so if anyone came to the beach, they would have not seen the debris unless they went as far as I did. When I finally reached the ramp that led up to the city, I had Ara go parallel to the side of it.

I hollered, "Come quickly, Sterling! There's a shipwreck up the beach, one man I know of is still alive, but there's more I do not know about."

Sterling barked orders to the other guard to seek more men and ran down to me; he jumped on the back of my saddle. Ara snorted at the sudden weight as my friend wrapped his arms around my waist. Back up the beach we went. A chill shook throughout my body as I started to register the cool wind hitting my soaked lower half.

"Good God, Lee!" Sterling yelled. "You are soaking wet!" He took his cape and wrapped it around the both of us as he pulled me tight against his hard chest.

Lieutenant Sterling Fenwick was one of the few guards that I was close with. I was glad it was him on the ramp and not just a regular guard. I quickly glanced back at him to catch sight of his straight shoulder-length raven hair blowing in the wind.

"The first man I saw was still getting hit by the waves. I had to get him out and see if he was still alive," I yelled over the sounds of crashing waves and wind.

"How many more are there?"

"I am not completely sure. I know of at least one more."

"That was a nasty storm that came through last night. I would not have wanted to be out there in it."

Eventually, I made Ara slow down as we approached the scene.

"Holy mother of God," Sterling murmured in shock.

Debris was still washing up on the shore; I stopped Ara when we came upon the man. Sterling slid off Ara and went over to him, with me right behind him. He peeled back the cloak I had wrapped around him and checked his chest just as I had. Suddenly, he sat straight up. "I cannot believe he's still alive! He's cold as snow, we have to hurry."

"If you can help me get him on my horse, I will get him to the medical ward."

Sterling scooped up the man and threw him over his shoulder with ease. I gave Ara the order to bow down, which she did with no hesitation. He propped him up in front of the saddle with my cloak still wrapped around him. Sterling kept him upright so I could climb into the saddle.

"Wait, Lee…unhook my cape," said Sterling, and I unpinned it from his shoulders. "Wrap it around your shoulders then you can wrap the rest around him."

"Thank you, Sterling." I wrapped the cape around me and got into the saddle. Holding the ends of the cape in each hand, I enclosed my arms around him and held him tight against my chest. Snatching up the reins, I gave Ara the command to stand.

"Are you going to be all right holding him?" he asked. "I can do it if you want."

"I can handle it, start checking for more survivors." I looped my horse around and gave her a swift kick and yelled, "Come on, Ara! Take us home!" Off we went for the fourth time that day. The muscles in my legs and stomach started to burn now as I headed down the beach. It was a workout trying to keep him straight in the saddle. If he leaned too far to one side, we would both go down. We passed some guards who were heading toward the shipwreck. One of the guards turned around and ran ahead of us. I could not understand what he was doing until we actually entered the city.

The guard up ahead was yelling and clearing the streets so I would not have to slow down. The medical ward was attached to the castle, so I had Ara run up the steps that brought you through the castle walls. People were already outside waiting for me. We came to a sliding stop over the cobblestones. Two men came and slid the man down and carried him into the building.

I started to follow, but a woman stopped me, "I am sorry, my lady, but you cannot come in right now." I fixed my eyes on her, wanting to argue, but I did not.

"Please send someone for me if he wakes."

"Of course, my lady." She bowed her head and scurried away. I spun around to Ara and petted her down the side of her massive neck.

"Well, girl, we got our run today, did we not?" I was exhausted and was ready for a bath and to crawl back into bed. She rounded her head and nibbled on my shoulder, which in turn made me laugh. "Hungry and tired, are you?" My stomach started to growl, reminding me that it was well past midday and I never ate breakfast this morning. "Me too! Let's get you back to the stables." I seized her reins and walked her back to the stables. There was a thought about going back to the beach, but they had everyone up there by now.

After giving Ara a rubdown, I made my way back to the castle so I could change my clothes. I never got the bath I wanted because the need to eat was more important. After I got myself dressed, a knock came from my door. My stomach growled in response. Knowing it was the food I requested to be sent up, I found myself practically running for the door. Queen Rosa was standing there with a tray of food in her hands. She extended the tray to me.

"As I was coming to see you, I saw the servant with your food. I heard you have not eaten all day." She beamed me her beautiful smile.

I took the tray out of her hands and turned to put it on my desk. "No, I have not, and I am famished!" Grabbing the chair from my vanity, I place it by the desk. "Please, Rosa, sit. I would love to talk with you if you do not mind that I eat too."

Rosa gave me her famous smile again. "Of course not, go right ahead and eat."

I did not say another word. Grabbing the mutton sandwich, I took a bite. The first bite made me close my eyes in pleasure with the taste. I took another bite then another; it was delicious! I was going to have to make sure that I compliment Varon when I saw him. I think this must be the best sandwich he had ever made, or I just thought that because I was so hungry. I was just about done with my food when I finally glanced over to Rosa, who had not said a word. She was all smiles.

"I heard about the man you saved on the beach," Rosa said. "It was a good thing you got upset at the barracks and decided to go for a run. Who knows how long he would have been out there before someone found him."

I nearly choked on my food, and then I let out a moan. I completely forgot about what happened at the barracks. My mind had been all wrapped up with that man I found. "You heard what happened at the barracks already too?" I swallowed the rest of my food, and the thought of my father came to my mind. If he was here, he would be so shaking his head at me right now. At least I covered my mouth with my hand before I spoke.

Rosa tipped her head back in a laugh. "I hear everything, my dear Lee."

"Did they find any more survivors?"

"No." Sadness came over her, and she bent her head down. "The one you found first is the only one who lives, so far at least."

I placed down what was left of my sandwich. For some reason, I was no longer hungry, "When do you think I can go and see him?"

"I would wait until tomorrow morning. In the meantime, why not finish your sandwich and the two of us will go for a walk."

"I am no longer hungry, so let's go for that walk now." I took hold of the tray as I stood up. I followed Rosa out the door and placed the tray on the floor beside my door. The next servant to pass my room would surely grab it.

As we got to the main doors of the castle, the guards bowed and opened them for us. The late afternoon sun poured down upon us, and I took in a deep breath. The queen wrapped her arm around mine, and I lightly touched her hand.

"Spring is such a beautiful time, do you agree?" Rosa asked.

"Yes, I think it's my favorite season."

We strolled across the courtyard toward the gardens. The gardeners here did such beautiful work. In the evergreen hedgerows that were a good foot higher than my own height, they had every color imagined weaved through them. We went through the maze of paths that led to the fountain in the middle. It was still too early, but in a few more weeks, the roses around the fountain would be in full bloom. The two of us sat on one of the benches, and we stayed silent for a moment.

It was like we both had to take in the tranquility of it all. I could hear the chirps of baby birds in the branches above my head. The light scent of roses filled the air with the trickling of water from the fountain in front of us.

"So, Lee, would you explain to me what happened earlier today at the barracks?" Rosa asked softly.

"I thought you said you knew about it," I replied even softer.

"Well, I would like to hear your point of view." The queen reached out and gently patted my hand on my lap.

After taking a deep breath, I explained everything to her—about how I felt about Dogan Ramstien and about what he had said to me. The anger started to bubble again in my chest. It was asinine to allow him to join the guard.

"I see why you do not trust him, Lee. But I thrust General Wolfe's decision. He would never do anything that could potentially harm our kingdom."

"I trust him too! It's just…what if he tricked the mage to think somehow that he spoke the truth and he really did not?"

"Now you are just being paranoid!" She laughed. "No one has ever been able to lie to Azzan, not even other mages."

Slouching my shoulders, I hung my head in defeat. "Maybe, but I am still not going to trust him, he's going to have to prove himself to me."

Rosa let out a gorgeous laugh and wrapped her arm around my shoulders and squeezed. "That's my Lee I know and love. I know you will make him work hard for it too." I smiled back at her. She was so easy to talk to. Then the baby popped in my head.

"Enough about me, let's talk about this baby," I murmured to her. Rosa's whole face lit up, and we spent the rest of the afternoon discussing the baby and all that needed to be done to prepare for its arrival.

That night was my first nightmare of Dogan Ramstien. There was a traitor among us. I was stabbed through the back and stared down in horror at the blade that was protruding from my stomach. A bloodcurdling scream escaped my lips as the blade was jerked out. Dogan was before me with an evil grin and a sword dripping of dark crimson…my own blood. Waking up in a panic, I threw off my blankets as I touched my stomach that still slightly ached in pain. I was soaked in sweat as my hair and nightgown clung tight to my body. I prayed that it was only a dream and that I dreamt it because I was *paranoid* like Rosa said.

It had been a few days since I found the man on the beach. I had been down to see him every morning since. The lad was still unconscious. I woke up before dawn, so I decided to walk down to the medical ward before Mira came. Brushing my hair that was wild from sleep, I finally gave up and just pushed it behind my shoulders. I slipped into my robe in hopes that it would help keep my hair pulled down. While walking down the softly lit corridor, I began to think about the man. Who was he? Where was he from? He could be from anywhere. When I finally reached the medical ward's door, it swung open before I could even grab the handle. One of the nurses practically ran into me.

"I apologize, ma'am," she said with heavy breathing like she'd been running. Surprise came to her eyes when she really looked at me. "Lady Leelah!" she screeched.

"Yes." I winced and wanted to bring my hands to my ears in reaction to her yelling my name in such a manner.

"I was just coming up to get you. He's awake, Lady Leelah! He wants to speak with the woman who saved him."

"Pardon?" Staring at her in shock, could this really be? I can feel the vibrations in my chest from my pounding heart.

"Please come and hurry!" she said urgently and grabbed my hand.

I could not say another word. The woman practically dragged me down the narrow corridors of the ward. It's a lot cooler here than in any other place in the castle. I was not sure why; it might all just be in my head. Maybe it had to do with all the men and women who have died here. After we reached the end of the corridor, she turned right. We went past a dozen or so doors before we stopped at his. Staring at the old wooden door, I was all of a sudden afraid to open it. Finally, the nurse laid a hand on my shoulder and whispered, "Go ahead, my lady." She coaxed me toward the door. "He's a real gentleman."

While looking at her, I tried to give her a smile. She smiled back, gave me a light pat on the shoulders, and turned back the way we came. Taking a deep breath, I brought my shaking hand to knock on the door. I do not know why I was so nervous. Maybe I was just letting my imagination of him get the better of me.

"Come in," a raspy voice responded from inside.

Taking another deep breath, I pushed down on the lever of the latch and pushed open the door at a snail's pace. The man was sitting there with his back propped up with pillows and with a plate of food on his lap. The candle on the stand beside his bed lit his face and projected shadows all around the tiny room. My room was at least ten times the size of this. He put down his utensil and looked me up and down. He smiled, "You must be Lady Leelah. Am I correct?" His voice sounded extremely raw, and I imagined it probably hurt to talk.

"Yes, you are correct." I gave him a nod and smiled.

"Please grab that chair and bring it over to sit," he whispered while pointing at the chair on the other side of the stand. "I would like to get a better look at the woman who saved me."

I did without hesitation. Placing the chair in front of the stand, I sat facing him. He had dark bags under his eyes and looked like he had not slept in days. Was that even possible? His face that was smooth when I first found him was now covered in dark stubble. I had so many questions that I did not know where to start. Finally, I asked, "What's your name?"

The man smiled faintly. "If I knew that, I would tell you, my lady. For some reason, I have no memory of my life before. The doctor says that may come back gradually in time."

"You have no memory whatsoever?" I asked in astonishment.

"None." He chuckled due to my expression, which caused him to start coughing a little. "It's very frustrating, let me tell you, to not know your name or where you come from. I have been up for a few hours now, and I cannot think of a single thing."

"I am sorry to hear that." I began to laugh a little. "I had all sorts of questions for you, now I guess they will be unanswered."

"Just for the time being," he assured me. "I want to thank you. If it was not for you, I might be dead right now so…thank you."

"I am just glad I went for a run that day. Let me tell you, I had a hard time getting you out of the water, but I did. I was quite surprised that you still had a heartbeat."

"Is it true that you have been here every morning since I got here?" he asked, and I felt my cheeks start to warm with embarrassment.

"Yes, it's true. I have been worried about you, hoping that you would pull through," I whispered and looked down at my clasped hands in hopes to hide my flushed cheeks. Thankfully, he did not seem to notice.

"Can you tell me the story? How you found me and how I got here?"

I went into full detail on how I was running my horse on the beach to blow off some steam, how I came upon him with the waves still hitting him, to how Sterling helped me get him on my horse so I could get him to the ward.

"When I get strong enough, will you bring me back there?" he asked.

"Of course I will," I said and then sighed. "I am sorry but I need to take leave." As I stood up, I reached down for his hand and gave it a reassuring squeeze. "I will be back tomorrow. I promise!"

"For some reason, I believe you, Lady Leelah. Can you do me a favor?"

"Yes, what do you need?"

"Before you come back tomorrow…" He hesitated and then took a sudden sharp breath. "Can you think up a name for me? Just until I can remember my actual name, that is."

Laughing I said, "Are you sure you trust me enough for that favor? I could think up some crazy names."

"Yes, I am sure you will do well," he chuckled.

"All right, I will have a name for you by tomorrow. Get some rest."

"I will not be going anywhere anytime soon." He smiled. "Thank you again."

I beamed him back a smile as I shut his door. Wrapping my robe tighter around me, I ran back to my room. Now I have to think of a name. It's got to be a strong name but a name that fit him. I will have to ask Rosa today. She might know of some good names. As I made my way down the corridor that led to my room, I caught sight of Mira knocking at my door.

"Mira," I shouted, making her jump; she jerked her head in my direction.

"What is it, Lee? Is everything all right?" she yelled back in concern.

I plowed myself into her and closed my arms around her. With my jumping around in excitement, Mira was now giggling and asked, "What is this all about?"

"He's awake, Mira! Awake and alive! I am so happy I had to hug someone."

I let her free, and she was still giggling a little when she said, "That's wonderful news, Lee. Well? What's he like? His name?"

I opened my door and led her in. "He has amnesia. The man does not remember anything."

Mira walked to my closet to find a dress and stopped to look at me, "Really? How terrible!"

"I know! He wants me to give him a name to go by until he remembers his real name."

"Well, that should be fun. Do you have any ideas yet?"

"Not a clue."

"If I think of the perfect name, I will let you know. For the meantime, let's get you washed up and dressed. You are having breakfast with the king and queen this morning."

She handed me a dress, and I said, "Let's hurry then, the queen might know of a good name."

As I got myself ready, all I could think about was the man in the medical ward. I could not even imagine what it must be like not to remember anything. It's horrible! I walked out with Mira and we said our good-byes. As I got to the base of the stairs that led up to the living quarters, there was sight of the two guards standing on either side of the double doors, wearing the royal colors and with a sword strapped to their hips. They were never supposed to talk when they were on duty. When I am alone, they would smile and say hello. I guess they just got tired of me always trying to get them to smile that they routinely do now if they can. Well, today was one of those days. While ascending the stairs, both guards beamed down at me. When I got to the top, I said, "Good morning, gentlemen!"

"Good morning, Lady Leelah," they both said in a hushed tone. The one to the right, whose name was Byron, turned and pushed the door open for me. After thanking him, I walked in.

Walking down the lush red-carpeted hall, I looked at the portraits that hung on the walls. I could never get tired of looking at them no matter how many times I walked down this same hall. They were portraits of all the kings and queens of the past and their families, starting with the very first royal family all the way to Bryce's immediate family. It amazes me how so much has changed from the beginning.

There was new light shining into the hall up ahead, and the smells of breakfast filled my nose. My mouth instantly started to water. I loved having breakfast with Bryce and Rosa. It can be unbelievable sometimes on how much food there was. If I was on my own for breakfast, I would usually just have some fruit or something light and head for where I needed to be.

Turning right, I went through the open double doors into the dining room. The ceiling was vaulted with large windows on the far wall to let in the natural light. There was a massive fireplace to the right that, if I went to stand inside it, I would be able to without having to hunch over. King Bryce was the first to see me. The king was a dignified man and was easy on the eyes. But do not let that fool you; he can be a tyrant when needed be. His chestnut hair lay lightly on his shoulders. Bryce walked over to greet me and gave me his signature smile.

"Good morning, Leelah! It looks like we are going to have another fine spring morning."

"Good morning to you too, and I would have to agree with you." He stood in front of me as I continued, "I have not seen you since Rosa told me the news. May I give you a hug in congratulations?"

He let out a hearty laugh. "Of course, Lee! You do not have to ask." He opened his arms, and I smiled as I wrapped my arms around his neck. While laughing he lifted me up and spun me around. He placed me back on my feet while my world continued to spin around me. I had to close my eyes for a moment to steady myself and to find my balance again. I heard Rosa's laugh.

"Now look at what you did, Bryce." I felt her wrap an arm around my waist. "The poor girl is dizzy."

Chuckling a little, I said, "No, I am fine, Rosa." I grinned at her. "This is a joyous time! You both have no idea how happy I am for you."

Before I could say anymore, Kaidan walked into the room. He was all smiles. "So how much longer do we have to keep this secret to ourselves? I do not know about you, but I find it hard to keep it in. I almost let it slip a few times yesterday."

"Another month at least, we just want to be sure before we tell the country," Rosa explained.

"Please sit, Lee and Kaidan, so we can eat." Bryce gestured toward the long table that was filled with fruits and pastries. Bryce walked over and pulled the chair out for Rosa. She lightly brushed her hand down his cheek before sitting down in the chair.

I hope I can find that someday. I thought I had it once, but I was wrong. Even though their marriage was arranged before they even met, the two of them actually love each other. Rosa told me how hard it was when she first came to the castle. She was scared, but he was gentle and kind to her. Bryce let her move at her own pace. Rosa eventually came to accept him and now loved him unconditionally. They had been trying to have a baby for years. Now, it looks like God has finally blessed them with a child. The child will be blessed to have parents like them.

"So what are the plans for today?" Kaidan asked.

"We were thinking of going for a ride later this morning, maybe on the beach," Bryce said. "This afternoon, there's a group of people coming that request my audience."

"All right, after breakfast, I will let the men know. I will make sure that they have our horses ready by midmorning."

"Thank you, Kaidan," said Bryce, and Kaidan nodded and continued eating.

After the king and Kaidan left the room, I turned to the queen. "Rosa, the man I found on the beach is awake, but he has amnesia and wants me to pick out a name for him. Just until his memory comes back. I have no clue what kind of name to give. Do you have any ideas?"

Rosa gave me a blank stare as she thought about it, then her face lit up with excitement. "I have got it and it will be perfect." She jumped out of her chair and ran out of the room to the library across the hall. As she scanned the bookshelves, she explained, "I read once of a name that had the meaning of *sea*. In folklore, it is said to be the name of a legendary sea god. I just cannot remember the name." Rosa kept searching for the book as I thought of him again, hoping that the name would suit him.

Just as I was about to ask the queen what the name of the book was so I could help find it, she yelled, "Here it is!" She pulled out the old leather-bound book with gold trim and letterings. It read, *The Real Story of the Gods and How They Came to Be.* She laid the book gently on one of the many tables in the library. She opened it up, and with carefulness, she turned the pages like they could fall apart in her hands.

"Here." Rosa laid a delicate finger on the page. "You should give him the name of Dylan. I think it will suit him just fine." She looked at me with a beautiful smile on her face. "He came from the sea, did he not?"

Returning her a smile, I said, "Rosa, it is perfect!" I gave her a hug, causing her to laugh. "I knew you would think of a good name. Thank you."

"It was my pleasure, my dear Lee, so, what are you still doing here?" Giving her a puzzled look, she replied, "We still have time before we go on our ride. Go down and tell the lad his new name."

"Thank you again, Rosa," I said briskly and rushed for the hall.

I could still hear her laughing as I got to the door that took me out of the royal living quarters. I ran holding the front of my dress up a little so I did not fall flat on my face. I managed to make it to the medical ward without running anyone over; this was an achievement in itself. I straightened my dress and walked into the ward. Walking briskly, I made my way down the narrow corridors. Arriving at his door, I took a few deep breaths trying to calm my nerves. I knocked on the door lightly. Faintly, I heard the words, "Come in." I opened the door slowly. "Ah, it's my angel! I was not expecting you to come back so soon." Shyly, I closed the door behind me. Luckily, it was dark enough for him not to notice me blushing.

"I know, but I could not wait until tomorrow. My friend helped me pick out a name for you, and, well, I think it is perfect," I said while holding my hands down in front of me.

"Well, do not keep me waiting, my lady, what is it?" he asked with great enthusiasm.

"Dylan," I answered, smiling.

"Dylan?" He looked puzzled for a moment. "Why Dylan?"

I laughed. "It means sea, and he is supposedly some legendary sea god."

He let out a hoot then started coughing terribly. I leapt to him to rub his back as his body was arched forward. "I apologize, maybe I should have waited until tomorrow."

He reached up and patted my arm as his body started to bounce up and down with silent laughter. "It's fine, my lady, and the name is perfect." He looked at me with tired eyes, but they did have a twinkle of excitement in them. "Thank you, Lady Leelah! Please make sure you tell your friend I said thank-you also."

He squeezed my arm as I rose. I looked to him one last time before I shut the door. "Get some rest, and I will see you tomorrow, Dylan." I gave him a smile, and he quietly chuckled.

"Yes, my lady," he whispered with a slight bow of his head.

I walked the medical corridors much slower than when I came in. Thoughts of my father came to mind and how proud he would be of me right now. I think I should write to him tonight and tell him about Dylan. Then I realized that I should be getting a letter soon from him. Normally, I would receive a letter from him in the middle of the month. I always tried to get a letter back out to him the very next day. By the time my letter got to him and if he sent one out the day after he received mine, it would usually take a month. It's a long wait, but they're always worth it.

While strolling in the main entrance area of the castle and in my own little world, I jumped when I heard my name called. Kaidan shook his head at me and was holding out my cloak. He's the best!

I snatched it out of his hand. "Why thank you, kind sir." I said in a high voice. He smiled and rolled his eyes. "Are they down yet?" I tied the cloak around my neck.

"Actually, I think they're coming down now." He nodded ahead of us.

Gazing up the stairs, I watched them around the bend. They were so elegant together. I guess they have to be, right? They are royalty! The king and queen were wearing matching cloaks made of red velvet and fox fur. They were also wearing matching gold bands with rubies on their heads. Sometimes, it felt like they could steal your breath away if you stared at them long enough.

It's different when I am with them in their private living quarters. Sometimes, I forget that they are royalty. It would always hit me when I saw them in their fancy clothing and jewels. Everyone was bowing. People practically sat on the floor as they walked by. They were very loved for the most part by the people of our country. Since he'd been on the throne, there'd been no war. Kaidan and I both bowed when they came upon us. "Your Majesties!" we said in unison.

As we all walked out of the castle, Rosa wrapped her arm around mine and whispered in my ear, "Well, what did Dylan think of his new name?"

"He loves it. He wanted me to tell my friend thank-you too." I winked at her.

"Good, I am glad," she said as I walked her to her horse.

The king took her hand as she walked up the steps beside the horse. Walking up to Ara, I reached into my pocket, pulling out an apple I took from the table after breakfast. When Ara took the apple from my hand, the king said behind me, "I wonder where that apple came from."

I could feel my face getting red hot, which I hated and could not figure out why that was. I never used to blush this easily. Bryce laughed and patted me on the back. "I am only jesting with you, Lady Lee."

"I know, Your Highness."

Kaidan burst out in laughter. "You think she's red now, you should have seen her the other day when this guard—" He stopped in his tracks when I glared at him to stop. He cleared his throat and added, "I will save that story for another time." He winked at me when he climbed up on his horse.

We spent the rest of the morning riding the horses up the beach. We went a little ways up past where the shipwreck was. There were still some small pieces of debris in the sand, but for the most part, it was all cleaned up. We did a lot of laughing and enjoyed the beautiful morning. I spent the rest of the afternoon with Rosa in the library reading and talking.

Chapter 3

The Letter

Night had finally fallen, and I was ready for bed. Noticing it as soon as I walked into my room, sitting there on my desk was a letter. Slamming the door behind me, I snatched it up. I knew it was from my father before I even opened it. Taking the letter, I went over and sat in front of the hearth. I did not want to bother lighting any of the candles in the room. I just wanted to read my letter. Breaking the wax seal that was marked with the letter *B*, I slowly unfolded the letter and smiled instantly when I saw his exquisite handwriting.

> Dear Baby Girl,
>
> I am glad you liked the city Chesterton. I have not been there since before your oldest brother was born. This was one of the many reasons why I wanted you to take this job. Ever since you were a little girl, you always talked about traveling the country. Well, Baby Girl, now you can. I still miss you a great deal, and I always will. I hate not seeing you; it's been three years now. Maybe after Regner's wife has the baby, we all can plan a trip to come see you. I cannot wait till you meet Flora, you will love her. She's really glowing lately. Regner and she truly believe the baby is a girl. I do not care either way; I

just want to be a grandpa! Only two more months to go, we are all excited. It's all Estelle talks about. Wade is courting a young lady named Adele. She's a sweet girl, a little on the shy side. Rythe and Irving are also doing fine. We ALL miss you and send you ALL of our love.

Love and God bless,
Pa

Postscript: Oh, I almost forgot to tell you that your friend Lieutenant Rowan Lythandas came by today. He wanted me to tell you that he's sorry and that he thinks of you often. I do not know what he did to you, darling, but his feelings toward you are genuine.

Staring down at the last part of Pa's letter, I was unable to move. Rowan! My vision started to blur with tears. He went and saw Pa. It's been a little over a year since he left. I loved him, and apparently, I still did. We had made plans to go away together. Then out of nowhere, he told me a position opened up at a post and that he was taking it. He said he needed to take it because we were not meant for each other. He would not tell me where he was going, and that vision of him riding away still haunted me. Now he went to see my father, telling him that he thinks of me often. Why must he torture me so?

To get the man I loved out of my head, I stared into the fire, trying to picture my family. Estelle, Pa's wife of eleven years, sitting and knitting little booties for the baby. My oldest brother, Regner, doting over his beautiful wife, Flora, who I had not yet met. My second-to-oldest brother, Rythe, working with the horses out in the field with Irving. Then there's my third-to-oldest brother, Wade, all excited about the new girl in his life. She would be all he talked about. My brother Irving was the one closest in age to me. He was only a year older. There's a total of ten years between Regner and me. I love my family, and my heart always ached for them after I read my father's letters.

After I read the letters, I loved to go for a walk through the gardens to relax myself, especially after the whole Rowan thing—I would never be able to sleep. Walking over to my wardrobe, I opened it and grabbed my cloak inside. Once it was secure around my neck, I pushed all my dresses that were hanging to the left. Crouching down, I felt along the back wall. Feeling the slight indention in the wood, I pushed it in. Turning the tiny handle that now stuck out, I was able to pull the small door open. I stood up a little and walked into the darkness.

Before closing the door behind me, I crouched back down, grabbing one of the few matches I had left against the stone wall. I struck it against the stone and lit the candle. Reaching back in, I closed my wardrobe doors first then the hidden one. Grabbing the candle, I stood up and turned around so I could go down the narrow spiral staircase. Just as I was getting ready to take my first step down, the other hidden door to my right jerked open.

"Get another letter from home, Lee?" questioned Kaidan with a grin on his face. "Is that why you are sneaking out...to get some fresh air and to clear your head?" If only he knew what was in the letter, he would not be smiling.

"How in the hell did you hear me? I was being quiet as a mouse."

"Lee, I can hear everything," he said then made a funny face. Laughing at him, I rolled my eyes and continued down the stairs.

"How's your family?" Kaidan hollered. "Are they well?"

Still laughing the best I could, I yelled back up to him, "Yes, Kai! They are all well, thank you!"

Once reaching the bottom stone step, I looked up and down the dark narrow corridor. It was always creepy down there. No one ever went down there. Kaidan and I are the only ones that I know of who actually used the door that was in front of me. Kaidan took me down these long, hidden corridors once when I first arrived to the castle. They have not been used in so long that only a select few know that they existed. I placed my candle down on the last step. Turning, I ignored the creepy darkness to the left and right of me, unlocked the door, and pushed it open to the crisp evening air.

As I walked up the stairs that run along the castle, the hedges tickled my face as I went. When I topped the steps, I walked sideways against the wall because the hedges were so overgrown. Then pushing myself through the break in the hedgerow that I made, I turn to the right toward the maze of hedgerows. I loved walking in there at night, it was so peaceful. I had walked it so much over the years that I knew where every turn would take you.

With the enormous full moon, it gave me more than enough lighting that the lanterns in the garden could not provide. I could smell the sweet aroma of spring before I even set foot into the maze. I walked, turning left here and right there. When I came to a crossroad, so to speak, I looked over to my right for some reason. I saw a silhouette of a figure standing there at the end. It always sent me a chill whenever I saw a guard in here at night. Most nights, when I saw someone, I would usually say hello and talk for a bit, but not tonight. I just kept going straight. When I came to a T, I got an eerie feeling to look behind me, so I did. Back at the crossroad stood that guard. It was too dark, and he was too far away for me to tell who it was.

"I cannot tell who you are, but I am not much in the mood for company," I announced to the dark figure, but I got no response.

The men had always just let me be. Trying to shake the feeling away, I turned to the right. As I got to an opening in the hedges, I looked back again before turning right. Sure enough, the man was in sight. Walking into the opening, and as soon as I knew I was out of his sight, I took off in a sprint, making the turns that would bring me to the fountain rose garden in the middle of the maze.

Once I made it, I plastered myself against the hedgerow. Why was he following me? Who was he? I lifted my leg up and pulled out the knife in my boot. I was trying my best to slow my breathing so I could listen. Whoever this was, they were about to get an earful for scaring me like this. If Kaidan had anything to do with this, I was going to kill him.

I was holding my breath so I could really listen. Whoever it was, they were now on the other side of the hedge. I could hear his breathing; he must have been running to catch up. Now I was really starting to panic. As the boot stepped into the rose garden, I extended my arm and brought my knife up against his throat. He was a lot taller than I expected.

"You bloody fool! What in the hell do you think…" I cut myself off once I realized who it was. "you!"

Dogan Ramstien gave me an evil grin. "Aye, 'tis me." His Salvie accent was thick and low. "This is the second time ye and I came face-to-face, and in both encounters, ye pressed yer bloody knife against m'neck. I'm gonna say this once…this will be the last time yer knife ever touches m'skin." I felt something against my stomach; I looked down in horror to find his dagger pressing hard against me. A little more pressure and the tip of the blade would pierce my skin. "Remove yer damn blade now, if ye wanna live to see another day." Staring up at him in disbelief, I quickly stepped back, keeping my knife up in front of me. With the lanterns lit in the garden and with the moon's eerie light, I did not like the looks of him, and it made his dreadful scar more pronounced. I took a few more steps back.

"How dare you threaten me!" I said trying my best to conceal the panic in my voice. "What are you doing here and why are you following me?"

He made an odd noise, which I assumed was supposed to be a laugh, though it did not sound friendly. "I'm on duty tonight, and I was following ye because I wanted to ken who the hell walks around in here at night. Once I realized 'twas ye—" he suddenly cut himself off. "Now thanks to ye, I'm gonna ha' a hell o' time getting outta here," he stated angrily.

"I came out here to clear my head, which is not happening, apparently," I said through gritted teeth. "So now that you know it's me and you are not planning on killing me then why not leave and try to find your way out."

"Planning on killin' ye? Well that could be tempting," he grabbed his chin like he was actually considering it.

"Once I scream, all those guards will be in here. They know their ways through the maze." My heart was pounding so frantically that I was actually afraid that he might hear it.

"Woman, if I was gonna kill ye, ye'd be dead before ye even thought about screaming fer help. Why would ye anyway? Ye'r the queen's guard, I'm right?" He tilted his head to the side as his lip slowly curled up.

"I do not trust you, Ramstien. You should not be this close to them, you should not be allowed in this city," I snapped, trying to keep my voice down.

Dogan took a step toward me, and I instinctively took two back. His tone was low and threatening. "It seems some people trust me, and that's why I'm here. I really dinna give a damn that ye dinna trust me. I think 'tis a joke that they ha' a wee lass like yeself protecting the queen."

I laughed in a heartless manner. "You do not know anything about me or what I am capable of, Ramstien."

"Aye, and ye dinna ken anything about me, Bayard. I'm not the only one here that's quick to judge," he replied with his voice thick with anger.

"I came out here to be alone. Get away from me and stay out of my way. The less we see each other, the better," I hissed.

"Fer the first time, I actually agree wit ye. I'll stay outta yer way, but if ye get in mine, ye'll regret it," he threatened.

Before I could ask what he meant by that, he turned abruptly and disappeared into the darkness. Afraid of turning my back on the opening to the maze, I backed up to one of the many benches. Even though we both agreed to stay out of each other's way, I knew this was only the beginning. It was going to get worse when it came to that beast; I just knew it. I sat and tried to shake Dogan Ramstien from my thoughts and everything that he represented.

All of a sudden, memories of Rowan Lythandas filled my head. It was a warm summer evening; we lay together in a field staring up at the starry sky. He was laughing at something I said and rolled over to his side so he could look at me. Rowan was smiling. Oh, how I loved his crooked smile. That was the night when he first told me that he loved me.

I hung my head and covered my face with my hands. The sobs hit me so hard that it shocked me, not realizing that I was holding it all back. The pain of him leaving was as strong as the day he did. "Why do you torture me so?" I softly cried. "You told me to forget about you then you do something like this. If you think about me so often, then why not come and take me away?" We had made plans.

We were going to get married and head north to my home town of Mastingham to start our new life together. I was once his *Lovalee*, then out of the blue, he hits me with this.

He once said, "I am sorry, Lovalee, but I have to go. I am not the right man for you. There's someone else out there that you are supposed to be with."

"No!" I cried. "I love you! You are the one I am supposed to be with."

"And I love you, but sometimes, that's not enough. Please forgive me!" That was the last thing he had ever said to me. I watched Rowan ride out until he was gone, and I stayed in that spot for hours, crying, alongside the fence, hoping that he would change his mind. He never did.

Now here I am a year later, grieving for the man I lost all over again. When there were no more tears to cry, I looked up at the night sky and started to pray softly out loud.

"Dear Heavenly Father, please give me strength. I thought I was over Rowan, and I am obviously not. I realize now that I just kept it buried down deep but I do not think I can keep it buried anymore. If he still loves me, Lord, then why can we not be together? Help me! I do not understand! I need him in my life. Please bring Rowan back to me...Amen."

I took a deep breath of the salty night air and wiped the left-over tears from my eyes. I stood back up and made my way slowly through the maze and praised God I did not catch a single sight of Dogan Ramstien.

"This is delicious, Varon!" I said to the cook. If I got up early enough, I liked to go down in the kitchen and eat. This morning, Varon cooked me some eggs with a generous amount of mushrooms sliced in it and a side of buttered bread. He's one of the few that knew of my true purpose.

"Thank you, my lady!" He winked with a smile.

"Mmmm, Varon can you make me some too?" Kaidan asked from behind and took the stool next to me. The kitchen was busy with people cooking and setting up trays of food to take up to the king and queen. I always tried to stay out of their way. Kaidan and I liked Varon's cooking the best. We always sat at the small table in his area. He was a big, round man and had an optimistic outlook on life. Varon was always a pleasure to be around, and I think he enjoyed our company too.

"Of course, more eggs coming up," he said, answering Kaidan's question.

"Good morning, Kai." I grinned at him before taking another bite of my eggs.

"Good morning, you sleep well?"

"Well, considering everything that happened last night, I actually did," I stated. I was proud of myself for that. Usually, when I was upset, I could not sleep a wink. I had no haunting dreams at all.

Kaidan gave me a concerned look. "What happened last night?"

I told him about what my father said at the end of his letter. He was one of the few people who knew about my relationship with the lieutenant. Kaidan knew of the pain I felt when he left too. There were countless nights when he heard me crying in my room and would come through the hidden doors to see me. He would never say anything, only come in and wrap his arms around me. Kai would lie in my bed with arms tight around me and softly console me until I cried myself to sleep.

"That bloody fool," Kaidan yelled, hitting the table with his fists, which made my plate jump a little.

"Easy there, Sergeant. Do not break my table now," Varon added over his shoulder.

"Sorry, Varon," Kaidan said then looked at me. "What's he trying to do? Does he want to torment you?"

I laughed a little at that. "That's the same thing I said to myself last night." I decided to get off the subject of Rowan. "Last night while I was in the maze, I was being followed. I ended up running through the maze until I got to the fountain. When the guard set foot into the garden, I brought my knife up against his throat. In return, he put his dagger against my stomach."

"Who in the bloody hell would do that?" he asked angrily as he narrowed his eyes.

"Dogan Ramstien!"

"The Salvie? What the hell happened? What did you do?"

I told him everything that was said and how scared the man made me, which I hated to admit, and Kaidan knew that.

"You should have told me when you came back to your chamber," Kaidan said as he stared down at the food Varon just placed in front of him. His jaw was twitching as he was trying to control his anger.

"For what reason? There's nothing you could have done."

"I could have done something," he snapped. "Like go down and confront the man."

I patted his back and said, "Then you would have made trouble for yourself and that's something you do not need. Just eat your bloody food before it gets cold."

He stared down for a moment longer then finally grabbed his utensil and dug in. I smiled and gazed at Kaidan as he ate. I truly do love the man. He's my brother. Kaidan has been my shoulder to cry on, my friend to laugh with, and if I ever needed to fight with someone, he was always much obliged.

Chapter 4

The New Trainer

Today was supposed to be a quiet day for me. The queen did not need me, and I could do what I pleased. The only thing I had to do was meet the general for some training early that evening. It was late morning by the time I knocked on Dylan's door. When he said to come in, I opened the door. There were a few more candles in the room, which was good. With no windows, a man could go crazy being in the dark all the time. He was sitting at the little table eating his lunch.

"My angel, how are you? I was afraid you were not going to come today," he said with a gratified look.

"My morning flew by today. I do not know where it went." I sat down on his bed since there was not another chair in the room. "I see that you are out of bed. That's great!" The dark bags under his eyes were getting less pronounced with each passing day.

"The doctor said that I will be able to leave within the week."

"What terrific news, Dylan! Any memories coming to you yet?" I inquired as I laid my hand on his shoulder.

Patting my hand, he said, "No, angel, not yet." A ghost of a smile ran across his lips.

"What are your plans once you can leave here?"

"I am not sure. I think I might stay here in the city. I will have to find a job and a place to live."

I was glad to hear that; my heart went out to the man. I cannot even imagine what he was going through. With determination, I would do all I could to help him get settled in. "I did hear that they are looking for help in the stables. I can go and talk to them for you…if you want."

"Really?" His face lit up. "That would be wonderful."

"Great, I will go and talk to someone right now. I will come straight here to let you know what they say." I got up and walked over to the door.

"Thank you, angel! You have done so much for me already. I do not know how I will ever repay you."

"You have already by staying alive." Giving him a wink, I quickly walked out the door.

As I made my way to the stables, I could not help but pray that the job was still open. I turned off the main road to a side street that led straight to the stables. When I looked out in the field at the horses grazing and enjoying the sun, I searched for Ara. She should be out there today. There was a sudden commotion, and one of the horses took off in a full run in my direction. It was Ara. The Hybrid was amazing; she must have smelled me from way out there. I walked up to the fence waiting for her to greet me. She came to a sliding stop, brought her head over the fence, and nibbled on my shoulder.

"Hello, girl, how are you?" I rubbed my hands up and down on both sides of her massive neck.

"She's the most intelligent horse we have here. You know that, right?" I turned to look at Wyck Fangmeir, the man who managed the stables. He had a huge smile on his sun-kissed face as he walked toward me. I had grown fond of the man over the last three years. Wyck was a stocky man, only a few inches taller than me. He loved to share his knowledge of horses with me since I was raised around Hybrid horses all my life.

"Yes, I know." I smiled back at him. I was proud of my horse, and everyone knew that. "You are just the man I was looking for."

"Is that so, my lady? What can I do for you?" His smile widened.

"Do you still have that job opening available?"

"Yes, it's still open." Wyck gave me a questionable look. "Do you know of someone who's looking for a job?"

"The lone survivor from the shipwreck gets released soon, and he's interested if you are willing to hire him."

"Does he have any experience with horses?" he inquired.

"After the accident, he lost his memory, so I do not know."

Wyck rubbed his dark whiskery chin while in thought. "I will tell you what, my lady. Since I like you, I am willing to give the lad a try."

I jumped up and down in excitement and wrapped my arms around his neck. "Thank you, Wyck!" I gave him a loud kiss on the cheek. "I knew I could count on you!" He laughed and lightly patted my back. After I let him go, I said, "He's going to need a place to stay. Do you know who I should talk to about that?"

"There's a cot in the back room of the stables." He pointed his thumb over his shoulder. "He can use that until he gets back on his feet."

"Wyck, you are the best!" I started to laugh, and I hugged him again. "Thank you."

Laughingly, he asked, "What's the lad's name anyway?"

"He's not sure of his real name, but we call him Dylan," I explained, feeling all jittery with excitement.

"Well, tell Dylan to come and see me once he's released."

"I will, and thank you again." I beamed him one last smile before taking off back to the castle to tell Dylan the wonderful news.

Not being able to contain myself, I burst into Dylan's room once he answered the knock. "I got you the job!" The man literally jumped from my suddenness. He was now sitting up in his bed; I sat down in front of him.

"Really?" he asked in disbelief.

"Yes, and guess what else?" He just looked at me, smiling, waiting for me to tell him the news. "Wyck said you can use the cot in the back room until you get on your feet."

He let out a hoot. "You are amazing, angel! You got me a job and a place for me to rest my head once I can leave this hellhole." He gazed around in his windowless room. Dylan was definitely itching to get out of here.

"What are friends for, right?" I asked.

"Is that what we are?" he asked looking pleased. "Friends?"

"I would hope we can be."

"Well, I cannot imagine us anything less." He smiled, grabbed my hand, and squeezed. "Thank you for everything again. You will always be an angel to me."

I found myself staying there for a few hours then I had to leave to meet the general for training. Just as I was about to leave, Dylan asked, "What do you do, my lady? Do you live here in the castle?"

I smiled at him. "Yes, I do. I am the queen's lady."

His eyes widened in astonishment. "You are the queen's lady? You know her?"

I laughed at his reaction. "Yes, very much so. Now get your rest, and I will see you tomorrow." Quietly, I shut the door and headed to see the general.

"That's good, Lee, but I know you can do a hell of a lot better," stated the general, strolling over to the four wooden statues and yanking out my knives. Two of them have a knife in their faces, another has one stuck in its chest, and the last one was stuck in its neck. I replaced the knives in my boots and the sheaths on my thighs. As I walked back to the place where I threw them, the general went and rearranged the statues.

"Go back another ten feet this time," he commanded.

Doing as I was told, I stood with my back to them, trying to calculate the distance and the force I would need to make an accurate kill shot. Approximately thirty feet from them now, the general walked up beside me and said, "All right, Lee, whenever you are ready."

Taking in a deep breath, I closed my eyes. When I turned around, he had two of the statues side by side in front of the other two, which are only slightly visible from where I was standing. It would be hard to hit the back ones, but it could be done. Trying not to think too much, I grabbed the knife off my right thigh and the one off my left boot at the same time. I chucked both of them forward at the same time. The two knives hit both front statues in the foreheads. I had the other two knives in the air just as the first two hit. My second right knife just skimmed the front statue and nailed the shoulder on the one behind it. My left one on the other hand ended up hitting the shoulder of the other front statue, never reaching the one behind it.

"Bloody hell," I yelled in frustration. With determination, I stomped forward to snatch my knives and to try again. Some days were better, when I did hit with complete accuracy and amaze myself, but today was not one of those days. For the last half hour, I had to stomp forward in disgust on how I missed my targets.

"Well, what do you think?" asked the general. Just as I was about to answer his question, someone beat me to it.

"She's good fer a woman, if that's what ye'r askin'?" His accent sent a chill down my spine like it always did. I jerked my head around and glared at Dogan Ramstien. He was leaning on the jam of the open door with his arms crossed against his thick chest.

"What the hell are you doing here, Ramstien?" I narrowed my eyes.

"I was told to come here." He glared back at me.

With my knives in my hands, I walked toward them. While putting them in their proper places, I asked the general, "General, why was he told to come here?" I had a bad feeling about this. What did he have up his sleeve now?

"I am going to have Dogan start training with you."

"I beg your pardon?" I yelled in shock. "Hell no! I do not want to be anywhere near this monster."

"General, please tell me ye'r jesting wit me here. Ye canna possibly think that I can work wit this *bairn*?" asked Dogan, who was now standing beside the general.

Oh, I so wanted to strangle the man right then. He just called me a child! Taking the knife off my right thigh and pointed it at him, I retorted, "I would watch what you say, Ramstien. That's a warning."

He just gave me a look like I was a joke or something and looked back to the general. "Look, General, I joined the royal guard to help defend the kingdom not to—" he looked at me again and said with a curled lip—"baby sit!"

"You bastard." I could not control myself any longer, and I lunged at him. The general caught me and held me back.

"Lady Leelah, control yourself! This is not like you at all." General then pointed his finger at Ramstien. "And you! Hold your tongue! This is why I am doing this. I am not having two of my guards hate each other this much. After I heard what happened between you two last night, I am not having it. You are going to learn to get along and trust one another."

"How did you hear…Kaidan? I am going to kill him!" I struggled to get out of the general's grip, but he just held tighter the more I fought.

"No, you are not, Lee, now calm down!" he yelled in a warning tone; then as I started to settle in his embrace, he let me free.

"Dogan, I have seen improvement in the men you have trained with the last few days, and since Lee is the queen's guard, I want her to be better too." He lightly patted my shoulders, and a soft groan escaped my lips.

Dogan asked, "D'ye really think 'tis a good idea fer us to be alone wit weapons?" The mere thought of being alone with him and with weapons in hand sort of scared the hell out of me.

"Oh, it's a good idea." The general grabbed the front of my dress and Dogan's uniform. He yanked the both of us to him then shifted his eyes back and forth while he talked. "And if I ever hear that one of you intentionally hurts the other, you will have to deal with me. I will have you both thrown out on your asses. Do I make myself clear?" He spoke in a low harsh tone.

In the three years I had been there, I had never seen the general this angry, at least not around me. "Yes, General!" I said quickly. Dogan also agreed.

"Good!" The general let go of us, turned for the door, and said over his shoulder, "I will leave you two be so you can figure out a schedule that will work for you both." Out the door he went.

I smoothed down the area of my dress that the general had grabbed then I looked up at my enemy. We just glared at each other for what seemed like minutes then he finally asked, "D'ye even own a sword?"

"Yes," I replied, annoyed.

"Good, bring it wit ye and meet me here tomorrow at dawn." He turned on his heels and walked out the door.

"Wait! What? That's only twelve hours or so from now," I yelled, but I got no response. I twirled and threw all my knives in frustration. Every blade landed on each of the four statues' foreheads. I just shook my head. Of course when I hit them all perfectly, no one is around to witness it. I grabbed my knives and put them in their appropriate places. Then headed out on a mission, and that was to hunt down Kaidan Kimball so I could wring his neck. I made my way through the castle and said something to the first guard I saw.

"Do you by chance know where Sergeant Kimball is?" I asked.

"Sorry, my lady, I have not seen him today," the guard replied.

I thanked the man and decided to go to check Kaidan's room. I might get lucky and catch him there. As I made my way up the stairs to the long corridor that led to our rooms, I saw him at the end of the hall walking straight toward me. I was so angry with him right then that I was shaking. My hands were in tight fists at my sides as I quickened my pace in hopes to catch him off guard. He looked up and smiled when he saw me. It looked like he was about to say something but stopped and made weird a face. It was like he was trying to figure out what was wrong with me. I was only a few feet away when he finally said my name in question. Grabbing hold of his arm and made him turn a little, I slammed his back against the stone wall. Taking my right forearm, I jammed it under his chin. Trying to push me away, he yelled, "Bloody hell, Lee! What's your problem?" I started punching him in the chest with the side of my left fist.

As Kaidan tried to grab my left hand, he yelled in frustration, "Lee, stop this right now. At least tell me why you want to try to beat me to a bloody pulp." He continued, trying to get control of me, but I did not care. I just wanted to inflict some type of pain on him.

"Do not make me do it, Leelah, because I will if you do not stop this instant," he yelled again, but I did not stop. I hated him at the moment. I needed to fight with someone, and he was the perfect candidate. Before I could even think about stopping, Kaidan got a hold of my left arm. He turned me around, twisted my arm, and pressed it against my back. Then he took my legs out from underneath me, causing me to fall forward onto my stomach. Luckily, I was able to catch myself a little with my free hand, or the force might have knocked the breath from my lungs. Kaidan took my other arm, twisted it, and sat all his weight on my back.

"I am sorry, Lee, but I did warn you," he yelled breathlessly.

"You are a fool." Because of all his weight on my back, I had to force the words out. "You know that?"

"If you promise not to swing at me, I will let you up and you can tell me why I am a fool." He paused a moment. "Promise?" I nodded my head.

"No, say it!" he commanded.

"I promise, Kai! Now get off me," I screamed, and a servant peeked out one of the doors up ahead. Kaidan waved them off, and they quickly shut the door. Once the pressure was off, I rolled onto my back and sat up. As I rubbed my arms, I glared at Kaidan, who was sitting against the wall.

"Well?" he asked in annoyance. "Why are you so angry? I have never seen you go crazy like that, and you have done some stupid things to me." Kaidan laid his crossed arms on his knees while he waited for my explanation.

Angrily, I pointed my finger at him. "You just had to tell him! I confided to you this morning. You are supposed to be like my brother. Meaning, if I tell you something, you should keep it to yourself not go and tell the general." My cheeks were burning with heat. It took all my strength not to lunge myself at him again.

"What are you talking about? I never said anything to the general about Rowan, only about the Sal..."

I just widened my eyes and gave him a look like, *you idiot! That's what I am talking about.* Then added, "Because of your big mouth I have to train with him, starting at dawn tomorrow."

Kaidan stared at me; then his face started to get distorted. I knew what he was about to do. I knew what his face looked like when he tried to hold in the laughter. Trying not to smile because I wanted to stay mad at him, I pointed my finger. "Kai, I am warning you. I swear to God if you start…"

It was too late; the laughter burst out of him. Quickly, I got up; and as I marched past him, I slapped him hard across the head. When I got to the door to my room and looked back down the corridor, Kaidan was still sitting on the floor, holding his stomach and started to laugh even harder when he looked back at me. I stormed into my room and slammed the door behind me. He's an idiot! I would get him back for this one way or another. While dropping down in the chair at my desk, I decided to write Pa back, which was probably not the best time to do it, but I needed to do something. I could not just sit in here and do nothing.

> Dear Pa,
>
> I am glad to hear that everyone is doing well. That will be terrific if you all can take a trip out after the baby's born. Oh, Pa, I miss you so much. I would so love to be home right now. I have to start training with a new guard tomorrow morning. He's a Salvie, and I do not trust him, Pa! Because of Kai's big mouth, the general is making us train together, all because we hate each other. I am sorry! I just got done yelling at Kai about it, and I am still frustrated about the whole thing. Oh, about that, you would have loved to have seen it. I attacked Kai when I saw him; in return, he got me flipped onto my stomach with my arms behind my back. To top it off, the bastard sat on me till I calmed down. I am sure it was a sight to see. It was like I was fighting with one of my brothers again. You would have been rolling in laughter. I love you, Pa, and send my love to everyone else.
>
> With love and God bless.
>
> Your daughter,
>
> Lee

Not wanting to seal the letter, I left it upon my desk so I can add more than just my rant and mail it in the morning. I did not mention a single word about Rowan. Pa will notice that too. I was sure he's expecting some kind of reaction to the last part of his letter. As much as I loved the man, I was still angry and hurt about how he left things. Why would I want to honor him by mentioning him in one of my letters? If I ever saw Rowan again, I was not sure if I would punch him or hug him. Hopefully, I would not have to find the answer to that question anytime soon because right now, I would definitely punch him.

I got myself into my nightgown and crawled into bed. Since I had to get up early, I might as well go to bed early too. While I lay there with thoughts about Pa, I heard my hidden door open and close real quickly. I rolled my eyes. What did he just do? I dragged myself out of bed and opened my wardrobe. On the floor sat a piece of paper so I picked it up and read it.

> I am sorry for laughing, Lee. Wait! No, I am not! You have to admit that this is funny. It's just your luck, do you not think? But on a serious note, I am sorry that you have to deal with that bastard. I will try to talk to the general tomorrow. I know you love me, Lee, you cannot hate me forever.

Still smiling, I opened the hidden door and hollered, "Do you want to bet?"

"Actually, yes, I do!" he yelled from his room and started laughing again; I just shook my head as I closed the door.

Chapter 5

Hiding the Pain

Dreams of Rowan left me waking up early and crying. I cursed his name and dragged myself out of bed. Standing before my window, I could see the night sky starting to lighten up. A light moan filled the silence, and I decided to get dressed. I was not looking forward to this at all. Dogan Ramstien was not going to be an easy man to get along with. Searching through my wardrobe, I pulled out a dress. Just a basic dress, nothing fancy; it would do fine.

After I pulled my hair back to a tail at the base of my neck, I wrote Mira a short note, just to let her know where I was and that I did not know how long I was going to be. Grabbing my sword out of the hidden compartment in my wardrobe, I walked out my door to head down to face my enemy.

As I made my way down the stairs that led to the front doors of the castle, I could hear them open. There walked in Dogan. As quickly as he looked up at me, he turned away. When I got to the bottom, I followed him. My heart was pounding in my throat. The man scared me, and that was why I loathed him so much.

We walked into the room where I had always done my training, and I shut the door behind us. All the candles along the stone walls were lit. Someone must have been told to have them lit for us. He turned and faced me. Even though he was starting to grow a beard, I still could not help but look at the gruesome scar on his face. The pain he must have felt had to have been unbearable.

I almost jumped when he finally spoke. "I hate this just as much as ye, maybe even more." I wanted to laugh, but I did not. He continued, "I tried like hell to get outta this, and believe me, I tried. General Wolfe is not budging on this. So if I'm stuck training wit ye, then we're doing this my way. I dinna care if ye like it or not. That's how 'tis going to be. We'll train four to five times a week, depending on the week o' course." I stopped him right there.

"Whoa! Are you serious?" I asked raising my eyebrows. "Because I cannot even stand being in the room right now and you want to get together four or five times a week. Are you crazy?"

"Oh aye, I'm serious! I dinna jest. And am I crazy…most definitely. General Wolfe wants ye stronger and a better fighter. So, m'lady, I'm not going to make ye better. I'm going to make ye one o' the best he's ever had." I stared at him, and when I realized that my mouth was open due to the shock, I snapped it shut. I did not know what to say to him. He continued, "What is this, m'lady? No comment? This may be a first."

"Oh, go to hell!" I snapped as I narrowed my eyes.

He laughed a little without opening his mouth. Dogan reached out his hand and commanded, "Let me see the sword."

Hesitating at first, I handed it over to him. He examined the handle before he pulled it from the leather sheath. He dropped the sheath on the floor so he could use both of his hands. It was an arming sword, made mostly for cutting and thrusting. I was proud of that sword as I made it myself. My father's a blacksmith, and I always worked with him in the forge before coming here. Even though I had not used it in a while, it still shone as he held it up, turning it back and forth. I engraved my last name into the blade just below the hilt.

Dogan ran his thumb ever so softly on the edge of the blade. When he lifted his thumb, I could see a little blood. He placed the flat of the blade on one finger to check the balance. Sure enough, when he let go of the hilt, the sword did not even sway a little. He tossed it up in the air and caught it by the handle and then started doing some thrusting moves with it. For how big the man was, he was quick. Quicker than most men I knew.

"I do ha' to say, I'm impressed. The sword's light but strong. 'Tis extremely balanced and too sharp to the touch. Let me guess. 'Twas a gift from yer father, maybe?" He arched his scarred brow.

I was not about to tell him that I made it. He would not believe me anyway, and he would probably just laugh. I gave him a snide smile and said, "I will never tell you because that's none of your damn business."

"Well, at least tell me this: who crafted it? I would like him to make me two," Dogan said *him*; I began to laugh inside my head. If only he knew.

"That will be a little difficult since it was made in Mastingham."

Still looking at my sword, he said, "If I'm ever up north, I'll ha' to keep that in mind."

Dogan picked up the sheath off the floor and slid the sword back in. He leaned it against the wall by the door and walked over to the other end of the room. Opening the wooden chest at the far end, he pulled out two wooden swords. He placed one sword on the closed lid and called me over to him. Reluctantly, I walked up to him. He tossed the wooden sword to me, and I caught it by the hilt. He nodded. "Good, now show me how ye hold and move it."

Holding it in my right hand, I sliced it through the air in front of me. I felt like an idiot! Why the hell am I even here? Dogan stalked toward me and ripped the sword out of my hand.

"Wrong!" he hollered. He snatched my hand and wrapped it around the hilt of the sword again. Dogan squeezed his hand around mine and tried to pull it again from my grip. It did not budge. Now wrapping both of his massive hands around mine, he said, "Think o' this as an extension o' yer arm. Always ha' a firm grip. Yer life depends on it."

Once he took his hands off mine, he quickly grabbed the wooden blade again. My grip was still tight around the hilt, so when he tried to pull the blade away, he nearly pulled my whole arm out of place. I rubbed my shoulder as he went over to grab the other sword.

"Today we're going to go over just the basics. How ye should move the sword and blocking." Dogan stood about ten paces away from me. His eyes, all of a sudden, got tense, and he said to me, "But first I wanna to see what ye got." He gave me a slight evil smile and then beckoned me. "Come get me, woman! I wanna to see if ye can even hit me."

For the first time, the man actually made me smile. I hated him so much that all I wanted to do was hurt him. "It would be my pleasure!" I mimicked his evil smile and charged toward him.

Over an hour later, I walked back to my room sore and tired. The man was good, and he did not even break a sweat. I, on the other hand, was drenched. I hated to admit it, but the man taught me a lot today. Never actually hit him myself; I tried, but he was too quick. He nailed both of my arms so much that I lost count. I was hurting severely, but the pain only made me more determined to get better. It will be a great day when I can actually inflict pain upon Dogan Ramstien.

"Oh my, Lee, you look terrible," Mira cried in concern when I walked into my room.

Giving her a small laugh, I said, "I feel terrible. The man did not hold back, I can tell you that." What I wanted was a hot bath, but I knew I did not have time for that. "I think I might need some help getting out of this dress."

As I started to drag the dress over my head, I winced in pain. It hurt to bring my arms above my head. Mira worked the dress till she got my head out of it without lifting my arms too much. Once my arms were bare, I could see the damage. Both of my upper arms were bright red and already starting to bruise. I was glad he wanted to wait till the day after next for training again. I was going to stiffen up by the end of today. There was no way I would be able to train tomorrow anyway.

"Oh my Lord, Lee! Look at what he's done to you," she screeched and lifted my arm to get a better look.

I winced in pain. "Easy, Mira."

"Sorry." She gave me a pained look. "Sit on the bed. I am going to wrap your arms in a damp cloth. Hopefully, that will help keep the swelling down."

The coolness felt great against my skin. When she was done, she sat in the chair in front of me and said, "Kai is going to lose it when he sees this. You know that, right? He was telling me this morning how upset he was with himself for getting you into this situation."

"I know, and that's why he's never going to find out about it. Promise me you will not say anything to him," taking hold of her hands, I pleaded with her.

"Oh, Lee, he should know what this man did to you."

"It's my fault that I am hurting. I will get better. If Kaidan knows about this, he will go after Ramstien. I cannot see Kai getting hurt because of me. Ramstien is not like any guard we have had before. He's well trained and fights like a true Salvie. He would definitely hurt Kai if he attacked him. So promise me you will not say anything."

"All right, I promise for now, but if I ever find you in worse shape than now, I am telling him."

Sticking my hand out to her, I smiled, "Deal!" Mira shook my hand and got up, shaking her head. A little while later, she removed the cloths from my arms and helped me get clean for the day.

"I am sorry, Lee, but you have to wear this today." Mira held up a corset in her hand.

I moaned, "Can we not and say we did?" I hated wearing those bloody things. They were uncomfortable, and I could not breathe. I never wore them unless I absolutely had to.

"No, not this time, Lee. You will be leaving soon to go with the king and queen to the Duke Thelas's estate. So you need to have everything in its proper place."

"Great, that means I am going to have to deal with Gavin," I groaned.

Gavin was Duke Marvin Thelas's son. He disgusted me and reminded me of a weasel. He was not a man in my eyes. Whenever I see him, he would not leave me alone. One of these days, I was going to be my normal self and punch him square in the face. First, I get myself beat up by a man I loathed, and now I was going to get groped by a man that nauseated me.

"I know the man makes you sick, but just try to stay calm," Mira spoke quietly and lightly patted my cheek.

I laughed and accusingly said, "Stay out of my head, Mira."

"I cannot help it that I know you so well." She gave me a small smile and then nodded toward the corner of the bed. "Do you think you can hold on to the post while I tighten this?"

Not responding, I just stood straight while she fitted the corset around my torso. My hands were tight around the bedpost while she pulled and tugged at my back, the whole time trying to ignore the pain in my arms. After she was done, I went over to stand in front of my vanity and looked at myself in the mirror. These damn corsets were ridiculous, and how they pushed up my breasts. Whoever said women should wear them should be hung. I was already feeling like I could not breathe and started grabbing the bottom of it to try pulling it down. Mira snapped at me to leave it alone. I turned side to side to inspect my arms. I knew by the end of the day they were going to look a lot worse.

"Mira, I better wear something with long sleeves. I do not want to take a chance of Kaidan seeing this." I winced when I laid my right hand on my upper left arm. Kaidan always playfully punches me in the arm; now I was praying he does not because then he would see that I was in pain.

"I am already ahead of you...how's this?" she held up an olive-and-white gown. It had long sleeves, so it was fine for me.

After saying my good mornings to the guards in front of the royal living quarters, they let me in. I could hear Kaidan talking as I made my way down the hall. When I strolled into the dining area, Bryce and he were sitting at the table that still had food on it. My stomach growled instantly at the smell of it. I had not eaten anything since the afternoon the day before.

"Good morning, Lee. How are you?" inquired Bryce.

I took a seat and snatched one of the many scones off the plate. Before taking a bite, I said, "I am doing good, but I am starving. How are you this fine morning?"

When I bit into the scone, he smiled. "I am doing great, Lee. Thanks for asking."

"So how did it go this morning? It looks like you are still in one piece," Kaidan asked while he tried to hide his smile. I so wanted to throw the scone at his head.

Mira fixed me up good. With the dress and my hair twisted up off my neck, no one would have thought of me being beat up early this morning. "Actually, it was not as bad as I thought it was going to be. He's tough, do not get me wrong. I did learn a lot today." I was not about to tell him that the man was a beast and he did not stop attacking. I had to lie a little, but I did learn quite a bit though.

"See, you got all mad at me for nothing." Kaidan started laughin'. "It looks like I won that bet."

Bryce started to chuckle too. "Kaidan told me about the fight you two had last night. I wish I could have seen it." Bryce turned to Kaidan. "What bet do you speak of?"

"I bet Lee that she could not hate me forever." He grinned at me as he took a bite of food.

"Oh, I still hate you, Kai!" I said, fighting not to smile.

"Liar!" he said, pointing at me. "I can see your lips twitching."

Quickly, I stood up. "You know what? I do not need to take this from you men. I am going to go find Rosa. She will have sympathy for me." I grabbed another scone, and as I walked out of the room, the two of them roared in laughter. I could not help but smile; at least they could not see that. After knocking on the door to the queen's dressing room, a maid answered it.

"Good morning, my lady," said the maid as she let me in. There are four maids with her, helping her get ready. When the woman was done tying the back of her corset, Rosa turned to me. Soon she will not be able to wear corsets anymore once her belly starts to swell, and I will envy her when that happens.

"What are those men laughing about? I could hear them all the way from here."

"What are they always laughing at…me of course."

"Sweet Lee, are they picking on you again?" she asked, and I smiled. She was so beautiful with her light-strawberry hair lying down past her bare shoulders. "So tell me, Lee, how did it go with this Dogan Ramstien?"

"He's brutal, and I am a little sore. Other than that, it went all right I guess."

"Good, I am glad to hear that." She gave me a soft smile.

I wanted to say something about the baby, but I was not sure if the maids knew yet. So I will have to wait till we were alone.

We took a carriage to the Duke's estate, which was a little over an hour's ride. We pulled into the long drive that led to the house. Kaidan, who was sitting next to me, wrapped his arm around my shoulders and squeezed me against him. I must have hidden the pain that shot up my arms because he never said anything about it.

"We are almost there to see your friend, Gavin," he teased. He knew how Gavin was toward me. The man truly irritated Kaidan. If my arms were not hurting, I would have punched him in the chest; so instead, I muttered the word *bastard*.

"Fight nice, children. Do not make me have to separate you two," Bryce joked, causing us all to laugh.

The carriage stopped at the front door. Kaidan opened the carriage door and jumped out. Usually, the carriage operator would come, unfold the steps, and open the door. Kaidan never had the patience waiting for the man, so he always got out and did it himself. When I went to the small door, Kaidan held out his hand for mine. "My lady!" he said with a funny accent and bowed his head. I took his hand as I walked down the steps.

"Thank you, kind sir," I said, bowing to him.

Bryce stuck his head out, smiling, and stared at us. "I do not know what to think of you two sometimes. It's never a dull moment, I will tell you that."

Kaidan looked at me and winked. When Bryce helped Rosa out of the carriage, the front door of the house opened. Duke Thelas came out with his arms wide open.

"Bryce, Rosa, I am so delighted you came," he said in a joyous voice.

"We can never say no to an invitation like yours, Uncle. How's my beautiful aunt?" The Duke was the brother of Bryce's late mother. He was a jolly man in his mideighties.

"Well, come on in and ask her yourself." He said hello to Kaidan then came to me. "Beautiful Lady Leelah. It's always a pleasure." He took and kissed my hand.

As I curtsy, I said, "Thank you, it's a pleasure to be here."

We were about halfway through our brunch when Gavin showed his face for the first time since we got there. Kaidan kicked my left ankle as soon as he walked into the room. I jerked my head and glared at him. He was looking in the direction of Gavin with a straight face. The longer I glared at him, the more his lips started to twitch. Gavin strolled over and gave his cousin, the king, a hug then he kissed Rosa's offered hand. He was just a few inches taller than me, with dark hair and a short mustache and goatee. Gavin was in his midforties and handsome. I could see how the women fell for him, but I knew his true nature. That was the reason I try to avoid him as much as possible.

"Lady Leelah." I gave him my hand and he kissed it. "It's been too long since we have seen each other. How are you?" *Has not been long enough*, I thought.

"I am good. Thanks for asking," I lied.

He smiled and went to sit beside Kaidan. Since the room was noisy with different conversations, I leaned over and whispered in Kai's ear, "For the love of God, please do not get up. As soon as you do, that man will be in your seat with his hands all over me. If you truly love me, you will not leave me with him."

"Do not worry, Lee. I like to torture you, but when it comes to him, it's not funny," he whispered back. I lip the words *thank you* to him, and he winked.

The first thing out of Dogan's mouth was, "How's yer arms?" As I walked in the room for training, I grimaced at the thought of being hit in the arms again.

"They are fine," I lied.

"Lift yer sleeves so I can see 'em," he demanded.

"No," I yelled. Dogan stalked over to me. I knew if I ran or backed up, it would only make it worse because he was going to have his way no matter what. He grabbed the upper part of my right arm and lifted it up to the side. I cringed in pain. Even though it's been two days since my first training session, my arms were still stiff and sore.

"They're fine, eh?" He grabbed my sleeve and yanked it up my arm. My arm had black and blue marks, starting at the top of my shoulder all the way to my elbow. The left arm was the same way. Dogan examined it and said, "I take it that the left looks the same." While huffing out a breath, I said yes.

"I got something that'll help wit the bruising. I'll give it to ye when we're done here." When I did not say anything to him, he yanked down my sleeve and handed me a wooden sword. Dogan turned and walked a few steps before abruptly turning back toward me with the sword in the air. Not looking forward to getting hit today, I brought up my sword with my right arm and laid the flat of the blade against my left hand. His sword crashed down hard on mine, but I did block it. The force sent shock waves of pain down my arms.

"Good," was all he said.

For the next hour, we went over different blocking techniques. The man was exceptional, I will give him that. He has taught me a great deal more than my brothers ever have. It did not mean that I trusted him. We do not really talk to each other all that much. I think that's what we both preferred.

"I ha' guard duty tomorrow evening, so meet me here at dusk," he ordered.

"All right." I took a deep breath and turned to leave the room.

"Woman, wait!"

Rolling my eyes as I turned, and he tossed a small glass jar to me. I snatched it out of the air and held it up to see what looked like a white paste. I gazed back at him and asked, "What is it?"

"Just rub it on to yer arms tonight and wrap a cloth around them. Ye'll be better by morning."

"Umm, thanks?" I gave him a questioning look and walked out of the room.

With the jar in my pocket, I made my way to the kitchen to get something to eat. At least I did not get hit today. That made me happy. I did not think my arms could have handled the abuse anyway. Just the slightest touch caused pain. When I got to the busy kitchen, Kaidan was sitting and talking to Varon. I avoided him as much as possible yesterday. I just did not want him to know about my arms. I was not sure how he would react. Sometimes he will make jokes about things and other times he goes into big brother mode. If he did not see me walk in, I probably would have snuck back out of the kitchen.

"Well?" he asked.

I rolled my eyes. "It went better today. Just practiced different blocking techniques." I took the seat next to him.

Kaidan, being his usual self, punched me in the arm. "See and you thought it was…" I flinched, and I did not mean too; it's was a reflex. "What's wrong?" he asked with concern.

"It's nothing I am still a little sore from our first training session." I shrugged my shoulders. "That's all."

Kaidan gave me an odd look, and before I could stop, him he yanked up my sleeve. He had a horrified look on his face. "Holy mother of God! He did this to you?" he bellowed in disgust.

"Kaidan, it is fine," I said gently while laying a hand over his that was lightly touching my arm.

"The hell it is! I knew something was up. The day we were in the carriage, you tensed up when I put my arm around you, and you avoided me all day yesterday." He started to get up. I grabbed and yanked him back down to his seat.

"Look, Kaidan, I am fine. It happens when you train. I might be a little beat up and sore, but I am not broken." Moving my arms up and down in hopes to reassure him.

"You are a woman, for God's sake. He has to be hitting you with full force to be leaving bruises like that." He leaned his one elbow on the table while he faced me. All the while his hand was clenched tight in a fist.

"Yes, a woman who's supposed to protect the queen. Do you think the enemy is going to go gentle with me because I am a woman? Hell no, so relax! This is why I did not want to tell you. I knew you would flip out," I yelled as my voice began to tighten in anger.

"I cannot believe you're defending him. You are supposed to hate the man," he yelled back as his dark eyes started to spark.

"I still do, Kaidan," I screamed. "But I still have to train with the man, and if you go and approach him on this, he will only be harder on me. I just know it, so stay out of it, Kai!"

Kaidan glared at me for a few moments; he appeared like he was about to burst out of his skin. When he was not saying anything, I punched him in the shoulder, "Kai, snap out of it!" I yelled.

"All right! I will leave it go for now, but if I see anything worse than that, he will have to deal with me," he said, calmer.

I smiled at him. "Thank you, brother." Wrapping my arm around his neck, I brought him to me so I could kiss his forehead. "I do love you!"

"Yeah, yeah." He pushed away from me and turned back to his food to finish eating. Varon was shaking his head with a small smirk as he placed a plate of food in front of me. I smiled back and said thank-you.

Later that night after I got into my nightgown, I opened the jar that Dogan gave me. Taking a quick whiff of it, I gagged. It was revolting! Was he really expecting me to put this on myself? Then I figured what the hell, right? If it does not help, I will never use it again. I stuck two fingers into the paste. It was cool to touch, which astonished me. The coolness felt great on my bruised arms. Then I wrapped both of them in the cloths that I asked Mira to get for me. The cloths helped keep the revolting smell down. After I said my prayers, I crawled into bed, hoping to have a good-night's sleep.

Chapter 6

Bittersweet

While waking up, I stopped in midstretch. Both of my hands were above my head, and I had no pain. Urgently, I unwrapped one of my arms and stared upon it in amazement. In complete shock, it was unbelievable. I quickly unwrapped the other; it too was the same. My arms were perfect. No bruises, no pain! Laughter escaped as I picked up the jar and kissed it. I did not know what it was, but it worked like a miracle.

Mira came in when I was looking in the mirror at my arms. She did not say anything at first; she just took my arm and examined it. "How?" she asked.

"The paste that Ramstien gave me actually worked," I said, still in complete amazement.

"What's in it? Is it made by a mage?"

"I really do not know, Mira." Mages are what we called people who had some type of special power. Some like Azzan, the king's mage, can make you speak the truth. Others can heal or even revive someone who had just passed away. I have heard that there are people who can see into the future. People say that mages are truly blessed and are supposed to use their powers for the greater good, but there are some that do not. Azzan was the only mage I had ever met—well, that I know of anyway. "Maybe it is some type of magic, but do you think that Ramstien is a mage?"

"Do not ask me. You know that only other mages can tell each other apart. All I do know is that paste that he gave you is definitely some type of magic. Why not just ask him? You have to see him tonight, right?" she asked as she continued to examine my arm.

"I have a feeling it will just be a waste of breath with him, but I will ask," I groaned out.

The door to the training room was opened so I walked in quietly. Dogan asked without turning around, "How's yer arms today?" How the hell did he know I was here? Maybe he was some sort of mage.

"They are perfect, actually. What's in that paste, Ramstien? Are you some type of mage?" I just went right out and asked him.

Dogan started laughing, actually laughing, and the sound did not seem right coming from him. He finally turned and looked at me; he had a deep dimple on each cheek. His entire face changed, if it was not for that terrible scar over his right eye, he would probably look handsome. I tried to shake the image from my head. Behind that brilliant smile was still the monster that I did not trust.

"Let's just say 'tis an ol' family recipe," he said then his face went back to its sober self. Just as I expected, he was not going to tell me anything. I cannot really blame him because I felt the same way. Maybe if I kept asking him questions, over time he would answer me, so I will shut up. I need to find out this man's story. Why here? Why now? Why even leave his home? Does he have any family in Salvatoria? One way or another I was going to find out. I walked up to him, and he handed me two swords; instantly, I backed up several steps.

"So, Ramstien, how did you get that appalling scar on your face?" I asked him in his native tongue.

"A dagger," he returned in his language. "How did you learn to speak my language so fluently and with our accent on top of it."

"I had a good teacher," I replied in my language.

Dogan waved me to come and attack him, so I did. We went back and forth taking turns blocking and attacking each other. He knocked one of my swords out of my grip and shouted at me, "Stop flinching too! If ye flinch one more time, I'll ha' ye on yer arse before ye can even realize what I'm doing."

I was sweating and sore all over again. The man was relentless, so I picked up my sword for the tenth time that evening. Dogan brought his sword up high and swung it down toward me. I had to be quick, but I was able to get one of my swords above my head to stop the leading blow. He was so quick that before I realized what he was doing, my feet were in the air, and I hit the floor hard. Pain shot up my spine and blurred my vision for a moment. He bent down, grabbed the front of my dress, and yanked me up to his face.

"Ye flinched," he growled. "Every time ye do that, I'll ha' ye thrown on yer arse." He let go of my dress and shoved me back. "Now get up!"

"Ramstien!" We both jerk our heads to the door to see Kaidan marching toward us.

"Kaidan, no!" I scurried to get up, but Kaidan was already up in his face. Dogan was at least ten inches taller than Kaidan, but he did not seem to care.

"You are supposed to be training her, not beating her up. There is no reason for you to take her out like you did," he yelled and practically spit in his face with anger.

I tried to get myself in between them, but I could not budge them. Kaidan had his chest up against Dogan. Trying to do something, I yelled, "Kaidan, just leave it be. I am fine." When he would not look at me, I tried to jam my arm between the two of them. "Kaidan, for God's sake look at me!" Before I could get a reaction from him, Dogan wrapped his monstrous hand around my face and pushed me back. He did it with so much force that I stumbled back several steps.

"Stay outta this, woman," he barked. I was just about to yell back at him when Kaidan took his right fist and connected it with Dogan's jaw. He stumbled back, and Kaidan tackled him to the ground. All hell broke loose. They were rolling on the ground with their fists flying.

I screamed, "That's enough you fools! This is ridiculous!" I started to see blood on the white marble floor, but I could not tell who it was coming from. "If you two want to kill each other, then have at it!" I marched out of the room. What idiots! I told Kaidan to stay out of it, but he did not listen, did he. When I got to the end of the corridor, I turned right and almost slammed into General Wolfe.

"General!"

"Lee, have you seen Kaidan? One of the men said he saw him head in this direction."

I so wanted to smile, but I did not. "Yes General! He's in the training room with Ramstien."

"Thank you, Lee. Did training go well today?"

"Yes, General, it went very well."

"Good." He smiled and turned down the corridor I came from. I was almost tempted to turn and follow him. I would have loved to have seen his face and the faces of those two idiots. Instead, I continued walking back to my room with a big smile on my face. Kaidan and Dogan are going to catch hell for this.

As I walked into my room, a sweet aroma filled the air. Sitting by the fire was a brass basin filled with perfumed water for me to clean off the sweat. I kicked off my shoes and pulled my dress over my head. Slipping out of my shift and leggings, I slid into the chair in front of the hearth. With the cloth in hand, I submerged it in the lilac-scented water. Squeezing out the excess water, I pressed it against my face. Slowly, I washed the sweat from my body. My arms were sore again and most likely will have to put that paste on them before I go to bed.

After I felt clean and refreshed, I grabbed my nightgown off the bed and slipped it on. Just as I did that, I heard the hidden door and my wardrobe doors burst open. Quickly, I hugged my arms across my chest and screamed, "Kaidan, you idiot! You almost caught me naked!"

He slammed the doors behind and stalked toward me. His left eye was swollen shut, and he had lacerations on his right cheek and mouth. He looked terrible, and he was mad. Kaidan pointed his finger at me as he yelled, "This is entirely your fault!" I walked backward and around the chair so I could head for the door. Out of all the time I had known him, I had never seen him like this.

"How's what my fault, Kai? I told you to stay out of it!" I panicked as my back hit the cool wall, with Kaidan standing only a few inches from me.

He poked his finger at my chest as he brought his angry eyes level to mine. "It's because of you that I have to train with Ramstien with the general watching our every move. You know what? Ramstien was right—all you are is a filthy cunt!"

My mouth dropped in disgust of what he just called me. I reached with my left hand and unlocked my door. Narrowing my eyes, I spoke to him in a low forced voice, "Get the hell out of my bed chamber, Kaidan, before you say or do something else you will regret."

Kaidan glared at me with his dark angry eyes then hit the stone wall beside my head. He walked out and slammed the door behind him. I stood there for a few moments with my heart beating out of my chest. I was growing weak at the knees; never in my life had anyone called me that. Angrily pushing myself off the wall, I threw on my boots. With my robe wrapped tightly around me, I walked out the hidden door that was still open from Kaidan. There was noise of something being smashed in his room. Quickly, I shut my door behind me. I did not even bother with the candle. I was so irate right then that all I needed was fresh air.

I kept my hand against the stone walls to help guide me down the spiral staircase. Once I opened the door to outside, I took in a deep breath. *Please, Lord, do not let Ramstien be in the gardens tonight. I do not think I would be able to control myself if I saw him.* Peeking around the hedges to look toward the castle's front doors, the few guards that are standing there had their backs to me, so I bolted across to the maze.

I continued running and did not stop till I reached the fountain. I walked to the far end and sat on the bench that was on the other side of the only tree in there. So if anyone came in here, they would not see me unless they actually walked around. I sat there trying to catch my breath. My head hung down as I placed my elbows on my knees. The words that Kaidan said came back to my memory. I still could not believe he said that. Kaidan, my brother! How could he ever think of saying something like that to me? My body was shaking with anger. I tightened my robe, but I knew that I was not cold. I looked up when I heard a noise, and there he stood. In the faint light from the lanterns, I could see his face was badly beaten as my brother's.

"Because o' ye"—Ramstien pointed his finger at me—"I'm stuck training wit Kimball while being supervised by General Wolfe."

I stood up, "Go back to your duties, Ramstien! After what I heard from Kaidan, you are the last person I want to see right now."

"If Kimball is able to ha' his say wit ye, then I ha' a right to."

Walking calmly to the beast, I looked straight up at him. I brought my right hand up to slap him in the face for what he said about me, but he snatched my wrist just inches from his face. What I did next will always shock me. I could not help myself even if I tried. Still fixed on his emerald eyes, I grabbed his shirt with my left hand and jammed my knee up between his legs. He had the look of shock and pain that distorted his face as he fell to his knees on the ground.

"Ye rotten bitch! What the hell did ye do that for?" he groaned out.

Taking a handful of his hair, I yanked his head back so he could look at my face. "That's for calling me a filthy cunt, you bastard!" I let go of him and took a few steps back.

"I never called ye such a thing, but now I'm wishing I had." He continued moaning as he cupped his member I just smashed. His shoulders were slouched as he rocked back and forth.

I stared at him for a moment, stunned; then Kaidan broke the silence. "What he says is true, Lee."

"I beg your pardon?" I asked.

"That's why I came out here. To tell you I am sorry and that Ramstien never said that. I was angry, and it just came out." His beaten face was softer, maybe even sad.

"You mean you are telling me that I just kicked him where it counts for no reason whatsoever?" I could feel the panic work its way up from my stomach. My body started to shake uncontrollably.

"Oh, I am sure he needed to be kicked, just not for the reason you did." He gave me a shy smile.

"Kaidan you fool!" I screamed and looked back at Dogan. Still hunched over on his knees he slowly lifted up his head and gave me snide grin.

"Just wait till tomorrow evening, ye bitch. Ye'll pay for this!" The anger was vibrating off his body. Oh my God, what have I just done? There was tightness in my chest. I needed to get away from them both before I really lost it. I took off pushing Kaidan out of my way.

"Lee," he yelled. "Wait!"

"Stay away from me, Kai!" I screamed over my shoulder. "You have already done enough."

I ran as fast as I could with the need to get as far away as possible from Ramstien. I am dead woman! The man was going to kill me tomorrow. What was I thinking of doing that to a man like himself? I burst out of the maze and ran down the side of the castle. There were sounds of Kaidan running behind me as the hedges grabbed and pulled against my robe. I opened the door and slammed it shut behind me, tripping up a few steps as I ran up them. When I finally got up to my room, I collapsed in front of the fireplace. My throat burned from inhaling the cold night air. There was noise of my brother behind me shutting my wardrobe doors quietly and then sitting on my bed. Looking at him now, he sat with his elbows on his knees as his head hung down. That lump was starting to form in my throat that I get before I start crying.

Trying to keep it down, I said, "If Ramstien never said that, that means you did. How and why would you ever say something like that to me?"

Not looking at me, he said, "Lee, I am so sorry. I was angry. I needed someone to yell at, and you were the person I picked. I should have never barged into your room, and I should have never said what I said. I wanted you to hate Ramstien as much as I hate him."

"I already hate him, and you of all people know that," I said, still trying to keep my voice down. "Never in my life has anyone ever called me that, Kai. I still cannot believe that came to your mind to say. Now because of what you said, I did something I should have never done. The man is going to kill me tomorrow. Oh my God! He is so going to kill me!"

I started to rock back and forth. I could not breathe all of a sudden. The panic started to really hit me. And to think I was scared of him earlier, now I was petrified. Kaidan knelt down in front of me and took my face in his hands. He made me look at him.

"Easy, Lee, breathe." I tried to take some deep breaths, "That's a girl. Keep breathing. Everything is going to be fine. I will talk to the Salvie tomorrow, all right? He's not going to kill you. I will promise you that." He paused and searched my face with his swollen and sad-dened eyes. "Lee, can you ever forgive me?"

Like the bloody fool that I am, I started to cry, "Of course I forgive you, brother! Just never call me that again!" Kaidan wrapped his arms around me in a hug to soothe me. A moment later, his body started shaking. I know what that shaking meant; he was laughing. I sat up and hit him in the chest when I saw his silly smile. I rubbed my eyes to get rid of the excess tears so I could see him clearer.

Laughingly, he said, "You really nailed him good though, Lee. It took all of me to not start cheering."

I could not help but smile at him. "You did a number on his face too. It looks like it's going to be a long night for him."

"I know," he said, then we both were sitting on the floor laugh-ing. I always find myself never being able to stay mad at him very long. No matter how much we may hurt each other, in a snap of the fingers, we can be laughing. After the laughing, subsided Kaidan got up to go back to his room.

"Kai, wait. Sit in this chair. I have some stuff that will help with your face." As I walked to stand to grab the paste, I realized how much I really cared for him. Anyone else, I would probably still hold a grudge, no matter how much they apologized. Kaidan was different. We might not be siblings by blood, but we still had that bond that brothers and sisters share.

"Oh, I do not know." He sat in the chair cautiously. "What is it?"

"I am really not sure, but it works. Ramstien gave it to me yesterday. This morning when I woke up, my arms were healed," I said, lifting up my arms

He moaned when I said the name *Ramstien*, and I handed him the jar. "That stuff smells horrible, and you want to put it on my face? Hell no! It's probably some type of trick to punish me more for what I said."

I laughed at him. "Trust me, Kai." Taking the jar from his hand, I very lightly spread the paste over the bruised and cut skin. Once it was on, I handed him a few extra cloths I had. "When you lie in bed, drape these over the areas I covered. Make sure you see me as soon as you wake up. I want to see how it looks."

"All right, Lee, good night, and again, I am sorry for everything," he said.

"Good night, Kai." I gave him a soft smile, and he smiled back as he bent down and walked through my wardrobe back to his room.

The next morning, a knock came from my door. I told them to come in, expecting to see Mira, but it was Kaidan instead. Wearing his long robe, he walked in with a huge smile on his handsome, untouched face. "All I got to say is I want a jar of that paste. The only marks left on my face are two small scars."

I walked up to him to get a closer look. He had a scar above his left eyebrow and another one by his bottom lip. Other than that, his face was its normal self. Beaming him a smile, I said, "I told you it would work, the paste is magic."

Mira walked in behind him. "Good morning you two."

Her face really lit up when she's around Kaidan. When she got a good look at his face, her expression turned serious. "Kai, what happened to your face?" Of course she would notice right away. She would have been horrified if she saw him last night.

"I am fine, Mira. I got in a fight last night with Ramstien, but Lee fixed me up. I am glad you did not see me then."

"You got in a fight? How did that happen?" she asked with a horrified look.

Kaidan touched her face as he said, "When we meet for lunch, I will tell you then." He leaned forward and lightly touched her lips with his then walked out of the room. This was the first time I had ever seen them do something so intimate. Mira gazed shyly at me with her cheeks all flushed. They loved each other, and I envied them for that. I had that once, a love that made you blush all the time. A love that gave you butterflies in the stomach whenever you saw him. The memories of Rowan will haunt me till the day I die. Not knowing the true reason of his leaving made it all the harder.

"You are thinking of him again." Mira stated. "I am sorry, Lee. Kai should have never kissed me like that in front of you."

"No, I am glad he did, Mira. I am happy to see you two together…finally." I softly smiled. "It's not just that kiss, it can be anything. One moment I am fine, the next I am getting slammed with some type of memory of him."

It was late in the afternoon when I strolled down the cobblestone streets of Burreck City. Usually, I would ask for my horse but decided the long walk would do me good. The aromas of fresh-baked breads, fruits, and vegetables filled the air. Horse-drawn carts were being filled with goods. People were laughing, and some argued about prices. The city had everything you would ever need. The closer I got to the barracks, the harder my heart started to pound. What was I thinking of coming here to talk to Dogan Ramstien? I could have just sent someone with a message for him. I guess if I did not do this, it would be eating at me until I did see him again.

Upon reaching the front door of the barracks, I took in a deep breath before knocking. The door opened instantly, and standing there was Sterling with a brilliant smile. He had his raven hair tied back away from his face. Sterling always had a beard, but now he was clean-shaven. I almost did not recognize him. He was Rowan's best friend, and I loved seeing him for that reason.

"Lee, what a pleasant surprise, please come on in." He beamed and opened the door wider. I walked in and grabbed his chin.

I rubbed my thumb against his smooth skin while I gave him my full smile. "Love the new look, Sterling. It makes you look younger." He was thirty-two, the same age as Rowan. Quickly, I gave him a kiss on the cheek in greeting.

"That was the look I was hoping for." He winked. "Well, you do not come here to see me anymore, and so let me guess…you are here to see Dogan too?"

"Sorry, Sterling, I promise to start making my visits again." I gave him a shy smile. This place used to be my usual hang out when I was off. I needed to stop avoiding this place and see my friend whom I do care about. Then I thought about how he said *Dogan too?* "Was someone else here today to see him?"

"Kimball was here about an hour ago." Then he bent down to whispered in my ear, "He told me all that happened last night and what you did to Dogan. That was just wrong." I did not know what to say. I knew I was wrong; that was one of the reasons why I was here. Sterling started laughing at me and wrapped his arm around my shoulders. "I am just jesting with you, Lee. I wish I could have seen it though—a man like Dogan Ramstien falling to his knees."

"You are a bad man, Sterling." I laughed shaking my head. "Is he here then?"

"Yeah, I think he's still upstairs." He kept his arm around me and took me with him. Then he yelled up the stairs, "Dogan!"

A moment later, he yelled from upstairs, "Holy hell, Sterling! I ken ye'r a lieutenant, but if ye yell m'name one more time today, I swear to God—" He cut himself off when he saw me. He was leaning over the railing so I could see his face was no longer bruised or swollen either. "Bayard," he growled.

"I need to speak with you," I softly said to him, and he turned back in the direction he came. I pointed to the stairs and asked Sterling, "May I?"

"Go right ahead, my lady, but remember: there's no ball kicking allowed under this roof," he announced with a wicked grin.

Laughingly, I said, "I will try to refrain myself." He laughed even harder.

I was halfway up the steps when Sterling yelled up from behind me, "Lady Lee is coming upstairs, so if any of you are not decent, then shut your bloody doors!"

As I reached the top, I heard a handful of doors ahead of me slam shut, causing me to bite down on my lips as I turned to the right to find Dogan. I found him in a room sitting on one of the dozen or so beds. The beds were just big enough for one man, and the room just had plain wood with nothing hanging on the walls. While slipping his foot into one of his boots, he said without looking at me, "I'm kind o' disappointed to see Kimball's face all healed up." He paused, "Why are ye even here, woman? We'll be seeing each other in a few hours."

"That's one of the reasons I came. The queen needs me tonight, so I will not be able to make it for training. I also came to say I am sorry for—" He held up his hand to stop me. Dogan slipped on his other boot then slowly gazed up at me.

"Ye got guts, woman. I'll give ye that. Never in my life has a woman ever done what ye did." He paused for a moment. "Kimball told me earlier about what he said to ye, so I'll let this slide fer now. I also got to say that I respect ye fer coming here to face me in person, instead o' sending a servant wit a message."

He stood up and I had to look up at him. "When do you want to meet again?"

"I'm not sure, sometime within the next few days. Dinna worry, I'll let ye ken when." Dogan quickly wrapped his right hand around my throat. He lifted me up so I had to stand on my toes. Clamping my hands around his wrist, we glared at one another. Just when I was about to say something, he did, "If ye ever pull a stunt like ye did last night, I'll break both yer legs. Do I make myself clear?" he asked in a threatening tone.

"Do not ever call me a name that I despise, and I will never kick you in your nether region. Do I make *myself* clear?" I mimicked his tone.

It seemed like his lips actually twitched, then he let go of me and stalked out of the room. After a moment, I gathered myself together and made my way back downstairs. Without looking at anyone else, I headed straight for the door. Sterling stopped me. "Whoa, where do you think you are going, Lee?" I stopped and gave my attention to Sterling who, was standing by the table that was filled with men eating. "You and I have not had a talk in a while," he said. Dogan, who was leaning against the counter drinking his tea, gave me an odd look.

Trying to ignore him, I looked to Sterling. "Look, how about some other time, all right?"

"Nope. There are some things I need to say. Come." He held up another cup of tea to join him. Forcing myself back toward him to grab the tea, I followed him out the back door. Out back was where the men did their training. There were a few men out right now, using real weapons instead of the wooden ones Dogan made me use.

It's been a while, but Sterling and I would get together sometimes to just catch up and reminisce about Rowan. It was not just me he left. Sterling and Rowan were childhood friends. When we reached the end of the porch, I leaned against the railing and sipped on my tea while I waited for him to speak. He still did not know about Pa's letter mentioning Rowan. I will have to tell him about that.

Quietly, he said, "I found him, Lee."

I nearly choked on my tea. "How? Where is he?"

"I could not take it anymore, so a few months back, I went through the general's papers when he was not around. I found where he was posted, and I wrote to him," he whispered as he gazed out at the men in training.

"Well, where is he? Did he write back?"

"I did not think he was going to write me, it's been months. I just got a letter this morning." His broad chest expanded as he took in a deep breath.

"What did it say, Sterling? Did it say why he left?" I demanded and placed my cup on the railing.

"I know somewhat why, but not the whole story. That's for him to tell you anyway. I cannot tell you where he's at. He said that you will find him soon enough, and he will tell you the reasons for every-thing." He fixed his eyes on me then.

"How am I supposed to find him? Do I have to go through the general's office too?" I asked.

Sterling laughed at that. "No, Lee, you cannot do that. He made sure that I told you not to do that."

"Then what am I supposed to do?" Could this really be happening, or am I dreaming? Sterling found him!

"All he said was that you will find him soon." He paused. "There's one more thing." He took a deep breath and placed his tea on the railing, "Please do not hit me, Lee. This is his action and words, not mine, all right?"

"What are you talking about, Sterling?" Before I knew it, he took hold of my face with both of his hands and lightly pressed his lips against mine. I used the front of his shirt for an anchor because I felt like I was going to fall over.

When we parted, he kept his face close to mine and said softly, "His exact words are 'I love you, Lovalee.'" Tears rolled down my cheeks, and Sterling rubbed them away with his thumbs. He only called me Lovalee when we were alone. No one, not even Sterling, ever heard him call me that. Sterling brought me against his chest and squeezed me tight.

"Why?" I cried into his shirt. "If he still loves me, then why did he leave me?"

"I am sorry, Lee, it's not my place to tell you. I was not even going to say anything to you at first then you showed up here. I thought it was a sign, telling me that you needed to know." I squeezed him tighter, and he did in return. "I do not know what's worse, Lee. Thinking the man does not love you anymore or knowing that he has all along and you still cannot be with him."

"I do not know either," I cried. When I got my father's letter saying something about Rowan, I cried. Now I was crying the hardest I ever had for the man. Sterling held me till I had no more tears. Breaking away from him so I could rub my eyes, I complained, "Great look at me, I am a mess now."

"Come on in, you can wash your face before you leave." He held out his hand.

I gazed out at the men who were training; some were looking at us. "Great, Sterling, those men probably think we got something going on." Luckily, they were far enough away that they could not hear us.

"That's fine. It gives them something to talk about." He winked and continued to hold out his hand. "Come let's get you cleaned up." I took his hand, and we stopped in our tracks when we saw Dogan leaning against the door jamb staring at us.

"What the hell is going on out here?" he asked and sipped on his tea.

"That's none of your business, Dogan." Sterling pushed him out of the way then led me to a room.

After I got myself cleaned up, I went back out to the main gathering room. Ignoring Dogan, I went straight to Sterling. I hooked my arms around his neck and whispered in his ear, "Thank you, Sterling, for telling me and for the kiss." I brought my face around, and I gave him a quick kiss on the cheek. "I really do appreciate it."

Sterling brushed some stray hairs away from my face. "I know, Lee." He gave me a gentle smile. "Try not to be a stranger, all right? We have had some good times in the past." And that we have. Times that I miss terribly. I was going to make it a point to see him as much as I can.

"I promise not to be a stranger anymore."

I said my good-nights to some of the men as I walked out the door. Once I was outside, I could hear one of the men inside ask Sterling if I was his woman. He replied that he would never tell. That made me smile. Sterling was a great man. Kaidan and Sterling were the only guards that I considered my best of friends. Then there was Rowan. *How am I supposed to find you if I have no idea where you are?* Why could not he just come here and talk to me or even write me a bloody letter? As I made my way back to the castle, the sun was low in the sky; it would be sinking into the ocean soon.

Chapter 7

Introductions

Today was the day Dylan was getting released from the medical ward. I made sure to send word to Wyck so he knew that Dylan was coming. I walked down the cold narrow corridors of the ward and stopped at the open door of Dylan's room.

"Hello, angel." His face was clean-shaven, but he still seemed a little pale.

"Hello, Dylan." I beamed him a bright smile. "Are you about ready?"

"It seems so. I do not really have much of anything anyway. Just the books and an extra outfit you gave me." He held up the bag that held his personal items.

"It's a beautiful sunny day. Are you ready to see it?"

"Definitely! I cannot get out of this hellhole fast enough." Dylan looked around his tiny room, which was like a prison cell to him.

I laughed. "All right, follow me then."

After we made our way through the narrow corridors, I pushed the door open and walked outside. Dylan swiftly brought his hand up over his eyes. "Wow," he laughed. "It's so bright it actually hurts my eyes." He used his hand as a visor and walked down the few steps. He gazed up behind him to see the castle. "It's beautiful. I cannot believe I have been living in there for almost two weeks."

The massive stone structure of Burreck Castle was breathtaking. The two of us walked backward so we could get a better view. The bell tower was the highest point, stretching up close to two hundred feet. There was a total of four stories with a labyrinth of corridors and rooms.

"Yes, I know the section you have been living in is not glamorous. Maybe some time, I will give you a tour of the castle."

"I would like that." He gave me a flash of white teeth as he held his bag over his shoulder. "So how do we get to the stables?"

With the thoughts of how lucky he was to still be alive, a smile of joy spread on my lips as we walked through the castle gates into the city. I watched him as he absorbed everything we passed. His own smile never left his face.

"We will turn left up ahead. That will bring us straight to the stables," I said while pointing out in front of me.

"This place is amazing. There are so many different shops—it's going to take me forever to see them all," he said with excitement in his voice.

"Luckily, you have all the time in the world now to do just that," I said as I patted his shoulder.

"I do not know how I am ever going to repay you for all you have done for me. I cannot thank you enough."

"Just having you here and alive is good enough for me. So stop worrying about repaying me, all right?" He nodded, and the barn and pasture came into view. While we walked along the fence, Dylan gazed out at all the horses that were grazing. The stable doors were closed, so I pushed them open enough for us enter, and then I heard my name, causing us both to look back.

"Bayard! I need to talk to ye," Dogan yelled. He was way up ahead and was now jogging toward me. Dylan tensed up and jerked his head back toward the stable door.

"Go ahead and see some of the horses, I will just be a moment," I said, wondering if he was all right. He seemed suddenly anxious.

"All right," he said softly and walked in.

I casually walked out to meet Dogan as he continued to jog toward me, "What is it, Ramstien?" I said with a little annoyance in my voice. The little hope that I had of not having to see him had been crushed.

The man was not even breathing hard; he glared past me and asked, "Who's that?" he nodded toward the stables.

"That's Dylan, the lone survivor from that shipwreck." I tilted my head to the side. "Why?"

He continued to glare in that direction for a moment longer before he shook his head and asked me, "Are ye doing anything in an hour?"

"No." Suddenly, the feeling of anxiety started to roll around at the pit of my stomach. "Why?"

"Good, meet me for training in an hour then." He turned around and jogged back in the direction he came from. It's been a few days since I trained with him. It's going to be the first time since the incident, so to speak. I let out a moan as I walked back to the stables. I strolled in to find Dylan rubbing Ara's nose.

"I see you found my horse, her name is Ara," I stated and started to rub the side of her neck. "She should be going out to pasture soon."

"Hello, Ara. She's gorgeous, angel," he said, giving me a soft grin.

"I know." I smiled proudly at her. "Thanks!"

With his eyes fixed on Ara, he said, "What was that all about? Is he a guard?"

"Yeah he just had a message he wanted me to give to the king's guard," I lied.

"He's not very respectful towards you by calling you by your last name like that." He sounded aggravated. "He sounded funny, he must not be from around here."

"Well, look at you, paying attention to detail." I laughed when I noticed him getting embarrassed. "Yes, he's actually a Salvatorian. It's a country north of here." Dylan went still and just stared at Ara; finally, I asked, "Umm, are you all right, Dylan?"

He snapped out of it and smiled at me. "Sorry, angel. I thought maybe I remembered something, but I guess I do not."

"Your memory will come back in time. I know it will." I grinned while patting and rubbing the back of his shoulders.

"So you must be Dylan." Wyck walked in from outside and came over to us, "I am Wyck Fangmeir, Lady Leelah has told me a lot about you."

"It's a pleasure to meet you." They shook hands. "Thank you for this job."

"It's no problem, lad. Come, I will show you around." He placed his hand on Dylan's shoulder and beckoned him to follow.

"Well, I need to get back to the castle." I gave Dylan a quick hug. "I will see you around, Dylan."

"Do not be a stranger, angel," he said, appearing anxious of my departure.

"Oh, I will not. Just ask Wyck. I am down here all the time." I said my good-byes to the both of them and made my way back to the castle.

As I walked through the castle front doors, I headed straight to the training room. Might as well get some practice throwing my knives while waiting for Dogan to come. Once I had the door shut behind me, I threw my knives at the wooden figures up ahead. I lodged all four into one of them. After I yanked them out, I situated them into a row to face me. Walking back toward the door, I turned to face them. Inhaling a deep breath, I threw them two at a time. All four hit lower than I wanted. Frustrated, I stomped back to retrieve them. After yanking them free from each dummy, I turned to find Dogan leaning against the door jam. He was early, and I did not even notice the door opened.

"Ye'r thinking too much into it," he stated and pushed himself away from the door. "Let me see the knives." I handed them to him. He stuck them in the inside of his belt. Dogan turned his back to the wooden statues and fixed his intense emerald eye on me. He pointed a finger to his head. "Dinna think about it, woman. Just turn and throw, all right? Turn and throw, ye got that?"

"Yes, Ramstien! Turn and throw, I got it!" I said annoyingly and rolled my eyes.

"It doesn't matter if ye miss right now because once ye learn to clear yer mind, I guarantee ye'll hit where ye want every time." Dogan spun around and threw my knives. All four lodged in the foreheads of each statue. The man was awesome, and that was terrifying. "All right now go get 'em so ye can try."

"I beg your pardon? You are the one that threw them, you should go and retrieve them," I snapped, and I wrapped my arms around my chest. The man was always bossing me around, telling me to do this and how to do that. I know he's training me and I was learning quite a bit, but come on. Since he's the one that threw them, he should get them.

"They're yer knives, so if ye want to continue practicing wit 'em, then ye ha' to grab 'em," he said, mimicking my stance and raised his scarred eyebrow.

"Well, I guess we will have to do something else today then." I was not going to give in to this man today. I could be just as stubborn as him.

"That's fine wit me. I ha' not been able to inflict pain on ye yet, fer what ye did to me earlier this week." He strolled over and grabbed some wooden swords.

I looked at him nervously. "You told me that you were going to let it slide this time."

"I lied." He tossed the sword to his left, and it skidded across the marble floor. "Now try to get to it before I reach ye."

Not bothering to question him, I ran to the sword with Dogan coming to cut me off. It must have been a reflex because I still do not know how I managed it. I could either get nailed by the sword or get down and maybe not get hit. The smoothness of the marble floor helped out tremendously. I slid down onto my hip and skidded past Dogan as his sword sliced through the air above my head. I snatched the sword in my hand as I slammed into the wall and instantly brought the sword up and blocked Dogan's blow.

He looked down at me and said, "Nicely done, m'lady!" Dogan gave me his usual evil grin and pushed himself back so I could get up.

"Oh, it's 'my lady' now, is it? We will just see about that, *Dogan*." I said his name sarcastically. Pushing myself off the wall, I charged at him, but the man was too quick for me. It seemed like I could never get my blade to connect with him. Back and forth we went at each other. He spun around and got his one leg behind mine, causing me to fall flat on my back; it stunned me at first. Dogan was above me with his sword against my neck.

"I ha' just killed ye, yet again. That's the fifth time fer me today. How many times did ye kill me?" he paused, waiting for me to answer. When I did not, he said, "Zero."

He could be a real bastard. I just wanted to hurt him but just could not manage to do it. There had to be a way of inflicting pain on him without kicking him where it counts. Then the idea came to me. I reached my hand up to see if he would actually help me up, and to my surprise, he did. With his hand still holding the sword, he grabbed my right hand. I used the momentum to bring myself up and spun around, wrapping my right arm around his arm. With my back against his massive torso, I lifted my left elbow up; and with as much force I could muster, it connected hard with his face, and pain jarred all the way down my arm. I was able to pull his sword out of his grip, and I jumped away from him. After a few steps, I turned to face him. Dogan had his hand against his jaw and spat what looked like blood on the white floor. I knew he was going to give me hell for that, but it was completely worth it. I stood there with a sword in both hands, waiting for him to say something.

You could tell, mixed in his pissed expression that he was impressed. "That was a dirty move but nicely done at that," he said and spat again. "Ye'r gonna pay fer that. Ye ken that, right?"

"I know, and it was worth it. Besides, who's the one without a weapon?" I gave him a smile and raised my eyebrows as I twirled the swords in my hands.

"Come on, woman. Come and get me, then we'll see who's weaponless." He beckoned me to him.

So I charged after him yet again, and I still could not hit the man. He kept jumping, ducking, and turning. It was not normal how a man of his size moved so fluently. It should not be possible. I was getting tired, and he must have sensed it. The next thing I knew, my left arm was twisted up behind, me and he took the sword in my right hand up against my throat.

I could feel his chest at the back of my neck and shoulders heaving with air. After a moment, he murmured in my ear, "That's the sixth time for me and still zero fer ye." Suddenly, I started to feel slightly uncomfortable with the closeness of our bodies.

"Well, at least I made you bleed. That's a first for me, and I am happy with it." I could not help but smile as the air heaved out of my lungs.

"I'm sure ye are." He pushed me forward. "That ends it fer today. Meet me here again in two days." He walked over to put the swords away, and I went over to grab my knives that were still stuck in the figures. "So, woman, before ye leave, tell me what's this between ye and this lieutenant."

I turned and looked at him shockingly. "Sterling, you bastard!" I said under my breath. Dogan gave me an odd expression, and I said, "Personally, that's none of your business. That was a long time ago. Way before you ever got here, so do not ever mention him again. You do not even know the man."

His eyes widened, and he smiled with deep dimples coming to view. "So ye are telling me that there's another lieutenant?"

"I beg your pardon?"

"I was talking about Sterling. Who's this other lieutenant ye'r talking about?" He raised his scarred eyebrow, waiting for me to answer.

Damn it! I kept forgetting Sterling was a lieutenant now. Great, now this man was going to always pester me about this, I just knew it. "Like I said, it's none of your business, so just leave it," I said, glaring at him while he had a smirk on his lips.

I turned as I heard someone else walk into the room. "Lee? Rosa wants to see you." Kaidan announced. Dogan walked to leave the room, and the two of them glared at each other as he passed. Thank God he came in and saved me from having to deal with Dogan's question.

"Right now?" I asked when Dogan was gone.

"That's what she said. I was hoping to end your training early, but it looks like you are done anyway. How did it go with the beast today and what's none of his business?"

"It went the same as usual, him nailing me and me missing him. I did elbow him in the jaw though, making him spit blood," I said. "And Rowan is 'what's none of his damn business.'"

"That's my girl!" Kaidan let out a hoot then he said, "Rowan? I still cannot believe Sterling found him." He paused in thought before saying, "Now you better go. She's waiting."

"Look at me, I am all sweaty. I am a mess! I cannot go and see her looking like this, Kai." I held my hands out to the side as I spun around.

"Yes, you can, let's go." He grabbed my arm and pulled me out of the room.

Kaidan left me to go find the queen myself. My braid was all loose and my hair was winging out the sides. I can just feel it. I had tried patting it down, but there was no helping it. My hair was sticking out in all directions, and I could feel the heat still in my cheeks. I tried to rub the sweat off my face, but I knew my face still looked greasy. As I walked up the stairs that led to their living quarters, the guards gave me funny looks.

Byron said before opening the door, "Well, you look like hell, my lady."

My jaw dropped in shock that he actually said that to me. He laughed and opened the door. I hit him in the shoulder as I walked in. This was just great. I did not want her to see me a mess like this, but what could I do? I was told to come straight here. There she was in the library sitting and reading a book. She looked up when I walked in. Rosa brought her hands to her mouth like she was trying to hold back a laugh, but she could not.

"Oh, my poor Lee. I take it you were just at training?" she asked with her eyes laughing too.

"Yes," I laughed shyly and pushed some stray hairs behind my ear.

"That man must give you a real workout. I have never seen you look like this."

"He's a lot harder than any man has ever been with me. I usually get myself cleaned up before I have to see you, but Kaidan said I had to come straight here."

"Oh, it was not that important. I just wanted to tell you that I want to go shopping tomorrow morning. He was supposed to tell you himself," she explained with a brilliant smile.

"That bastard," I said under my breath, but Rosa must have heard me because she burst into laughter.

"You two go at it like siblings, you know that?" She rocked forward, holding her stomach as she giggled.

"Yes, I know," I said frustrated. "I cannot believe he made me come up here looking like this. He made it sound urgent."

"I am sure you will get him back for this, poor Lee. You may leave then. Get yourself cleaned up, and I will see you in the morning," she said with a lovely smile.

"Thank you, Rosa! I will be here in the morning." I bowed and walked out of the room. I could hear Rosa laughing again when the guards opened the door for me. When I got to the bottom of the steps, Bryce and Kaidan came into view and were walking toward me.

"Oh my, Lee, are you all right?" asked Bryce, and the whole time Kaidan had this big mocking smile.

"I am fine. I just got done with training," I stated and then jabbed my finger at Kaidan. "And you are a rotten person. I am going to make sure Mira knows that too." I marched away, listening to them both laughing in my wake.

The next morning, I walked through the front doors of the castle with Rosa holding my arm. It was cloudy and much cooler than it had been in days. Rain was definitely in the forecast for today. You could feel it in your bones. We both tugged our cloaks tighter to us.

"Yesterday would have been a better day for this," Rosa commented as she looked up at the gray sky.

"It still might warm up yet, the day has only begun. So, Rosa, how have you been feeling lately?" I asked while patting her arm.

"I actually got sick this morning for the first time," she murmured in my ear. "That's an indication that I am pregnant, do you not think?"

"I have heard that women get morning sickness when they are. Is it terrible for me to say that I am happy you did?" I whispered then beamed a smile.

Rosa laughed and hugged tighter to my arm. "No, my sweet Lee. I was so excited that I threw up that Bryce thinks I am a little crazy."

I giggled. "I have never seen Bryce laugh or smile so much as he has in the last few weeks. When do you think he will make the announcement?"

"He wants to wait another month. We have already started making plans for a party, and he will tell everyone then."

As we walked through the castle gate, I found myself at full alert. It was up to me to make sure the queen stayed safe. While we walked down the cobble streets, I kept my eyes on everyone that came by us. Most people just bowed and said good morning. Usually after we have these walks through the city, I am drained. I hate it, but I trust no one when it's just me with her. I do not want to be caught off guard, and God forbid anything should ever happen to her. There's no way I would be able to live with myself.

Rosa touched my hand, and I looked to her. "Let's stop in this fabric shop. It's been a while since we have come here, he might have something new." We turned to the door, and I opened it for her.

"Your Majesty, it's a pleasure as always. Some time has passed since you have been here last," the enthusiastic gentleman who was behind the counter said.

Rosa walked up with hands extended forward to take his. "I was just telling Lady Leelah how we have not been here in a while. I take it you have some new stock."

"Of course we do, Your Majesty. Follow me."

The owner led us to his new stock and left us to go through it. Rosa loved to make her own dresses. She did not have to; she had so many gowns at the castle, but she still liked to make her own every now and then.

"Oh, Lee, look at this, it's beautiful! Feel how soft and smooth it is." She put the dark-lavender material against my skin.

"You are right, Your Highness, it's very beautiful," I agreed as I felt the fabric.

"This would look amazing against your fair skin. Oh, please, Lee, will you let me make you a dress for the party at the end of the month?" she asked with a pleading look.

She always did this, and I could argue with her, but she always won. I was not about to argue with her now. Rosa's very talented when it comes to this; all the dresses she's ever made for me were always stunning and beautiful. I loved them, but they were not me. I was more a shirt-and-trousers type of girl, but I had to give that up when I came here.

"Yes, Your Majesty, I would love for you to make me a dress." I smiled with a bow of my head.

She jumped and wrapped her arms around my neck. "Thank you, Lee, for not arguing with me!"

"You are welcome!" I laughed. While I was still hugging her, a little girl came into view in the aisle. I knew who she was instantly, "Cora! How are you, sweetie?" Her long curly chestnut locks bounced as she ran to us. I had her up in my arms and was squeezing her tight.

She started giggling. "Lady Lee, I have missed you!"

"And I have missed you." I gave her a loud kiss on the cheek. She smiled back at me and laid a tiny hand on my cheek. Her beautiful emerald eyes were glued to mine. They were so intense that I felt like she was searching for something, and then suddenly her eyes softened, almost becoming a little sad before she hugged my neck again.

"Cora, you have grown since we have seen you last. How long has it been now?" asked Rosa.

"Six months, Your Majesty," answered Vi, who was coming toward us and wrapped her arms around the queen in an embrace. She had her gray hair pulled back into a neat bun like she always had. "How are you? You look as beautiful as ever."

Cora's nana Vi was once the queen's personal maid. It started to get too much for her to do that and raise her granddaughter. Two years ago, Cora's mother abandoned her when she was three. Vi has been taking care of her since. Every now and then, Vi used to bring her to work if she could not find anyone to watch her. Cora was such a joy, and I miss seeing her in the castle.

"Vi, I have missed you both so much. How's the new job going?" Rosa asked.

"I do not enjoy it like I did when I worked for you, but it works for Cora and me," she stated as she ran her hand through Cora's thick hair.

"Well, I am glad it's working for you at least. Come and visit us when you have off, we miss your company," Rosa said as she reached for Vi's hand.

"I think Cora and I can manage that. Come on, sweetie, we are going to let these ladies finish their shopping."

Cora fixed her emerald eyes on mine again. Her eyes became intense again, and it felt like she was searching for something deep inside me, like she did when I first took her in my arms. I found myself not wanting to let go of her, and then she gave me a quick kiss on the cheek and slid down to the ground. Shaking the feeling from my body, we said our good-byes and went back to gather more materials for the dress Rosa was going to make for me. After we got the entire fabric and materials packaged up, I picked up the bundle, and we headed back out to the streets. Even though my arms were full of her materials, she still managed to wrap her arm around my left elbow. We walked in silence to enjoy the scents and sounds of the city. As we made our way back to the castle, I almost stopped in my tracks when I saw him. Dogan was talking to another guard up the street.

"What is it, Lee?" she asked with concern in her eyes, "I felt you get tense suddenly."

I murmured to her. "That guard up ahead with the scar is Dogan Ramstien."

"Really?" She gave me a look of interest. "I would like to meet him. Get his attention."

Great, I should have not opened my mouth. As we continued forward, I called to him, "Ramstien!" He jerked his head and saw us. Dogan said something else to the guard then came over.

"Your Highness, I would like you to meet Dogan Ramstien. Ramstien this is our Queen Rosa," I said to both of them.

He bowed graciously. "Yer Majesty, 'tis a pleasure."

Rosa reached for his hand and clamped both of hers around his. The two of them froze and just stared at each other for a moment, then she said, "Oh, the infamous Dogan Ramstien! My Lee speaks nothing but good things about you." She turned and winked at me.

Oh, she did not just say that. Dogan looked at me then gave the queen his smile that I have only seen once or twice. His smile was huge and genuine with two deep dimples poking into his cheeks.

"Is that so?" He laughed. "Maybe I'll ha' to start being a little tougher on 'er then," he said in a hushed tone.

Rosa let out a loud laugh. "Oh, I am sure you are tough enough on her as it is. By the look of the poor girl yesterday, she was drained."

If my hands were not full, I would have covered my face. They were both getting enjoyment out of this.

"Yer Lee is unlike any woman I ha' ever met. I think she's got a lot o' anger issues."

I jump in on that. "I beg your pardon? I am standing right here, and you should talk, Ramstien!" Rosa laughed and rubbed her hand across my shoulders to try to calm me down.

"See what I mean?" He gestured to me. "If ye'd like, Yer Majesty, I'll walk wit ye two back to the castle. I wouldna want *Lady Lee* straining too much here wit these packages then she'll be worthless fer me tomorrow."

"No, Ramstien, we are fine," I hissed in frustration.

"Lady Leelah!" Rosa said in a tone that a mother would use on a child. "Please ignore her and take the packages. We would *love* for you to walk with us."

Why do you punish me, Lord? Can you answer me that at least? Dogan reached for the packages and he had to yank them from my grip. We continued walking, and Dogan followed one step beside the queen. All of a sudden, I felt like I needed to be between them. What if he has somehow fooled the Mage Azzan and he's really here to be undercover? So following on my instincts, I moved and squeezed myself in between them.

"Lee, what has gotten into you?" Rosa laughed in shock.

"It's all right, Yer Highness. She's just going on 'er instincts. Beside 'er anger issues, she has trust issues too." He smiled down at me. "So, Yer Majesty, what do we ha' here in these packages? It feels like clothing possibly."

"You are almost right. I found this lovely lavender material that will look absolutely beautiful on Lee. So I had to get it. Now poor Lee will have to deal with me poking her with pins yet again."

I squeezed my arm to bring her closer. "You know I never mind, besides you always do such beautiful work."

"So ye'r saying that ye the queen o' Altecia bought this to make a dress fer yer lady? Does this kingdom not ha' any tailors?" He gave her a dumbfounded look, like he could not believe a woman like herself would ever put the time into something like that.

"Of course we have tailors." She giggled. "I just love making and designing dresses. Lee is most always the one I make them for. I enjoy it!"

"Ramstien," a man hollered from behind. The three of us turned back to look. Once the guard got a good look at who was with him, he stopped and bowed, "Your Majesty."

"Please rise," she said waving her hand to him. "Did you need Dogan?"

He stood in attention and said, "Yes, Your Majesty, the general would like to see him."

"Oh, well, thank you so much for the talk, Dogan. It was a pleasure to finally meet you."

"The pleasure was all mine, Yer Majesty." He handed me the packages then murmured to the queen but loud enough for me to hear, "Can ye do me a favor? When ye'r fitting Lady Lee in that dress, I'd appreciate it if ye'd poke her a little more than usual wit the pins." He turned and gave me an evil grin, and I glared back at him.

Rosa let out a hoot. "Oh, you are a bad man, Dogan Ramstien!"

He gave her a bigger smile and bowed again before walking away. I growled, "That man really rubs me in the wrong way."

"I know he's rough with you, but I like him." She paused. "There's just something about him."

I gave her a look of shock, and she just laughed at me. I have hated that man since the first day I laid eyes on him. I am not sure if there will ever be a day that I will actually start liking him. We turned and continued our way back to the castle, trying my best to throw the bloody fool from my head so I could stay aware of my surroundings.

Chapter 8

Tolerance Hit Its Limit

The next evening, I walked into the training room to find Dogan already in there. He had a long shield in his hand. We walked to each other, and he handed me the shield.

"Why am I using this?" I asked him. It was not like I would ever use one. Men only use them if they are in the front lines during a war.

"I just want ye to ken what one feels like and how to maneuver wit it," he responded.

"All right, but what's the likelihood of me ever using one?" I asked. "It's slim to none."

He nodded. "Probably, but ye never ken what the future holds."

Balancing the shield on the floor in front of me, I slipped my left arm through the two leather straps so they were resting along my forearm. He handed me a wooden sword and backed up. The shield was awful heavy. I was not sure how long I could hold this thing up. "This shield is too heavy for me. It's made for men more your size, not mine." My arm was already starting to burn from the mere weight of the shield.

"Ye better start building some muscle in that arm then." He gave me half a smile and continued. "So, Bayard, tell me about this

100

Lieutenant Rowan Lythandas." His smile grew wider when he saw the shock in my face when he said Rowan's name.

"Sterling," I growled.

"It took me two days o' pestering 'im, but he finally gave me a name. So I went around talking to other men that ha' been here a while. It's been said that ye two were quite an item at one time and then out o' nowhere, he just ups and leaves. So tell me this, woman, what did ye do to make the man leave?" With his wicked grin, he seemed real proud of himself.

"Why are you doing this? It's none of your business." It took all I had not to cry. This was one man I did not want to cry in front of. He just could not leave it be. It's like he wanted to make my life a living hell, and he got enjoyment in doing so. I dropped the shield and sword and let them fall hard to the marble floor. The clatter echoed loudly off the walls. "If I knew the answer to that question, I sure as *hell* would not tell you."

Dogan's face got serious. "Pick 'em up, Bayard," he growled.

"Go and rot in hell, Ramstien! I am not dealing with this today!" Turning on my heels, I headed for the door. I knew he would come after me, and I was ready for it when he snatched my arm and spun me around. Using the momentum of his force to bring my right fist around, it connected hard with his jaw. Instant pain shot through my hand. He made a sound that was like a laughing growl.

"Ye ha' got a wicked right hook fer a woman," he sneered, but it seemed like he was repressing the urge to smile.

"Let go of my arm now!" I demanded, and his grip got tighter before he finally released me. "Whenever we meet for training, you are to never mention that name to me again. Do I make myself clear? That's a part of my past that I do not like to talk about. If you do this for me, for the meantime, I will not ask you of your past. But believe me, I will in time."

"I'll find out who ye are and the past that haunts ye." His emerald eyes shone bright with anger.

"I am sure you will, but it's not going to be tonight. Good night, Ramstien!"

I turned and walked away from him with my head held high, and it felt great. Will the two of us ever come to an understanding of each other? Sighing, I thought probably not. All of a sudden, the need to see Sterling hit me like a ton of stones. I needed that companionship and only connection I had left to Rowan. Once leaving the corridor, I knew that Dogan could no longer see me; I lifted up the front of my skirt and ran like the devil himself. To my room I headed to retrieve my cloak. I was delighted to make it there without running into anyone who wanted to talk to me. Bursting through the door, I snatched the cloak from my wardrobe. I tied it on while running back out the door.

Once I got outside, I went to the first guard outside the door, "Do you by chance know where I can find Lieutenant Fenwick at this hour?" The sky was pink due to the coming sunset.

"He should be still by the ramp that leads to the ocean. Is everything all right, my lady?"

"Yes, I am fine." I took off in a run again then I yelled over my shoulder, "Thank you!"

Once I got through the castle gates, I turned to the right and went into a full sprint. The shoes that I was wearing were not the best for this. I kept losing my traction, but all I cared about was seeing him. He was my friend, and because of his connection to Rowan, I knew he would be able to settle my nerves. I never did much crying while I was a child, but in this last year, it did not seem to take much to set me off. I could deal with physical pain with no problem. Growing up with four older brothers, I was always getting hurt and pushed around, but I never cried. If I did then, I would catch hell from them. Never in my life did I experience love like I have for Rowan. Now because of that, my emotions were always going up and down. Is that what love does to you, messes with your emotions?

It seemed like it was taking me forever to get there, but I finally got to where I could turn for the ocean. I practically ran right into him. Wrapping my arms around his waist, I pressed my face into his chest.

"Whoa, Lee! What's wrong, darling?" he asked, sounding a little startled as he lightly placed his hands on my shoulders.

With my face still against his chest, I could feel the tears start to pour out. "I am sorry, Sterling! After dealing with Ramstien, I needed to see you." The sobs came out, and my body started to shake uncontrollably.

"Shh." He tried to soothe me by rubbing my back then he whispered, "Come with me."

The next thing I knew, I was up and cradled in his arms. I buried my face into his neck and got hit with the strong scent of his spice cologne. Instantly, I began to cry harder as I hung tight around his neck. It was close to the same cologne Rowan used to wear. In response, Sterling tightened his arms as he continued to whisper calming words in my ear. There was the feeling of us descending the ramp that led to the beach. The clicking of his boots stopped once he hit the sand. He walked for a little ways then he placed me down on the sand. Finally looking up myself, I saw the sun was about to sink into the ocean. It was beautiful how it set the sky on fire. Sterling sat beside me, wrapped his arm around my shoulder, and pulled me close to him.

"It's beautiful, don't you think?" he asked softly.

"Yes, it is." I rubbed my damp cheeks, but the tears kept coming, "I am sorry! I did not know who else to go to."

"Please do not be sorry. If anyone is to be sorry, it should be me, and I am. The bastard kept asking me questions, and I finally told him Rowan's name so he would shut the hell up. I regretted it as soon as I said it," he said, sounding disgusted with himself.

"It's all right, Sterling. Ramstien has caused a lot of animosity with some of us. The man really gets to me. He mentioned Rowan right in the beginning of our training today. I ended up walking out, and he stopped me, so I punched him in the face." Pleased with the memory of punching him, the tears began to slow down.

Sterling started laughing and squeezed me tighter to him. "I wish you would do these things to him when I was around."

"Sorry, the opportunity has not come to be yet." I smiled a little. "I told him to never mention his name again, and for the meantime, I will not ask him of his past. Then I took off to find you before I really lost it," I whispered, staring out at the view. The waves crashed loudly before us, but the sound was soothing to me. It was helping to wash away the pain.

"I do not believe the man's had an easy life. I have seen him without his shirt on in the barracks. He's got scars all over his chest and back, like the one his face. Some actually look to be claw marks," Sterling mentioned.

The image sent a chill through my body, and Sterling squeezed me even tighter in response. So I laid my head on his shoulder and watched the sun slowly disappear into the ocean. There were countless times that I sat like this with Rowan.

"Why can he not be here with us?" I asked.

"I really do not know how to answer that question. Maybe someday in the future, he will be back in our lives," he said so quietly that I almost did not hear him over the crashing waves.

I looked at him. "Do you really think that after all this time?"

He smiled at me and lightly touched my cheek. "Yes, I do." Sterling kissed my forehead, causing me to lightly sigh and close my eyes. "Life was never meant to be easy, Lee. God gives us different challenges to see how we handle them. You can either handle them the right way or the wrong way, that's up to you to decide. You have a purpose in this world, Lee. You might not know what it is yet, but I have a feeling you will know soon enough."

"Life can be evil sometimes. This last year, I have been lying in bed thinking about home and wanting to go back to my old life," I admitted for the first time out loud.

Sterling did not say anything at first; he just stared out at the sinking sun. What he finally said surprised me. "I hope you reconsider that. I already had one friend leave. Do not make me lose another." He looked to me, then with a soft smile, he lightly poked my nose with his finger.

Gazing at him with tears streaming down, I smiled. For the first time in a year, I felt the need to stay again. "Thank you! I think deep inside I needed to hear that. You know someday you will find yourself a lady and you will make her very happy." I laid my head back down on his shoulder. My head started to bounce up and down with his light laughter.

"If I ever find her. You would think with all these women in this city, she would be here somewhere." He laughed.

"You will find her, I just know it." I squeezed my arms tight around his waist.

We stayed there till the sun was completely gone. He kept his arm around my shoulder as we took a slow walk back to the castle. It was dark now and all the street lamps were lit.

"Have you eaten dinner yet?" he asked me.

"No. Why? Do you want to go to MacLeod's and get something to eat?" I suggested with a huge smile.

"You stole the words from my mouth." He smiled. "Let's go, it's been a while since you have had their fish."

My mouth watered instantly. Their fish was to die for, and it had been months since I had eaten there. We enjoyed each other's company; it had been a while since the two of us had done that too. I loved the fish and enjoyed the few tankards of ale I had. It was late by the time we walked through the castle gates. A moan sneaked out when I saw Dogan standing with a few other guards by the front doors. Not even looking at him, I passed to go up the stairs to the doors. The guards opened the door for me, and I turned to Sterling.

"I am holding you to that promise, remember," he reminded me. We promised each other earlier that we would try to get together more often.

"Just as I am holding you to it too." I smiled back. He bent down and kissed my forehead.

"Good night," he whispered.

"Good night and thank you for dinner." With his beautiful smile, he bowed and turned to walk down the steps.

Once I walked into the castle I turned to look back. Sterling grabbed Dogan by his uniform with both hands and yanked his face down to his. I was afraid that Dogan would swing at him, but Sterling was his superior, and he would get into severe trouble if he did. Sterling's voice was tight with anger. "I do not know what kind of games you are playing here, but if you *ever* torture her about Rowan again, I will…"

The doors closed tight, and I could not hear what else he said. I was almost tempted to have them reopen the doors, but what was the point? I wondered what he threatened he do. A smile spread across my lips as I walked up the stairs to my room. With the different trials I have had to go through in my life, it's people like Sterling that make me love my life. I was truly blessed with the people I do have. In some ways, I do love them all, except for the monster that was just getting yelled at outside. I will definitely have to thank God for them tonight. Lately, I am always crying and yelling at him. I have not thanked God in a long time for anything. I will have to apologize, and hopefully, he will forgive me.

For the next two weeks, if I was not with Dogan, I was with the queen. Dogan and I were back to not talking much during training, which was fine with me. When he did talk, it was just to tell me what I was doing wrong. He asked me no questions, and I did the same. Today, the Thelas family was coming for dinner. I was not looking forward to it all. If it was not for the duke himself requesting that I would be there, I would not even show my face.

Kaidan and I were already up in the royal dining room when they all showed up, including Gavin. I cringed at the sight of him. We all said our greetings before sitting at the table. Bryce sat at the head of the table, and I sat beside Kaidan while Gavin took the chair on the other side of me. Rosa, Marvin, and his wife took a sit across from us. I indulged Gavin in some small talk, hoping it would keep his mind off touching me. It was when dinner was finally served that the touching began.

First, he started by lightly tracing his fingers along the back of my neck and shoulders. It sent chills down my back, and I did not mean a good chill. If that was all he did tonight, then I would have been able to handle it. It's when we were having our dessert when he started to get more aggressive. He laid his left hand on my right knee. Slowly, he started to move it up my leg. I grabbed his hand and removed it from my leg with enough force for him to get the clue. I could not even look at him. While I stared at my plate, he placed his hand back on my leg, but he had a firmer grip this time. His hand was high up my thigh when I laid my hand on his to stop him. This was not the first time he'd touched my leg, but it was the first time he'd moved up my thigh like this. I did not like it one bit. His fingers were close to touching an area where no man has ever been with me. Repeatedly, I kept trying to remove his hand, but he only tightened his grip, which was starting to really hurt now. Trying to keep a straight face, I took my left hand and brought it under the table so I could touch Kaidan. He gazed at me; with my eyes locked with his I leaned back a little so he could see what was happening to me. Kaidan looked down, and I could see the anger and horror before he jerked his head to the king.

Kaidan cleared his throat, "Your Majesty, we should take these men into the library, and you can tell them about that boar you killed last week."

Bryce gave Kaidan an odd look then peered to me. It was like he understood what Kaidan was trying to do. "What a good idea, Kaidan. Uncle, cousin, please join us." The king rose with his goblet of wine.

Gavin finally let go of my thigh and murmured in my ear when he stood, "We will continue this later," and he walked away. Suddenly, I felt sick to my stomach. What the hell did he think I was? A whore? That was it; my tolerance with this man had reached its limit.

Behind me, Kaidan laid a hand on my shoulder and whispered in my other ear, "After we are gone, ask for the queen's permission to leave. Tell her you are not feeling well." He stood back up, and I squeezed his hand to tell him thank-you without saying it. He squeezed it back before walking away.

I waited for a few moments after the men left the room before I said anything, "Your Majesty, I request your permission to retire early."

Rosa gave me a concerned look. "Of course, Lee. Are you feeling all right?"

"I just think I might have eaten too much." I gave her a shy smile.

"Go right ahead, Lee. I will see you tomorrow, and get some rest," she said.

I said thank-you and my good-nights to Rosa and the duchess. I could hear the men laughing in the library when I walked into the hall. I quickened my pace and the guards opened the door for me. Down the steps I went and I walked swiftly to my room to retrieve my cloak. There was a need to get out of the castle just in case Gavin came looking for me. I decided to go to the barracks as it would be one of the many places he would not look. Walking out the front doors, I was welcomed by the cool night air that hit my face.

"Hello, Lady Lee! You look beautiful as ever," said Caine Templeton. He was all smiles when I looked at him.

"Thank you, Templeton! When did you start guarding here at the front door?" I asked.

"I am just here for the night, filling in for someone."

"Oh, I see. Well, I hope you have a good night," I said as I bowed my head.

"Thank you, my lady. And the same goes for you."

As I walked down the steps, I glared at Dogan, who was standing at the bottom. "Ramstien," I hissed curling my lip at him.

"Bayard." He mimicked my curled lip.

I smiled once Dogan was behind me. Two of us were starting to get an understanding of each other...well, sort of. As I was getting closer to the castle gates, I kicked loose a small stone. Once it stopped ahead of me, I bent over and picked it up. It was in a perfect oval shape and completely smooth. There were no cuts in its smooth surface, and it fit perfectly in the middle of my palm. While rubbing it, I looked back to Dogan to see he had his back facing me. Looking at the stone then back to Dogan, I took a few quick steps in Dogan's direction to give me momentum and chucked the stone in the air. I watched the angle of the stone, and I knew instantly that it would land directly on Dogan's head. That was my plan anyway. I do not know why I did it...I just did.

What Dogan did next was something I have seen no man do before. He jerked his arm back and snatched the stone before it hit him. Dogan did this without even turning his head. Did the man have eyes in the back of his head too? How in God's name did he do that? He turned his head and blessed me with his usual grin while throwing the stone up in the air and caught it again. I found myself marching to him, and he turned his body around to face me.

"How the hell did you do that?" I demanded while pointing to the stone that was still in his hand.

"I thought we were not going to ask each other questions anymore?" He gave me a snide grin.

"No, I want to know how you caught that without looking. I want you to teach me that." With my arms crossed, I stood there staring up at him with only a few inches between us.

His eyes got big, and he let out a loud laugh. "No way, woman! Besides, it takes too much time—"

"Last time I checked, we got all sorts of time," I said cutting him off.

"And patience, which is something ye ha' little o'."

I laughed at that. "And you think you have patience? You are just as bad as me. Besides if you can do that, I am sure as hell I can."

Dogan's face changed then. He was actually giving me a genuine smile. "All right, Bayard! We'll start tomorrow. Just so ye ken, I'll be getting a lot o' enjoyment outta this."

"Why is that?" I asked.

"Oh, ye'll see tomorrow." He started laughing, a rather deep, jolly laugh that made me sort of nervous. Great, what did I just get myself into? I heard the front doors open and looked up to see Gavin walking out.

"Damn it, Ramstien! This is your fault!" I murmured angrily to him and hit him in the chest. I could tell he was about to ask me what I meant, but Gavin cut in.

"There you are, my lady. Going for a walk? How about I join you?" He came down the steps to me.

"No, thank you, Thelas. I'd rather be left alone," I stated with annoyance in my voice.

"Well, that's too bad because I am not taking no for an answer." He grabbed my right arm and jerked me away from Dogan. Angrily, I bit down on my lips to help refrain me from saying something that I may regret. He walked us toward the gardens and spun me around just before the entrance. There was sight of Dogan, who was now slowly walking toward us.

"You know what, Thelas, I do not even like you. What you did to me during dinner is unacceptable, and I never want your filthy hands on me ever again. Now let go of me!" I tried to pull my arm from his grip, but I could not. It was amazing for how narrow his form was; he did have quite a bit of strength in it.

"I know you liked it, Lee. You cannot fool me." Oh my God, this man was crazy. By the look in his eyes, he truly believed that. He finally let go of my right arm but quickly wrapped it around my back, bringing me tight against him. Before I could get my hand up on his chest, so I could push away, he had his lips pressing hard against mine. My eyes opened wide in shock. He held tight to my hair with his other hand, stopping me from turning away. I tried to break away, but he was holding me too tightly. I was able to squeeze my hand up; I wrapped it around his throat. While squeezing, I pushed with all my might. He released me as he stumbled back a few steps and brought one hand up against his throat. Dogan was standing maybe a foot behind him, and I did not think Gavin even realized that. He gave me a look that said, *I can take him out right now, if you would like.* I shook my head, and Dogan took a step back. Gavin gave me a smile and said, "I always knew you were a feisty one."

As he marched back to me, I brought back my right arm then connected my fist with his nose. Gavin hunched over instantly in pain. He screamed and called me every name possible. I have wanted to do that since the day I met him. Now that I actually did, I regretted it. I walked around him and faced Dogan, who had his dimple smile out in view.

"You know who I just punched?" I asked nervously.

He nodded. "The Duke Thelas's son and who's also the cousin o' the king."

I covered my face with my hands and mumbled, "What was I thinking, Ramstien?"

"I think you broke my nose, you bloody wench!" I turned and looked down at Gavin, who was on his knees. He brought his hands away from his face, and they were covered in blood. Gavin gave me an evil look. "I am going to make sure Bryce has you packed and out of this castle before I leave."

No! I cannot let that be. I quickly looked back at Dogan. He laid a hand on my shoulder and brought his face down to my level, "Go back inside, Lee. Ye better just go to yer room so they can find ye easily."

Any other time, I would have had a comment about him using my first name. He never has said it like that before. I did not argue. I just turned and headed for the front doors of the castle. None of the guards said anything as I walked in. As I ran up the stairs to my room, Kaidan was coming down them.

"Lee, there you are! When I noticed Gavin snuck out, I wanted to make sure you were all right," he said stopping on the step that I was on.

"Kai!" I cried. "I did something horrible."

He gave me a serious look. "What happened, Lee?"

"I tried telling him that I did not like him and to leave me alone. He just would not stop. I ended up punching Gavin in the nose, and I think I broke it," I explained in a panic.

A laugh slipped out as he tried his best to hold it in. "You actually broke his nose?" I bit down on my lips and nodded my head. Kaidan laughed lightly and dragged his hands through his hair. "Did anyone witness this?"

"Yes, Ramstien was right there when it happened. He's still out there with him now."

"All right. Lee, go to your room and lock the door just in case Thelas wants to be a bastard. I will take care of this. I am sure Bryce is going to want to talk to you though," he said calmly.

"Gavin said that he's going to make sure that Bryce has me packed and out of the castle tonight. I do not want to leave, Kai! I regret what I did. I know I should have never let it happen." I was panicking and laid my hand on his chest.

"It's going to be all right, Lee. If Bryce ends up doing something like that, then he loses me too. Now go!" he ordered. Kaidan continued down as I went up. When I got to my room, I closed the door and leaned my head on it while I locked it. The pacing back and forth in my room started, and it seemed to help a bit with my anxiety but not completely. I was too anxious to sit down. As much as I missed my family back home, I would miss my new family here just as much.

It had to be a good half hour by the time I got a knock on my door. I jumped in response to the noise. "Lee?" Kaidan's voice came from the other side. I unlocked and opened the door slowly to find Dogan standing beside Kaidan.

"What's going on? Why is he with you?" I asked pointing to Dogan.

"The king wishes to speak with you and the witness, which is him." He slapped Ramstien hard on the back. "Let's go, he's waiting."

Taking a deep breath, I stepped beside Kaidan with Dogan walking behind us. We walked in silence. The guards opened the doors into the living quarters, and we walked in. I could hear Gavin's voice as we went down the hall. "That's her coming in now, is it not? I want to see her," he yelled angrily.

When we got to the opening that led into the dining room, Gavin was right there and about to get in my face. His nose was swollen and had what looked to be small pieces of cloths stuffed up each nostril to help stop the bleeding. All of a sudden, Dogan's back was in my face, blocking me from Gavin. Gently, I laid my hand against him and took a step back; he was that close to me. I looked at Kaidan to see that he was also shocked at what Dogan just did. Was he trying to protect me?

"Oh, do not try to protect that bitch! Move out of the way," Gavin yelled, and it sounded like he tried to shove Dogan back, but he did not budge.

"Gavin Thelas!" his mother yelled. I assume she did because he just called me a bitch.

"Oh, ye got it all wrong, m'lord. I'm protecting ye from 'er. Lady Lee is not like any other woman. See how easily she broke yer nose, she can do a hell o' a lot worse if ye give 'er a chance. So if ye ha' any brains in that head o' yers, ye'll stay away from 'er." Dogan's voice was tight and threating.

I could not believe the words I was hearing coming from Dogan's mouth. The man needed to stop because he was making me want to think differently of him. I had to step to the side so I could peer around Dogan's broad back to look at Gavin.

"I would watch what you say, Salvie! Do you even know who you are talking to?" Gavin sneered.

"Gavin," Bryce yelled. We all jerked our heads to the left to see the king marching toward us from up the hall. "Get your ass back in the room!" Then he stopped and pointed at us. "You three come with me!" Bryce ordered and turned back to where he came from. We continued up the hall to follow the king. I walked with Kaidan and Dogan on either side of me. I hung my head down and was afraid of what the king had to say to me. Kaidan must have felt the anxiety from me because he clasped his hand around my wrist and kept it there for a moment. We turned left at the end of the hall. Bryce turned right several doors down into his office. When we walked into the office, the king had his hands on his desk and with his back facing us. Rosa was sitting in a chair in the far corner by the window, and she had a worried expression. Once Kaidan shut the door behind us Bryce pushed himself from his desk and faced us.

"Lee," he said then started laughing anxiously and dragged his hands through his hair as he spoke. "What the hell were you thinking punching him like that? Of all people."

I hung my head again, unable to look at him. "I was not thinking, Your Highness. The man has touched me in places where no man has before, and when he forced his kiss upon me, I did push him away." I took in a deep breath, "When he came back to me, I threw my fist without thinking of the consequences. I am so sorry to put you in this predicament."

"She speaks the truth about him touching her inappropriately. The bastard had his hands on her at the dining table. I saw it with my own eyes. That's the reason I suggested us to go in the library so Lee could leave, but he still ended up getting her." Kaidan's face was bright red with anger, and his fists clenched at his sides.

The king stood there staring at us with no expression on his face. You could tell he was thinking of how to handle this situation. "Gavin wants me to have you out of the castle tonight!"

"I understand, Your Majesty." I hung my head yet again and softly said, "I will just take what I brought here, which is not much. So it should not take me long." Suddenly, my stomach started to turn, and there was fear of me getting sick right in front of him.

"Bryce, please do not do this!" Rosa shot up out of her chair and was at his side.

"Bryce, please reconsider!"Kaidan said urgently. "If you get rid of Lee because of a reason like this, then you will lose me too."

It seemed like Bryce just ignored Kaidan and his wife. He looked to Dogan and asked, "So, Dogan, you must be the Salvie that's been working with our Lee? We have not been properly introduced." He said *our Lee*! That should be a good sign, right? The king walked up to Dogan, who was to my right. The two of them shook forearms. "It's a pleasure to meet the man who's been beating up this poor woman." Bryce gazed at me and only winked no smile.

"It's a pleasure to meet ye too, Yer Majesty," he said with a bow of his head.

"I want you to tell me everything you saw. You are the only one here that has nothing to lose," he said to him.

Dogan went into full detail, starting with me talking to him about training tomorrow. He left out the part of me throwing the stone at him. Dogan told Bryce everything I said word for word. It surprised me that he remembered it all with such detail. He said how Gavin handled me and how he followed us but kept his distance. He explained everything up until when he told me to leave and to go to my room. Dogan ended by saying, "Can I be bold wit ye, Yer Majesty?"

Bryce nodded. "Please do, Dogan."

"I personally think yer cousin is not a man at all." I sucked in a short breath in fear he might say something to piss the king off. He continued, "A man should never handle or touch a woman like he did wit Lee. I'm not sure what happened at dinner, but if I'd ha' kent about it, he'd probably ha' more than a broken nose." The king gave him a slight smile as he tilted his head but did not speak so Dogan could continue. "Lee is the first woman I ha' ever had to train wit. At first I thought ye were all crazy to ha' a woman to guard the queen. That was until I started to actually ken 'er. I ha' been training wit 'er fer about a month now, and she's already improved drastically. If ye get rid o' 'er because she gave that weasel ye call a cousin what he deserves, then ye'll be making one o' the biggest mistakes o' yer life. So I'm asking ye to reconsider yer decision o' making 'er leave." My jaw dropped in shock.

"Holy hell, Lee," Kaidan murmured in my ear. "Where is this coming from?"

I shook my head in disbelief. This was the second time this evening that I could not believe Dogan was even capable of even saying such things. For the first time since we had met, I wanted to hug him. Bryce turned to me and said, "Well, Lee, did you hear that? This is coming from a man that you despise."

In shame, I hung my head again. I was so sorry for what I had done, but how do I tell him? Bryce was now standing in front of me. He took my chin in his hand and lifted my face up to look at him. The handsome smile was reassuring. "My dear Lee, do you really think I would get rid of you like that? And that goes for all of you." He fixed his eyes on Kaidan then back on his wife. "What kind of a man do you think I am?" When no one answered, he turned back to me, "Gavin has no clue what your true purpose of being here is. Just like everyone else, he just thinks you are the queen's lady. Well, love, you are a hell of a lot more than that. Not only are you one of my guards, you are my wife's closest friend, and you are my friend. So no worries, you are not going anywhere."

He turned back to Dogan. "Thank you, Dogan for coming and talking with me. Please continue what you are doing with Lee. I have seen the improvement in her. She's more confident. It's because of that confidence she punched Gavin in the first place. I do not think she would have done it if it was not for you. So keep up the good work."

"I will, Yer Majesty, thank ye." Dogan bowed gracefully before him.

"Kaidan, you and Dogan may leave now," the king insisted. "Rosa and I need to speak with Lee alone."

"All right, let's go, Ramstien." Kaidan squeezed a hand on my shoulder as he turned for the door. I gazed up at Dogan, who was looking back at me with intense eyes. When I was about to reach for him, he turned to follow Kaidan.

Rosa rushed and took me in her arms. "Oh, Lee, I was so afraid that I was actually going to lose you!"

"I know, me too." I squeezed her tight.

"I still cannot believe you all thought I could do something like that." We turned to find the king with an astonishing look. Rosa laughed and brought my head to hers, and we both continued to gaze at the king. I could not help but smile then he finally did himself.

After a moment of silence, his face sobered again, and he said, "Lee, I know this might be uncomfortable to tell me, but I need to know. How did my cousin touch you at dinner? I saw him touching the back of your neck. What else did he do?"

I stood straight and took a deep breath, then Rosa suggested, "Bryce, darling, maybe it will be better if she just tells me then I will tell you."

"No, it's fine, Rosa. I can do this." Walking over to the chair that Rosa was in earlier and sat down, I began, "He first grabbed my leg here." I used my left hand on my right leg since it was his left hand he used. "I pushed it away, but he ended up replacing it. He dragged his hand all the way up my thigh and I stopped it when he got about here." I looked down at my hand and thought how close his fingers were to touching me in a place he had no right to be. Finally, I snapped out of it and said, "His grip was so tight I could not remove it. That's when I got Kaidan's attention."

"That bloody fool," Bryce roared. "He does this right under my nose, in my house!" His face was on fire when he stormed out of the room.

"I am so sorry, Lee! I cannot believe he did that to you." Rosa's eyes glistened with tears and extended her hand to me. When I took the offered hand and stood up, she wrapped me in another hug. "Come, let's go."

She guided me out of the room. We stopped in the hall just before where we were supposed to turn to go back where the dining room was. Bryce was yelling angrily, "How dare you, Gavin! In my house and to my wife's lady." We pressed our backs against the wall and listened. For how loud they are, we knew that they were in the hall.

"She's a lying whore, Bryce, and you need to get rid of her," Gavin screamed, and my mouth dropped at his statement. It took all I had to stay still and not to go marching down that hall to beat him to a bloody pulp.

Bryce's voice was now low like a growl. "Do not ever call her that again! Kaidan saw with his own eyes as you had your hands on her. I am sorry, Uncle, but I do not ever want this man in my house again. Did you hear that, Gavin? Never again! Now I want you to get the hell out of here."

"All right, I see how it is. Pick her over your own family," Gavin yelled with disgust.

"Oh," he laughed. "You and I are not family, now get your ass out of my castle!"

A few moments later, I heard Gavin holler, "Open that god-damn door!" Then he was gone.

"I apologize for everything, Bryce. I know my son has a reputation when it comes to the ladies. I do not know why he is the way he is. We did not raise him to be like that. He gets bad when he drinks too much, you know that," the duke said softly.

"I do know that, but he went too far this time," Bryce said calmly to his uncle.

"He did! It's a shame because I have always liked Lady Leelah. I hoped that maybe she would fall in love with my son and I could call her my daughter." If Gavin was like his father, I probably could fall in love with him, but he was definitely not.

"I am sorry, Uncle, but I can never see that happening. Lee is too much of a strong, independent woman for Gavin anyway."

"I see that now. Please tell her that I am so sorry for my son's actions and that I hope she does not stay away from our house because of it." I smiled when I heard him say that. I had always liked the duke. He was a pleasure to be around.

"I will let her know, Uncle. Thank you."

"Are you serious about not allowing Gavin to come here?" the duke asked.

"For the meantime, yes. Once he knows what he did was wrong, I will allow him to come here to apologize to me and Lady Lee. Then I will decide if he's welcome here or not."

"Thank you, Bryce. Please tell Rosa that we said good night," the duchess said.

"Will do! Good night and safe travels home."

Rosa and I still had our backs against the wall; she had ahold of my right hand. We were just standing there waiting in silence for the Thelases to leave. Bryce came up from the hall to our right and stopped as soon as he saw us.

His face was still flushed with anger, but he smiled instantly. "Well, look at you two eavesdropping!"

Rosa and I shared glances, and we started to giggle. "Sorry, darling, I just thought it would be better to wait until everyone left before I brought her out."

"I am glad you did. I think the three of us deserve another glass of wine." He beamed us a smile and continued down to where he came from. Rosa and I followed arm in arm.

Once I finally got to my room for the evening, I was exhausted. When I peeled out of my dress, that's when I noticed the bruises on my arm that Gavin caused. They were long narrow marks where his fingers used to be. I lightly ran my hand over them. When I took off my leggings, sure enough there were more bruises on my upper thigh. They stretched all the way down into my inner thigh. Instantly, I ran over, and pulled open the drawer in my nightstand and grabbed the jar of paste that Dogan gave me. With the need to get rid of the marks the dirty bastard put on me, I struggled with the lid to the jar. Once I had it open, I welcomed the coolness of the paste to my skin. Quickly, I rubbed the substance into my arm and thigh, praying that there would be more signs of them by tomorrow morning.

Chapter 9

Auras

That morning, I woke up pleased to find my skin mark free, and it was now late in the afternoon as I headed down to meet with Dogan. Anxiety had been growing in me all day with the thought of seeing him. After what happened last night, I found myself considering him as a friend, still not sure if that was a good thing or not. It most likely was not, but only time would tell. The funny thing was that I still despised the man. Can it be possible to be friends with a person who always aggravates you? I liked it better when I thought of him as the evil enemy.

When I walked in, he was standing in the middle of the room. I did not even bother shutting the door. Instead, I went straight to him and asked, "Why did you say what you said last night?"

The beast of a man sighed. "Because I was pissed off wit that weasel. The only person that's allowed to rough ye up is me, and that's because o' yer training." While I glared at his statement, he continued. "What he did last night was unacceptable. Ye handled yerself correctly though," he stated roughly with his Salvie accent.

I would not say *correctly*. Not knowing what to say to the man, I just replied, "Thank you, Dogan."

"Dinna say my name like that, woman," he growled.

119

"I beg your pardon? That is your name, is it not?" I asked with my head tilted to the side.

"Aye, but ye only call yer friends and the people ye care about by their first name. I'm definitely not yer friend." He narrowed his eyes.

He was right. The guards that I was closest too I call by their first names. "Well, Dogan," I said his name sarcastically, "I am afraid that I do consider you a friend. No worries, though, you are the first friend that I have ever had that I still want to inflict pain to. I think I will always despise you!" I gave him a huge sarcastic smile.

He growled, shaking his head, "Go and shut that bloody door." It looked like he was trying not to smile, but I do not know for certain.

Without thinking, I turned around and grabbed the handle of the door; that was when I got wacked across the back of my head. The pain was instant, and I stumbled forward a step. My hand went to the back of my head, and I started to massage the area. Turning around, I scowled at Dogan, who now had a brilliant smile on his face. "What in the hell was that for?"

"Ye asked fer it, woman." His smile widened making his dimples show. "And aye, I was right...I'm gonna enjoy this verra much."

"Your idea of training me is by throwing..." I bent down, picking up the tiny brown sack off the floor. It fit perfectly in my hand and felt through the cloth what was inside. "Is that sand? You are going to throw sacks of sand at my head? Do you know how much that bloody hurts?"

He nodded his head. "It will make ye more determined to learn faster. Fer now on I'm gonna be chucking these things at ye even when ye least expect it. If I see ye in the city, I'll be hitting ye. I'll not care if the queen's wit ye. I'll always ha' 'em, and I'll always throw 'em even when ye do learn to sense 'em."

This was going to be just wonderful. Why do I get myself into these predicaments? Now every time I go out, I am going to have the feeling to look over my shoulder. Dogan was going to get so much enjoyment out of this; it's not going to be funny.

"Well, how do I learn to sense them?" I asked.

"Ha' ye ever heard o' an aura?" he asked.

Giving him an odd look, I inquired, "No, what's that?"

Dogan walked over and sat on the bench by the window. I could see the sun behind him and it would be sinking into the ocean in a few hours. "Come sit, lass. This may take a while to explain," he spoke calmly, so I slowly walked over and sat beside him. In the time I have know him, this was the first time the two us sat like this, just to talk.

"Yer soul generates a light that radiates from yer body. That light is called an aura. They come in every color imagined. Some are brighter than others, depending on the person. Once ye are aware o' it, ye can control it. Usually, the average aura will only expand maybe a few inches the most from yer body. Once ye learn how to grab hold o' it, ye can expand it tens o' feet from yer body. By doing that, ye'd be able to sense everything around ye even wit yer eyes closed. Like last night, fer instance. Even though my back was to ye, I was still watching ye walk away. I saw ye kick loose that stone and picked it up. I saw ye look back at me and the stone several times before ye threw it at me." Dogan had a light smile on his lips while he thought of last night. I wanted to say something, but I did not, as he would not continue if I stopped him. "This is not something ye'r gonna learn overnight. It can take months, even years, to perfect it. Hell, I'm still perfecting mine."

"Can anyone learn to do this?" I finally asked.

"Nay," he responded quickly with a shake of his head.

"Then how do you know I can even do it?" All of a sudden, I was afraid to know the answer to that question.

"When I first walked in the barracks that day and saw ye sitting wit the general and Kimball...I almost couldna look at ye, ye are so *bright*. It has been a long time since I ha' seen someone as bright as ye. I figured ye were a mage because they usually ha' brighter auras. 'Twas not till ye pressed yer knife against my throat and then yer fingertips brushed my skin. 'Twas then when my hunches were confirmed and that I kent what ye were. I also kent then that ye had no clue what ye were capable of."

"So you are a mage of some sort?" Then I thought about what he just said, "What do you mean you know what I am? And what am I capable of?"

"Ye are just like me," he announced, turning his light smile into an evil grin. My body shook with a chill. I did not like the sounds of that. "That's why I ken ye can do this. Like I said, it's gonna take a lot o' time fer ye to grab hold o' this power. But when ye do..." He paused. "Ye'll be seeing life through different eyes. Ye'll be able to tell who mages are and who are like us."

"So what are we...mages? Is there other people here in the city that are like us, so to speak?" I asked slowly still in disbelief.

He laughed. "I dinna like to consider myself one, but I guess we're some type o' mage. I ha' only met a handful o' people in my life that I could tell had abilities like me. Two o' 'em I met here, and yer one o' 'em."

"Who's the other? Do I know them?" I practically begged.

Dogan actually let out a short chuckle. "Aye, ye ken 'im and quite well, actually. It's Lieutenant Sterling Fenwick."

"Sterling?" I yelled in shock. "Does he know?"

"I think he knows he's different, but I ha' not talked to 'im about that yet," he answered.

"Are you going to?"

"Aye," he said, sounding annoyed. I realized then that he always used the Salvie word of *yes* and *no* when he spoke, which I thought was odd. He seems to know my language quite well, but I have noticed that sometimes he does add some of his words when he's speaking our tongue. Like the word *bairn* for instance—it means child. Getting myself off track here, I shook my head quickly and looked back at him.

"You said I am bright. What's my color?"

"The same as Sterling and I, a deep red," he said. "It means grounded, strong will power, survival oriented. That can change though, or ye might always stay that color. It really depends on the person's soul."

"Do you always see people's auras, or can you block it out?" I asked.

"Ye can block it out. Ye have to, or ye'll get terrible headaches. Only time I usually look at someone's aura is when I'm first meeting 'em. I can get an idea what they're gonna be like before they even start talking," he said, gazing down his nose at me.

I am not sure if he was trying to intimidate me with those eyes of his, so I did not let them get to me and asked my next question, "What about the king and queen, did you look at their auras?"

"Och aye, the king is gold. It means he has divine guidance, wisdom, intuitive thinker. The queen is emerald green. That means a healer, a love-centered person." He paused. "D'ye ken she's pregnant?"

Quickly, I looked at the door to make sure it was still closed then jerked my head back to Dogan. "How do you know about that? Only Kai and I know," I asked in a hushed tone.

"Coming from 'er emerald aura, she has sparks o' white light. That usually indicates pregnancy."

Leaning toward him, I whispered harshly, "You must not say a word of this to no one. They are making an announcement at the end of next week. Please tell me that I am the first person you shared this information with."

He shoved me back roughly. "Ye'r the only one. I figured ye would ha' ken since ye are close to 'er."

After staring at him for a moment, I asked, "How do you know all of this, Dogan? Someone must have taught you."

Dogan looked away from me and stood up. All right, I just found something he did not want to talk about. I wondered why. Who taught him, and why all of a sudden did he get tight-lipped about it? I will not pester him about it today, but he will tell me someday. I would make sure of it. An idea popped in my head, and I smiled at his back.

"All right, Dogan, I want you to prove something to me." He finally turned and fixed his eyes on me. Untying the dark blue sash, I had around my waist. I brought it up and pressed it tight over my eyes. There was no way of see anything not even shadows. So I walked over to him and handed him the sash. "Tie this over your eyes so you have no vision. I want to see what *you* are really capable of."

While he tied on the sash, I went over to the chest and grabbed four wooden swords. Suddenly, there was a sharp pain in the back of my head for the second time that day. A groan escaped my lips as I picked up the sack of sand off the floor. When I turned back, Dogan was standing in the middle of room with his arms folded across his massive chest. Even though he was now blindfolded, I could still feel his gaze on me. I chucked the sack back at him, but more to the left. Sure enough, he extends his arm and snatched it in the air. Shaking my head in disbelief, I walked up to him and handed him the two swords in my right hand. He knew exactly where they were at. Dogan took them out of my hand like he had no blindfold on at all. Taking both my swords in each hand, he stepped back a few paces. He had a mocking smile as he spinned the swords in his hands.

"Well?" he said. "What are ye waiting fer, woman? Come get me!"

Oh, how I loved to hear him say those words. It made me smile every time. I charged after him like I always did. Taking my right sword high and my left low, he blocked them both. Swinging and jabbing both my swords at him, Dogan just blocked and swung back at me, like any other day. He was still quick, maybe a little quicker than usual if that was possible. The man was unbelievable. Not being able to help myself, I started laughing while I fought with him. For the first time, the man made me laugh because I could not believe that this was possible. I was actually enjoying myself. As I kept attacking, I heard the quiet noise of the door opening. In walked Kaidan and the general. I gave them the signal to keep quiet and waved Kaidan toward me.

Dogan must have sensed them because his head turned slightly to right in Kaidan's direction. I threw one of my swords to him. Kaidan snatched it from the air and charged at Dogan with the sword high. When he brought the wooden blade down on him, Dogan spun and blocked Kaidan's blow.

"Hello, Kimball," he said with a wicked grin.

Kaidan looked at me with wide eyes then asked, "How in the bloody hell did you block my blow and know it was me?"

"It's amazing, is it not?" I said with a big smile. Kaidan pushed Dogan back and signaled me for the other sword. After I threw it to him, the two of them went back and forth at each other. I walked to the door to stand by the general.

"How is he doing that, Lee?" he asked without taking his eyes off the men. "Is he a mage?"

"He's definitely some type. Dogan thinks he can train me to do what he's doing right now," I announced without tearing my eyes away from the men.

"Are you telling me he can teach anyone to fight like that, with no vision?" he asked in disbelief.

"No, he can only teach people who are like him." The general was looking at me with wide eyes. When he did not say anything, I continued, "He says he's only met a handful of people like himself. Two of them he met here, me being one of them."

"Who's the other?" he whispered eagerly.

Gazing and smiling at him, I said, "Sterling."

His eyes grew wider as he smiled, "Does the lieutenant know of this?"

"I do not think so. Dogan said he has not talked to him about it yet."

"I want you to stay here. I am going to summon for Sterling. I will be right back." He practically ran out the door.

"Where did the general go in such a hurry?" asked Dogan. The two of them were no longer fighting, and he pulled off the blindfold. He knew the general was here and left with his eyes covered. The smile never ceased from my face. Could I really do that someday? It does not seem possible.

"He's going to summon for Sterling," I told him.

"Why?" Kaidan asked. "Is there something wrong?"

"Nothing is wrong, Kai," I said. "Sterling, like me, is the same as Dogan."

Kaidan gave me an odd look then turned to Dogan. "What the hell is she talking about, Ramstien?"

Dogan gave Kaidan a shortened version of what he told me earlier this evening. Kaidan started to pace then gazed at me after he thought about it. "So he's saying you are most likely a mage and you never knew about it?"

"I do not know, Kai. I am still trying to register it in my mind," I said while shrugging my shoulders. The whole idea was hard for me to even comprehend.

Chapter 10

Releasing the Light

As soon as the general walked in with Sterling behind, he ordered Dogan to blindfold himself again. When he does, the general handed Sterling a wooden sword and ordered him to attack Dogan. Sterling hesitated; he gave me a questionable look. The general gave him the order again, and Sterling charged. I could tell that he was shocked when Dogan blocked his blow. Then he started on Dogan harder. Never watching Sterling fight before, it surprised me that he moved a lot like him. He was fast, but not quite as fast. After a few minutes of them fighting, Sterling landed a blow on Dogan's left shoulder. I actually jumped in the air and cheered for him. He laughed at me as Dogan pulled the blindfold off.

Dogan stuck out his arm and praised, "Ye ha' got some good swordsmanship, Lieutenant."

Sterling grabbed his forearm in a shake. "Thank you, Dogan. You mind telling me how in the hell were you able to do that?"

Before Dogan could respond, the general spoke, "Kaidan, let's leave these three be. They have a lot to discuss." Sterling gave me a puzzled look, and the general continued, "Dogan, do not worry about your guard duties for tonight. I am giving you the night off. Please be sure to see me in the morning."

"Aye, General," Dogan said, and the general nodded and walked out with Kaidan following suit.

"Can one of you please explain to me what's going on?" Sterling asked in a frustrated tone.

Dogan fixed his eyes to me. "Woman, can ye run and ask Kaidan if he can find someone to bring us up some food? We're going to be here fer a while, and I'm bloody hungry."

My stomach growled instantly when he mentioned the word food. I did not say anything, just turned and walked out the door. Kaidan and the general were at the end of the corridor when I shut the door behind me.

"Kai," I yelled, "wait for one moment!"

Kaidan turned and came jogging toward me. We met halfway down the corridor. "What is it, Lee?"

"Would you mind going to the kitchen and asking Varon to make up three plates for dinner? Just tell him to send the food here with some wine." Wine sounded perfect at that moment.

"No problem. Do you want anything particular for dinner?" he asked.

"No." I smiled. "Tell him to surprise us."

"Very well." He smiled back.

"Thank you, Kai! I really do appreciate it." I smirked while walking backward.

"I know, now get your ass back in there." He gave me a wink and then continued back down the corridor.

When I returned to the room, we all took a seat, and Dogan explained everything to Sterling. After a while of just talking about auras and how we can learn to control them, a knock came from the door. Sterling instantly went to the door and opened it. "Thank you, but I can take it from here." he pulled in the cart. "What did you order us, Lee?"

"I am not sure what it is. I told Kaidan to tell him to surprise us. Why?"

"It smells great," he said while sniffing the air and lifted one of the lids. "Pork chops! You know how long it's been since I have had those? It's been forever." While smiling, he wheeled the cart to us so we could eat. We sat at the only table in the room that was against the right wall. It was just big enough for the three of us. Once we got ourselves situated with our food and wine, we started to talk again while we ate.

Dogan starts, "So, Sterling, did ye always ken ye were different?"

"I was real young when I started to see people's auras. I did not know that's what they were called until tonight. I always asked my family if they could see the lights around other people. They just thought I was crazy. Then when I was around eight, Rowan's family moved into the property that was next to ours. My parents brought me over to meet him. Rowan was the first and only person I have ever met that had the same color light as me. Of course, we hit it off right away. That day while we were playing out in the woods, I decided to ask him if he ever saw lights around people. He told me that he thought he was the only one that could. It was that very moment that the two of us became brothers. Over the years, we were able to figure out how to block it out. It always gave us headaches, and we decided not to use it anymore. What was the point anyway, right?" Sterling looked at me and gave me a small smile.

I could not believe it. "Rowan had the same gift." Then I looked to Dogan, "If you are so certain that I have the same power, then why did I not see lights when I was younger?"

"Some people are more open to it. I did meet a man that told me he didn't realize about his abilities until he was fifty years old." Dogan paused and then held up his hand. "People like us can even talk to one another through touch."

"What do you mean by that?" Sterling asked.

"If ye touch a person like yerself, ye can talk to them through yer mind instead o' talking out loud."

"Really?" I was amazed. For the first time, I was not mad about Dogan coming here. If it were not for him, I probably would not know any of this.

"Aye. I want us to try after dinner. Have either o' ye ever try meditating before?"

Sterling and I shared glances, then I smiled, shaking my head no. Sterling asked laughing a little, "No, do you meditate?"

"Aye," he snapped. "I meditate a few times a week. It will help ye access yer core. When was the last time ye saw anyone's aura, Sterling?"

"I was about twelve when I figured out how to block it out. I have not let it out since."

"Ye think ye can open back up to let yerself see my and Lee's auras?" he asked and then stuffed another piece of pork into his mouth.

"It's been twenty years, but I will try." Sterling put his utensil down and closed his eyes. After a moment, he took a deep breath and slowly opened his eyes. First, he looked at Dogan. I could see his eyes widen and a smile came to his face. "You are the same color as Row and I." Dogan nodded, and Sterling looked to his right at me and his eyes squinted a little, but he still had a smile, "Wow, Lee, I did not think it possible but you are even more beautiful with your red light." And then he spoke to Dogan without tearing his eyes off me, "Why is she so bright? I have never seen an aura that bright before."

"I'm not sure why she is. I'm thinking maybe 'tis because she's never used 'er abilities." Then Dogan fixed his eyes on me. "This is why ye are so close wit Sterling and at one time wit' this Rowan. Ye all are drawn to each other. Like I was drawn to follow ye in the garden that night." Now he looked to Sterling. "And even though ye annoy the hell outta me, I still canna help but like ye, Lieutenant."

Sterling laughed. "The feelings are mutual."

We continued to eat our dinner and drink our wine, all the while I tried not to think of Rowan. Dogan explained how he was going to train me by throwing those tiny sacks at me. I was happy to hear that he was going to do the same thing to Sterling. After we were done eating, Dogan stood up, walked to the middle of the room, and sat down with his legs crossed. Sterling and I looked at each other with smiling eyes, then we both gazed back at him.

"Stop staring at me ye fools and just come and sit." He was getting annoyed with us, so we did what he said. The three of us sat in the form of a triangle, my right knee touching Sterling's and my left touching Dogan's.

"We're gonna try meditating. I want both o' ye to lay yer left arm across yer leg wit palms up." We both did that, and so did Dogan. "Now take yer right hand and lay it over the other person's palm." At first, Dogan and Sterling's hands were cool against mine, then they instantly heated when Sterling completed the circle.

"Did ye feel anything before Sterling touched my hand?" he asked me like he already knew.

"Yes, both of your hands became very hot as soon as Sterling completed the circle."

Dogan gave me a small smile and said, "Good." Then he continued, "I want ye two to close yer eyes and not talk at all. If ye need to speak, please speak in yer mind. I'll hear ye. Even though this is the first time fer the two o' ye, ye should also hear me."

After closing my eyes, I tried to relax after taking a deep breath. This was not how I expected my night to be like. It was just supposed to be like any other day I met with Dogan. Now here I am, sitting and holding hands on the floor with my best friend and a man I still do not know what to consider.

"I'm not yer friend if that's what ye are considering," Dogan's voice roared in my head.

"Oh my God! I can actually hear you," I thought back to him.

"This is crazy! You would not think it's possible," Sterling's voice filled my head.

"I want both o' ye to try to clear yer heads. Try to get rid o' all anxieties ye may ha'. Whatever may trouble ye, try to ferget about it. Just breathe." Dogan paused. I heard him take a deep breath. When he spoke again, it was the softest I ever heard. It was calming, soothing almost trance like. *"Dear m'Heavenly Father, I pray fer yer white light o' protection over the three o' us. Help guide me to access their abilities ye've obviously blessed 'em wit. And guide 'em in their journey o' their newfound power. Amen."* I never pictured Dogan as a religious man, but I guess you learn something new every day. Sterling squeezed my right hand, and I squeezed back.

For several moments, there was nothing, and then Dogan's soft voice filled the silence in my head, *"Now take a deep breath in through*

yer nose and fill yer lungs completely." I did as I was told. *"Hold it...*
now exhale through yer mouth. Good, again! Take a deep breath..."

We did this exercise several times. I was already feeling my
body relax and began to feel heavy, especially my head, shoulders,
and arms.

"Now I want ye to picture yerself on a beach..." Slowly his voice
seemed to drift away and I found myself standing on a pearly beach.
Somewhere in the back of my mind I knew I was still in the castle but
at the same time I was invisioning the beach as if I was really there.

I was barefoot with the sand warm against my feet, and my
toes instantly dug in. The sun was hot, and I tilted my face up to
the lovely summer breeze as I walked up the beach. The waves were
crashing, and the gulls were calling from high up the cliffs.

Eventually, I had to come to a stop since the beach had a break
in it. There was a narrow waterfall, maybe four feet in width, coming
down from the top of the sandstone cliff. The fresh water fell down
into a pool of calm salt water. Cautiously, I stepped in. There was a
slight current from the ocean, but nothing overpowering. The water
was up to my knees, and my long skirt stuck to my skin as I moved
toward the waterfall.

As I moved forward, a figure of red light began to form on the
other side of the falls. It was a person, a tall person, at that. The water
distorted the figure so there was no clear view on who it was. A hand
encased with red light and long elegant fingers stretched out through
the falls toward me. I felt no fear but love. This was a woman who
was special to me, but I still did not know who she was. When I laid
my hand in hers, it was warm, and I felt protected as she guided me
through the falls. The water was cool and refreshing against my hot
skin. As I started to come to the other side of the falls, I began to
register Dogan's voice again.

"Now that ye feel cleansed, ye begin to walk back down the beach to
where ye came from." I struggled to return to the falls and the mysteri-
ous woman, but I could not. As much as I tried, the vision was gone.

"How d'ye feel? Relaxed?" Dogan asked. Sterling and I said *yes*
in unison. *"Good! Now I'm gonna grab hold of both o' yer cores. Ye are*

gonna feel a pull from yer chest and then ye'll ha' instant vision even though yer eyes are still closed."

At first, I was calm and sitting in the dark, then I felt extreme pressure on my chest like someone was pushing hard against it. Suddenly, I started to feel slightly nauseated as the pressure increased. The pain was unbelievable as the pressure literally felt as though it was ripped from my chest and I found myself falling backward in its wake. Dogan clamped his hand down on mine, and I grabbed a hold of Sterling's so I did not fall. After registering the pain was gone, I realized that I could see them. Just as if my eyes were open, except that they were in deep red. Everything was their clothing, skin, hair, even the floor. I looked at Sterling, and I gave him a huge smile. He smiled back then stuck out his tongue at me, making me laugh softly.

"This is amazing, Dogan," Sterling marveled. *"Will I be able to do this by myself?"*

"Aye, in time ye will. It takes a while to learn how to release it. If ye meditate, it'll help ye a great deal," he said.

"How is it possible for me to see what's in front of me and behind at the same time?" I asked to him, *"And is everything red because of our auras?"*

"I dinna ha' the answer to how ye can see all around. Ye just can. And aye, because yer aura is red, so will everything else when ye release it," Dogan answered.

"So is this what it looked like to you when you were blindfolded earlier?" I asked him.

"Aye."

I started laughing hard, and I gazed at Sterling, *"This is unbelievable, Sterling! I am happy I can share this with you."* I squeezed his hand, and he squeezed mine back.

Dogan growled at us, causing me to giggle and then he asked, *"Did either o' ye see anything else beside the beach, ocean, and the waterfall?"*

I hesitated for a moment then bit down on my bottom lip before speaking through our touch. *"I saw a woman, I believe. I could not see her clearly."*

In the red light, I saw Dogan turn his head toward me as his eyebrows arched up. *"Really? Please tell me everything ye saw, including colors."*

I smiled softly because the man actually sounded excited, which is a first I believe. *"She was standing on the other side of the falls. She was quite tall. Now that I really think about it, she was close to your height. Her whole body was encased in a red light similer to this color."*

Dogan stiffened a bit, and he began to squeeze my hand tighter. *"How d'ye ken 'twas a woman?"*

"Because she stuck her hand out to me throught the falls. Even though the hand was bigger than mine, the fingers were too long and elegant to be a man's."

"Was there any jewelry on this hand or wrist?" Dogan asked in all seriousness.

I had to think back for a moment and then shook my head. *"No, there was no jewelry."* Dogan's grip lessoned considerably.

"That's excellent, woman." Dogan was pleased. *"Ye possibly had an encounter wit one o' yer spirit guides."*

"Do you really think so?"

"Aye, that's good fer the first time. Maybe ye'll actually see 'er next time we do this," he said and then addressed Sterling. *"How about ye? Did ye see anything?"*

"Nothing more then what you were describing," Sterling groaned in my head.

"That's fine, Sterling. Ye'll get better at it as time goes, and it's normal not to see anything extra the first few times." Dogan slowly turned his head at me. His eyes were closed, but I knew he could see me as clearly as I could see him. *"This woman is obviously more open to this than I thought."* Dogan's soft voice was gone and was replaced with his rough, thick Salvie accent. A chill ran the full length of my spine as if I could actually see his intense, angry, emerald eyes boring down on me.

We spent a good while in the red light. We just sat there, quietly taking in the surroundings. My body felt great…I felt love. Why? I was not completely sure, but I definitely felt it.

Dogan broke our peaceful state. *"I'm going to put back yer energies now. Since this is the first time ye both ever had 'em out, they're going to hit ye hard as they go back in. Hold on tight."*

Dogan held tight to my hand as Sterling did to my other. All of a sudden, it was dark again, and I got hit in the chest with so much force that it knocked the air from my lungs. My eyes sprung open to the shock of it, and I tried to suck the air back in. Sterling was staring at me with wide eyes. He too was trying hard to breathe in air.

"Relax," Dogan said calmly. "Yer breath'll be back any moment."

We both gawked at him. He was not even struggling to breathe. The man was sitting there like nothing happened. After a few seconds, I was able to speak...sort of.

"How..." I managed to say while taking a quick breath, "do you...make it...not hurt?"

"I ha' been doing it all my life," he stated. "Every time ye do it, the easier it'll get. I promise. The next time ye release yer core, it'll hurt a little less than now."

"Why did you wait till now to say anything to me?" I finally asked. "We have been together practically every day for a month, and you never said a damn thing."

"I knew ye were not aware o' it, and if I said anything to ye back then, ye would ha' thought I was crazy."

"I still think you are crazy!" I cut in, and he narrowed his eyes.

He continued, "Last night, ye said to me, 'Besides if ye can do that, I am sure as hell I can.' I knew that instant that 'twas time to tell ye, and that ye'd actually listen to me." Dogan stared at me for a moment then added, "Has anyone ever told ye that ye swear too much fer a woman? It's not verra lady like!"

My jaw dropped for a moment. I knew I could be vulgar at times, but I could not help that. Sterling started to laugh. "Our sweet lass cannot help it sometimes. She was practically raised by her father and four brothers."

Dogan looked at me with interest. "Really? Ye had no mother?"

I wanted to hit Sterling for speaking anything of my past in front of him, but instead, I looked at Dogan. "That's none of your *damn* business!"

Dogan did that throaty laugh he does sometimes, then he released our hands and stood up. Sterling and I stayed seated; we still had not let go of each other. I was afraid to stand up, like I might fall over. Slowly, Sterling rose; he never let go of my hand.

"Come on, darling." He smiled and pulled me up to his side. I wrapped my arm around his waist to balance myself. Something was different with our touch, it was sort of tingling. Sterling said, "I do not know what to say, Dogan. How did you learn to do this? Rowan and I have never experienced anything like this. I do not think we were aware that we could talk to each other in the way we just did. We always seemed to know what the other was thinking. We just did not realize what we were doing." Then he looked down at me. "I could always feel your emotions when we would touch. Did you ever notice it?"

"Maybe," I said. "I was not aware of it, but now…" Still holding his hand, I fixed my eyes on his and said in my mind, *You're my best friend, Sterling. If it was not for you, I would be lost right now. Tell me out loud what I just said.*

He smiled. "You're my best friend, Sterling. If it was not for you, I would be lost right now." I laughed in amazement, and he added, "All right now it's my turn."

Sterling squeezed my hand and stared into my eyes. *"Dogan is a bloody bastard, and I smile every time when I think of you kicking him in the balls. Now say that out loud."*

I burst out in laughter. "Hell no, Sterling! I am not repeating that!"

"You have to, so I know you heard what I said," he teased with his beautiful contagious smile then looked at Dogan. "Come on, Lee, tell Dogan what I just said."

"No, I cannot!" I answered shaking my head.

"All right, ye got my attention…What the hell did Sterling say, woman?" Dogan was obviously annoyed.

I took a deep breath and squeezed myself closer to Sterling. Like I was afraid he would flip out when he heard. "He said, 'Dogan is a bloody bastard.'" I started to giggle. "'And I smile every time when I think of you kicking him in the balls!'"

A slow smile spread across my lips as I looked at Dogan. It did not help to feel Sterling bouncing in silent laughter. I waited for a snide comment to come from Dogan. He practically growled just as I expected him to. Shaking his head, he laughed a little. "Ye are a bastard, Lieutenant."

"I know…just as you are most of the time. Come on, Dogan, let me buy you a drink," Sterling said. "And that goes for you too, my lady."

"Oh really? Do I get a say in this?" I asked to him.

"Nope, you are coming whether you like it or not." Sterling winked. "Besides, the DeBolbec family is playing tonight. I will need someone to dance with."

"You had me at the word *dance*."

"Good!" He gestured to Dogan. "Let's go you bloody fool! I do not know about you, but I could use another drink."

As the two of us walked toward the door, I got a sharp pain in the back of my head for the third time this evening. I bit down on my lip and groaned. Instantly, my hand was rubbing the spot. Sterling cursed, spun around, and picked up the little sacks off the floor.

"Damn it, Dogan! That bloody hurts…" He rubbed the back of his own head as he looked at me. "Do you throw them that hard at her?" He pointed at me with his thumb.

"Of course, I dinna ease back on 'er because she's a woman. I know it hurts, it'll make ye more determined to learn to sense 'em," Dogan said with a smug expression.

"I do not know about you, Lee, but this is going to get old real fast," he muttered then glared viciously at Dogan.

"I thought the same thing when I got whacked in the head for the first time," I moaned. "This is the third time for me this evening."

"Oh God!" he laughed. "Dogan, get your arrogant self in front of us! I am not walking all the way to MacLeod's with you throwing these"—he chucked the small pouches back at him—"sacks at us!"

Dogan gave us a snide smile as he walked past us. "As ye wish, Lieutenant," he said sarcastically.

Sterling and I walked arm in arm all the way to the pub. We talked the whole time in each other's head about the man in front of us. I was going to enjoy this newfound gift. Even though I could only do this with the two of them, I would be able to talk privately to Sterling no matter where I was.

The air in MacLeod's was thick with music and a delicious aroma of food. People were laughing, dancing, and enjoying a tankard of ale. The three of us went straight for the bar and took the three empty stools. I sat in between the two of them.

"Good evening, gentleman and my lady," said the man on the other side of the bar. "What can I get for you this evening?"

"We would like three ales, please," Sterling replied and put the coins on the bar. The man took his coins, and a moment later, we had our ales in front of us. He picked up his tankard and held it up in front of me, so Dogan and I did the same. "To a new beginning, and may Lee and I not kill you by the end."

I laughed and said in the Salvie tongue, "Slainte mhath!" (to good health), and three of us clinked our glasses together. Once the ale touched my lips, I let it pour down my throat. I kept drinking the sourness down till it was gone, and I slammed the tankard down on the bar then look at Sterling. His ale was also gone, and he had a huge grin on his face. "Well, what about that dance you told me about?" I asked him.

"That's the lass I know and love!" He chuckled as he handed some more coins to Dogan. "Get us each another drink. Do not chuck those things at us while we are dancing, and that's an order. Do you understand?"

Dogan nodded his head and gave us the same snide smile from earlier. Sterling took my hand and brought me out to where the other people were dancing and spinning around. Filling the air was the sound of string instruments, flutes, and drums. It had been too long since I had actually done this. Sterling spun me and brought me back close to him. He had me laughing so hard that my stomach was now hurting. He could be so adorable sometimes, and I loved him for that. After a few songs, we made our way back to our seats. I was practically out of breath and thirsty. Instantly, grabbing my tankard of ale, I took a few gulps.

"Hello, handsome! It's been a while since I saw you here," a woman to my left said. I turned my head to watch Dogan spin around on his stool to face her. She was wearing a provocative dress, where her breasts were practically falling out. Her long wavy fiery hair was draped over one shoulder. The woman pushed herself between Dogan's legs, and her face disappeared to the other side of his face. She must be whispering or doing something to him because all of a sudden, a dimple popped out on his cheek. I never understood how women could stoop so low and live like that. I was raised that sex was supposed to be shared by two people who love each other and were married, not just with some stranger from the streets.

Dogan had his elbows on the bar; he reached over and grabbed hold of my arm. His touch tingled against my skin. Once he did that, Sterling took my other hand. He was still looking straight ahead with a smile on his face while the woman whispered in his other ear.

His thick voice filled my head. *I can feel yer eyes judging me, woman. So stop right now and return to yer drink. I'm only a man, and I do ha' needs!"*

Sterling burst out in laughter, and I yelled back in my head, *"Good God, Dogan! I sure as hell did not need to know that."* I jerked my arm from his grip.

I sat there drinking my ale and tried to ignore the man and woman to my left. Sterling and I shared a private conversation, talking about good times we had shared. The music slowed, and an angelic voice filled the room. I stared at my empty tankard as I listened to the song. It was about two people having to take two different roads and how she and her true love will never meet again. My eyes filled with tears as I thought of Rowan. Sterling took hold of my hand and squeezed it. I could not help it that the song hit me so hard. I understand the woman's heartache.

Dogan startled me with his laughter; I jerked my head to him and glared when I realized it was me he's laughing at. "Are ye serious?" he asked. "Are ye crying because o' this song?"

His woman gave me a blank stare, and I fixed my eyes angrily on him. "You know what, Dogan? You were right. I still hate you and you can go rot in hell!" He roared even louder in laughter. I pushed myself away from the bar and headed for the door. I stopped halfway out, afraid that I might get hit in the head. I turned to see Sterling in his face. With the loud music, there was no way of knowing what he was saying. Dogan continued to laugh while Sterling walked to me.

"Come on, love. Let me walk you home." He cupped his hand around my elbow, and we walked out into the cool night air. "I do not think that man has a heart, the bloody fool!" he growled once we were outside. Sterling quickly draped his arm around my shoulders and pulled me to his side.

"One moment, I can tolerate him, and the next I can rip off his head," I whispered angrily. "I think it's always going to be like that with him."

"The man is right though," Sterling said. "As much as he aggravates me, I cannot help but like him. It has to be the connection we all share. Just like Rowan, you and I were all drawn to each other."

"Rowan…," I said softly and I laid my head on his shoulder as we walked back to the castle. We did not talk much. I think we just wanted to enjoy the feeling of us together as we walked. Ever since Dogan ripped out my core earlier this evening, my touch was different. Every time Dogan or Sterling touched me, their touch gave a tingling sensation against my skin.

"Sterling?" I asked softly.

"Yes, love?" he replied.

"Has your touch changed? Right now, every part of me that is touching you is tingly."

"Yes, it has, and I feel it too," he whispered. "I like the feeling."

"Me too." I snuggled up closer to him and asked, "Do you think it's going to be like this every time we touch someone?"

"No. It's just us and people who have the same powers as us," he said. "I touched someone at the pub to see if I got the same sensation as I do with you and Dogan. I did not."

When we got to the castle, the guards opened the door for me, and to my surprise, Sterling walked in with me. "I know I usually say my good-nights outside, but I decided to walk you all the way to your room tonight. I am not quite ready to let go of you yet."

"All right." I smiled up at him and squeezed myself closer to his side again. When we got to my chamber door, he stopped and turned me so I was facing him. There was softness around those beautifully round chocolate eyes of his.

"I love you, Lee." He laid a hand on my neck and rubbed his thumb along my jaw. I believe my heart may have skipped a beat. The sensation from his touch was very soothing. "Not in the way that Rowan does, but I do. I am always here for you. If that bastard ever does anything to upset you, just let me know and I will take care of it. A door has just opened for us that we did not even realize was there. It's even a bigger door for you since you had no idea of what you are capable of. I want us to help each other, all right?"

I started to softly laugh and nod my head as the tears started to roll again. Quickly, I jumped up and wrapped my arms around his neck. "Thank you, Sterling, and I love you too," I murmured into his neck. The sensation was even stronger when it was skin to skin contact.

He started to laugh and brought my face in front of him. "You were tickling my neck, and the tingling sensation did not help matters." He had a beautiful smile on his face as I fixed my eyes on his lips and I wondered what the feeling would be like there. I looked back into his eyes. He must have read my thoughts because he said, "Well let's try and find out." Sterling quickly glanced up and down the corridor.

With my arms still around his neck, he wrapped his one arm tighter around my back and put his other hand on the back of my neck. This kiss was different from the one he gave a few weeks ago. That one was from Rowan, and, well, this was all Sterling. I pushed myself deeper into the kiss, and my head started to spin. The feeling was amazing and made me tingle from head to toe. Instantly, with our lips still connected we both smiled and separated so we could laugh.

"That was amazing!" I said still in his arms.

"I know, damn it! Why cannot I have this feeling with any other woman?"

I laughed at him. "Maybe you will find a woman with the same gifts someday, then you will be able to experience what it would be like."

"Maybe in my dreams!" He laughed then fixed his eyes on mine. "I am going to write Rowan tonight and tell him about everything. Is there anything you want me to say to him?"

Giving him a small smile I said, "Just tell him that my heart aches for him." A lump started to form in my throat again.

He nodded. "I can do that but only if you do something for me." His beautiful smile returned.

"I will do anything for you, what is it?"

"Kiss me one more…"

I did not let him finish, pressing my lips hard against his as he gave me a throaty laugh. It was nothing sexual when I kissed him, and I could tell he felt the same way toward me. We both just enjoyed the feeling. We finally separated laughing again.

"Good night, Lee."

"Good night, Sterling."

Upon opening my door, I watched him walk down the corridor. He turned and gazed back at me. As he continued to walk backward, he said in a hushed tone, "I am going to be looking for more of those kisses, Lee. At least until I find someone that can give me the same sensation." He winked at me. I laughed and nodded my head yes. Sterling's smile widened as he turned and continued down the corridor.

For the next several days, training with Dogan went as usual. The three of us got together again one night at the barracks for another meditation session. I had another vision of that woman, but I still cannot get a clear look of her. I went into the city three different times by myself, and all three times I got wacked in the back of the bloody head. It's like the man was watching my every move somehow.

I went down and visited with Dylan. I do enjoy his company; he makes me laugh a lot. He's doing great with the horses. It seems to come natural to him. Wyck told me he was a hard worker, one of the best he's had. I was happy to hear that.

Chapter 11

Urgent Message

hile still in bed, I started to stretch and stopped half-way through when I noticed how bright it was in my room. Quickly, I sat up and look to my window. Damn it, I had overslept! Dogan was going to kill me! I was supposed to meet him at dawn. It was definitely past that now. I flew out of bed and grabbed my robe. A soft knock came from my door. Moaning I dragged myself to it as I flattened the hair that loosened from it's braid. Once I got myself prepared for his wrath, I opened the door.

A man I had never seen before was standing before me, not Dogan. He was my height with very short black hair. His face was covered in whiskers like he had not shaved in days. He looked exhausted.

"Can I help you, sir?" I asked

"Are you Lady Leelah Bayard?" he inquired, sounding just as exhausted as he looked.

"Yes, I am."

"I have urgent news from Mastingham." He handed me a letter. "I have been running for three straight days to get this to you. I am sorry, my lady." He bowed and walked away.

My body started to shake. I slowly backed my way into my room and shut the door. This cannot be good. It was Pa's handwriting on the front of the letter. I went over and sat on my bed. With my heart pounding out of my chest, I gently broke the wax seal that was engraved with the letter *B*.

> *My Dearest Leelah,*
>
> *I hate to write the contents of this letter, but I have too. We have just experienced a great tragedy here at home. Yesterday, Flora went into labor, and it was too soon. She gave birth to a healthy beautiful but tiny baby girl. They named her Ella. The labor was hard on Flora, and she passed away a few hours later. Regner is a mess, Lee. He cannot handle this loss, just like I could not handle the loss of your mother. He needs you, and we need you. Please come home to us.*
>
> *Love and God speed,*
> *Pa*

No! I screamed to myself. *This cannot be!* I stared down at the letter that was now shaking in my grip. I have to get home. A cry escaped from my lips, and I covered my mouth with my hand. The sudden pounding noise at my door made me jump.

"Woman, are ye in there?" Dogan roared from the other side. "Ye are late!" He pounded on the door again, and I did not answer him. The bloody fool checked the handle and let himself in. He yelled, "What the hell are—" He stopped himself and stood there for a moment before he walked over to me. "What's wrong?" he asked with his rough deep voice.

There was no way I could look at him, afraid of the tears that might come, so I just handed him the letter. He took it and read it. After a moment, he finally asked, "How long has it been since ye ha' seen 'em?"

I tried to talk, but I could not seem to get the words out, so he reached down and laid his hand on top of my head. His fingertips tingle against my skull; he asked again, *"How long, Lee?"*

"Over three years now," I cried. It was much easier for me to talk that way. Dogan turned and left the room swiftly with my letter in hand.

I brought my legs up and hug them tight against my chest. "Regner," I cried out loud. "I am so sorry, brother!" I laid my head on my knees and let my tears flow out. After a while, I jumped again at another knock at my door. I rubbed my eyes clear and call for them to come in. Mira and the general walked in. She flew into my bed and took me into her arms.

"I am so sorry for your loss, Lee," she cried. All I could do was nod. I was unable to talk again at that moment.

"Mira's going to help you get ready. I want you to wear your knives and bring your sword. I am having a guard go with you, and your horse will be ready shortly." The general walked to me and took my face with his right hand. He had sympathy in his eyes. As he rubbed my cheek with his thumb, he said, "I am sorry, Lee. I will keep you and your family in my prayers. I am going to let the Majesties know about your departure."

"Thank you, General," I managed to say, and he gave me a small smile before leaving the room.

Mira took my face in her hands and wiped my cheeks free of tears. "All right sweetie, let's get you ready." She kissed my forehead before crawling out of my bed. I still could not move from the shock of it all. Thank God for Mira or I would never have been able to get ready at the moment. She was going through my drawers and pulled out the trousers that I wore here three years ago.

Mira held them up and said to me, "I know it's been a while since you have worn these, but after all the training you have been doing with Dogan, I think they may actually fit you again." I finally crawled out of bed and went to her.

"Do you really think I have lost enough weight to fit back into these?" I held them up in front of me. This was my normal attire back home. I did gain a little weight after I came here. It would be nice if I could; it would be miserable to wear a dress on a journey like this.

"I think so, but we will not know for sure until you try them on." She gently smiled.

After I washed up my body, I said a quick prayer before slipping into my old trousers. Sure enough, I was able to button them all the way up. I looked up and smiled softly at Mira.

Mira clapped her hands together. "I knew it. You look good, Lee." She walked to me and grabbed one of my arms. "I think you are building muscle again too." She smiled and handed me a shirt. Once I got my shirt tucked in, I slipped into my riding boots that go all the way up just below my knees. I strapped my knives to my thighs and buckled my sword around my waist. All there was left to do was my hair, so I sat at the vanity. Mira brushed my hair out and started the braid at the top of my head. She pulled and yanked, but I did not care. As long it stayed out of my face, I would be happy. Once she was done with the braid, I stood up to take a good look at myself. Mira wrapped her arm around my waist and laid her head on my shoulder. In return, I leaned my head on to hers. My eyes were swollen; my nose and cheeks were flushed. Personally, I felt and looked like hell. After we gazed at one another through the looking glass, I said, "I am mourning for a woman that I never met, Mira."

"You might not have known her, but you knew of her. Personally, I think you are mourning for your brother. It kills you inside knowing what he must be going through."

I watched as my face got distorted in the mirror and turned away from it and wrapped both arms around Mira in a hug. She held me as I cried until another knock came to my door. "Holy hell," I muttered to Mira. "I am really getting sick of hearing that door today."

"I will be right there," Mira called. She went over and grabbed a damp cloth for me. I pressed it hard against my face and took a deep breath of the lilac scent. Once I rewashed my face, I told Mira to let whoever it was in. As she went to the door, I went to my wardrobe and grabbed my cloak. It was starting to warm up nicely outside now, but it still cools down a lot at night.

As I closed my wardrobe, I heard my name. I turned to find Bryce and Rosa walking into my room. Rosa had been crying. I could tell by how flushed her face was. My tears instantly came back at the sight of her. When we embraced, Rosa started crying. "Darling, I cannot believe it. I think my heart stopped when I heard the news. I will pray for strength for you and your family during this trying time."

"Thank you." I pulled myself back to look at her then I looked up to Bryce with tear-filled eyes. "I am sorry but I have to go."

Bryce looked down at me with sympathy; he grabbed my arm and pulled me to his chest. He squeezed me tight like my pa always did, then he kissed the top of my head. "Do not be sorry my dear Lee. Family is important especially in times like these. Rosa is right, we will keep you all in our prayers. Take as much time as you need. Your job will be here waiting for you when you come back."

"Thank you, and I love you both." I squeezed myself tighter to him, and I felt Rosa hugging me from behind.

She cried, "And we love you!"

Once we broke apart, I started to wipe my eyes again. "This is going to be a long day." Mira handed me a cloth again, and I washed my face.

"I am sorry that I will not be here for the ball. You have worked so hard on that dress too." They would be making the announcement about the baby then, and it was less than a week away.

"That's no problem, Lee. You will be greatly missed, but we will have other balls for you to wear that dress to. No worries, all right?" Rosa softly smiled as she touched my cheek. I nodded and gave her a small smile. While she rubbed my shoulders, she said, "If you are ready, then we will walk out with you. Mira, you can come too."

Mira smiled and bowed. "Thank you, Your Highness."

"I need to see Kaidan before I leave. Where is he?" I asked the king.

Bryce said, "He went to make sure food was packed for your trip. Kai might be outside already."

"Well I guess…" I tied on my cloak and looked around my room. I did not need to bring anything with me since I would have all the clothes I needed at home. "I think I am as ready as I am going to be."

As I walked down the corridor, Rosa had her arm wrapped around my right arm and Mira was holding tight to my left hand.

This was my second family, and I loved them all. I would miss them, but I would be back. How long was I going to be gone for? Only time would be able to tell. The weight on my left hip from my sword felt awkward. It had been years since I had worn it, and I never did that much before that. When we made our way down the stairs, I saw Kaidan getting ready to walk out the front door. He stopped in his tracks once he saw us. He had a small sack on his back, which I assumed was filled with food.

"Bloody hell," I murmured when I felt the tears coming again.

"Do not worry, I brought the cloth with me." Mira showed it to me in her hand. I lipped the words *thank you*, and she smiled. Once I reached the bottom of the steps, Kaidan looked at me with glistening eyes before pulling me into a hug.

"My heart is aching for you and your family. Please let them know that I will be praying for them," he whispered in my ear.

"I will, thank you!" I pulled back so I could see him through my blurry vision. "I will miss you, Kai. Make sure you take care of our friends." I looked back at all three of them and smiled.

"I will. No worries about that." Kaidan smiled. "Here is some food Varon made up for you two."

Taking the sack, I put it securely over my shoulder. "Who's coming with me anyway? The general never said."

He gave me his usual *up to no good* smile, "Well, he's outside, come and see."

By the look on his face, I had a feeling that I was not going to like what I was about to see. I wiped my face again then I followed Kaidan out the door. Just as I expected, I did not like the sight in front of me. Sitting on a dark cinnamon Hybrid beside mine was Dogan. He was no longer wearing his guard uniform that I was so used to seeing him in. His outfit was similar to mine, except his trousers were dark brown instead of tan like mine. I glared at him as I descended the stairs, then I turned to Kaidan, "Please tell me this is just one last joke to play on me before I leave."

Kaidan laughed. "Sorry, Lee, I would not pull a joke on you at a time like this." Then he gave me a look of sympathy.

Then I looked to the general, who was standing by Ara, "General, out of all the hundreds of guards we have in the city, you stick me with him." I jabbed my finger in Dogan's direction. "Why?"

"Because you need to continue your training," he simply stated.

I groaned at his response then I saw Sterling running through the castle gates toward us. "What about Sterling?" I pointed to him. "Dogan's been training him and Kaidan too."

"I only had him work with Kaidan so they could get an understanding of each other, and they did. With Sterling, Dogan says he took care of that already."

"What did you take care of, Dogan?" Sterling asked, looking to the man on the horse.

"I got someone to chuck sacks at ye while I'm away," Dogan said with a crooked smile.

"Who?" Sterling demanded.

Dogan laughed. "I'm not telling ye, Lieutenant."

Sterling groaned and then looked to me. He had sadness in his eyes. "I just heard the news, love." Sterling opened his arms and waited for me to go to him. The action made me laugh and cry at the same time. I went to him, and my body went tingly from head to toe in his embrace.

"I wish it was you coming with me instead of him," I cried in my head.

"I know! I am sorry for your loss and for having to deal with that arrogant bastard," he said back.

I laughed in my head. *"I will miss this, but I will be back. I am not sure how long I will be gone for."*

"I will miss you too. Please be careful on the road. If you have to travel with anyone, I would want Dogan to be the one with you. As much as he is a pain to us, he is a smart man."

"I know, I know," I moaned. *"I promise to be careful."*

We pulled back from our embrace, and he kissed my forehead. I wiped my eyes with the cloth, and I handed it back to Mira. Taking my time, I said my last good-byes to everyone. Sterling was standing beside Ara; he smiled as he weaved his hands together in front of me. I placed my foot in his hand, and he gave me a boost up. Once I got myself secure in my saddle, Sterling rounded the front of Ara and came to stand between Dogan and I.

"You have already lost a few hours of light, but if you ride the horses hard the whole time, there is a town called Hebridge. It will already be dark by the time you get there, but there is a guard barrack. I know some of the men that are stationed there, they will accommodate you. It will save you from having to sleep on the hard ground for one night at least."

"Thank you, Sterling," I reached down and ruffled his hair. He grabbed my hand and pressed his lips to my palm.

"Godspeed, Lee," he whispered then turned to Dogan. He reached his arm up, and Dogan took hold of his forearm. "Dogan, try not to kill each other while you are away." Sterling gave me a wink.

"I will try to restrain myself," he said, and I just rolled my eyes at him. Sterling walked back and stood with everyone else.

Dogan and I turned our horses toward the gates. I looked over my shoulder and yelled, "I love you all, and I am going to miss every single one of you."

They all yelled back that they loved me too. As I looked straight ahead, I wiped the tears from my eyes. Once we were through the gates, we turned to the left to head north. When the castle walls were finally behind us and we were on the open road that would lead me home, Dogan finally said, "Well, woman, can ye handle riding yer horse at full run?"

Giving him a snide smile, I said in his Salvie tongue, "Take us home, Ara." I loosened on her reins and gave her a few solid kicks as I leaned forward in the saddle. She took off in full run after the first kick. It took him a moment, but Dogan made it to run beside me. *I am on my way, Pa!* I yelled in my head.

We rode the horses hard for hours. Even as we passed through small villages, we never slowed down. When the sun was high in the sky, I took off my cloak and tucked it under my legs. It was an hour or two past noon when Dogan came to a sudden stop.

"What are you doing?" I asked him urgently. "We need to keep going!"

"I can hear a stream in the woods. The horses need water, and I dinna ken about ye but I ha' to piss." He turned his horse into the woods, and reluctantly, I followed. If I did not care so much for Ara, I probably would have ignored him and kept going. I never heard the stream until we were several feet into the woods. How did he hear that? I shook my head in amazement. Once we got to the stream, we both dismounted. Ara was breathing hard. As I patted the side of her neck, my hand got soaked with her sweat. The sweat on Dogan's horse was now just starting to turn white against her dark coat. They had been running for hours now, but they could continue to run for several more hours. I guided Ara to the water and left her to find a place to relieve myself.

After coming back, I found Dogan checking everything that was tied to his saddle. I let out a groan when I saw the wooden swords bundled together on the side. Grabbing my water sack off my saddle, I then went and bent down at the edge of the stream. As I pushed the opening into the water to refill it, there was a sudden sharp pain at the back of my head. Closing my eyes with a groan, I bit down on my bottom lip. When I turned my head to glare at him, I ended up jerking my hand up to catch the second sack just before it hit me in the face.

"Oh!" I laughed evil like. "If that had nailed me in the face...I would have so killed you for that!"

Dogan smiled. "Damn ye and yer quick reflexes!" He laughed. "If that had connected wit yer face, it would ha' made my day."

"You bastard," I yelled and chucked back both of the sacks at him. I kept my eyes on him while pushing my water sack back into the stream. After it was refilled, I hooked it back on the saddle. I handed Dogan the sack of food that was on my back. "Here, I am sure you are hungry."

Dogan untied the sack and shoved his hand inside it. He grabbed two biscuits and a chunk of cheese. He handed the sack back to me, and I threw it back over my shoulders.

"Ye should eat something," he said as he walked back to his horse.

"I do not have much of an appetite at the moment," I said as I stroked Ara's mane.

"Suit yerself," he said and then stopped to look at me. "D'ye need help getting back on yer horse?"

"No, I can manage just fine myself," I snapped, feeling a bit aggravated.

He raised his eyebrows at me before turning to his horse. His Hybrid's back was as tall as himself, but he managed to get into his saddle with ease. Dogan looked down at me, waiting to see how I was going to manage to get myself back on the horse. While laying my hand against Ara's neck, I looked back up at him, smiling.

I gave Ara the Salvie word for *down*, and she instantly went down. First, she went down on her front knees then brought down her backend. I climbed into her saddle, and then gave her the Salvie word for *up*. Ara lifted her rear end up first then pushed up with her front legs. Instantly, I burst into laughter, when I notice the dumbfounding look on Dogan's face. It was priceless.

"How in the bloody *hell* did ye train 'er to do that?" he asked as I rode past him. "Never in my life ha' I ever seen anything like that."

I said over my shoulder, "It was easy...it just took a lot of *time* and *patience*." Throwing his words back at him made me grin from ear to ear. I weaved Ara through the trees as we made our way back to the road.

"Dinna be a smart arse, woman!" he yelled. Even though he was behind me, I could tell he was smiling. It made me smile even bigger if that was possible.

"It's 'smart ass,' Dogan!" I yelled back, "a-s-s. There is no *r* in it. So if you're going to say it, then at least say it right."

"I can say it any damn way I like, so kiss my arse!" he hollered, and I laughed, shaking my head. When we made it back to the road, I waited till Dogan was beside me. Once he swallowed the last of his biscuit, he said, "Let's get going then." We both gave our horses a swift kick at the same time, and we were racing back up the road again.

Chapter 12

Hebridge

It was two hours past sundown by the time we reached the town of Hebridge. We slowed our horses down to a trot. Ara was breathing hard; she was exhausted, but she did very well today. I had not run her like this since I was a teenager. All the lanterns were lit along the road. Music and laughter streamed out of the open door of the pub as we passed. Catching the scent of food made my stomach grumble. I had not eaten all day, and it was now just starting to hit me. Hopefully, there would be food at the barracks.

"There 'tis up ahead to the left," Dogan explained. "I can see the flag."

Squinting to see through the darkness, sure enough, I could see the flag too. The blue flag with the king's coat of arms hung off the front of the porch. It was a wonderful sight to see. My body ached, and I was exhausted from the ride. When we reached the hitching posts in front of the barracks, we dismounted. Dogan groaned when he hit the ground, and he stretched. As he rounded the horses and went up to the porch, I stretched out all the knots and mimicked his groan. I never used to get sore like this after riding all day. I hooked my sack of food to the saddle for now, and the front door opened as I rounded the horses.

"Can I help you, sir?" the guard asked.

"My name is Dogan Ramstien, and I'm a part o' the royal guard —"

"The hell you are, Salvie!" The guard completely cut him off. I moaned, shaking my head as I reached the bottom of the steps. Dogan better not do anything stupid like punch the man because I would rather sleep in a bed tonight and not on the ground. The next thing I knew, Dogan grabbed hold of my arm and jerked me up to his side.

"Please explain to this arrogant fool because I'm too damn tired fer this right now," he hissed.

"My lady!" he said and bowed his head. I recognized his face, but I could not remember his name. Glaring at Dogan, I yanked my arm out of his grip, turning all my attention to the guard.

"What Dogan says is true," I heard what sounded like a sudden jerk of a chair across the wooden floor. "We are just passing through. Lieutenant Sterling Fenwick said that you would accommodate us for the night. We will leave at first light."

"Lee?" asked a familiar voice from inside. My whole body stiffened up, thinking my heart actually skipped a beat. Could it really be him or were my ears playing tricks on me? There was only one way to find out. Stepping in front of Dogan, the guard stepped back, opening the door wider for me. Once I stepped foot into the barracks, I saw him. He was standing beside a table to the left that had other men at it eating. It must have been his chair that I heard jerk across the floor. His dark reddish-brown hair was now cropped short like Dylan's. Instead of a beard, he now had a short goatee. He looked so much different since I last saw him.

Finally, he got rid of the blank expression and replaced it with his beautiful smile. As he started to walk the length of the table, I walked toward him and never took my eyes off him. Once I reached him, I noticed his blue-gray eyes were glistening as I wrapped my arms tight around his neck. As he squeezed me tight against him, pressing my face into his neck to take in his spiced scent I always loved. The tears started to roll out with the feeling of his lips against my neck.

"You found me, Lovalee!" His voice filled my head. There was a very light tingling sensation. Nothing like when I touched Dogan or Sterling. I imagine it was because he had not released his core yet.

"I found you, Rowan!" I said while feeling him smiling against my neck.

"Sterling was right…I can actually hear you," he marveled. *"What are you doing here? Are you going home?"*

Nodding, I replied my head, *"Regner's wife passed away after giving birth to their daughter Ella."*

"Flora!" he yelled in my head. I started to cry even harder when he said her name. *"I am so sorry, Lee!"* He squeezed me even tighter and tried to comfort me. After I got control of myself, I pulled myself back so I could get a good look at him. Rowan was close to six feet tall, and he gave me a small loving smile. He took both his hands and rubbed both my cheeks dry of tears. Rowan looked past me, and he froze. Turning my head to see Dogan standing in the doorway, I noticed he was giving us an intense look. That's when I noticed everyone else was staring at us too.

Looking back to Rowan, I cleared my throat. "I would like you to meet one of our new members of the guard and my *trainer"*— groaning out the word— "Dogan Ramstien."

Rowan draped his left arm around my shoulders and walked us to Dogan. He extended his right arm and said, "I am Lieutenant Rowan Lythandas. It is a pleasure to finally meet you."

Dogan fixed his eyes on me for a second before taking Rowan's forearm. "'Tis good to finally meet ye too, Lieutenant." He nodded his head.

"Please come on in and have a seat. We have plenty of food, and I will have my men tend to your horses." Rowan gave orders to two men, and out the door they went with no questions asked. Looking at Dogan, he said, "There are some things I want to talk to you about, but first…" He turned his face to me. "You, my lady, are coming with me."

With his arm still around my shoulders, he turned me around and guided me toward the hall. We bypassed the staircase and walked down the hallway. He guided me through the last door on the right.

There was a full-size bed straight ahead with a crackling fire in the hearth against the left wall. The room smelt of him. As he lit the lamp on the stand beside the bed, I asked, "You have your own room?"

He smiled. "I am head of the barracks here." Standing in front of me, he untied my cloak that I put back on once it got dark. Rowan laid it on the dresser behind him. He unbuckled my belt that was holding my sword and placed it on top of my cloak. "Please sit," he said softly. I did as he said. Bending down on his knees, he slipped both my boots off. It was then that I noticed the chain around his neck that was tucked under his shirt. Reaching for it, I pulled out the necklace. My vision started to blur with the sight of the steel heart charm dangling at the end. It was mine once. Made it myself when I was a teenager then gave it to him the night he told me that he loved me. He still wore it! There was a smile on my face as the first tear fell down my cheek.

Rowan smiled as he wiped the tear away and started to unbuckle the knives around my thighs. He sent chills throughout my body. When he took off the second knife, I traced my finger along his bare cheek and asked, "Am I dreaming, or are you really here?"

"This is not a dream," he whispered and then quickly took my face in his hands. Once his lips were on mine, I wrapped my arms and legs around him to take hold. He wrapped his one hand around my long braid as he bound me in his arms. Rowan slowed down the attack with his mouth then slowly started to kiss me along my left jawline. I closed my eyes so I could enjoy the feeling. He said breathlessly, "Good God, I love you!"

"I love you too," I managed to whisper. He stopped kissing me and pressed his forehead to mine.

"There is so much I need to tell you, but first, let me get you some food." Rowan kissed my lips again softly before standing up. "Get comfortable, I will be right back." He gave me his loving smile then turned for the door. The door never latched behind him and was open a few inches. There were men talking in the main room. I stood up and pulled back the blankets. After getting the pillows propped up against my back, I laid the blankets back over my legs. Sitting there thinking about thanking Sterling when I saw him again for guiding me to Rowan, I stopped when I heard Rowan's voice.

"I got a letter yesterday from Sterling," he said to Dogan I assume. "He told me about everything. I would like you to show me what he meant before you leave in the morning."

"I want to leave as soon as it starts to lighten up so we'll do it a half hour before that," Dogan said. "Please make sure that *woman* is up then too." I found myself curling up my lip and growling like he always made me do. He's such a bloody fool! Does he really think I am going to sleep in? The need to see my family is stronger than the need to see Rowan. I smiled to the sound of Rowan's hearty laugh.

"Sterling told me how Lee and you are the best of friends." He laughed.

"The woman is nothing but a pain in my arse," Dogan retorted.

"I am sure her feelings toward you are mutual," he replied. "Help yourself to any spare bed upstairs, and I will see you in the morning." He said his good-nights to his men, and then I could hear the clicking of his boots against the wooden floor in the hallway.

Rowan walked in with a bowl in one hand and a cloth holding two biscuits in the other. He handed me the bowl and laid the biscuits on my lap. An instant smile came when I saw and smelled the contents in the bowl. It was his famous chicken soup.

"Still cooking, I see," I said, smiling at him.

"Of course! The men like my cooking." He smiled. "I forgot to grab you something to drink. What would you like?"

"Water will be just fine," I said. He nodded and walked back out of the room. My eyes closed in pleasure when the first spoonful of his soup hit my mouth. The warmth going down my throat felt wonderful. After that, I dove right in. The biscuits were moist and tasted amazing when dipped into the soup. I was just finishing up my meal by the time Rowan returned to the room.

"Holy hell, Lee! You must have been starving." He laughed slightly.

"I was! I have not eaten anything today. I got news of my family when I woke up this morning, and I have been running ever since. Dogan tried to get me to eat something earlier today, but I was not sure if I would be able to keep it down." A small smile formed on my lips.

He gave me a look of sympathy and asked, "Do you want any more?"

"No, thank you." Rowan took the bowl from my hands. "That used to be one of my favorite meals you use to make...it still is. It was savory!"

He placed the bowl on the nightstand and took my hand as he took a seat on the edge of the bed. "Thank you," Rowan said, looking down at our joined hands. I took my right hand and lifted his head up so he could look at me. He clamped his eyes shut and turned his head away from me. Rowan stood up and walked toward the end of the bed, keeping his back to me. He brought the bottom of his hands to his eyes and said softly, "Bloody hell!"

That was why he turned away from me...he did not want me to see the tears in his eyes. I ended up dragging my legs up and buried my face into my knees. After a moment, I lifted my head to find him staring at me from the foot of the bed. Since he was still not saying anything, I did. I needed answers.

"Why, Row? Why tell me one night that we were going to get married and turn around and leave me the very next day? Did I do or say something to make you change your mind?" I asked, trying to keep my voice down so the other men did not hear me. "Damn it you broke my heart! I have been grieving for you every day since! Have you? If you loved me like you say, then why in hell did you never come for me? Explain it!" I said harshly. All of a sudden, I was furious with him. This whole thing was his fault, and I needed to know why he did what he did!

"You think I have not been grieving!" he yelled harshly but kept his voice down. "My heart"—Rowan slammed a fist against his chest—"has been aching for you every goddamn day!"

My heart was pounding in my throat. Taking a deep breath, I closed my eyes to try to calm myself down. There was this sudden urge to attack him and beat the answers out of him. Keeping my eyes closed, I pleaded, "I need answers, Rowan. Please."

Upon opening my eyes, I found him staring at me again as he raked his hands through his short hair. Rowan dropped his hands to unbuckle his belt and took off his sword. He walked around to the other side of the bed and leaned the sword against the wall. He pulled back the blankets and sat on the bed. With his back facing me as he took off his boots, it took all of me not to touch him. Rowan arranged the pillows like I did earlier against the headboard. Once he got himself situated beside me, he took hold of my right hand and squeezed it.

"I do not know where to start," he whispered as I was looking down at our hands that were weaved together.

"How about starting from the beginning?" I asked quietly.

Rowan took a deep breath. "First of all, I never left because of you. You are perfect to me in every way. I love everything about you. I have never met a more spirited woman than yourself, and to top it all off, you are beautiful. I felt like the luckiest man in the world to have found myself a woman like you."

Still looking down at our intertwined hands, I laid my other hand on top of them and asked, "Then why the sudden departure?"

Rowan took in another deep breath and laid his other hand on top of mine. "I left you that night with full intentions of giving the general my resignation in the morning. Lee, I was so happy! I was planning on leaving the next day for Mastingham just so I can get your father's permission to marry you." He paused and took another breath. "That night I had a dream, but it was not like any other dream I had."

I sat there in silence waiting for him to continue, wondering if it was the dream that made him leave. God, please do not tell me he left me because of a bloody dream! Finally, when he still had not said anything else, I asked, "What was the dream, Row?"

"A woman came to me that night. She had long dark wavy hair like yours and the greenest eyes that I have ever seen. She was tall, beautiful, and I knew her face from somewhere, but I could not remember where. The woman said that I was about to go down the wrong path and that I needed to end it now before I ruined both of our destinies. She told me that we were both fated to other people and the whole world depended on it. I was so angry with her! I screamed and cursed at her for saying such things to me. Somehow, the woman calmed me down. All she did was lightly touch my cheek with her hand, and the feeling of love radiated from her. She was glowing white, and it was then that I realized that she was an angel. In my dream, I lost all strength in my legs and fell to my knees in front of her. These are her exact words..." He paused for a moment. "I know the love the two of you share for one another. You will always have that but for the time being, you have to leave. Leelah has to stay where she's at. She is destined to do great things for this kingdom just as you are. I want you to speak with your general in the morning. Tell him you want the position that is open in Hebridge. You cannot tell her where you are going and make sure the general knows that. She will grieve, but I promise you that I will guide her back to you when I know that she can handle the truth. Then you two can be back in each other's lives, but never as husband and wife. Once you leave, I will come to you again and tell you more."

As the tears rolled out, Rowan let go of my hands and wrapped his arm around my shoulders. Burying my face into his chest and taking hold of his shirt, the tears flowed out. He kissed the top of my head as he rubbed my back.

He continued, "As I sat there on my knees crying, she came to me and kissed me on top of my head. The next thing, I was awake in my own bed. My cheeks were wet with tears. When it registered what I just dreamt, I started to cry again when I realized that it was not a dream at all. She was an angel with a message for me, and as much as it killed my heart, I had to do what she told me to do. I got dressed and went straight to the general. He was shocked when I asked him about Hebridge. No one knew about that position being recently opened, and he wanted to know how I knew about it. I told him about my dream and told him that no one is to know where I am going. Not even Sterling. If I told him, eventually he would tell you where because he's also your best friend. Lee, that was the hardest day in my life. It killed me leaving you broken like that, but you have to understand now why I did."

With my head on his shoulder now, I asked quietly, "Who is she? Did you ever find out, and did she ever come back to you like she said?"

"Oh, she comes to me often," he said, and I looked to him to find him smiling. "After the first month being here, I could not take it anymore, so I took a few days off and headed north for Mastingham. It was the only place I could think of going, where I would feel close to you without see you. That would be the first of many trips."

I cut him off right there. "Are you saying that you have visited with my family more than the time just recently?" He gave me a questioning look, and I continued, "A little over a month ago, Pa wrote about you being there and that you still cared for me."

Rowan started to laugh and leaned his head back. "Damn you, Randall!" He looked back to me. "I have visited with your family at least once every month or so. I told them to never let you know of my visits." He laughed softly and shook his head. "I always wondered if he would eventually tell you. You have a wonderful family, and it breaks my heart about Flora. God, Lee, you would have loved her."

"It kills me that I never got to." Laying my head back down on his shoulder, I thought of them all and then of Rowan being with them all. "I cannot believe you went to see them."

"After I left you, it was the only place I could go. That first evening upon showing up at the house, your father was shocked to see me. They all remembered who I was and had me join them all for dinner. While walking into the living room, I stopped in my tracks when the sight of my angel came into view. She was in one of the two portraits hanging over the fireplace. She looked a little different since that she was pregnant with you in the portrait...it was your mother, Arabella."

Sitting straight up, my whole body became covered in goose pimples. "I beg your pardon?" That was the last thing I had ever expected him to say.

"It had been years since I had been there, but that was why she looked familiar to me. Randall asked me what was wrong when he noticed my reaction to the portrait, and I ended up telling him everything."

"Pa knows?"

"Yes, and maybe Arabella told him to write about me in his last letter." He smiled. "So you would not try to kill me when you did see me for the first time," Rowan teased.

I lightly hit him in the chest and gave him a small smile. "Do not jest!"

"I am just saying." He laughed a little. "If you never got word from your father or Sterling about my true feelings for you and you saw me not knowing this...you would have attacked me. Just admit it!"

Burying my face into his shoulder to hide my smile, "Oh probably," I mumbled. Enjoying the feeling of him bouncing in light laughter and with his arms around me, I thought about what he said earlier about us being destined to other people. I looked to him and asked, "Can we just ignore our fates and just be together?"

His broad smile softened as he lightly touched my cheek. "We could, but the world would be affected by our actions. We would be happy and have children. Your mother has showed me this. Years from now, a great evil will try to take over the world. Everything around us will be in chaos and death, all because we chose to be with each other instead of thinking of the greater good of our people. You have to stay by the queen's side. You have to find your soul mate, and the two of you will have a daughter, and she will do great things someday."

Unable to tear my eyes from him, I asked, "I am to have a daughter?" It was hard to picture me as a mother.

"Yes, love," he said with a smile. "You see...you and I are part of a group that will help fight this great evil someday. We will always be in each other's lives. I promise that. And we will always have hold of each other's hearts, but eventually, someone will come around and take hold of the bigger half."

"I cannot imagine loving anyone but you, and what is this evil you keep talking about?"

"I am not sure what kind of evil it is, but it's not to happen for another twenty or twenty-five years. Some things still need to come into play, I guess. As much as it is hard to picture yourself with someone else, it's going to happen whether you like it or not. But for the meantime, there is no law saying we cannot do this." He lifted my chin up and brought his lips to mine. After a moment, he pulled back and whispered, "Even after we find our soul mates, I will still kiss you like this."

That made me laugh. "Really? I cannot imagine our mates allowing that," I said as we exchanged smiles.

"Oh, they will. Trust me! Both our mates will know of our history together way before either of us is with them. They will accept it as long as it is only kisses and nothing more." His smile widens.

Shaking my head, I said, "You are bad, Rowan!" Then I asked him, "Do you know who they are?"

"I do not know of mine yet. All I do know is that I will not find her for another twenty years or so. You, on the other hand, are going to find him a hell of a lot sooner. I have seen you with a man, and you were very happy."

"Who is he?" The thought of being with any other man beside him was making me anxious.

"I am not sure because I was paying all my attention to you. The mere sight of you took my breath away, but I did notice that he had a tattoo." Rowan ran his fingertips along my jaw and down my neck.

"A tattoo?" I asked. "Rowan, do you know how many men have tattoos? Almost every man I know has one, including you."

"Sorry, Lovalee. That's all I got for you now." He brushed a stray hair away from my face. Closing my eyes to really feel his touch on my skin, the light tingles felt great.

With my eyes still closed, I asked, "You have to wait twenty years?"

"Yes, but it's all right though. It gives me more time to torture your mate when he finds you." I opened my eyes when there was the feeling of him bouncing in laughter again. I realized then how much he and Sterling were alike. There was no way of stopping my smile.

"Will you stay with me tonight?" I had never lain in another man's arms before, and I wanted him to be my first. It was forbidden for me to stay behind closed doors with him because we were not married. Since my father was not around to catch me, I really did not give a damn what the other guards thought of me at the present moment.

"I thought you would never ask. Just so you know…we can never make love. Once we do, you will get pregnant, and our destinies will be over with. Do you understand?" he said with all seriousness.

"All I want is for you to hold me tonight, that's all."

"I can do that." He leaned over me to turn out the lamp on the stand. Instantly, I closed my eyes to savor his spiced scent as he lay against me. Once he sat back where he was, I watch him slip his shirt over his head. He looked gorgeous in the light glow of the fire in his room. When he was situated with blankets and pillows, he opened his arms and said, "Come to me, Lovalee."

Lying on my side against him, I wrapped my left arm and leg around him. We gave each other endless kisses before I finally lay my head on his chest and falling into a deep sleep.

The next morning, I woke up with him kissing me again. It was still dark outside, but I could hear the eager chirps of birds waiting for the day to start.

"Good morning, beautiful," he murmured and kissed me again.

"Good morning, handsome," I whispered and laughed when he rolled over and was now on top of me. I wrapped my arms around him and allowed him to attack my jawline and neck with his mouth. The man was sending jolts throughout my whole body; never removing his lips from my skin, he said, "God I have missed you so much." Finally, he lifted his head and looked down at me, "I promise to never leave you again. It will torture me knowing that I can never make love to you, but I can at least see you and touch you." He traced a finger down my neck and kept going down until the fabric of my shirt stopped him, which was just above my breasts, "I will be happy with that." The man was sending all sorts of new feelings throughout my body.

"I love you," was all I could say, and he pressed his lips to mine once again. Taking hold of his face, I made him go deeper with the kiss before he pulled away.

"I better go out and see if Dogan is up yet. He is supposed to show me how to release my core. Speaking of that, do you know how damn bright you are?" he asked me.

I laughed. "You can see it?"

"Yes, I saw it when you first walked in last night. It truly adds to your beauty." He smiled and gave me another quick kiss before rolling off me. Rowan relit the lamp as I swung my legs over the edge of the bed. The man was beautiful. He was lean but nicely built. Rowan had a black band tattoo in a knot design that wrapped around his arm just above his left elbow. While he's standing in front of me, I took both of my hands and brought them up to his bare stomach. Raking my hands through his light-auburn chest hair, I stood up and felt the chills pass through his body as I worked my hands up.

Once my arms were around his neck, I said while combing my fingers through his hair, "I have always loved your hair long, but I think I love it this way too."

"You on the other hand have not cut your hair." He took hold of my braid, yanking my head back to see the angle of my face, "I think I love it this way too." He smiled devilishly and kissed me again. "All right, I need to go and see if he's up."

I rolled my eyes. "Believe me Rowan the man is up. He is never late for a damn thing," I ranted. "Besides, he's going to want me to do it with you too."

Rowan laughed. "Sterling told me all about the relationship you and Dogan have and how you kicked him in the balls." He started to laugh even harder. "That man is a monster…what the hell were you thinking? He could have killed you."

I raised my eyebrows and started to laugh. Of course Sterling would tell him about that. "I was not thinking. I was too angry to think. I will not do that again I will tell you that."

He gave me the same devilish smile and rubbed the end of his nose against mine. "He also wrote about the kisses you two shared earlier this week."

I could feel the heat rise up into my cheeks. I buried my face into his neck and began giggling. "Of course he would tell you about that too. It was nothing sexual, I promise. The feeling is amazing, and once you release your core, you will see what we mean."

"Oh, I know it was nothing sexual, darling. I just wanted to pick on you." He yanked on my braid again, making me look up at him, and he kissed my forehead. As he went over to put on a clean shirt, I started putting on my weapons.

After my knives and sword were secure, I grabbed my cloak and walked out to find Rowan and Dogan. As I walked into the dark hallway, there was light streaming out from a room two doors up. I could hear muffled voices before I walked in. Standing in front of a desk was Dogan and Rowan. Rowan looked so petite beside him. Even though I knew Dogan quite a bit better now, the man could still send chills through me at the mere sight of him.

"Well, let's get this over wit so we can eat and start ridin'. I wanna get a lot o' distance traveled today," Dogan announced.

I walked over to them and responded, "You and me both!"

Dogan closed the door, and the three of us sat on the floor with our knees touching each other. We took hold of one another's hands, and Dogan explained how to relax as we closed our eyes. Dogan did not go through the full meditation process because we did not have the time but did the breathing exercises. After a few minutes Dogan's voice filled my head.

"In a moment I'm going to pull out yer core. Ye'll feel great pressure like someone is pushing hard against yer chest." Dogan squeezed my hand, and in return, I squeezed Rowan's. He continued, *"Are ye ready?"*

"Yes," the two of us said in unison.

Instantly, I felt it get pulled out of my body with less pressure than the first time. The room was instantly in a deep red. I looked toward Rowan. Even though his eyes were closed, I knew he was looking toward me also.

His laugh filled my head. *"I can actually see and I can feel your touch now. This does not seem possible."* He continued laughing. *"Can I just kiss you now so I can feel what it feels like?"*

Dogan groaned, *"What the hell is it wit ye and Sterling? This woman is not that special."*

"I beg to differ! Besides, she is the same as you and me. You will someday open your eyes to her true beauty. Have you ever kissed a woman with the same powers before?" Rowan asked.

"Nay. She's the first woman I ha' met wit the same abilities."

"I heard it's rather amazing, and I am doing it as soon as we are done here." Rowan smirked.

Dogan growled, and I laughed. I could not wait to feel it myself. We stayed in the light for several minutes. The whole time, Dogan explained everything to him. Sterling had already told him a lot and told him that it can take a long time for him to learn how to access it by himself. He promised him that we will do this again when we come back through. That made me happy to hear him say that.

"All right I'm going to return the energy now. It'll hurt as it slams back in so hold on tight," Dogan explained. We grabbed hold tight, and I swayed back a little as it hit me in the chest. The brunt force still sprang my eyes open, but it took my breath away a little less this time. Rowan's eyes were wide in panic as he fought to breathe.

"Relax, Lieutenant. Yer breath'll be back in a second," Dogan said then looked at me. "I'm going to get the horses ready. Then we'll ha' a quick bite to eat before we hit the road."

I nodded my head to him as he got up. Once the door shut behind me, I scooted myself in front of Rowan. He was finally breathing normal again.

"Dogan did not even seem fazed, please tell me it will get better and not take my breath away every time."

Laughing, I said, "I promise. I have only done it a few times now, and it already hurts less. Dogan has been doing it his whole life…he feels no pain with it."

Rowan smiled as he started to rub my hand that he was still holding. His touch seemed stronger then Dogan's and Sterling's. I am not sure why; maybe it was the love we shared for each other.

"Come to me," he ordered in my head, and I did. While crawling into his lap, I wrapped my legs and arms around him.

"Oh my God," he laughed. "I can feel every inch of your body on me. This only makes me want you even more."

I smiled and took his mouth with mine. He moaned instantly to the sensation and power of the kiss. He pulled back quickly, "Bloody hell!" With his one arm across my back, he took his other hand to my bottom and pulled me tighter to his chest. "This is only going to torture me more, but to hell with it," he whispered and took my mouth again. After a while, I pulled my mouth away from him; he moaned in protest.

Smiling, I said breathlessly, "Sorry, love, but I have to go."

"I know," he groaned. To my surprise, he managed to stand up with me still wrapped around him. He placed me back on my feet and said, "Let's go and get some breakfast because if I stay behind this closed door with you any longer, I might not be able to control myself."

Dogan and I ate with Rowan and some of the guards that were already up. Once we were done, the three of us walked outside. The sun was still not fully up yet, but it was light enough to start riding again. As we walked down the steps, Rowan went straight to Ara.

"Hello, Ara girl!" Before Rowan could even pet her, she walked forward and pressed her forehead to his chest, causing him to laugh. "I have missed you too!" He rubbed his hands up and down her head and ears. Besides me, Rowan was the only other person she's ever pressed her head to like that. He gave her the Salvie word for down, and she listened. I climbed on the saddle and looked back toward Rowan.

"The hell with it," he snapped and took my face with his hands and kissed me yet again. When he tore his lips away, he pressed his forehead to mine.

"If some of my men are watching through the window, they already assume we had sex last night, so what does it matter if they see us kiss, right?" he asked.

"Right! I do not care about what they think!" I answered him privately.

"Good! I would make a trip up there to see you and your family, but I feel its best that I do not at this time. We will see each other when you pass through again. Please send them all my condolences. I love you and be careful on the road."

"I will, and I love you too!"

Rowan gave me another quick kiss before commanding Ara to stand. I watched him go to Dogan and reach up to take hold of his arm. They stayed like that for a moment, staring at each other. While wondering what they were saying to each other, they let go, and Dogan turned his horse to the road, and I followed suit beside him.

"I will see you again soon…I promise," Rowan shouted from behind me.

I looked back smiling and yelled, "I know!" His smile widened, and we waved to each other. Looking straight ahead again, I asked

Dogan without looking to him, "What did Rowan say to you back there?"

"That's none o' yer business, woman!" he thundered.

I rolled my eyes and replied, "Of course it's not!" Giving Ara a few swift kicks, we were off running at full speed again.

We rode hard all day, only stopping once to eat lunch and to let the horses rest for a moment. Later that evening, while lying on the hard ground, I stared into the fire thinking about Rowan. The small fire we built about an hour before sundown was cracking and spitting up sparks into the black sky. The sound and warmth was soothing. You could almost go into a trance if you stared at it for too long. Dogan was directly on the other side of the flames. He was lying down too, so I was not sure if he was still awake or not. If the warmth was not so comforting, I would sit up to see if he was.

There was this need of telling someone what Rowan told me last night. I was still trying to accept it all. With my head lying on my bent arm and tucking my cloak tighter around me, I finally said his name softly, "Dogan?"

"Hmm?" he sounded tired.

"Do you believe angels can come to us through dreams?" I did not know how he was going to respond to this. I was most likely going to get some kind of snide comment. The feeling of supidity ran threw me all of a sudden. What was I thinking to even consider talking about this with him?

"I do…why?" responded Dogan, and my mouth dropped. He actually answered my question and wanted to know why and with no sarcasm too. Dogan was probably going to regret saying why, but I did not care. There were things I needed to get off my chest, and he was the only one here to listen.

I explained everything that Rowan told me last night…well, not everything. Just about his dreams, my mother, and the great evil that was going to try to take over the world. He never interrupted, and I ended up telling him about my mother.

"You see, my mother died just a few hours after I was born. The same way Flora passed away. I used to dream of her once in a while when I was a child. It has been over fifteen years since I saw her. Why would she go to Rowan and never come to me?" I asked him. While lying there hoping that he would answer me, I listened to the distant stream behind me. A smile came to my face when he finally spoke.

"She went to Rowan first because she knew how stubborn ye are and that ye probably wouldna ha' listen to 'er back then. I'll not be surprised if she comes to ye soon. Just be patient." I could hear him taking a deep breath like he had more to say, so I kept my mouth shut. "Like Rowan, I ha' also been blessed wit regular visits by an angel. She too has showed me visions o' this great evil, and like ye I'm also destined to be wit someone. The woman I'm destined to supposedly has a little girl. That's one o' my reasons fer coming to Burreck City. They need me, and they're somewhere in the city. I know what the child looks like, and I ha' been looking fer 'er since the first day I arrived here. Once I do find 'er, then it'll not be long till 'er mother finds me."

My body was full of goose pimples. As a chill ran through my body, I said, "And here you are, lying in the woods days away from the city. I am sorry for that because I do not know how long I am going to have to stay with my family for."

"Dinna worry about it, lass. God already has my life mapped out. He'll guide me to the bairn when the time's right. It can be a few days from now or maybe months or even years. I believe it's going to be more months than years though. Ye truly never know where yer life'll lead ye. Only God knows that!"

"I do not want to be with anyone else, Dogan. Why cannot God understand that?" I curled my legs up to my chest while I waited for him to answer.

After a moment, he asked, "Did ye name yer horse after yer mother?"

Rolling my eyes, of course he would avoid answering that question. It was all right though. "Yes...I was a teenager then, and I thought Ara was the perfect name for her." I always loved my mother's name, *Arabella*. Naming Ara after her made me feel close to her in some ways back then.

Dogan started laughing! Picking up a small stone by the firepit, I chucked it through the flames. He grunted when it connected with him. While still laughing, he growled, "Ye know I'll get ye back later fer that."

"I do not care. Besides, you should have sensed it coming," I said sarcastically.

"I'm too exhausted to ha' sensed it. Speaking o' that, let's try to get some sleep, aye?" he said, sounding tired again.

"Thank you, Dogan, for talking with me. I actually feel a little bit better…good night." I smiled a little when there was no response from him. With that, I closed my eyes and let the exhaustion from the day put me into another dreamless sleep.

There were sounds of birds in branches high above me when I started to wake. Stretching, with my eyes still closed, I stopped when I felt and heard something breathing above me. Slowly opening my eyes, a smile came with the sight of Ara's huge white nose. With it only a few inches from my face, I reached up and rubbed the end of it.

In the Salvie tongue, I said, "Good morning!" She let out a breath of air, which in turn made me laugh. I turned my head when a groan came from Dogan.

"What in the bloody hell are ye all cheery about?" With the fire only glowing embers, I was able to see him pop himself up onto his elbows. He glared over at us then started shaking his head. "That horse is not normal." Slowly, he pushed himself to his feet as he continued. "The sun will be up soon. We should start getting ready."

After I had all my things tied back on the saddle, a few loose hairs fell forward into my face. Running my fingers through my hair, I realized how loose my braid was. Once the band was pulled out at the bottom, I combed out the braid with my fingers. Dipping my head down, I pulled all my hair up to the top of my head. I straightened up and tied the band around my hair. Even with my hair up high in a tail, the ends still brushed the bottom of my shoulder blades. When I turned around to ask Dogan if he was ready, there he stood by his horse, staring at me with a blank expression.

Cocking up one eyebrow, I asked, "Dogan…are you ready?"

He literally shook his head, and Dogan's eyes became intense once again, "Aye, I'm ready!" He continued as he mounted his horse, "If we're lucky, we might make it to Mastingham way before suppertime."

Chapter 13

Homecoming

The sun was high in the sky when we started running up a steep hill. Ara was blowing out her air hard, and I decided to say something to Dogan once we reached the top about taking a break for a moment. Hopefully, we could find a stream nearby. As we crested the hill, the both of us pulled back on the reins at the sight below. It was Mastingham…I had not realized how fast we must have been running. Past the city below, I had a clear view of the port and all the ships docked there. They ranged in all sizes. To the right of the city in the valley below was my family's farm. There were hundreds of acres of pasture with hundreds of Hybrids out grazing. There was a small house by the woods line; I assumed that was the house Regner built for his wife. A gust of wind came ruffling Ara's mane and brought with it the scent of the ocean below. My tranquility ended when Dogan spoke. "We made good time. Our horses are faster than we thought."

Smiling back at him, I said, "I cannot believe we finally made it." Looking back at the view, I added, "It's such a beautiful sight."

"How far is your family's home from here?" he asked.

With the sight of my farm below, I said, "It's not far, but there is somewhere I need to stop in the city first." Giving Ara a light kick to get her moving, we both made our slow decent into the city.

Mastingham had not changed much in the last three years. There were a few new buildings as we entered the city. Other than that, it still looked and felt the same. It felt terrific to finally be home. Only wished it was for happier reasons instead of the true reason I was there. Once we reached my pa's shop, I dismounted.

"The blacksmith's?" Dogan asked. "Why are we here?"

"You wanted to know who made my sword, did you not?" I asked while tying Ara to the hitching post.

Dogan dismounted and tied his horse next to mine. "I do, but not now. Ye should be seeing yer family and not worrying about me meeting this man."

Rolling my eyes, I said over my shoulder while walking toward the open door, "Believe me, Dogan, coming here has nothing to do with you."

The strong and intense heat was pouring out the door. There was a lump already forming in my throat as I walked in. I stopped instantly with the sight of Wade. His dark shoulder-length hair was pulled back out of his face. Wade's face had streaks of black soot, like he was trying to wipe the sweat away. In his leather apron, he had his sleeves rolled up while he was working on the grinder. The lean, toned muscles in his arm twitched as he moved the blade. I wanted to run to him, but I was afraid of interrupting him while he was working out the edge and point of a sword. Finally, he quickly glanced up at me; Wade stepped away from the grinder and placed the sword on the table. He stopped in his tracks when he really looked at me, and his whole face lit up. The feeling of joy washed over me with the sight of my brother.

"Pa," he yelled over his shoulder, "our girl is home!" I ran to him then. We slammed hard into each other, causing us to laugh as we wrapped our arms around one another. Out of all my brothers, Wade was the one I would get into the worst fights with. We were always rough with each other. It seemed like we still were even after all these years apart.

"Thank God you are here, sis." He squeezed me tighter. "I never realized how much I have missed you till now."

"Me neither," I cried. "Sorry for being gone for so long!" The scents of the shop surrounded me, scents I was raised with and longed to smell again.

I had my eyes tightly closed, so I never noticed Pa until he had his arms wrapped around Wade and me. Pa pressed his lips to the side of my face and said, "I cannot believe you are here already, darling! I expected another day or two at least."

I turned my face to look at him. He had a lot more gray running though his dark short hair and beard now. Pa's hazel eyes were glistening as he smiled at me. The vision of him started to blur. "Ara and I needed to get home as soon as possible, and she did wonderfully," I said. "Oh, Pa, I have missed you all so much." My brother and father both squeezed their arms tighter around me.

Pulling my head back, I looked to Wade, "How is our brother?"

Wade started shaking his head back and forth, not saying anything at first. His face got distorted, then he started to cry hard. He pressed his forehead to mine as he tried to get control of himself. There had only been a few occasions when I had seen any of my brothers cry. This was rare for me to see this emotion coming from him, and I did not know how to handle it. All I could do was cry in response.

"He's not good, sis. Our brother is a mess! Regner has always been the strongest one out of all five of us. We all look up to him. He needs us now, and you most of all." He paused. "Oh God, sis! I wish you got to meet her. She was beautiful inside and out. You would have loved her…we all did!" Wade laid his head on my right shoulder as he started to cry again.

While laying my head on Wade's shoulder, I looked to Pa to my left. "I am so sorry I never got to meet her, Pa! It's something I will always regret."

"Shh, it's all right, baby girl." Pa rubbed his hands up and down mine and Wade's backs. "We are all happy that you are home now. Do you know how long you can stay?"

"For as long as I need to," I whispered and squeezed Wade tighter.

"Good!" Pa and Wade said in unison, causing us all to laugh a little. Breaking myself away from Wade, I wrapped my arms around Pa to give him a strong hug. He lifted me off my feet as he squeezed, making me laugh. God, I have missed these hugs. Once he placed me back on my feet, he grabbed my hair that was still in a tail and draped it over my shoulder, "Your hair has grown a foot at least since we saw you. Have you cut it at all?"

I laughed. "Of course I have cut it. If I had not, it would be down pass my ass!"

"Sorry, sir! We did not see you there. Can I help you?" Wade asked, and I looked behind me to see Dogan standing in the doorway. His expression was unreadable, and he just stood there, staring at us. I completely forgot about him.

"I was not allowed to travel alone, and the general wanted me to continue training while I am here." I waved Dogan to come over to us. "So I would like you to meet Dogan Ramstien." Looking up to Dogan when he came to stand beside me, I said to him, "This is my pa, Randall, and one of my four brothers, Wade Bayard."

Dogan shook both their hands and said while bowing his head, "I'm sorry to hear about yer loss."

Wade started to laugh instantly. "You must be the Salvie Lee bitched about in her last letter."

Oh my God! He did not just say that! Dogan did not need to know about that. Even though I had been gone for over three years, it looked like Wade and my relationship was just continuing where it left off, with the two of us saying or doing something just to piss each other off. Taking the flat of my hand, I smacked him in the center of his chest. Wade groaned and then quickly got me in a headlock.

"Holy hell, Wade! Are you serious?" I yelled. "I am home for a few minutes, and you have to start this with me."

Wade laughed a little. "What do mean that I started it? You were the one that hit me in the chest first. By the way, that actually hurt…you have gotten stronger."

"I only hit you because of your big mouth," I said while struggling in his grip.

"Please do not mind these two, Dogan. Lee fights the worst with Wade out of all her brothers. I think it's because they are the most alike. I cannot believe it, but it actually does my heart good to see this right now. Brings back good memories," Pa lightly laughed.

Taking my right elbow, I jammed it as hard as I could into Wade's gut. He grunted and released me instantly. He stumbled back a few steps as he rubbed his belly. Wade had a huge smile on his face. "Damn, Dogan! I have to say whatever you are doing to my sister, keep it up. I have had some nasty fights with her in the past, but she's never inflicted pain on me like she has just done. Twice at that!" Wade looked to me still smiling. "It's great to have you home. I do love you, sis!"

"I know. I love you too," I replied as he wrapped his arms around my shoulders and kissed my forehead.

Pa shook his head at us and then looked up at Dogan. "Wade and Irving have been sleeping over in Regner's house while Regner and Ella have been with us. So we have the spare rooms upstairs for you, Dogan. You can choose either one," Pa said to him.

"Thank ye, sir, but I'm gonna stay at the barracks here in the city," he stated to Pa.

"I insist that you stay with us. Besides, we could use the extra help on the farm, and please call me, Randall."

"As ye wish, Randall. Thank ye!" Dogan paused for a moment. "I ha' to say that I really admired the craftsmanship o' Lee's sword. How much would it cost to ha' two swords made like that fer myself?"

Pa smiled at me, and I returned his smile. While wrapping his arm around my shoulders, he said to him, "Well, Dogan, if you liked Lee's sword so much, then it's my daughter you have to talk to since she's the one who made it." My smile widened as his eyes widened as he looked toward me. The bloody fool thought it was a man that made the sword.

"Woman, I canna believe ye never told me," he said, like he was actually shocked that I kept that from him.

"Please, Dogan, do you really think I would have told you?" I snapped. "You would have not believed me anyway, you bloody fool!"

Wade and Pa started to laugh. "It is great to have her home, do you agree, Pa?" Wade asked while he patted our father on the back.

"I most certainly agree. You should head home. I wish I could be there to see their faces with the sight of you, but we will be home by suppertime." Pa blessed me with the gorgeous Bayard smile.

"All right, Pa." I gave him a hug and a kiss good-bye. Wade followed Dogan and me out the door. He went straight to Ara.

"Hello, Ara girl. Thank you for bringing sis home safely." He laughed as Ara started to nibble on his shoulder. Wade came to the side and gave me a boost into my saddle. Once in the saddle, I watched Wade round the back of Dogan's horse. Dogan gave me an odd look then swiveled in his saddle to look back at Wade. I knew what he was looking for. All the horses that are born on our farm get branded with the letter *B* in the inside back right leg. I noticed it on her the first day we left Burreck City.

"What in God's name are ye doing? Dinna ye ken that's a good way to get yerself kicked?" Dogan asked.

Wade laughed at him. "This horse is not going to kick me. Besides, I was right, she is one of our horses. I think she can be one of Shasta's babies. What do you think, sis?"

"Now that you mentioned it, I can see what you mean. She does look a lot like her." Her beautiful cinnamon coat shined in the sun.

"What the hell's this about…our horses?" Dogan asked sounding frustrated.

"My sister does not tell you a damn thing, does she, Dogan?" Wade asked as he was now standing between us and was looking up at him.

"Apparently not," he growled.

"Oh, that's right!" Wade grinned devilishly at me and said, "Your exact words were 'I do not trust him, and that we hate each other.'" His smile widened as I glared down at him. He just could not keep his bloody mouth shut, could he?

"Dogan, you can throw one of those sacks at him anytime now!" A laugh burst out of me a second later when Wade cursed and rubbed the back of his head.

"What did you do that for?" he narrowed his eyes at Dogan.

"Because yer sister wanted me too," Dogan said with an expressionless face.

Wade picked up the sack and moved it around in his hand. "Does he actually throw these at you?" He chucked the sack back at me, and I caught it.

"All the bloody time! I think the back of my head is constantly bruised." I instinctly rubbed the back on my head, which was tender. The bastard hit me last night when I was rolling out my bedroll, and again this morning.

"Holy hell, better you than me." He smiled and said his good-byes before walking back into the shop.

Ara knew exactly where to go. She turned right and walked down the narrow alley between our shop and the frobisher next door. Once we got behind the shop, I stopped Ara to look down at my family's farm up ahead. It was a magnificent sight. The barn itself was bigger than our house. It was able to hold a little over one hundred horses. I was assuming there were probably around 250 horses at least on the farm now. Ara started to twitch, and her ears stood straight up. Her whole body was shaking underneath me with the need to run home. As badly as she wanted to take off, she would not. She would wait anxiously for my command. Dogan stopped beside me.

"Thank you." I tossed back his sack of sand to him. "That was bloody funny!"

Dogan gave me a small half smile, like he was trying hard not to smile himself. "If his mouth is always running like that, then it'll not be the last."

Laughing again, I said, "Then be prepared to be throwing them a lot every day." That will be a sight to see. Wade sitting at the table, running his mouth, and then getting wacked in the side of the head. The vision had me smiling.

"So where to, woman?" he asked me. "I take it yer family has a farm?"

I shot him the biggest smile I could muster and pointed out the farm in the valley. Dogan stared out to the valley for a moment, then his jaw actually dropped.

"That's yer family's farm?" Dogan pointed out to the valley. "Who the hell are ye, woman? If I didna just meet yer father, I'd ha' thought he was a lord by the size o' that estate." He almost sounded…amazed.

"Well, I am Lady Leelah Bayard. The daughter of blacksmith Randall Bayard, who is also the proud owner of the largest Hybrid horse farm in the country! And, actually, the majority of the people in this city who know my family refer to my pa as Lord Randall Bayard. I guess he earned the title for how big the family estate is and for the money that follows him name."

Dogan shook his head and looked down. "Unbelievable," he mumbled.

With a smile still on my face, I gave Ara a kick and said, "Take us home, Ara." We flew down the hill into the valley. As we ran along the wooden fenceline, I spotted someone walking out of the barn. With the sight of the long straight brunette hair, I knew instantly that it was Rythe. He stopped in his tracks when he noticed me. Ry yelled to the barn and took off toward the house. I kicked Ara a few more times to get her to go faster even though I knew she was going the fastest she could because she had the need to be home too. Once we cleared the fence line, I veered her toward the house. As Ry came bursting out of the house, I yanked back on the reins, bringing Ara to a sliding stop. Jumping off her while she was still moving, I sprinted toward my brother. Ry had a huge smile on his face, and I screamed as I jumped into his arms. He laughed as he spun me around in the air.

"Ah, my baby sis has finally come home," he cheered as he placed me back on my feet.

"Oh God, Ry, I have missed you so much."

He took my face in his hands and gave me a quick peck on the lips and smiled. "You have no idea how much your presence has been missed here."

"Sis," Irving yelled from behind me. I turn around as he slammed into me, sandwiching me between Ry and him. "Thank God you are here!"

We both kissed each other on the cheek as we squeezed each other harder. I pulled back from him and smiled at the sight of him. His brunette hair was cropped short, and he had a thin beard. While taking hold of the short hairs on his chin I said, "I see you are finally starting to grow some facial hair."

Irving was the one closest to my age. Before I left, our brothers were always giving him a hard time about not being able to grow any facial hair. He gave me the beautiful Bayard smile. Behind me, Ry rested his chin on my shoulder and said, "It's still real thin, but it's getting there." Ry swung his arm around and lightly punched Irving in the arm.

"I like it, Irving. It looks good on you." I grinned proudly at him.

"Thanks, sis," Irving murmured and looked down in embarrassment. Out of all of us, Irving was the most soft-spoken and shyest. He always caught hell from our brothers for that too. When we were younger, I always stood up for him, and I still would.

"Lee!" Estelle screeched. I turned back to the house to see her holding up her dress as she ran down the steps. Estelle had her sandy hair down, which was rare. She usually had it pulled back in a bun and away from her face. She was crying as I met her halfway. "My baby girl has finally made it home," she cried out. "I cannot believe you are here so soon. Did you see your father?"

"Yes," I said and she started to run kisses all over my face, causing me to laugh. "I have missed you too."

She stopped, and we stared at each other for a moment. Estelle's flushed cheeks were soaked, and she looked exhausted. I was sure she'd been doing a lot to help out with the baby. She looked over my shoulder and asked, "Who is that monster of a man that's talking to your brothers?"

Looking over my shoulder, I watch Dogan shake hands with them. "Come, I will introduce him to you." Wrapping my arm around Estelle's waist, I guided her toward the men.

"I assume you have met my brothers?" I asked Dogan. He just nodded yes.

"The general wanted me to continue training while I am here, so I got stuck with him," I grumbled.

Ry started to laugh. "Are you telling me that this is the Salvie you—"

Cutting him off, I yelled, "Yes, Ry!" He started to laugh even harder due to my response. "I would like you to meet the woman who's been like a mother to me, Estelle," I said to Dogan and then looked to her. "I would like you to meet Dogan Ramstien."

Dogan took her hand and lightly kissed it, causing her to blush a little. "'Tis a pleasure to meet ye, m'lady, and I'm sorry fer the loss."

Estelle cleared her throat. "Why thank you, Dogan. Are you going to stay here with us?"

"I wasna planning on it, but yer husband wouldna ha' it any other way," he said, giving her a half smile so that one of the dimples showed. It amazed me how charming he could be. Dogan had not once showed that charm to me. All he did to me was bitch and inflict pain.

"That sounds like my husband. The boys here will show you where to bring your horse," Estelle said to him. There was a sudden noise of a dog barking. A smile came with the sight of Brute, our Altecian wolfhound rounding, the house. He stopped just before jumping up to throw his paws on my shoulders, causing me to stumble back several steps as I hit the hard chest of Dogan. My whole back was in tingles from his touch. Brute attacked my face with his tongue while I ran my hands through his shaggy copper coat.

"I have missed you too, Brute!" I giggled.

Brute stopped licking me and started to sniff the person behind me. When standing on his rear legs, he had to be close to Dogan's height. Brute gave him a low growl when he realized that he was a stranger.

"If that bloody dog bites me, I'll kill it!" Dogan's voice filled my head.

Smiling I said, "Settle down, Brute. Dogan is a friend." The growling stopped as soon as he heard the word *friend*. Brute leaned his head forward to get a good scent from him.

"I mean it, woman! If he bites—" He stopped talking in my head when Brute started licking his face. "Bloody hell," he muttered, caus-

ing everyone to laugh. The laughing stopped though when we heard the front door shut.

"Get down, boy," I whispered, and Brute took his paws off my shoulders.

Regner slowly made his way to the steps. He did not look like the brother I left over three years ago. The man looked horrible. I took off in a sprint when he collapsed down on the top step. He hung his head down as his elbows rested on his knees. Regner's whole body was shaking by the time I reached him. Going down in front of him on my knees on the step where his feet were, I lean back a little, afraid to touch him. Not once in my life had I ever seen Regner cry. Finally, with my blurred vision, I softly spoke, "Regner?"

"Sis," he cried out and pulled me to his chest. Once his arms were around my shoulders, he started crying loudly and rocked back and forth. I matched his sobs as I tried to soothe him at the same time. He was pulling hard at the back of my shirt, causing it to tighten around the front of my neck. I heard someone walking up the steps then felt Estelle kissing the top of my head. Opening my eyes, I watched her walk into the house with her hand over her mouth. Closing my eyes again, I buried my face into his neck.

"I am so sorry, brother! I will always regret not coming out for your wedding. I am so, so sorry!" I cried. He squeezed me even tighter.

He did not speak for a while, just cried while he rocked. "Why, sis? Why did God take her away from me? She was perfect!" he yelled. "Our daughter needs her. I cannot do this alone."

"I do not know why. None of us will ever truly understand the reason for his actions. The only thing I do know is that you are not alone. You have a family that loves you, and we all are going to take part in caring for Ella," I said, and he started to cry hard again when I said his daughter's name. I rubbed my hands up and down his back to try to calm him down.

"I hate God, Lee," he whispered. "I think I always will."

"You will not always hate him, I promise you that. It will take you some time, but eventually, you will find your love for God again." I pushed Regner back so I could see his face. Taking it in my hands, I rubbed his cheeks dry. His face was pale with stubble on his cheeks.

His eyes were bloodshot with dark bags under them. My brother looked like he had not slept in days or even eaten for that matter.

"You may never know how much it means to me to have you here." He closed his eyes as his chin started to quiver. I leaned forward and pressed my lips to his then rested my forehead against his as he started to cry again. His whole body convulsed with the sobs.

After he settled down, Regner let out a deep breath. "This emotion is really killing me, sis," he murmured with his forehead still against mine. "Our brothers cannot handle it. I think that's why Irving and Wade are sleeping over in my house. They are all used to me being the rock in this family. There is no way I can do that right now. I noticed Ry stepping up and taking the spot though. Even Pa and Estelle are relying on him. Please talk to him, sis. I am afraid he's keeping it all in to stay strong for all of us. Ry is more likely to open up to you than any of us brothers."

Pulling back, I gave him a small smile. "I will talk to him."

"Thank you." Regner gave me a tiny smile. We both looked at the door when the sound of a baby came from inside. It was an odd noise to hear. "Well, would you like to go meet your niece?"

I nodded my head as my eyes started to fill with tears again. As I stood up, I was glad to see no one standing in the front yard. They all left to unsaddle the horses. While following Regner into the house, the aroma of freshly baked bread hit me. It gave me the feeling of comfort. The long massive table was spotless with ten beautifully designed chairs neatly placed around it. Estelle had always kept the house clean. Past the kitchen, it opened up into the large living room. This was always my favorite room with the enormous fireplace to the left and the bookshelves that filled half of the east wall ahead of me. Estelle was bent over the bassinet that was alongside one of the couches. She stood up with a little bundle in her arms.

"Ella, I would like you to meet your Aunt Lee," she softly said to her. Smiling and still lightly crying, I traced a finger down her cheek.

"Hello, beautiful." I looked to Regner. "She's so tiny. Are babies normally this small?" I had never seen a newborn. The youngest baby I have ever seen was six months old.

"Well she, is here a month early. We were all worried at first, but the doctor is pretty certain that she's going to be fine," Regner said as he admired his daughter.

"It's because she has that strong Bayard heart and will inside her." Estelle smiled. "You want to hold her?"

"Oh, I do not know," I said nervously. "What if I drop her?" I have never held a baby before.

Regner laughed a little. "You will not drop her. Come and sit then, Estelle will hand her to you."

Doing as he said, I sat on the couch, and he sat beside me. Estelle stood in front of me and placed Ella gently into my arms. While smiling down at her, she stuck out her tiny fist from the blanket she was wrapped in. I lightly touched her hand, and to my surprise, she grabbed hold of my finger. I looked over to Regner and laughed. "I cannot believe how strong her grip is."

He softly smiled. "I know, it's crazy."

After pulling back the blanket from the top of her head, I was shocked to see the light red hair. "Flora was a redhead?" I asked him without taking my eyes off her.

"Yes."

"I think she's going to have our nose," I whispered while gently touching the tip of her nose.

Regner wrapped his arm around my shoulders and said, "Me too." He took a deep breath and sniffled a bit. "You know, for the first two days, I could not hold her or even look at her. I actually hated her and blamed her for Flora's death." He reached over and lightly touched her face. Ella's precious mouth opened instinctly like she was about to be fed. Regner and I lightly laughed. "If it was not for Pa and Estelle, I do not know what would have happened. I have finally come to my senses to be the father that Flora wanted me to be. It is hard though. I think she cries for her." He rested his forehead on my shoulder as the tears started coming back. With that, I turned my head and kissed the top of his.

With Ella still holding my finger, I gazed up at the two portraits hanging above the fireplace. Chills ran throughout my body with the sight of them. The one to the left had Pa and Ma, who was very much pregnant with me sitting in chairs with one-year-old Irving sitting on Pa's lap. Regner, who was around ten, was standing behind them with Ry and Wade standing on either side of him. In the other portrait, Pa again with Estelle are sitting in chairs. I am standing beside Estelle with my hand on her shoulder. I was close to fifteen there. Irving is in the same position beside Pa, and our three older brothers are in the same position as they were in the first portrait. We had that portrait done not long after they got married. I never noticed it before, but Pa was happy in both of them.

"You know what I noticed the other night while sitting out here?" Regner whispered. "Pa is very much in love in both portraits."

"Oh God, Regner! Stay out of my head…I was just thinking the same damn thing." My whole body was full of goose pimples.

"Language, Lee," Estelle warned from the kitchen. I bit down on my lip as Regner laughed a little and squeezed my shoulders.

"It's good to have you home. How long do plan to stay?" he asked.

"For as long as you need me to." I smiled at him.

"What if I say I never want you to leave us again?"

"Then I will not," I whispered, looking him in the eyes, and I meant it.

Regner smiled. "I would not do that to you, but you are not leaving anytime soon. I will tell you that."

I looked to the door, hearing my brothers' laughter. It was crazy, but I thought I heard Dogan's rare laugh too. Regner whispered to me just before they all walked into the house, "I meant to ask you, who's that Salvie-looking man that was with you?"

As they all walked in the door, I whispered to him, "Remember my last letter I sent?" His eyes widened. "Yes, that's the bloody fool I am stuck with." Regner stood up when the three of them came toward us. Each of them was holding things from Dogan and my saddles.

Ry said to Regner, "I would like you to meet sis's trainer and best friend…" Ry widened his smile and winked at me. "Dogan Ramstien!"

"Your uncle is a bloody bastard," I whispered ever so lightly to Ella so Estelle could not hear.

"Dogan, this is our oldest brother, Regner." Dogan stuffed the wooden swords under his one arm and took hold of Regner's hand and bowed his head.

"It's a pleasure to meet you, Dogan. So I bet my sister brings you nothing but joy every time you meet for training," Regner said sarcastically to him.

Dogan lightly smiled. "She nothing but a thorn in my side."

Ry widened his eyes again as he laughed at me. "Did you hear that, sis? You are nothing but a thorn!" He continued laughing.

"Yes, well, he's nothing but a pain in my ass too!" I said while looking down at the now-sleeping Ella.

"Lee," Estelle warned again.

"Damn it, you see what you did!" I yelled at the men standing in front of me. Then I bit down on my lip again when I realized that I just cursed for the third time. Well, actually for the fourth time, but the one did not count because she did not hear it.

"Leelah Bayard," she yelled. "Not in this house and especially around the baby!"

"Yeah, sis, what the *hell* were you thinking?" asked our soft-spoken Irving, and we all lost it when Estelle yelled at him. Irving was always the goody two-shoes in our family. He hated it when anyone was mad at him. With me laughing so hard, Ella started to move around in my arms. I noticed then too that Regner was laughing, but it was not his normal hearty laugh. With God as my witness, I was determined to get his laugh back.

Estelle came up behind Ry and asked, "Are you all purposely trying to give me gray hair?"

"That's what we live for, Estelle!" Ry said giving her a bright smile.

"Just wait till your father comes home," she threatened.

"What's he going to do? Bend us over his knee and whoop us?" Ry asked.

Estelle laughed. "Maybe."

Laughing, Ry slapped Dogan on the back. "Come on, Dogan, you can take Irving's room. Follow me."

The three of them went upstairs, leaving me with Estelle and Regner. Estelle had a huge smile on her face and started shaking her head. "Even though I cannot stand the swearing...I am so happy to have you home." She walked over to me and lifted my chin up. She lightly kissed my lips. "I love you, baby girl!"

"I love you too!"

That evening, we all sat around the kitchen table and had a wonderful family dinner. We did a lot of reminiscing. My family told Dogan all about the crazy things I did while growing up and the fights I used to get into. We talked about the worst fight Wade and I ever had.

It was the day that Pa was bringing Estelle over to meet us all for the first time. Wade ripped the head off my doll, and I was pissed. I ended up finding him out in front of the house and I tackled him. It rained hard the night before so the ground was saturated. My other brothers did not break us up; they just let us do what we needed to do. While rolling on the wet ground, we pulled and punched at each other. No matter how mad Wade got, he never punched me in the face, just anywhere else he could connect his fist to. I on the other hand did not care. He got a black eye and a fat lip from that fight. The both of us were covered in mud and blood. Oh, when Pa rode up to the house and found us fighting, he was livid.

Pa flew out of that carriage with speeds like a hawk catching its prey. Since I was on top at the time, he grabbed a hold of me by the hair and yanked me off my brother. Then he took hold of Wade the same way and pulled him to his feet. He was screaming, in our faces, with so much anger that he was spitting. After he was done with his screaming, he ordered Regner to take the two of us to the barn to wait for him. Regner took hold of both of our shirts and practically dragged us both to the barn. If we did something awful or mouthed off, we would be sent to the barn where he would whip us across our bottom. Well, he mostly whipped my brothers; Pa never used a whip on me, only his hand across my rear end. That was the first time I ever felt the pain my brothers always felt. I will never forget that pain till the day I die. I could not sit for days. It was the worst whipping I had ever received from my father, and it was the last.

Pa hated himself for how he lost his anger with us that day. That night, I lay in pain and was sick with myself at being fourteen years old and still receiving lickings from my father, when he walked in. He apologized for how he handled my brother and me. He said he did not know what he was thinking; he just lost it. Pa also said that we were not little children anymore and we could have easily laid him out if we wanted too, which I knew Wade wanted too because he told me. But we would not do that, out of respect for our father. That night, he promised to never lay the whip on me again, and he kept it. We both still got grounded for a month for that one. I was always surprised that Estelle never turned around that day and ran away. Despite that one incident, I would never change my childhood for the world. With all the laughing and the reminiscing, it did feel terrific to be finally home.

Chapter 14

Mother's Message

Later that evening with the house now quiet, I sat in the middle of my old bed. My room was the same as I left it. They never changed it, only kept it clean. Finally, out of the clothes I had worn for the last few days, I was in a clean nightgown with my old robe tightly around me and with my still-damp hair loosely braided over my shoulder. Laying my palms up on my legs, I took a deep breath while closing my eyes, getting myself relaxed with the image of me lying in bed with Rowan. Taking another deep breath and trying to imagine my core releasing from my body, I could actually feel it in my chest. It shocked me because it felt like it was trying to push through my rib cage. I kept my bedroom door open and could sense someone walking in, but there was no sound. Swaying a little as they climbed into my bed, I knew it was Dogan before he even touched me. He's got a clove type of scent to him. Once he had himself situated in front of me, he laid his hands over mine.

"I ha' to say that I'm impressed, woman! Yer chest's on fire wit color. Ye are learning quicker than I expected." His deep voice rang proudly in my head.

"It feels like it's stuck behind my ribs and that the core will break them if I release it," I told him.

Dogan squeezed my hands, and I swayed back a little as he ripped the energy from my chest. Instantly, I could see Dogan in front of me in my red vision. I noticed he was not wearing his boots, so that explained why I could not hear him when he first walked in. He too was in clean clothes, and his wavy chestnut hair had a shine of dampness to it. Staring at Dogan, I realized how peaceful he looked in this state. His face was relaxed, and his intense eyes were closed.

"Would ye like to see yer mother?" he asked me.

"I beg your pardon?" I asked in my head. Did he really just ask me that?

"When ye'r in this state, ye'r more open to the spirit world. All ye ha' to do is ask fer 'er."

"Dogan, if you are jesting with me, then that's not funny," I said, getting a little annoyed with him.

"I'm not jesting wit ye, woman! Just bloody ask fer 'er!" he yelled in my head. I noticed his peaceful face start to tense up.

"Good Lord, Dogan! Do not get so worked up, you bloody fool!" I paused for a moment while taking a deep breath. Is that all I have to do, call for her and she will come? Finally, I said, *"Ma? If what Dogan just said is true, then please come to me."*

My whole bedroom was filled with the deep-red light, so I noticed her instantly when she walked in through my bedroom door. Pushing myself off the bed, I ran to her. She was wearing a long lightly flowing white dress. There was a bright white aura all around her. Her wavy brunette hair was draped over her right shoulder. I stopped a few feet from her and stared at her with awe. Ma walked the rest of the way to me. She was taller than I ever imagined; she might be close to Dogan's height, but her piercing green eyes glowed brightly as she gazed down lovingly to me. She laid her hand on my left cheek, and I got a tingling sensation from her touch.

"Hello, baby girl," she said to me ever so softly with an accent I never heard of. It sort of reminded me of the Salvie's, but it was different.

The tears started to flow as I laughed and wrapped my arms around her. My mother…it was actually her. It did not seem possible, but I was hugging a woman who's been dead for almost twenty-six years. Ma pulled herself back and took my face in her hands. "It's you I have been seeing in my meditation session. I recognize your hands, but your color is different."

She smiled, "Yes, love. I'm so proud of the woman you've become." She moved her thumbs under my eyes to catch the tears as they fell. "I apologize for the heartache I put you through when Rowan left. Please tell me that you understand the reasons for my actions."

"I understand, but I still do not like the idea of never being with the man I love," I cried.

"You two will always be in each other's lives and you will always love one another. I promise you that. It just will not be the way you two always imagined it to be." She paused. "You have the same abilities that I had, Leelah."

My mouth dropped. "Really? Could you see people's auras, and did Pa even know about it?"

She laughed at me. "Yes, darling, Pa knew about it, and yes I could see the auras. I knew you were blessed with my abilities right after you were born. I told Pa about you and made him promise not to say anything to you about it. God gave me a vision of your life just before I died. You had to grow up not knowing of what you were capable of so you could become the woman you are today. At the end of this week, it will be your twenty-sixth birthday, and your father will be giving you something that was once mine. I told him to wait till this birthday to give it to you and you will see why." Ma looked over my head, so I turned and almost fell over at the sight. Dogan was still sitting on the bed, and I was still sitting in front him holding his hands.

Jerking my head back to my mother, I asked, "How is that possible?"

"For you to be able to touch me...you have to be like me. When you are in this relaxed state, and you have your aura spread out like now, part of your soul can leave your physical body for short periods of time."

I started to laugh at the shock of it. "That's amazing!"

"You still have a lot to learn, and you will be amazed at what you will be capable of. Someday, you will even teach Dogan something new." She looked to him again and said, "Dogan, please come to me."

Chills ran throughout my body as I watched him pull himself away from his body and came toward us. Dogan stopped beside me, and Ma went to him. She took both of his hands and kissed the top of them. "Thank you for helping my daughter find her gift. She still has a ways to go yet, but you will teach her."

"I'll do my best, m'lady." He gave her an easy smile.

"A good friend of mine wants to see you, Dogan." Keeping her eyes on him, she called over her shoulder, "Where are you, Cici? I am surprised you have not shown yourself yet."

A woman's voice with a Salvie accent filled the room, but then again, it was different than Dogan's. "I didn't want to interrupt ye and yer daughter's reunion." She walked in then, wearing the same type dress as Ma's. The woman was tall and lean. She too had to be close to Dogan's height. Her straight raven hair stretched down the length of her back. It was her smile that answered my question of who she was. That smile and the deep dimples on each cheek was Dogan's smile through and through.

Ma wrapped her arm around my waist as we watched Cici go to Dogan. He matched her wide smile and said quietly, "Mathair." That was the word for *mother* in his Salvie language. Cici took her son's face and gave him a kiss before wrapping her arms around him in a hug. I was right; she was exactly the same height as him. The two of them quietly talk to each other in their native tongue.

Turning to Ma, I gave her a smile. She returned my smile and whispered, "You can trust him, Lee. I know he can be difficult to deal with at times but he is a good man."

"I am trying, Ma. The two of us have come a long way in the last month. If you say I can trust him, then I will…in time that is." I gave her a bigger smile.

She lightly laughed and brushed back a stray hair from my face. "Can you give Regner a message for me?" A lump started to form in my throat when she said his name and I nodded my head yes. "Tell him that Flora is fine and is at peace with everything. Let him know that she loves him with all her heart and that she's around him and Ella all the time. If he notices Ella all of a sudden, looking in a certain direction, it's because she is there."

Hanging my head as the quiet sobs started to come out, Ma took me into her arms. The feeling of love pouring off my mother was comforting. She just held me in her embrace until I gathered myself together. "Thank you, Ma. I will let him know." Pausing for a moment, I then whispered, "I love you."

"Oh, baby girl, I love you too," she whispered back and kissed me on the cheek. Ma all of a sudden looked at my door behind her and said, "Cici, someone is coming soon we should leave." Ma gave me one stronger hug. "I will see you soon, my love!"

Smiling, I said, "I would hope so!"

Cici walked to me and took my face. Again, I got a tingling sensation from her touch too. Angling it up, she kissed my forehead. "I know my son is not the easiest person to get along wit, but somewhere in that thick chest of his, he does have a heart. Sometime within the next few weeks, my son will tell ye his story."

"That's none o' 'er damn business," he barked.

"Don't get testy wit me, son! I mean it! For her to be able to completely trust ye, she needs to know yer story," she snapped back at him.

Instantly, I covered my mouth with my right hand to hide my smile. He just got yelled at by his own mother. That was awesome! I could not help but laugh inside my head. Dogan narrowed his eyes at me, then his growl filled inside my head.

"Dinna ferget that we're still touching on the bed, so I can hear yer laughter…bitch!"

"Dogan Ramstien! I totally just heard what ye said to her." Cici grabbed hold of his chin. "I might be in the spirit world now, but I'm still yer mother, and ye'll listen to me. Before ye head back to Burreck City, ye'll tell her yer story."

His response to her anger was a huge smile with a light laugh. "All right I will. Besides, what would ye do if I dinna…give me a lickin'?" He cocked up his scarred eyebrow.

Cici started shaking her head as she laughed. "Oh aye!" she yelled.

Dogan laughed and pulled her into a hug. He closed his eyes as he squeezed her. You could easily see the love he had for her. Ma kissed me again and said, "Cici, they're coming up the stairs, we need to go." She smiled. "Love you, baby girl!"

Before I could respond, I was getting slammed back into my body. My eyes snapped open and then glared at Dogan as I tried to catch my breath. Taking both of my hands, I hit him in the chest. "You bastard," I whispered harshly. "You could have warned me first!"

He shrugged his shoulders. "I could ha' but I didna."

"What the hell is this?"

Quickly, I turned my head to see my brother standing in my doorway. "Regner!"

"Why are you in my sister's bed?" he asked Dogan then looked to me, "Lee, are you having sex with this man?"

"Good God, Regner! No!" I laughed in shock to his question. "I have never been with a man in that way."

"Liar," Dogan stated in my head. Glaring at him I jerked my knees that were still touching him away. Climbing off the bed, I went over to my brother.

"Then explain this to me, sis." He pointed at the bed.

"Did you know of Ma's special abilities?" I decided to go right out and ask him.

Regner's eyes widened. "Are you able to see the lights now?"

"Pardon?" I asked stunned. "No, not yet. Do all of you know about Ma and me?"

"No, only Ry and I know. Wade and Irving were too young to understand. Pa told us about you and said that we are never to talk about it, so we never did. If you cannot see people's lights, then how do you know?"

Looking back at Dogan, who was now standing, I said, "Because Dogan is the same as me." I looked back to my brother. "He's been helping me access it, and that's what we were doing before you came in."

"Dogan has the same abilities?" he asked, sounding suspicious as he looked behind me again at the beast of a man.

Nodding my head, I continued. "I found out tonight with this ability I can see our mother. I saw her, Regner, and she's beautiful... and tall."

Regner smiled as his eyes started to glisten. "She always was beautiful, and yes, she was taller than Pa. She was a rare beauty all the way around," he said quietly.

Taking a deep breath, I added, "I have a message for you." I instantly hung my head as I started to cry. Regner pulled me to him and wrapped his arms around me. I found it easier to talk this way instead of looking directly at him. "Ma said that Flora is fine and is at peace with everything. Flora loves you with all her heart and is around you and Ella all the time. She also said that if you catch Ella looking in a certain direction all of a sudden, it's because she is seeing her." Regner started to shake with sobs. For a long while, we stood there in each other's arms, crying before we finally pulled apart. Regner cursed as he rubbed his eyes clear.

"Where the hell did he go?" he asked. Dogan was nowhere in my room. The man left without either of us noticing. I shrugged my shoulders. "I do not like knowing that a man of his size can sneak past me without me noticing," he said, sounding edgy.

"I know what you mean."

Shaking the thought from his head, he stared at me for a moment. "Thank you, sis. I think this may help." He wiped away his tear as soon as it fell, "When you see Ma again please, tell her thank-you and I love her."

Nodding, I said, "I will."

He kissed my forehead. "Good night."

"Good night, brother."

Sometime during the night, I got woken up by a screaming baby. Quickly getting out of bed, I grabbed my robe while walking out of my bedroom. The upstairs hall was pitch-black but there was soft light coming from downstairs. As I walked down the stairs, I stopped on the last step with the sight of Regner. He was standing in the middle of the living room with his back to me. The room was lightly lit by the fire in the fireplace. He was bouncing Ella in his arms, trying to soothe her. There was a soft sound of a door shutting, so I stepped off the bottom step, turning down the hall that runs along the staircase. Sleepy Estelle stopped in her tracks when she saw me.

"Go back to bed, Estelle," I murmured to her. "Let me try to help him."

"Are you sure, sweetie?" she whispered and then yawned.

Mimicking her yawn, I smiled at her. "That's why I came…to help."

She lipped the words *thank you* and gave me a small smile before turning around to go back to bed. I walked back out to the living room to find Regner looking at me with pleading eyes. "I have fed and changed her and she still screams. I do not know what to do!" He stared up to the ceiling and yelled softly, "Flora! If you're here like Ma said, then do something!" As I walked up to him, Regner gazed at me with crying eyes.

While laying my hands on Ella, I said to him, "Give her to me, Regner. Let me try."

Gently, he placed her into my arms. She was screaming bloody murder. Her little face was bright red with tiny fists swinging in the air. I walked away from Regner and started rocking her in my arms.

"Easy, sweetie! You look like you're about to burst." I could not help but laugh.

"Do not laugh at her, sis!" he snapped as he plopped himself on the couch.

"I am sorry." I laughed at him. "I just cannot help it. Her face is so red."

"I know! She's been screaming for a while now."

"Shh," I said to her softly while still rocking her back and forth. I was thinking about the time when Pa used to sing to me at night when I had a bad dream. Having to really think about it, the song slowly came back to me. Ever so softly, I started to let the words flow from my lips. It amazed me, but she finally stopped crying halfway through the song. While I was still singing, I looked over to my brother. He too was sleeping on the couch. After finishing the lullaby, I continued humming the melody. A little while later, I walked over to her bassinet. As soon as I lay her in it, she started to fuss.

"You have got to be jesting with me," I mumbled to her. Bringing her back up to my chest, I looked back at Regner then to Ella. "Would you like to come and sleep with me?" Her way of answering my question was by snuggling her face against my breast. Smiling, I turned for the stairs and coming to a stop at the bottom step at the sight of a shadowy figure sitting at the top step. Squinting through the darkness, I could tell it was Dogan. Is he…sleeping?

Slowly and as lightly as possible, I made my way up the steps, remembering where all the creaks were and avoiding them. The man was sleeping! His arms were resting on his knees while he had the side of his head resting against the wall. Dogan's mouth was slightly open as he lightly snored. Brute was lying on the top landing beside him, and his tail started to lightly thump. Holding Ella in my left arm, I took my right hand and flicked him hard in the nose.

As Dogan jerked his head up with eyes wide, he snatched my hand that I flicked him with. My hand was full of tingles. He was disoriented and looked all around, trying to figure out where he was. Narrowing his eyes at me, he let go of my hand when he saw who was in my arm.

"What are you doing?" I whispered to him.

"I couldna sleep wit 'er screaming, so I got up to go fer a walk. I stopped here when I heard ye singing, and I realized that 'twas actually soothing 'er. It surprises me that it did because yer singing is horrible." Biting down on my lip so that I did not say anything in response, I continued up the stairs. As I passed him, I slapped him across the back of his head. He let out a low growl, "Ye'r not gonna always ha' that baby to hide behind."

"You think I am afraid of you?"

"Oh, ye should be," he warned.

Annoyed, I said, "Go to bed, Dogan," walking into my bedroom and keeping my door open just in case Regner wakes up. Once in bed, I lay on my left side next to her, keeping my arms around her,

I kissed her little face before laying my head on the pillow. Slowly I dozed off to sleep.

The next morning, I was awakened with Ella moving against me. Opening my eyes, I smiled at the sight in front of me. Sometime during the night, Regner came to bed with us. He was lying on his side on the opposite side of Ella with his hand up against her. It was amazing that I never woke with him coming to bed. I turned my head to look out the window and saw the sky was lighting up.

"Thank you." I jumped to Regner's voice, and he lightly laughed. He leaned forward and kissed his daughter's face. "Good morning, Ella." Lying my head back down as I watched him with her, she stretched her arm up and wrapped a tiny hand around his finger, and he laughed at her. "She has taken to you, sis," he said, looking at me. "I guess that means you are going to have to stay here forever now." He winked.

"I tried laying her in the bassinet last night, and she started fussing right away. So I decided to bring her to bed with me." I leaned down to kiss her cheek, and instead I wrinkled my nose to the stench. "Oh God," I laughed. "I think she has left a wonderful smelling gift, and that's all yours, brother! There's no way in hell I am changing something that smells like that!" I gagged a little.

Regner roared in laughter. He rolled on to his back as his hearty laugh escaped his lips. The loving sound brought a smile to my face, and I could not help but laugh too. He was still laughing when he rolled back to his side and took hold of Ella.

"Come on, darling, do not listen to your Aunt Lee. You smell wonderful." He got out of bed and lifted her to his face. "Oh my, maybe you do smell a little!" Regner continued his hearty laugh all the way out to the hall and to his room.

Ry walked in with his face lit and shut the door. Scooting myself across my bed, I swung my legs over the edge.

"Now that was Regner's laugh...how did you manage it?" he asked softly with a huge smile.

"I told him that his daughter left him a gift. It smelt horrible and that there was no way in hell I was changing that. I might have gagged a little too," I said, laughing still.

"You gagged?" He started to give a hard laugh. While he was laughing, I patted the bed to signal him to come and sit by me. Ry walked over, still chuckling, and plopped down beside me. I figured this would be the perfect opportunity for me to talk to him.

"I know about Ma's abilities and of mine," I said to him softly.

Ry's laughter abruptly stopped as his jaw dropped and eyes widened. "How?"

I explained everything to him, starting with how Dogan was teaching me and ending with the visit from our mother. I told him of the message for Regner.

"That is awesome, Lee!" He hung his head. "It does my heart good to hear the message about Flora."

"Ry, I know you have been trying to be everyone's rock through all of this. I just want you to know that you do not have to hide your feelings from me. Since I have never met her, you have no need to be strong for me. If you ever need to break down, I am here for you."

Ry lifted his head and looked at me with raised eyebrows. After staring at me for a few seconds, his jaw tightened as his chin started to quiver. He was trying so hard to keep it in. It was not until I took hold of his hand that the first tears started to fall. Quietly, he started to cry; he brought up my hand and kissed it before pressing it hard to his face. While laying my head on his shoulder, I took my free hand and rubbed it up and down his arm. After a moment, he started to sniffle and whispered into my hand that was still against his face. "Thank you."

"That's why I am here, brother." I leaned into him and kissed the side of his face.

Ry let go of my hand and started to rub his eyes. "Bloody hell," he mumbled. Reaching back, I grabbed my blanket and yanked it between us.

"Here," I said, handing him the end of the blanket. He gave me a small smile and buried his face in it to wipe away the tears. After a moment, he let go of the blanket and looked at me. Ry's face was lightly flushed.

"How do I look?" he paused. "Please do not say anything to our brothers."

"You look, fine and you did not cry for too long, so your eyes are not red. I promise not to say a word!" I give him a smile. Ry smiled back, quickly wrapping his left arm around my neck and held me tight in a headlock against his chest. "Ry! What the hell?" I yelled and he started to rub his fist on the top of my head. "We just had a beautiful bonding moment and now you are ruining it!" I grunted as I tried to pull out of his grip.

He laughed. "Sorry, sis! Us brothers have been stuck tormenting each other for the last three years…we need to make up for lost time!" He continued laughing while not letting go of my neck. Smiling I took hold of his long hair with my right hand and yanked his head back. Once doing that, I gave him a left hook right to the gut. He grunted and released me, so I quickly jumped away from him.

"Oh, you are so dead!" he threatened with a curled lip. Screaming and laughing, I bolted for the door. Once swinging it open, I plowed hard into Dogan's chest. He filled my whole doorway, and there was no way around him.

"Damn it, Dogan! Move out of the—" Before I could continue, Ry took hold of my right shoulder and spun me to the side. As he slammed me hard against the wall, he gave me a mischievous smile while pressing his forearm along my throat. "I would have got away if it was not for him." I nodded toward Dogan.

"You just keep telling yourself that, sis," he laughed. "You might be stronger than you used to be, but I am still your older brother. I will always be faster and"—he pressed his arm hard against my throat—"stronger!"

I started to cough a little, but I did manage to whisper out the word *bastard*. He laughed in response, and jokingly, he slapped me lightly across the face before letting go. Dogan stepped back to let Ry walk out. Laughing still, Ry slapped Regner, who was standing beside Dogan, on the side of the arm before turning for the stairs.

Regner was smiling at me while holding Ella against his chest. "What did you do this time?"

"Me?" I pointed to myself and raise my eyebrows. "He was the one who started it, and I would have gotten away if it was not for this damn fool!" While glaring at Dogan, Estelle yelled at me from downstairs for swearing. Rolling my eyes, I jerked my head to the sound of Wade's laughter.

"You are home for not even a whole day and you are already getting yelled at," he laughed from the bottom of the stairs. Narrowing my eyes at him and while trying to keep a straight face, I marched down the stairs to him. Stopping on the bottom step, I was fighting not to smile. "What are you going to do, sis? Punch me for ole time's sake?" he asked with a mocking smile.

I laughed at the thought of it and wrapped my arms tight around his neck. "I am so happy to finally be home!"

"So are all of us, sis," he said as he gave me a tight squeeze. "So are all of us."

It was wonderful to wake up in my old bed. I realized then as I saw Pa sitting at the kitchen table that it was going to be easy for me to fall back into my family's routines. Will I ever be able to leave them all again when the time comes? I might just want to stay. I guess only time will tell!

Chapter 15

Birthday

$\mathcal{J}$or the next several days, Irving and I took turns helping Pa and Wade in the shop and Ry on the farm. Every other day, I trained with Dogan. In the evenings, I had been trying to access my core by myself but still had not been able to release it. Every morning, I woke up with Ella and Regner in my bed. My brothers said that they have seen a difference in him since I had arrived. It's been nearly a week already since my arrival.

Today was my twenty-sixth birthday. I was blessed today to work on breaking a young stallion Hybrid for riding. The bloody beast bucked me off and dragged me so many times that I lost count. Dogan could not believe that I even had the guts to get on the animal. Ry explained to him that I was eight years old when my brothers forced me on an unbroken Hybrid for the first time. "It came natural to her, and she was the lightest out of all of us," Ry said to him earlier. Dogan told me that a person would have to be stupid to get bucked off and dragged and then climb back up and do it all over again. Then in turn, he said it was not guts that I had, it was stupidity. Ry laughed at him and said, "Stupidity or not, someone has to do it, and since Lee is back, she can save me from the pain of doing it." I was now bruised and sore from head to toe.

After dinner, I stayed and helped Estelle clean up the kitchen while the men went outside. Wade left to bring home his lady, Adele. She was very sweet and shy. The complete opposite of all of us, but I think she's the perfect match for my brother. Once everything was cleaned up, Estelle and I sat at the table with a glass of wine.

"How are you feeling, Lee? I watched you get thrown around like a ragdoll today. You have to be sore," Estelle asked as she sipped her wine.

Stretching out my back, I moaned, "Oh, my whole body aches," giving her a smile. "I never remember getting this sore."

"Well, love, you are not as young as you used to be." She smiled with a wink. Estelle loved me as if I was her own flesh and blood. It amazed me that none of us ever called her Ma. We were all older when she and Pa got married. If he had met and married her when I was younger, I probably would have called her that.

We got interrupted when everyone came back in, including Wade. "Did you get your girl home safely?" I asked him, smiling.

Wade's cheeks flushed. "Yes, I got her home. What did you think of her?" He explained to me yesterday at the shop that he thinks she may be the one for him. The man was absolutely crazy about her.

"She's quiet, but I like her," I said to him, and he gave me a wide smile.

After a bit, all the men returned to the table and topped off their glasses with wine. Regner sat directly across from me with Ella in his arm. He said, "We brothers did not know what hell to give you."

"Regner," Estelle warned, and he shot her a smile.

Regner continued, "Estelle gave us a suggestion, so we hope you like it. If you do not, then you can blame her." He gave her a wink.

Irving, who was sitting next to Regner, leaned forward and placed an oval glass vessel with a red ribbon tied around it.

"Happy birthday, sis," the four of them said in unison.

Smiling, I picked up the little jar...it was perfume. Opening it while bringing it up to my nose, my smile widened. "Lilac!" I laughed. "My favorite! Thank you, brothers!" Getting up I went and gave each a hug and kiss individually.

After I sat back down in my seat, Pa walked back in from the hallway. I never even noticed him leaving. I told Pa everything I learned in the last few weeks, including everything from Rowan. He had a small red box with a yellow ribbon tied around it. The only thing I did not tell him was what my mother said about him giving me something that was once hers.

Pa took a seat next to me and placed the small box in front of him, "What I have here was once your mother's. Before she died, she asked me to wait to give you this on your twenty-sixth birthday." He turned and looked at my brothers. "Irving, Wade, there is something I have to tell you about your mother before I give this to her." Pa went on telling them about Ma's abilities and how I am the same. It left the two of them speechless, which was a first for Wade.

"Happy birthday, baby girl," Pa said and handed me the box. Placing it on the table in front of me, I was nervous about what was inside. Finally, I let the curiosity take over and started untying the ribbon. Once lifting the lid, I stared with awe at the sight of it. Inside lay a silver oval locket with gold swirls. The size of it was no larger than my thumb. It was beautiful!

"I had seen your mother open it numerous times, but after she died, I could not seem to open it. Afraid of it breaking, I just let it be. I have a strong feeling that it will open for you." Pa gently smiled.

Gently, I rubbed my thumb across the gold swirls, and it tingled with my touch. There was a tiny click sound, and the locket slowly opened. A chill raced through my body, and the whole room was in silence. Everyone was leaning forward to see, even Dogan. Inside lay a small piece of paper that was folded in two. Picking up the piece of paper, I slowly unfolded it. A smile came to my face at the sight of the tiny words.

Happy Birthday, Baby Girl!
Like I said before you can trust the man...

Stunned at the words, I pointed across the table to Dogan without looking at him and waved him over. He pushed back his chair without hesitation and rounded the table to stand behind me.

I handed him the piece of paper, and he growled in response, which made me laugh and cry at the same time.

"She must ha' had a vision and wrote this before she died," he stated.

"What's it say, sis?" Ry asked.

After reading the note out loud for everyone, I said, "When I saw Ma the first night I arrived here, she told me then that I can trust Dogan." Turning my head back, I looked up to him. "I want to see if you can open it and if the note stays the same." I had a gut feeling, so after refolding the paper, I placed it back in the locket and closed it.

"If I can open it, I doubt the note'll change." Dogan reached over my shoulder and laid his thumb on the locket that was still on the table. It disappeared under his massive thumb, and I could hear the click. We both looked at each other as he lifted his hand away. Once it slowly opened, Dogan took the paper. He stood straight up and read it. At first, his face was serious like always then slowly a smile started to form on his lips. Before I knew it, the man let out a hearty laugh. All of us started to yell, asking what it said. Finally, he hands me the note. I read it out loud for everyone.

If ye keep on growling at her,
I will give ye a lickin', my son!

Everyone joined in laughing. It was his mother...that's amazing! How can something like this be possible? As everyone started to calm down, Wade said, "You do growl a lot, Dogan. Now that I think about it, I only hear it when you are dealing with my sister."

"Because she's been nothing but a pain in my arse ever since I arrived in this country," he retorted.

"Dogan," Estelle yelled, laughing and made the rest of us laugh some more.

Dogan gave her his big dimpled smile and apologized, "Sorry, Estelle." He looked back down at me, and his smile faded. "Never in my life ha' I heard o' something like this. This could become very handy to ha' someday. Put the paper back in the locket and ask a question in yer head. Reopen it and see if she answers it." I did what he asked, and I closed the locket. After thinking about what to ask, I finally came up with a question.

"*Can any person with special powers open this locket?*" I asked in my head.

Once I asked the question, I reopened the locket. Unfolding the paper for the third time it read…

No, only people like you can use it.

Dogan leaned his head over my shoulder so he could read the fine script and asked, "What did ye ask?"

"Can any person with special powers open it?" I said, and my brothers asked what it said, and I answered them.

"Aye, like I said before, this is gonna be very handy to ha'." He turned and walked back to his seat.

Once I replaced the paper back in the locket, Pa took it out of the box and slipped it over my head. The locket lay at the center of my breasts. There was a light tingling sensation where it rest. We spent the rest of the evening talking about Ma and the abilities I shared.

By the time I finally went to my bedroom, it was late. It was not until I shut the door behind me that I got hit with the floral aroma. Walking in the dark, I went to my nightstand and felt for the matches to light the lamp. Once my room was full of light, there on one of my pillows lied a bouquet of lilacs tied with a pink bow. Smiling, I picked up the note that laid beside them.

Happy Birthday, Lovalee!
I love you!

Crying and laughing, I kissed the note. "I love you too, Row!" I picked up the bouquet and buried my face into my favorite flower, taking in the full aroma. With flowers still in hand, I walked out of my room in search of a vase to put them in.

The house was dark and quiet with everyone in bed. Once I had the flowers nicely put into the vase, I started to head for the stairs. The sight of Brute staring at the front door and softly whimpering made me stop in my tracks. Placing the vase on the counter, I went to the kitchen window to see what had him upset. There sitting on the top step of the porch was the massive form of Dogan. Without thinking, I went and opened the front door, and Brute ran out. As he ran past Dogan, he made sure to lick the side of his face before going down the steps. He mumbled something as he wiped clean the drool.

I came to a sudden stop halfway across the porch as I felt the sorrow radiating from him. This was a new emotion for me to feel coming from him. With elbows on his knees, he lifted his head up and stared out to the yard. Slowly making my way to him, I took a seat beside him. Staring out to the fields, there were sights of horses grazing under the moonlit sky.

"Dogan, what's wrong? And do not say *nothing's wrong* because I can feel the sadness without even touching you." I sat there waiting for a response.

He took a deep breath and hung his head down. I noticed then the bottle of wine in his left hand. After a moment, he finally spoke, "Twenty-six years ago today, my parents were murdered." Once it registered what he just said, my jaw dropped as I gazed at him. He continued, "We both lost our mothers on the verra same day." He looked at me with his intense sad eyes. "What are the chances o' that?"

Shaking my head and not knowing what to say at first, I reached for his right hand and squeezed it, "I am so sorry, Dogan. I could not even imagine what you must have gone through. You had to have only been...nine? How did something like this happen?"

Dogan squeezed my hand back then pulled his hand away. "Aye, I was almost ten. I'm not talking about how it happened tonight," he said quietly. It was still odd to hear his deep voice so soft.

We sat in silence for a while. My heart ached for the man who was always aggravating me. He was so young when it happened. I could not help but wonder what happened to him after his parents were killed. As much as I wanted to keep asking him questions about it, I knew he would not answer them. Then I remembered him saying that he was almost ten, so I turned to him.

"When is your birthday?"

"That's none o' yer damn business," he growled.

"Goddamn it, Dogan! Why do you have to be such a bloody fool all the time?" I yelled at him. Jerking the bottle out of his hand, I took a few chugs of fruity wine before shoving it back at him. Looking down at my locket, a small smile formed on my lips. Quickly, I opened it and took out the paper. Laughter burst out of me at the words I read in the moonlight.

My son's birthday is exactly two weeks from today!

I handed the note over to Dogan so he could read it. The sadness feeling was now replaced with anger, and it was spurting off him. "Goddamn it, Mathair! Can ye please stay outta this! I'll tell 'er what I want to tell 'er. Not ye," he yelled. Dogan turned to me and took hold of the locket that was still in my hands. He placed the paper inside, then a second later, he reopened it. He hung his head after reading it and mumbled, "Bloody hell." Once he handed me the note, I angled it into the moonlight.

Sorry, Love but I have been in it since the very beginning and I always will be. You're just going to have to get used to it!

"Is your ma the angel you told me about?" I asked him.

"Aye," he muttered. I decided then that I should leave him be and try to get some sleep. Dogan stopped me; he must have sensed me getting ready to leave. "Wait." He reached to his left and handed me a...bow? After looking at it, I gave him an odd look. "Dinna ever say that I never got ye anything." He sounded annoyed.

I start to laugh. "You got me a bow for my birthday?"

"Do ye own one?"

"No," I said, still laughing. "It's been years since I shot one."

"Once I finish making the arrows, we'll start training wit it," he said.

"Whoa! You are making the arrows? Did you make this too?" I held up the bow in front of him, and he nodded. Staring at the perfection in the bend of the bow, I realized that I liked it even more knowing he made it. "Thank you, Dogan!"

After standing up, I squeezed his tingling shoulder before walking back into the house. Then I stopped. "You would not by chance know how those flowers and note got on my bed?"

He grumbled, "The bloody fool gave me the note on the morning we left." His back was facing me, but I could picture his grumpy face and smiled.

"Thank you for doing that. It was a pleasant sight to find," I whispered to him.

"Go to bed, woman," he groaned. I laughingly said good-night to him and walked back into the house.

Chapter 16

Knockout and Pranks

J t had been days now since my birthday. I left the shop ahead of Pa and Wade because they had some errands to run in the city. As I was brushing Ara down in one of the stables, I got startled by the sudden burst of yelling. They were literally screaming and doing it in the Salvie tongue. It was Dogan and Regner, and I could hear them coming toward my direction.

"Do not walk away from me, Dogan!" Regner roared now speaking in our language. "I want to know! Are you a spy?"

"Go to hell, Bayard! I dinna need to explain a damn thing to ye," Dogan yelled back. I stepped out of the stall then, and Dogan continued past me and shouted. "We're training, I'm going to grab the swords."

"The hell we are," I snapped. I was sweaty and covered in soot, there was no way I was training today. Dogan stopped in his tracks.

"Did you know that he was once a lieutenant for the Salvatorian Army?" Regner yelled at me.

"Yes." I looked back to Dogan, whose eyes were fixed angrily at me. "Just because you are pissed off does not mean I have to train with you…find someone else!" Turning, I stalked in the opposite direction.

"Woman," he warned, "don't ye dare walk away from me!"

"Do not talk to my sister in that tone," Regner bellowed at him.

After rolling my eyes, I yelled over my shoulder, "Just in case you have not noticed, Dogan...I am!"

Once turning right to the short hall that led to the pasture, I went into a sprint and burst out of the door. I knew he was after me. There was the sound of his quickened steps once I rounded the corner. After running for a moment, I thought, where the hell was I going to go? There was no way of outrunning this man, so I abruptly stopped and turned around. That was one of the worst decisions I have ever made. Dogan was so close to me that he did not have enough time to stop and plowed into me and slammed me hard to the ground. Pain shot up my back and head from the impact. It took a moment, but once my vision cleared, I saw his eyes were as wide as mine as we tried to find our breath. He took the pressure of his massive chest off mine.

"What the hell, lass? Are ye all right?" his voice filled my head. He actually sounded a little concerned. He seemed to be searching my face and thoughts wondering if anything was broken.

"Goddamn it, Dogan! What the hell is wrong with you?" I screamed in my head and smacked him in the chest.

The concerned look quickly washed from his face. *"Well, I guess that answers my question. Why did ye stop so sudden?"* he asked.

"I decided that it was ridiculous to be running from you," I said, narrowing my eyes; and all of a sudden, Regner was there, and he was red hot with anger. By the looks of him, I knew he was about to do something stupid and sure enough I was right. I yelled, "No, Regner!"

Regner did not listen and took hold of Dogan's shoulder, first yanking him up a bit then instantly giving Dogan a right hook to the face. His eyes rolled to the back of his head, and then he went limp inches from my face. My brother pushed and kicked him off me. After sitting up, I stared down at the now knocked-out Dogan Ramstien.

"Are you all right, sis?" Regner knelt down beside me as he was trying to catch his breath. He started to rub his sore right hand with his left.

The shock of what just happened was overwhelming. I could not take my eyes off Dogan, "I cannot believe you knocked him out," I whispered.

"The man is the same age as me…you think I did not have it in me to do that?" he asked, sounding annoyed.

Looking to him then, I said, "Of course I know you can knock someone out, I just never thought he could be knocked out."

"He is a man, sis."

"You do not know Dogan like I do. He knew you were coming, and he could have stopped you, but he did not."

"So?" he asked, shaking his head and shrugging his shoulders. Regner was still rubbing the hand he punched Dogan with.

"He let you hit him because he did not want to hurt you." For the first time since I met him, he actually pulled at my heart. Then I asked my brother, "How's your hand? You did not break it, did you?" He flexed his hand in and out of a fist and shook his head no.

"Sis." I looked back at Regner. "How is a man like himself in the royal guard? Are they not afraid of him being a spy?"

"I hated him at first because I thought the same way you do. He has been over to see the mage, and Azzan is confident that Dogan is not a spy. I still always questioned it though. It was not until I saw our mother that I believe now that he is not. Ma would not push me to trust him if he was bad…right?"

"No," he said, shaking his head. "If Ma said you can trust him, then you can." Regner looked at Dogan. "I did knock him out good though. You see, your oldest brother still has it in him," he said with a smile and then hit me in the shoulder. "I am sorry. I got pissed at him when I found out he was a lieutenant, and then when he tackled you, all I could see was red. I wanted to kill him."

"He only tackled me because I stopped, which was a mistake." I started to laugh. "The man is three times the size of me. He knocked the wind right out of me, and I am lucky I did not break anything."

I stretched my arms up over my head and then swiveled from side to side to loosen the knots that were starting to form.

Regner started to bounce in laughter, and before I knew it, he was letting out his hearty laugh. "I was mad at the time, but the more I think about it, the funnier it is. I wish there was more than just me that witnessed it." He held his belly as he started to rock back and forth in laughter. "He laid you right out!"

I started to laugh myself. "Go ahead, brother…laugh it up!" And he did. After a few minutes, he finally settled down and stood up. He held his hand out to me.

"Would you like to come up to the house with me?" he asked.

"No thanks, Reg. I think I will just stay here and wait for him to wake up." I looked back at the still-knocked-out man beside me.

He smiled. "All right. I will apologize to him later."

I nodded to him and watched him walk back to the barn. Laughter burst out of me when Ara startled him by walking out the side door we left open. Completely forgetting about her, I left her in the stall with the door open when I took off. Well, it seems she decided to let herself out.

Regner yelled from the barn, "She's your horse!"

"I know," I yelled back.

I jerked my head to look at Dogan when he let out a moan. He brought both his hands up to his face. "Can ye not yell fer one goddamn minute?" he moaned. I was biting down on my lip when he finally turned his head and looked at me.

"You were out for several minutes…how's your head?" I winced at him.

"It hurts, no thanks to ye," he growled as he pushed himself up into the sitting position. Dogan rubbed the right side of his face. "Yer brother packed a wicked punch though." He laughed a little to the shock of it.

"Speaking of that, you could have stopped him. Why did you not?" I asked while crossing my arms at my chest.

"He caught me off guard." He narrowed his eyes.

"Liar," I yelled and pointed a finger at him. "You did not want to hurt him because you like him!"

"Please, woman. If I had stopped him, not only would I ha' to deal wit ye, but yer three other brothers would ha' been on my arse as soon as they found out about it."

"Say what you will." I rolled my eyes at him. "You do not have to admit it because I already know. Besides, you are not the type to worry about the consequences." Ara, who has been walking toward us since she came out of the barn, was now standing next to Dogan. He had to stretch his neck up to look at her. She brought her head down and butted her massive head against his body like she did to Rowan and me. The only difference was she hit him with a little more force, making him sway to the side. I brought both my hands to my mouth as the laughter escaped.

"What the hell, cuddy?" he yelled. I chuckled even more when he said *cuddy*, which was *horse* in his native tongue.

"For some reason, she likes you. Ara has only done that move to Rowan and me." I started to laugh even harder as he glared at me. With him glaring, Ara was now moving her plump lips over the top of his head. His hair started to stick up every which way from her saliva. Finally, my laughter got the best of him because a smile broke through as he swatted Ara away from him.

"Bloody horse," he mumbled as he tried to flatten his now-spiked hair.

As I stood up stretching out the kinks that formed from the tackle, I said, "Come on, Dogan. If we go up now, we will still have time for training before dinner."

He groaned as he stood up, and he too stretched his arms up and bent over to lengthen out his back. "Forget about training for today," he mumbled and stood up right again. "I was just pissed off, and I needed to let out some steam, which I did when I tackled ye." He gave me an evil grin.

"Bastard," I mumbled. As I started to walk back toward the barn, I stopped when he asked me to wait.

"I meant to say something to ye the other night...dinna and I mean dinna say anything about my birthday, especially to Estelle." He paused and narrowed his eyes. "Do I make myself clear?"

Rolling my eyes, I said, "Relax, Dogan, do not get your feathers in a bunch! I am not going to say a single thing, all right?"

"Good," he said as he walked past me and said over his shoulder. "I'll find another reason to kick yer arse later then." Shaking my head, I followed him.

After getting dressed for the day, I gazed at myself in the mirror, looking relaxed in my normal short-sleeved shirt tucked into my brown trousers. I had been home for about three weeks now and realized how happy I was here. Hating to think about leaving, I shook it from my head when I walked out of my bedroom door.

Estelle was sipping on a cup of tea when I walked downstairs. "Perfect timing, love!" She gave me a huge smile and held up a basket. "Would you mind going to the coup and collecting eggs for breakfast?"

"No problem." Taking the basket, I marched out the door with Brute beside me. The fog was so thick that I could not see the fence line or the horses that were out grazing. Brute's huge form disappeared into the thickness as he ran. Soon, the sun will be up high enough to burn off the fog. Once stepping off the porch steps, I took in a deep breath of the cool morning air. It was going to be another warm and sunny day. I just knew it.

Walking into the coup, I found some of the chickens running up to me and started pecking the dew off my boots. They followed me like I was about to throw them some food. It always made me smile how predictable they were. We go through this every morning. After collecting the last egg, I did a quick count...three dozen. All of a sudden, I was getting hit hard in the back of the legs. Spurs dug deep into the back of my knees. Quickly turning around, the rooster jumped up and tried to hit me with his feet again while his white wings flapped to help give him height.

"Damn you, you bloody bird," I yelled and gave him a hard kick to his chest, sending him to the other end of the coup. All the hens scattered, jumping around and clucking as I tried to get out of there. Multicolored feathers and straw were floating through the air with all the commotion. Just before I walked out the door, the rooster stretched his neck down and puffed out the snowy feathers around his neck. I was ready for him this time. When he came at me, I gave him another good boot to the chest before running out and slamming the coup door. As the hens started to pour out their little door, I quickened my steps toward the house. That bloody rooster attacked me all the way up to the house last week. I was not in the mood for that this morning.

While walking along the side of the porch, I noticed Dogan walking toward the fence line. I do not know why, but I always got the sudden urge to throw things at the man. Stopping at the steps, I took hold of an egg and stared at it at first then fixed my eyes on Dogan, who was walking further away from me. It was his birthday today, and I should not do it, but I did anyway. Never taking my eyes off him, I ran a few steps and tossed the egg into the air, standing there with the basket still in my hand and waiting for him to duck just before it hit him. Except he never ducked like I thought he would.

Through the thick fog, I watched the egg explode on the back of his head. Dogan froze and slowly brought up his right hand to the back of his head. When he turned around, I could feel his eyes fixating on me through the fog. Bending over in laughter, I yelled the best I could, "You were supposed to duck. Why did you not duck?" Uncontrollable laughter poured out of me. There was no way of keeping it in. Dogan all of a sudden burst into a full sprint toward me. Screaming, I turned for the house and ran up the steps. Flying through the door, I placed the basket on the table and went for Estelle. Taking her by the shoulders, I used her to shield me as Dogan barged through the door.

"Lee! What are you doing?" Estelle screeched.

Narrowing his eyes, Dogan gave me a crooked smile as he reached into the basket. "Yer lovely Lee here just hit me in the back o' the head wit an egg," he sneered as he tossed the egg up and down in his hand.

"Oh, you better not throw that! I am not having an egg fight in my kitchen. Do you hear me, Dogan? Do not throw that in here,"

Estelle warned him and turned to look at me. A smile formed on her face. "I cannot believe you were going to use me as a shield. This is your fight, so take it outside." She lightly patted me on the cheek and stepped away from me. Dogan's crooked smile gained an evil appearance to it.

Smiling and still giggling, I said, "I am sorry, Dogan. I do not know what came over me."

"Get yer arse outside, lass!" His smile broadened when Estelle yelled at him for swearing, and he said, "Sorry, Estelle!" Dogan nodded his head toward the door. "Let's go!"

I slowly walked between the counter and table toward the front door. He was on the other side of the table, and I never took my eyes off him. I ran to the door, hoping I could reach it before he got to me. Just as I swung open the door, I was getting yanked back into the house. Dogan slammed me against the wall. The more I tried to get away, the harder he pressed his tingling body against mine. With much effort, I blocked the pleasure I was gaining from his scent that was clove with a fine hint of soap. Finally looking up at him, I gave him a shy smile and whined in my head, *Happy birthday?* A giggle slipped through my lips and then bit down hard on them so it would not happen again.

Dogan let out a loud laugh and filled my head with his voice. "*I think this is gonna be the best birthday present ever!*"

Once saying that, he took the egg and slammed it hard on the top of my head. He continued by taking his hand that was covered in broken shell and raw egg down the front of my face. Groaning and laughing at the same time, I blew the raw egg from my lips. Dogan stepped away, pleased with himself and looked to my father, who was standing by the table with his arms crossed at his chest. Pa had a huge smile as he shook his head.

"Well, that's not fair, Dogan," I said to him as I pushed myself away from the wall. "At least I did not smear the egg on you."

Dogan shrugged his shoulders. "Ye mess wit the bull, ye get the horns."

"All right you two," Estelle laughed. "Go and get cleaned up. Breakfast will be done soon."

Walking past the staircase, I went down the hall toward the bathing room. Pulling the band that was holding my hair up in a tail, I went over to the tub that still had water in it and bent down. Once my face and hair were clean of raw egg, I grabbed a towel to dry my hair. One of Estelle's brushes was sitting on a stool, so I used it and then started to braid my hair over my shoulder. There in my sight was Dogan, leaning against the door jamb with his arms across his chest. Laughter started to bubble in my chest again. "You never answered me, so why did you not duck?"

"I was enjoying the morning and not bothering wit any o' my powers. If I had known that ye were out there, I'd had my full sight on," he said and pushed himself off the door jamb.

"When you get done on the farm, come and see me at the shop, all right."

Dogan narrowed his eyes then said, "Very well."

As he walked past me, he bent down and dunked his head into the tub to clean off the egg. Smiling while staring down at his rear end, I took my boot to it and pushed him farther into the water. With sudden laughter, I burst out of the room, not wanting to see his reaction. I knew he was going to be pissed! While sliding into the kitchen, all my brothers were now sitting at the table.

"Whoa," Irving said. "By the speed you are going, I take it you just did something…to Dogan I presume."

Giving him a wide smile, I snatched two biscuits and some side pork off the table. "I am heading to the shop early, Pa. I will see you in a little bit."

Ry started to laugh. "Um, sis? You better hurry up because he's coming, and he does not look happy."

As I burst out the door, everyone roared in laughter as I ran farther away from the house. "Ara!" I screamed as I got closer to the fence line and the sound of the front door slammed in the distance. Ara slid to a stop. Climbing up the wooden fence and on to her bare back, I stuffed one of the biscuits in my mouth while taking hold of her long mane. Looking back toward the house, Dogan came to a stop several feet from the fence. Half of his shirt was soaking wet, and he was irritated. I took the biscuit out of my mouth so I could laugh out loud at him.

"Laugh it up, ye bloody wench," he hissed. "I'll get ye back fer this, ye just wait and see."

"I would like to see you try!" Giving Ara a swift kick, we took off up the pasture toward the city.

It was late into the afternoon as I was forging a piece of metal. Shoving the steel back into the hot coals, I laid my gloved hand on another piece that was glowing orange. Once I pulled it out, I laid it back down on the anvil. Taking my hammer to another six-inch section, I started to draw out the sword. Even though the process was a lot of work, I always found this part of making a sword very therapeutic. If I was ever in a bad mood, this would calm me down every time.

As I was hammering away, suddenly, someone wrapped their massive arm around my neck. If it was not for the tingling feeling around my skin and down my back, I probably would have started swinging.

"*I ha' been watching ye fer a while now, trying to figure out what to do to ye. I ha' not came up wit a payback yet, but dinna worry...I will,*" Dogan said in my head as he squeezed his arm around my throat.

A smile came to my face as I started to cough with the pressure around my throat. "*You are starting to choke me you fool!*" I laughed in my head.

"*I know.*" I could hear the amusement in his voice. "*I was told today that the pranks ye pulled on me this mornin' used to be a common occurrence in yer household before ye left.*"

"*Someone had to keep my brothers on their toes,*" I said to him, still smiling.

"*Ye wonder why ye always got yer arse kicked then,*" he added then finally let go of my throat.

Now free from his grip, I instantly rubbed my neck and shoved the blade back in the coals before looking back up at him. There was a time that whenever I looked at him, I could not help but stare at the long scar over his eye. It just dawned on me that I did not even notice it anymore. Those intense eyes of his stood out more than anything else.

"Why did ye want me to come here?" Dogan asked. I looked over to Pa, who was standing beside a table and was watching us.

"Can you close your eyes and do not use your other vision either?" I asked him.

He narrowed his eyes, "If ye pull another stunt on me…" Dogan leaned his face closer to mine and glared. "I'll kill ye," he whispered.

While rubbing the sweat from my brow, I said, "Relax, Dogan. I am not going to pull a prank on you, all right? Just close your eyes… please," giving him a small smile while batting my eyelashes at him.

Dogan growled and closed his eyes for me. Looking over to Pa, I waved him over. He grabbed the two swords off the table and came over to us. As he was walking over, I started to undo Dogan's belt.

Quickly, he took hold of my hand without opening his eyes. "Whoa! What the hell are ye doing, woman?"

Laughing, I said, "Do not worry, Dogan! I am not going to try to take advantage of you…I promise. Remember, no peeking!"

He growled in protest and let go of my hand. After I got the belt and the dagger that was attached to it off, I said, "Pa is coming up behind you, so please do not hit him." A small smile started to form on his lips, taking the belt with the new sword I made him, slid the dagger on it, wrapping the belt around his waist so the sword was on his left hip. Once I had it secured, Pa pressed the other sword on an angle against his back. He laid the strap over Dogan's left shoulder, and I reached under his right arm for the other. Bringing the two straps together at the center of his chest, I smiled as I buckled it in place. It was a perfect fit!

"All right, you can look now," I said, pleased with myself that everything fit perfectly.

Once opening them, he fixed his emerald eyes on me as he reached up behind him with his left arm and took hold of the hilt of the blade. Slowly he withdrew it and took his eyes off me. I made the swords the same way as mine. The only difference was I made them a bit larger to match his height and built. Wrapped around the hilt was black leather instead of blue like mine. Dogan examined it from tip to the hilt and stopped to read what was engraved at the base of the sword. While still looking at it, he pulled out the other sword with his right hand. It too had the same engraving. A dimpled smile formed on his face as he started to shake his head. The engraving read, RAMSTIEN.

Without taking his eyes off them, he said, "Thank ye, Lee. Ye did a great job on 'em. How much do I owe ye?"

It was always odd to hear him say my name. *Woman* was the name he usually used for me. Out loud, I said, "You do not owe me anything." Taking hold of his wrist, I said in my head, "*Consider it a birthday present.*"

Dogan glared at me as he slid the swords in their proper place. "They're too much, and I canna accept 'em as a birthday present."

"It's your birthday today?" Pa asked behind him.

Dogan closed his eyes and growled at the mistake of what he just said out loud. Looking to Pa, I said, "Please do not tell Estelle, Pa. Dogan does not like to celebrate his birthday and would rather have no one know about it."

Pa nodded his head. "Fair enough. I will not say a word. I promise."

"Thank ye, Randall," Dogan said to him then looked back at me. "If ye dinna allow me to pay ye, then I'll pay yer father."

"Sorry, son. Lee was the builder of those swords. If she is giving you them as a gift, then I cannot accept any money from you. Besides, you are always saying how much of a pain in the ass she is to you. Consider this as a bonus for all the pain she's caused you." Pa smiled and winked at me.

Dogan growled, "I dinna like it!"

"Oh well!" I said to him, slapping his chest. "Come, I want to show you something." With the need to get his mind off the subject, I stopped just outside the front door of the shop.

As I watched people going up and down the cobblestone street in front of me, I said, "I made myself another sword too, one to hang on my back like yours. With all the training we have been doing, I realized that I like the feeling of two swords." Still staring at the cobblestone street, I finally came to the decision that I was going to tell

Dogan about how I got the job to guard the queen. Taking a deep breath, I began. "I was standing right here when I killed for the first and only time." Feeling his eyes on me, I looked up at him.

He had his scar eyebrow cocked up. "Ye actually ha' killed someone?"

Nodding, I replied, "Yes. There were two of them."

Taking my eyes off him I inhaled another deep breath. "I came out to stand here to escape the heat for a minute. The king and queen had recently gotten married, and he was bringing his wife on a tour of her new country. They were here in Mastingham. Just as I came out to enjoy the cold air, the two of them were walking up the street arm in arm. There were guards all around them, including Sterling, Rowan, and Kaidan." Sucking in some more air, I continued, "As I watched them pass in awe, I noticed two enormous men walking a little ways behind them. Something in my gut told me that they were up to no good, so keeping my eyes on them, I stepped backwards into the shop. There were knives hanging on the wall by the door, so I snatched two of them. Stepping closer to the street, my eyes were glued on them. When they both unsheathed their swords, I looked over to the king and queen, and I knew it was them they wanted to harm. Without thinking, I threw one knife, and it lodged in the neck of one. Just as the other turned to see what happened to his comrade, I threw my other knife, and it stuck in his chest."

Taking a second, I cleared my throat and breathed. "Once I did it, I started to panic. People were running all over the place, screaming. No one seemed to notice me—at least that's what I thought. It was not until I got eye contact with Rowan that I really started to panic. I took off to the back of the shop, climbed on to Ara, and raced all the way home."

"What were ye panicking fer?" Dogan asked. "Ye saved the life o' the king and queen."

"I started to second-guess myself, and I was afraid that I was going to prison or be put to death." Dogan started to laugh. Instinctively, I slapped him on the side of the arm. "Shut up you bloody fool! Are you going to let me tell you my story or what?" He nodded, looking out to the street with a smile still on his face. "Anyway, when I got home, I locked myself in my room. Everyone tried to talk to me, but I just ignored them. It was not until Rowan came knocking at my door that I started to talk. We talked through my bedroom door for a good twenty minutes before I actually opened it. He explained to me that they were able to get some information out of one of them before he died. Supposedly, they worked for King Alistair, and they were after the queen. Rowan told me that there were some people downstairs that would like to meet me. Once I was satisfied that I was not going to prison, I followed him down."

After pausing for a second, I gazed at Dogan. He looked at me with raised eyebrows. "Well…keep going, woman. I know there's more to it."

Rolling my eyes, I continued, "Sitting at our kitchen table with my family were the king and queen. They were sipping tea and talking casually with them like they were all family. It was the most amazing sight I ever saw. Once I stepped off the stairs, Bryce and Rosa stood instantly and came around the table to me. They both said thank-you and asked how I knew. I told them that I did not know how, but I just knew. It was then that they offered me the job. Bryce explained what would be required of me and that everyone would just think that I was the queen's lady. The two of them left with the guards so I could talk about it with my family. They left Rowan at the house so I could give him my answer, and then he would go to let Bryce and Rosa know. So…obviously you know what my answer was."

Dogan stayed quiet for a moment. Just as I was about to turn to go back into the shop, he finally spoke. "There was a third man that day."

My jaw dropped. "You?" I asked in a panic.

"Good God, woman! Nay," he yelled and slapped me in the back of the head like I was stupid to think that. I glared at him because that really hurt, and he continued as I rubbed the spot he hit. "I remember seeing that man when he came back. He told me what his mission was and what happened. I guess he was farther back. He watched ye kill his men and took off in the chaos." Dogan began to laugh, shaking his head, "I canna believe I dinna realize it before. He said that they were in Mastingham and that the woman threw the knives perfectly. Then I meet ye…yer specialty are throwing knives, and ye'r from Mastingham. I'm such an idiot." He shook his head.

"Well, at least you finally admit to it," I mumbled and then said louder, "Did you know of the attempted attack on them before you talked to this man?"

Dogan shook his head. "Nay." He gazed down at me. "What time do ye get done here?"

Looking back in the shop, I said, "Probably soon, why?"

"Good! Meet me at the river that has the big rock that stretches out over the water so we can train."

Giving him an odd look, I said, "All right, but why down there and not up by the house like usual?"

"I dinna want to give Regner a heart attack because we're using real weapons," he explained.

I swallowed hard. "We are using our swords?"

Dogan gave me a crooked smile. "What is this…are ye scared?"

"No." I glared at him.

"Liar," he said over his shoulder as he walked away. "Make sure ye bring both swords. I want to see how good yer craftsmanship works!" Dogan disappeared around the side of the building.

Chapter 17

History Lesson

I t was about an hour later as I rode Ara bareback toward the river in the woods that ran through our property. I had my swords strapped to my hip and back. Hating to admit it, I was a little nervous training with real weapons. The man could easily kill me if he really wanted to. As we left the open pasture and entered the woods, my heart started to really pound in my chest. Trying to relax, I took a couple of deep breaths. I did not want him to know that I was nervous. Looking down at my locket, I asked a question. *"Is Dogan going to seriously hurt me today?"* I rubbed my thumb over it, and it clicked open. The note read,

Hahaha. No baby girl he's not going to hurt you.

Smiling as I put the paper back in the locket, I started to laugh at myself. What the hell was I thinking? If Dogan really wanted to hurt me, he would have done it months ago now. There was the sound of the river up ahead, so I brought Ara to a stop. Sliding off her, I patted her on the side of the neck to tell her thank-you. While walking the rest of the way, I was able to relax myself before actually reaching the water.

The river was wide as our house was long. There to my right was the rock that stretched out over the water. After a good storm, the water underneath it could be over my head. As kids, we would jump into it on hot summer days. It was very peaceful here with the steady sound of the water flowing by and the evening sun streaming through the trees. There were a few birds in the treetops above me, causing a ruckus. As I was getting closer to the large rock, it finally dawned on me that Dogan was nowhere to be seen. He might be hiding so, keeping my back to the water, I scanned the trees.

"Dogan," I hollered. "you better not jump out on me because that will probably just make me angry." Finally, I climbed up the rock and sat on the flat top, still facing the trees, trying to keep myself aware and listening for any sudden sounds of something moving. After a while, I realized that he was definitely not out here. *Where the hell are you? You tell me to meet you here and now you are not even here*...That's a first for him to be late.

Well, since I was already out there, this would be the perfect place for me to try to release my core. Bending my legs and crossing them in front of me, I laid my hands palms up on each knee. With my eyes closed, I started to take a few deep breaths to relax me, clearing my mind and finding my center energy in my chest. It stopped at my rib cage as usual. I threw the thought of it, breaking my ribs from my head and pushed with all my might. With blunt force, my core exploded from my body; and instantly, my surroundings were in a deep-red light. Laughter bubbled out of me in excitement.

"I did it! I actually did it! Ma, are you there? Did you see?" I continued to laugh to myself. My core was spread out around me in a twenty-five-foot diameter.

"I am always around, sweetheart, and yes I did see," said my mother, who was now walking through my energy behind me. Pushing myself up, I turned to face her with my physical body sitting between us. She looked exactly the same as the first time I saw her a few weeks back.

"Hello, Ma." She returned my smile as I went around my body and wrapped myself around her.

"Hello, baby girl," she said and kissed the top of my head. "I am so proud of you. After this, you will now be able to see the aura's around people."

Pulling back so I could look at her face, I asked, "Really?"

Nodding, she replied, "Yes."

Laughter bubbled out of me. "I cannot believe I actually did it by myself, and Dogan was not here to witness it."

Ma smiled. "Dogan got caught up helping Irving and Rythe. He will be here soon, which is good because his mother wants to wish him happy birthday."

"Is Cici here?" I asked.

"Of course," said the angelic Salvie-like voice from behind me. "Just like your mother, I too am always around." Cici too looked the same. Together, Ma and I walked down the rock to her. She had her beautiful dimpled smile on her face as she took me into her arms. "Thank you for telling my son your story today. He *will* tell you his. Oh, and those pranks you pulled on him early this morning was the funniest thing I have seen in a long time." She began to laugh. "I think it did his heart good to loosen up a bit and just have fun."

Laughing, I said, "I do not know what came over me. There was this sudden urge to just pick on him." I gave her a huge smile. Cici laughed and lightly kissed both my cheeks.

Turning to look at Ma, I said, "How is it that someone like me can have these powers? Am I definitely some kind of mage, and why do my brothers not have the same gift?"

Smiling, she took both my hands. "The blood that runs through your brothers' bodies are of your father's line. Whereas for you, it is my blood that runs true in your veins." She paused. "I'm a full-blooded Fae."

Closing my mouth that dropped, I asked, "The ancient race, Fae? They really exist?" That explains why her accent was different.

She threw her head back in a hard laugh and answered, "They most definitely do. My country is far away from here. People that go looking for our existence either stay there once they find us or die on their travels back home. The people you call mages are actually Fae. In our country of Faery, there is a portal that leads to a whole different world then here on Breena, and it's called Earth. In that world, the beings look like us, but they don't have special abilities like the Fae. At one time, we all were magical, but when the people from Earth started coming here, some liked it so much that they never left. Because of that, our bloodlines became diluted. The portal is now closed, and only the Fae's King Denmark and Queen Heaven can open and close it."

She paused for a moment then continued, "The Fae are tall like the Salvatorians, some even taller. Some Fae are so powerful that they can control every aspect of our world." She let go of one of my hands and pointed to me. "You, my dear, have Fae blood running through you so thick that there's not even a trace of your father's mortality. The same goes for Rowan, Sterling, and Dogan. For as long as you live, the four of you will be together, and eventually, you will turn to five then six. It has taken thousands of years, but finally, the blood of the Earth beings is finally starting to run thin, and if people are open to it, they too will find their true abilities. So yes, my love, you are a mage, but the proper word is *Fae*."

Letting go of her hands, I dragged my hands over my face and up through my hair. I started to laugh hysterically. It seems like every day, I was learning something new and unbelievable. I am a Fae, and there is another world out there? I lost my train of thought when Cici spoke.

"My son is coming. Who here wants to bet that he's not going to be pleased with seeing the three of us talking without his presence?" She had a huge smile on her face. Cici knew her son, and yes, he was not going to be happy.

Looking through the red wall, I could see a distorted figure walking toward us. Pushing my core out several more feet as he walked into it, a smile came to my face because Cici was right. Dogan was pissed and glared at me as he passed.

"He can actually see me when I am out of my body like this?" I asked the two women in front of me.

"Yes, he can, but he cannot hear us," said my mother. "Being that he is the same as you, he can see that your energy is released and what's going on inside."

Dogan walked over to my physical body and sat down in front of me. As he took hold of my hands, I could feel his touch even though I was standing several feet behind him. His head jerked back a little as his core bursts from his body. Instantly, his soul left his body, and he started yelling before he was completely up.

"What in the bloody hell's going on here?" Dogan pointed his finger at me as he came down the rock. "Ye think ye can get information from my mother about me? Is that what ye are doing?"

Before I could snap back at him, Cici cut in between us. "Now, my son, instead of yelling at her, why not try telling her how proud ye are that she released her core on her own." She took his face in her hands. "I know ye are."

Dogan fixed his angry eyes on me for a moment then looked to his mother with softer ones. "Why are ye here, Mathair? Did she ask for ye?"

She gave him a light laugh. "My dear boy, she asked for her mother, and wherever Arabella goes, I go and vice versa. Besides, I mostly came here to say happy birthday." Cici kissed both his cheeks, and he let out a moan in protest.

"Ye know I dinna like my birthday. So why wish me a happy one?" he grumbled to her.

"Because you are my son, and it's my job to wish ye a happy birthday. Now are ye going to congratulate Lee or what?" she asked and Dogan glared at me again.

"Holy hell, Dogan," I snapped at him. "It's got to be exhausting to always be grumpy. Can you just be happy for me this one time? I actually did it all by myself!" I threw my hands up in the air in frustration.

Narrowing his eyes, he groaned out, "I'm proud o' ye, lass."

"Then why the glaring? Why do you look so angry?" I asked.

"I'm angry because I wanted to be there when it happened fer the first time," he shouted.

"Well, you were not, so snap out of it, you bloody fool," I yelled back, and our mothers burst out in laughter.

"'Tis enjoyable to watch ye two when you're together…it's quite entertaining," Cici stated, and Ma agreed.

"I really wish ye two would stay out o' our business," said Dogan walking toward me, and as he reached for me, I shoved his hand away. Quickly, he countered with the other hand and grabbed my locket. I froze as he glared at me, afraid that he might rip it off. Instead, he said, "I'm still not sure what to think about this locket."

"That's right! Ma, thank you, I love it!" Carefully I pried his fingers away from it. Once it was out of his grip, I asked, "How did you get something like this?"

"It was once your grandmother's. She gave it to me because she knew that I'd have you someday and that it was made originally for you," Ma said with a loving smile.

Dogan matched my raised eyebrows and asked, "Who was her grandmother? Was she the same as us?"

"No, she was more powerful than us. As a matter of fact, she was once the most powerful woman to ever live." She lightly laughed when Dogan and I shared a quick glance then she continued, "Lee is the granddaughter of the late King Finvarra and Queen Aine Fionnlasdan. It is now my brother, Denmark, who rules the country, Faery."

We were both speechless and just stared at one another with awe, then he finally spoke. "Holy hell! Ye'r a close descendant to the royal Fae family? Ye'r a bloody...princess?" He dragged his hands roughly through his hair and turned away from me as he started to laugh hysterically. As quickly as he started laughing, he stopped and fixed his eyes on my mother. "If the stories I ha' heard o' this king and queen are true, then how were ye alive in our time because it has been said that they died thousands o' years ago."

My mother slowly beamed him a beautiful smile. "Well, Dogan, my race is immortal. We don't die of old age like most of the people here in Altecia or any other surrounding countries do."

My heart started to pound in my throat. "Pa said you were thirty-eight when you died. If this is true, then how old were you really?"

Still smiling, she said, "I was two thousand five hundred and ninety-three years old.

"Good Lord, Ma! Did Pa know any of this? Who you were? Where you came from?" I yelled in shock.

"At first, no," she responded calmly. "I finally told him about my past and my family just days before you were born. I knew I was going to die, and I wanted your father to know the truth before that happened." Her eyes suddenly saddened. She loved my father, and I could see that now. Quickly, I turned around to catch the breath that I suddenly had lost. First, I find out that the Fae truly exist, and now I am a daughter to a princess. I turned back around to face the three of them. Dogan actually looked a little pale, which was a first. He was just as shocked as me.

"Ma, I think I learned enough for one day." I started to laugh a little. "I still have more questions, but maybe that should wait for another day because I need to grasp this entirety first."

Ma and Cici laughed and agreed to wait for some other time. After we said our good-byes to our mothers, my energy was getting slammed back into my chest. The bloody fool always had to do that to me. Instantly, I hit Dogan in the chest with both hands and yelled, "Goddamn it, Dogan! Why in the hell do you…" I stopped yelling when I noticed a bright deep red glowing around him. With my hands still against his chest, I noticed my arms were also the same color.

Laughter burst out of me as I took hold of his face. "I can see, Dogan! I can actually see your color." Caught in the happiness of the moment, I pulled myself to him and pressed my lips hard to his in a loud kiss. His whole body stiffened with the tingling sensation of our lips; still laughing, I wrapped my arms around his neck in a hug and buried my face in the side of his neck. "Thank you, Dogan. Thank you so much!"

After a moment, I smiled as a growl started to rumble in his throat. He took hold of my shoulders and pushed me back away from him. "Get control o' yerself, woman," he yelled. "Holy hell!" Not fazed by his anger, I just sat there in front of him with a smile on my face. With his glow around him, it actually made him look… handsome. He was beautiful, and I could not seem to tear my eyes away if I wanted too. "Wipe that smile off yer face too," he growled as he shook his head at me.

"You can yell at me as much as you want, it's not going to ruin the feeling that's running through me right now," I said ecstatically.

"Ye are bloody Fae royalty," he yelled and shook me by the shoulders. "D'ye even realize that?"

"Stop bloody shaking me!" I yelled, and he let go of me. "Look, I am still trying to comprehend that myself," I told him. "My mother told me there is more Fae running through me like you, Rowan, and Sterling."

"I peg yer pardon? My mother never said anything like that to me," he said, getting more aggravated.

"Then you better ask her about it."

"Oh, I will," he barked and then pointed at my neck. "What ye ha' around yer neck is Fae magic. D'ye realize what some people would do to ha' that?"

Closing my hand around the locket, I said, "No one is ever taking this from me…it's mine!"

"We'll tell Rowan and Sterling about it, but after that, no one can know o' its powers. D'ye understand? People'll kill fer it!"

I swallowed hard as I looked down at my grandmother's locket. "Yes, I understand," I murmured to him. Looking back at him, I gave him a small smile. "Well, I just had a very interesting visit with our mothers, I guess now that it is over, we should start training."

Dogan pushed himself up and extended his hand down to me. The man can truly surprise me at times. My smile broadened as I took his hand. With ease, he pulled me up. "I ha' changed my mind. We're not training today." He stepped aside so I could walk down the rock first. Why is he acting all proper?

"Why?" I asked.

"I'll explain in a moment, now will ye please get the hell off the rock!" he yelled in frustration.

Rolling my eyes, I slowly eased down the side of the rock to the mossy soil. All of a sudden, I had an urge to duck, so I did. The sack flew past me and hit the tree in front of me. Tree bark showered down on me. I turned slowly and glared up at Dogan, who was still standing on top of the rock. He had a crooked smile on his face as he tossed up and down the other sack.

"Tell me this, did ye see it coming, or did ye just sense it?" he asked.

"I just sensed it, why?"

"That's what I thought, which is still good. Eventually, ye'll be able to release yer core wit yer eyes open. Ye'll be able to work or fight wit full sight all around ye." He jumped off the rock and landed on the ground a couple feet in front of me. I watched his glowing self walk around me and picked up the sack he threw. "I ha' a lot to tell ye, so if we take a slow walk back to the house, I should be done by the time we reach there."

Running over to him, I grabbed his arm. "Are you finally going to tell me your story?" I could not believe it…it was about time!

"Ye speak another word, I'll not say a damn thing. D'ye understand me?" he sneered. Looking up at him, I bit down on my lips to try to stop the smile that wanted to form. Dogan shook his head and said, "Let's go, ye pain in the arse!"

Following suit beside him, I went, as we left the river behind us. It was difficult to keep my mouth shut like he wanted me to. I had to continually keep my lips bit down. Finally, I can get the answers I've wanted for months now. What was his life like before coming to Altecia? We walked for a few minutes before he finally started to speak.

"After learning everything today, first o' what ye told me earlier and now what yer mother said, I ha' decided to tell ye about me. At least my mother can finally stop nagging me about it." His massive chest expanded with air, and he let it out with a long puff. "Before the age of ten, my childhood was like any other's, I suppose. I was quite close wit both o' my parents at the time. I never attended any school back then. They taught me everything I needed to ken. 'Twas my father who taught me yer language." He gave me a quick glance. "He even taught me a language that he called 'the tongue o' ole.' I'm not sure why he taught it to me. To this day, I ha' never heard anyone speak it, and I ha' been to several different countries over the years."

"The night my parents died, some soldiers o' Alistair's army came to the house. I guess my parents owed a lot in back taxes, and they came to collect. They must ha' kent that they were gonna get killed because my mother brought me to the back door and ordered me to run. She told me to never come back and that she'll find me. I was young and dinna ken any different, so I ran like she told me to. I ran forever, it felt like, and then a soldier came running up beside me on a horse. The man was quick and grabbed hold the back o' my shirt, yanking me up in his saddle. Instantly, I started fighting and punching 'im. Somehow I kent my parents were dead, and I wanted 'im dead too because he was a soldier. The man finally got me under control and asked who I was. Yelling out my name to 'im and told 'im that I was gonna kill 'im fer killing my parents. He told me that his name is General Leland Tybalt and that he never ordered such a killing."

I could tell this was not coming easy for him. If it was anyone else, I would have touched them to give them strength; but with him, it might do the opposite, and he would stop talking. So I folded my hands together in front of me and kept my mouth shut while we walked.

"Instead o' going back to my house, the general brought me to his home. He introduced me to his wife and son Iniel. The two o' us were close to the same age and eventually became the best o' friends. No one ever knew o' my abilities. My mother came to me in a dream two days after she told me to run. She told me that she and my father ha' been killed. She also said that she'll always be near me and that I kent how to contact her if I needed to see 'er. I was warned to never let the general and anyone associated wit 'im ken o' my powers. I was also told not to leave, that I was safe fer the time being. I ended up living wit the Tybalts until I was ole enough to join the army."

I could not help it, I had to ask, "If you hated what the soldiers did to your family, then why did you go and join them?" If that was me, I could not picture myself going and joining the group that destroyed my family.

"I hated doing it, but 'twas the only way I figured to get in and find out who exactly killed my parents and to kill 'em myself. Of course, no one could remember anything because 'twas almost nine years by then. Fer the next several years, I lived by Alistair's law. I did what I was told. One of Alistair's mages made a serum that he wanted to test on some o' us men. I was one o' the few that were picked. They ended up taking us to a secluded part in the mountains. We were told that after taking it we should transform, and once we do, we ha' to fight one another to the death."

"Good God," I said horrified about what I was about to hear. "What the hell did you transform to?" Then quickly I bit down on my lip when Dogan glared down at me. I had to look away so he would not see me fighting the smile.

Thankfully, he continued, "It's some type o' wolf serum. We turned into half man, half beast. I grew to about seven feet tall, thick chestnut-color hair grew over most o' my body. My face transformed to the face o' a wolf, and my hands grew larger wit knife tips as nails." He held out his hand in front of him with his fingers spread apart.

"Are you jesting with me? Because if you are, I am so kicking your arse." His lips twitched at the last word I said, and when he did not answer, I asked, "Was it painful?"

"Oh aye, like hell." He paused. "After the transformation, the pain was gone. The strength and speed I gained was unimaginable. As we attacked one another, we realized that we couldna die. Every cut and stab wound we got would heal almost instantly. The general called me over to him and handed me his sword. He wanted me to cut the heads off the four other men, so I did wit no questions asked. The men were pleased wit the new weapon they now had. The power and strength became highly addictive to most men, me included. We got an order to attack a village up in the high country. There was word o' the villagers plotting against the king. There was a team o' twenty-five, and we all drank the serum. We entered that village and slaughtered everyone including women and children."

"Dogan," I said softly while looking at the ground as we walked. "How could you kill innocence like that? Did it not bother you when you were in that form?" I started to feel sick to my stomach at the mere thought of it.

"When ye are in that form, a different instinct takes over, and ye dinna care who ye hurt. It was not till the next day when it hit me what I just did. I was sick wit' myself and vowed to never take the serum again. It wasna long after, that my mother came to me, and she was fuming. She told me that what I was doing was unacceptable. 'Twas then that she told me about coming to Altecia. I told 'er hell no, there was no way I'm going to a country that's my enemy just so I can join their guard. I laughed and yelled at 'er. She did tell me that there was a woman in Burreck City wit' the same abilities, and that I had to teach 'er." Finally, he locked his intense eyes on me for the first time since he started talking.

"She told you about me?"

"Oh, aye." He nodded and continued. "She continued by telling me o' the young girl I needed to raise and that after I find 'er, eventually, 'er mother, who I'm destined to will find me too. I was so angry wit 'er and told 'er to leave me the hell alone. Before she left me that night, she said that I was gonna learn the truth about 'er death and 'twas going to cause me a lot o' pain. She said that she canna bear to witness me going through that, but if that's what it takes fer me to leave, so be it."

While he was quiet for a moment, I asked, "Is that why you growl all the time? Is the wolf still inside you?" Now that I really thought about it, his growl was very animal-like. As much as I tried to mimic him, I could never sound like him. A person should not be able to growl like he does.

Dogan gazed down at me and gave me a half of a smile. "It's a good possibility. I drank that serum more than anyone else at the time. I canna turn though, if that's what ye'r thinking. The transformation only lasted fer a handful o' hours. But ye do retain the strength and healing powers for days afterwards. I drank it so much that I became one o' the few that could change from beast to man and then back to beast in those several hours o' the transformation. Most men canna change back until the serum wears off."

"Does General Wolfe know what Alistair's army is capable of?" I asked him.

"I told the general everything when I came here. He's made sure to let the king know o' this information." Dogan took a deep breath. "Anyway, as I was saying, after that night, I dinna see my mother fer a long time. 'Twas months later when I ran into Iniel in the city. He too was a lieutenant. Iniel said that he was taking a few men to a household that owed a lot in taxes and asked me to come along. Since I had nothing to do, I went wit 'em. We came to a small farm deep in the woods. It sent chills through me because it reminded me a lot o' my childhood home. There was a young girl probably around five or six, and she bolted fer the house when she saw us coming. When we got off o' our horses, one of Iniel's men barged right through the door, which pissed me right off. There were sounds o' the young girl screaming inside. I was last to walk in the house and was horrified at the sight in front o' me."

Dogan hung his head down and stopped in his tracks. We were halfway across the pasture now, and I stopped myself to look at him. "Those goddamn monsters never even asked fer the money. They went there wit' the intensions o' killing, and that's what they did. When they slit the throat o' the man, two soldiers grabbed and dragged the young girl and woman out o' the room. I knew what they were about to do to 'em, and there was no way I was gonna be a part o' that. When I started yelling fer 'em to stop, Iniel took hold o' me and pushed me out o' the house. I asked 'im why the hell he was allowing this, and he said it was an order so people can see the consequences o' not paying their taxes. I screamed at 'im asking what would his father think o' 'im allowing the rape and murder o' a woman and bairn. 'Twas then that I found out the truth about my parents. Iniel told me that his father wouldna think twice about it since he was the one who allowed the same thing to happen to my family."

Dogan's fists were clunched, and he shook his head at the memory, "I completely lost it then. Tackling Iniel to the ground, I started to pound my fist to his face. My mother was raped before they killed her, and I lived under the same roof wit the man who ordered it. I was sick and angry wit myself, and I had the full intention o' killing Iniel right then and there. Somehow, he managed to grab his dagger." Dogan pointed to the scar over his eye. "'Twas 'im that did this to me. Instantly, I got off o' Iniel and back away from 'im while holding my right hand over my eye. There was so much blood, and the pain was excruciating, I thought he actually got my eye too. When Iniel finally stood up, I climbed onto my horse and told 'im that I was through wit 'im and his father. I also told 'im that a day'll come and I'll kill them both. I rode my horse hard for hours into the night. Stopping at the first house that still had lights streaming from their windows, I pounded on the door. I lost a lot o' blood and needed help to get patched up. Somehow, I manage to stop at a mage's house, and he fixed me up. He never gave me his name, but he did give me different recipes including the white paste that I gave to ye. The next morning, I rode to the port and got a job on the first ship I found that was heading to Burreck City." He gazed down at me and said, "Well, ye know the rest."

Dogan told more than I ever expected, and there had to be more yet. I was sure the longer we were around each other, the more he will tell me. As his eyes intensified on me, he asked, "When ye are looking at me, are ye still seeing my light?" I nodded yes, and he continued, "While ye'r looking at me, I want ye to imagine the aura shrinking down until there's no more light around me, all right?"

I did what he said, and to my shock, the color around him started to go down. After it vanished, I started to blink several times, and it never returned. "It's gone! How do I get it back?"

Dogan gave a throaty laugh at my reaction. "The same way: just think about seeing it, and it should reappear."

When I thought of seeing his aura, instantly the bright light engulfed his body. I jumped and started to laugh in excitement. "This is awesome! I can change it so easily."

He nodded at me. "Just make sure ye keep it blocked out more than anything. If ye use yer new vision all the time, ye'll come down wit severe headaches, and they'll make ye sick. Always keep that in mind."

Smiling, I grabbed hold of his hand. "Thank you again, Dogan for everything that you have taught me so far and for telling me some of your story. I know you did not live an easy life and you have done things that you regret. But you are here now, and I have a feeling that you are going to do great things for our country and that will some-day outweigh the things you did in the past."

Dogan gave me a horrified look as he jerked his hand out of mine. "Goddamn, woman!" He yelled, "What the hell has got into ye lately? I like it better when ye are a bitch!" He pushed me out of his way and marched toward the house.

I laughed loud and yelled, "I am still a bitch...I was just saying thank you!" I stood there for a moment smiling as Dogan with his red glow marched away.

Chapter 18

Payback

ater on that evening, I was lying on one of the couches with a book while Regner sat on the other with sleeping Ella in his arms. Our brothers and Dogan were over at his house playing games, gambling, and most likely drinking. The four of them tried to drag Regner and me with them, but we decided to stay in. When looking up from my book, Regner was watching me with a smile, then he looked back down at his beautiful daughter. For the last few nights, he had been able to settle Ella down by himself, and she was starting to sleep more during the night.

"I think Ella and I are going to try to sleep in our own house tomorrow night," he announced quietly without taking his eyes off her.

Laying my book down on my stomach, I smiled at him. "I think you two will be just fine, brother. You have been handling her all alone for the past couple nights." Looking down at my hands that lay on top of the book, I felt the sadness coming over me with the thoughts of having to leave soon. Even though I had been gone for several years, everything was just the same as I left it. I fell right back into my family's routine as if I had never left. It felt right here, like I belonged. Then at the same time, it felt right in Burreck City too.

"I know you are thinking about having to leave soon," he said softly. "We all wish you could stay, but we understand that you have to leave. I have talked to all our brothers and to Pa. We all agreed to make a point to come and see you every summer. There is no way any of us can go another three years before seeing you again."

Holding back the tears, I said, "That would be wonderful. I cannot go that long again either. There is a huge part of me that wants to stay and aches for this place when I am gone. On the other hand, I have a new family, so to speak, in Burreck City, and I miss them too now that I am gone. So it's like I cannot win either way."

"Burreck City is where you are meant to be, not here running a Hybrid farm or working as a blacksmith. You are destined to do greater things than that." Regner stood up and walked over to me. Bending down, he pressed his lips to my forehead. "Sweet dreams, sis. We will see you in the morning." Quickly, I sat up and he brought Ella down to my level so I could kiss her good-night.

"Sweet dreams to you too, Reg," I whispered and watched him walk to the stairs. I never mentioned to any of them of what I had learned about our mother. Even though they had a right to know, something inside of me was saying that this was not the time to talk about it. Plus, I was afraid that Regner and Ry already knew about that too. It was already bad enough that Pa had kept all of this from us younger three, but to learn that our two oldest brothers knew and never said anything actually bothered me more. So I just kept my mouth shut on the subject. After a long while of just sitting on the couch alone in the living room with thoughts of my mother, Rowan, and my friends back at the castle, the day finally caught up with me. Once I shut my eyes, there was no way of reopening them.

Suddenly, I was awakened by someone lifting my hands and sliding the book away from my stomach. The action startled me so much that I instantly sat up, which caused me sharp pain to my forehead. My eyes sprung open as I rubbed the pain away from my head. In the light glow of the lamp behind me, Ry was kneeling beside the couch, and he too was rubbing his head as he moaned and laughed at the same time. Still foggy from sleeping, I turn my head toward the front door at the noise of someone else laughing. Irving was bent at his waist laughing while he held his stomach.

"Sis just smacked her head off of Ry's, and you all just missed it. That was great," he laughed out the front door.

When I looked back at Ry, he started to laugh even harder, and at the same time he was trying his best to keep his voice down. It was then that I realized that my brother was drunk. No, wait a minute he was not drunk…the man was wasted. He reeked of it, and by the looks of Irving, he was wasted too.

Finally, I smiled at Ry. "Good God, Ry! You reek of wine. How much did you boys drink?"

He gave me a devilish smile and whispered, "All of it!"

"I beg your pardon?" I asked. "How much did Regner have over there?"

"He had a little over a case," he said and started to laugh even louder when I widened my eyes. I covered his mouth with my hand so he did not wake Pa, or Regner for that matter. He was going to be pissed when he found out his brothers drank all his wine.

With my hands still over his mouth, I brought my face close to his. "Our brother is going to kill you all, and I hope I am around to witness it." I started to laugh at his smiling eyes.

Ry pulled my hands down, "Sorry to disappoint you, but Wade and Irving are going to the city tomorrow to replace all the wine we drank plus more." He made a goofy face and then stood up. As he staggered back two steps, he extended his right hand to me. "Come, sis. We want you to see something."

"Right now?" I asked him. "It's late, and what is it that you want to show me?"

"You will see. It's a surprise." He gave me another devilish smile.

Rolling my eyes, and like the fool that I am, I took his hand and he pulled me up from the couch. There was a bad feeling in my gut as I made my way toward the front door. Irving, with an open bottle of wine in his hand, walked back out to the porch. As I got to the door, there was Wade at the bottom of the steps looking up at the stars. All of a sudden, I got a weird feeling, like I was about to be ambushed. Pausing at the door, I decided to demand from Ry what it was exactly that he wanted to show me. Just as I was about to turn around, with brute force, Ry shoved me out the door.

Stopping myself just before the steps, I quickly turned around and yelled, "What the hell, Ry!" Just as I turned that's when I caught sight of Dogan, and it was too late to run. I let out a quick high-pitched scream as the cold water saturated me. My whole body froze from the cold, and I was drenched. The ass that he was took a whole bucket full of water and dumped it over my head. While glaring at him, my teeth started to chatter. All four of them were roaring in laughter. Dogan was laughing so hard that he was bent over by the waist and had a hand on the railing to help keep him up. The man was just as wasted as my brothers. Finally, he looked at me with playful eyes and started cracking up all over again at the sight of me. "The look on yer face when the water hit ye made it all worth it," he laughed. It was odd hearing him laugh like that or seeing his eyes smiling for that matter. Since the day we met, I had never heard him laugh so hard.

"Go ahead! All of you laugh it up," I insisted as I waved my hand at them. Snatching the bottle out of Irving's hand, I jerked my head back and let the sweet wine just pour down my throat. With my eyes closed, I savored the sweetness left on my tongue. I finally opened them back up to find happy drunk Dogan still smiling at me.

"Paybacks can be a bitch sometimes, lass." With his huge dimpled smile, he extended his hand to me. "There, we're even now!"

Ignoring the temptation of hugging him so he too would be all wet, I just took his tingling hand and shook. "We are even, you bastard," I smirked at him. "I cannot believe how wasted you are."

"'Tis yer brothers' fault." He laughed a little and grabbed hold of the railing again to help steady himself. "After I lost what money I had on me, all there was left to do was drink." He kept swaying back and forth.

"All right, sis," Regner said from the doorway with a sleepy smile. My scream most likely woke him up. I was surprised Pa was not beside him. "Was it Dogan or Wade?"

"'Twas me," Dogan said leaning against the rail. "I had to get 'er back fer earlier today. 'Twas Wade's idea though." He turned his head toward Wade, who was still at the bottom of the steps, and laughed as Wade yelled at him.

"Oh, you dirty bastard," Wade yelled. "You never rat on a brother like that!" His yelling only made Dogan laugh more.

"I am not surprised being that you had done that to me numerous times while we were growing up," I said to him as I marched down the stairs. Back in the day, I probably would have thrown myself at him and tackled him to the ground. Instead, I stopped at the bottom step and rung out my hair over his head.

He smiled. "I guess I do deserve that." Wade gazed at me with his drunken eyes. "Do you really have to leave us again?"

Giving him a small smile and lightly slapping him on his cheek, I said, "Yes, brother. We will be leaving within the next few days."

His eyes widened at the shock of my words. "You cannot! What about Regner?" He pointed up the stairs to him.

I turned to look at Dogan, as he started to speak. "Wade's right, Lee. We dinna need to leave yet." I could not help but smile at him. The fool liked it here, and he too was not ready to leave.

"All right, everyone," Regner shouted as we all quieted down. He closed his eyes for a moment and began to speak again in a softer tone. "I am still grieving, but I am doing a lot better now. Ella settles down for me now without sis's help. Brothers, she needs to go back to the queen. That's where she is meant to be." He turned to Dogan. "And you out of all of us should understand that." Dogan nodded his head to my brother, and Regner continued, "Tomorrow night, Ella and I are going to sleep in our own house. Believe me, brothers, if I could, I would never let our sister leave again, but we have to let her go."

For the next hour or so, the six of us sat on the porch talking about this and that. Ry gave me a blanket off the couch so I can wrap my damp body in it. We did a lot of laughing and just enjoyed each other's company. I felt like the luckiest woman in the world to be raised with such amazing, wonderful men. Back in the day, I would not have thought that, but now that I am older, I see how truly blessed I was.

Sometime during all the talking, I ended up falling back asleep in the chair. I sort of woke up when half my body got a tingling feeling. Opening my eyes halfway, Dogan had me cradled in his arms as he walked through the house. Laying my head back against his chest, I said in my head. "*Thank you and do not drop me, you drunken fool!*"

His happy laugh filled my head. *"As tempting as that sounds, I'll try to refrain from doing it."* Laughing softly to myself, I ended up falling back to sleep before he even put me to bed.

The next night, I took a stroll outside and went to the fence line. After climbing to sit on top of it, I got a good view of Regner's house that was along the wood's line. There was a light twinkle in the front window that reminded me of a tiny star in the night sky. Regner lit that very candle every night since the death of Flora. It is said that the light of the candle will help the souls of the deceased to find their way back home. To this day, my father still lights a candle every night for my mother. I knew now that you did not have to do such a thing because our loved ones are all around us. They did not need the candle to find us; they knew exactly where we are.

There was a noise coming from behind me so I glanced back to see a huge shadowy figure with a dog close to his side. As he made his way toward me, I said, "Brute has taken a real liking towards you. I think he's going to miss you when we leave."

Dogan reached down and rubbed the dog's shaggy ear as he reached the fence. "Aye, I ha' takin' a likin' to 'im myself." He was to my right as he crossed his arms on the top of the fence. I got a quick whiff of his clove scent. The man stared out to the right toward Regner's house. "Ye think he's gonna be all right?" he asked it so quietly that I barely heard him.

Gazing back at my brother's home, I took a deep breath. "Yes, he's still grieving, and he will be for a long time, but he is a Bayard, he will make it through this." I gazed back out into the pasture. My eyes were now adjusted to the darkness, and I had sight now of all the Hybrids scattered about. "I am thinking about leaving in about two days or so. I told Pa today while I was in the shop."

"Aye, he caught me in the barn before dinner and told me." I glanced down at him, and he continued to look forward. "If ye feel ye are ready to leave, then we'll leave."

"It's not so much that I am ready, but that I have to," I said, and he nodded his head in agreement. Ara emerged through the darkness and came straight toward us, snorting in excitement. She came alongside the fence and rubbed her body across my legs that were hanging over. My beautiful Hybrid stopped there, and the two of us instinctly reached out and petted her. That was all she wanted, and that was the intention.

Lifting my right leg, I laid it over her and pulled myself onto her back so that I was on her backward. Stretching out my legs on her back, I crossed my ankles as I lay slowly back. My shoulders and head rested on the base of her neck as I laid my folded hands on my belly. As I stared up at the starry sky, she started to slowly walk. I used to lie on her like this countless times before I moved away. She would slowly travel around the pasture as I enjoyed the tranquility of it all.

She must have sensed that I had stuff on my mind because she did not travel far from Dogan and the fence. Ara kept circling back; on the third trip toward him, Dogan finally said something, "She's one o' a kind. D'ye realize that?"

"Oh aye." I smiled as I continued staring at the dark starry sky.

"That canna be comfortable." He spoke softly again. It was odd to hear his voice so gentle. The softness did not match his form or temperament.

"Well, actually, it is." I gave him a soft smile as we strolled past him. "It may be uncomfortable for a man of your size, but for me, it's a perfect fit. I can stare up watching for falling stars and feel her muscles move underneath me while she strolls around. It's quite soothing."

"I ha' noticed that ye talk to 'er more in my tongue than in yer own language," he stated. "Why is that?"

I let Ara start to loop back around toward Dogan before I spoke. "I have always liked the Salvie language, so ever since Ara was a foal, I started teaching her commands in that language. I speak to her in mine, but she responds better to Salvie." I reached up over my head and touched her mane, "Right, Ara girl! You like it when I speak to you like this," saying it in Salvie, and she let out a snort in agreement. I laughed and patted the side of her stomach.

Ara came to a stop beside the fence, and Dogan was only a foot or so away. He was about eye level to me now, but I continued to look up while I spoke, "Before you came down to the river yesterday, I asked my mother why my brothers did not have the same gift."

"Well, what did she say?" he asked, still having the softness in his voice.

A star shot across the sky, and I saw that as a sign. It gave me the confidence to continue on what had been on my mind all day. "She said that the blood of Fae runs through me like you, Sterling, and Row. Whereas for my brothers, it's my father's blood of mortality that runs through them. So I guess what I have been thinking is…" It was suddenly difficult for me to say the word out loud.

"Ye'r wondering if we four are going to be immortal," he whispered.

I let out the breath I was holding. "Exactly."

"Ye ha' yer locket. Why dinna ye ask 'er?"

I lightly laughed at him as I looked down at it. "A dozen times today I tried to ask her, but then got too scared to know the answer. I do not think I am ready for that answer yet." Finally, I turned my head to the left and locked my eyes to his. I wondered if he realized how amazing his eyes were. Even though they almost appeared black in the night, they were still intense to look at. I asked, "Do you think your ma is from Faery too?"

Dogan's relaxed face suddenly got irritated. "Why in God's name would ye ask me that? My parents are Salvatorians!" Ah, there's the Dogan I am starting to know so well. I was beginning to think he was starting to soften up.

"Are you going to tell me that you did not notice that our mothers had similar accents?" I asked calmly. There was no way I was going to let his anger faze me. I could tell that he was thinking it over because his eyes looked to be somewhere else. Taking the locket in my hand, I said, "I can ask her if you would like."

That snapped him out of it because his eyes glared at me. "Don't ye dare ask that question," he hissed. "If ye'r not ready to learn if we're immortal or not, then I'm not ready to find out o' another thing my mother has kept from me."

Laying the locket back on my chest, I said, "Fair enough." Patting Ara on her side, I said in Salvie, "Come on, Ara. Let's go for a long walk this time." Ara turned, and we slowly left the fence and Dogan behind.

Chapter 19

Farewell

The sun was rising, and there were no clouds in the sky. It was a perfect way to start our journey back home to the city. As I walked out of the house with Pa and Estelle, Dogan and my brothers were standing around by our horses. My saddle had more on it then the day that I arrived. There was bag with some of my old clothes so I could have more pants at home. I was not sure when I would ever get to wear them, but it would be good to have them just in case. With my cloak draped over my arm, I strolled toward them.

"Wow! If I came across the two of you on the road, I would definitely steer clear of you, that is for sure," Ry said, and I started to chuckle. I was covered in weapons, from the knives on my legs and in my boots; I also had both my swords on. Wrapped over my other shoulder was the bow and arrows that Dogan gave me for my birthday. Dogan was wearing his dagger and the swords I made him while his original sword was wrapped up and tied to the saddle.

Ara hit me with her head as I came up to her. Smiling, I ran my hand down her neck and threw my cloak over my saddle. I turned around only to find my family watching me with sorrowful eyes. This was always the hardest part...saying good-bye. Going to each of them individually, I hugged and kissed them. Pa and Estelle ended up hugging and kissing me at the same time.

"I will be praying for safe travels for you and Dogan," Pa said. "Keep writing to me, and I promise never to go this long without seeing you again." Like Estelle, Pa also had tears in his eyes.

"Thanks, Pa." I squeezed them both and cried. "I am going to miss you all so much, maybe even more than before." Pulling back, I gave them both another kiss. Saving Regner for last, I gazed over at him and Ella. There was no vision through the tears as I wrapped my arms around his waist. He pressed his cheek to the side of my head as he squeezed me with his one arm.

"I wish I could take you and Ella with me," I murmured.

While rubbing his hand up and down my back, he said, "I know, sis, but we will all see each other again soon. We promise that."

"I love you," I whispered.

"I love you too," he whispered back. Wiping my eyes clear, I gazed down at Ella. She was so beautiful. I slept countless nights in the last month with her in my arms. It tears at my heart to say goodbye to her. Sniffling, I kissed her precious face. "I love you, Ella. I am going to miss you so much." Looking back at Regner, he had tears rolling down his cheeks. Taking my hands to his face, I wiped them away. "Make sure you talk about me all the time to her, so when she does see me again, she will remember me."

Regner gave me a small smile. "I promise. Ella will know who her aunt is." He gave me a kiss on the forehead. "Safe travels, sis." He looked over my shoulder to Dogan, who had been saying his goodbyes to everyone else. Dogan came over to us and extended his hand to him. My brother pushed it away and wrapped his one arm around him in a half hug. He hesitated at first, but he hugged him back. "I know we had a rough start in the beginning, but I know you are a good man. Make sure you keep an eye on my sister for me."

"I'll try my best," replied Dogan. Regner nodded to him, and Pa and Estelle came over. She took Dogan's face and brought it down. Estelle gave him a light kiss on the lips before wrapping her arms around his neck. He flashed his dimpled smile as he lifted her up off the ground, causing her to yell. We all laughed as he kept her off her feet for several moments before placing her back down.

"I'll miss ye, Estelle." He gave her a broad smile. "Especially yer cooking!" Taking both her hands, he kissed them.

"You will be greatly missed here too, Dogan. Please take care of our Lee," she said, lightly crying. He gave me a softer smile and nodded. Pa wrapped his arms around Dogan, and he hugged back with no hesitation like with Regner.

"You are a good, hardworking man, son. This is for you, and I do not want you to argue with me that you do not need it." Pa handed him a purse, which I knew was full of coins because he gave me mine before I walked out of the house.

When Dogan looked inside, his eyes widened, "Randall, what's this for? This is too much for me to accept."

"It is your month's wages for working with us. You worked just as hard as my own sons, so I am paying you as I pay my sons."

"Ye dinna understand, Randall. I dinna even get close to half o' this in a month as a guard. This is too much, besides I'll be getting paid fer the time I was gone when I get back to Burreck City," he said as he tried to hand the coins back to Pa, who pushed his hand away.

"Well, I am paying you for the work you did on the farm and around the house, and then you will get paid again for the training you did with Lee. Just accept it, Dogan, because I will be offended if you try giving it back again," Pa insisted. Dogan growled in protest.

Reluctantly, he put the money in his pocket and extended his hand to Pa, and he took hold. "Thank ye, Randall. 'Twas a true pleasure to get to know ye all this past month."

"It was a pleasure for us too. Thank you for everything you taught Lee so far. Keep it up!" Pa smiled and then winked at me.

Dogan nodded. "I will, sir."

Turning to our horses, Pa helped me into my saddle. Looking at my family, I blew them all kisses. "I love you all, and I will see you again soon!" They all yelled out that they loved me too, then I looked over to Dogan. "Well, are you ready to go."

"I'm as ready as I'm ever gonna be," he said and gave his horse a swift kick, and off he went. Saying good-bye one last time, I kicked

Ara into a run so we could catch up to Dogan. It took all of me not to look back at them again. My heart was aching terribly, and I knew if I looked back one more time, I would not continue. Instead, I would turn around and stay with them forever, and I knew I could never do that.

Later that evening, we lay around a fire in the woods ways away from the road. Using my cloak as a blanket, I brought it up tighter around my neck. It had cooled down considerably since the sunset. While staring into the flames, I had thoughts of Rowan dancing around in my head. I would be able to see him tomorrow, and the more I thought about it, the more I realized that when we get to Hebridge, it would only be around midday.

"Dogan?" I asked softly. I was not sure if he was asleep yet.

"What is it, woman?" he reponded with annoyance in his voice.

"I know when we make it to Hebridge tomorrow, it will only be around midday if we are lucky. So, I was wondering if you would mind if we stopped just for a short while and then we could continue on our journey?"

Dogan sighed. "I was planning on staying the night there tomorrow anyway. It'll save us from sleeping like this. We'll leave at first light, and we should make it to Burreck City before dark."

"Really?" I asked in excitement. There was a feeling of butterflies in my stomach with the thought of sleeping in Rowan's arms again.

"Aye, now go to sleep," he growled.

Waiting a moment, I whined out his name again with a smile on my face. "Dogan?"

"Bloody hell, woman," he roared and sat up to glare at me. "What is it now?"

I could not help but smile at the sight of him. His intense eyes were glaring like usual at me, but it was different if I let his glow show through. Dogan was annoyed with me, but with his deep red, I actually liked the looks of him. Suddenly, I shook the thought out of my head and made his aura disappear. There had been a question gnawing at my brain for the past few days, and I wanted it answered, "What is the purpose of our gift? Can it be used for the greater good?"

Rolling his eyes, he fell back down on to his back. Letting out a huff of breath, he said, "D'we really need to talk about this now, because I ha' better things to do…like sleep fer instance," he groaned out.

"I want to know. This question has been bugging me for days now," I said, staring into the flames. The man got so aggravated with me, and I knew he was tired because so was I, but I needed to know.

"And ye are just asking me now?" he asked in frustration. "Good God lass, if ye had just asked earlier, we could be sleeping right now."

"You were constantly with my brothers, and I was not about to ask you in front of them. I decided to wait until we were on the road, and I forgot to ask until now," I explained.

"Bloody hell." He paused, and I smiled as I lay there, continuing to stare at the fire. "I can sense yer smiling, so wipe it off yer face," he growled as I shook my head no. Dogan fell silent for a moment. Just as I began to think he was not going to talk about it, he finally spoke. "I ha' met a variety o' mages over the years…"

"Fae," I corrected him.

"Fae," he growled. "And none o' 'em can see auras like we can. I'll teach ye the meanings o' all the colors in time, but ye'll be able to get a read on a person before ye actually talk to 'em. As ye already know, we can talk to the deceased. We might even be able to talk to God himself, but I'm not fer certain because I ha' never had the guts to ask. Now that ye ha' released yer energy yourself, ye'r now able to tell when ye face another *Fae*. They vibrate wit' power, and I'm sure we feel the same to 'em. 'Tis hard to explain the feeling. Ye'll just know when ye come in contact wit' one. Also. when ye ha' yer core energy released, no one can touch ye."

"I peg your pardon? What do you mean no one can touch me?" I asked shockingly.

"When ye ha' it released, it makes an invisible barrier around ye. Only people like us can walk through. Eventually, when ye can do it wit yer eyes open, then it can be another weapon to use to protect the queen wit. If ye are holding on to her when ye release it, then it'll protect ye both, but if ye should let go o' her, then she'll be thrown from the energy. No other person or weapon can pierce it."

"Really?" I started to laugh at the shock of it. "That's amazing! Can I still throw my knives accurately? Or would they go off track."

He paused. "I...I do not know. I have never tried it!" All of a sudden, Dogan jumped up to his feet. He did it in such a fluid motion that it did not seem possible of a man his stature.

"What are you doing?" I asked as he snatched his dagger from his belt.

"I hate not knowing the answer to a question. I ha' to try it now, or I'll never sleep," he said in frustration with himself. Even though I was watching him without looking at the color around him, I could still see when he released his core. The bright deep-red exploded from his body and engulfed him in at least a ten-foot-diameter dome. As much as I tried to block out the energy, I could not seem to do it when it was out like this. Holding the dagger by the tip of the blade, he brought it up by his shoulder. Once he flung his hand forward, he released the dagger from his fingertips. The blade flew through the air at the speed of lightning and lodged itself in the trunk of a tree. Never in my life had I seen a knife thrown with such force. Jumping to my feet, I scurried over to Dogan. Just before I reached him, his energy shrunk back down to his body, and the deep red disappeared.

"How in the hell did you throw that? The speed that blade flew is not normal," I said in astonishment.

Dogan looked down at me with his intense eyes and a small evil smile. "Ye seen me throw knives before, and they never came close to that speed. 'Twas my energy! Once the dagger left my touch, the energy expelled it, and it still hit where I wanted it to." He marched over to the tree, and I followed suit. More than half of the dagger was lodged in the tree. Dogan took hold of the hilt and pulled back. The dagger did not budge as he grunted.

"Bloody hell, ye ha' to be jesting wit me," he yelled. A smile spread across my face as I brought my arms across my chest. This should be interesting to watch. I did not care how big and strong Dogan was. That dagger was in there deep, and he was going to have a hell of a time loosening it up.

After a few minutes of hitting the hilt up and down with his fist, the dagger lost its purchase with the tree. That was a disappointment to me; I was hoping that it would have taken him longer to get it out. He pointed the dagger at me. "Ye need to learn how to release yer energy wit yer eyes open. Ye'll be able to keep the queen safe and still kill whoever wishes 'er harm. I want ye to try right now," Dogan demanded.

I laughed in his face. "Hell no, Dogan! I am too tired to try that right now. I will wait until we get home."

"I dinna give a damn," he glared. "I was too tired to talk, but I still did!"

"Talking does not take too much energy, but releasing my core does. My answer is no, and I am going to get some sleep." Turning my back to him, I started to walk back to the fire. The damn fool took hold of my shoulder and spun me back around.

Dogan grabbed the wrist of the hand I brought up to hit him with and bent down with angry eyes. "What did I tell ye about walking away from me?"

"Let go of me!" Matching his angry eyes, I brought up my other hand. The fool took hold of that hand too before I could hit him. Well, it looked like we were getting back to our old ways with each other. Yelling in frustration, I said, "Goddammit, Dogan Ramstien! Let go of me this very instant!" With my hands bound in his grip, I lifted my right foot quickly and jammed the heel of my boot with as much force I could muster on top of his foot. Dogan's eyes clamped shut as he groaned from the pain.

Releasing my wrists, he shoved me back. "Ye can be a real bitch sometimes...d'ye know that?" he yelled.

Marching back to the fire, I yelled over my shoulder. "You are a bastard all the time...do you know that?"

Once I got myself situated back on the hard ground, Dogan glared at me with a curled-up lip as he went over to his side of the fire. "I pity the poor bastard ye are destined to," he snapped. "I would sooner slit my own throat than be stuck wit a woman like yeself." My jaw dropped in disgust as I watched him cover himself with his cloak and turned his back to the fire. Am I that bad of a woman that my own soul mate, whoever he may be, will hate me? I know that I am not very ladylike, but I have been working on that since I took my position beside the queen. But after living almost fifteen years with only men, it's hard to change your ways. How am I supposed to sleep now? The man can really drive me crazy sometimes. To get myself to stop thinking of the fool and what he said, I tried to think of something that made me happy. With a smile on my face, I closed my eyes and envisioned myself kissing Rowan again, and the hoots from the owls in the distance finally helped me drift off to sleep.

A knock came from my chamber door. A moan escaped while dragging myself out of bed. Who is calling at this hour of night? Then my heart skipped a beat when it occurred to me that something might have happened, maybe to the queen. Suddenly quickening my step, I reached for the door.

The sight on the other side took my breath away. The man was gorgeous, dressed in a long white robe and encased in white light. He had to be as tall and muscular as Dogan. Even his long wavy hair resembled his. The smile he greeted me with was contagious, and I beamed a smile back as I asked, "Can I help you, sir?"

His smile grew wider. "Leelah Bayard, it's a pleasure to finally met ye." He spoke with an accent that was similar to Salvie, but at the same time, it was different. He reached out and took both of my hands. His touch tingled against my hands and grew stronger as he pressed his lips to them.

The heat rose in my cheeks, and I quickly averted my eyes downward. "I am sorry, sir, but who are you, and how do you know me?"

"I have known of ye since the day ye were born, and as of late, ye are all my wife talks about." Still holding my hands, he lightly bowed his head. "My name is Steaphan Ramstien."

Smiling, I said, "Dogan's father." He nodded, keeping his eyes locked on mine, and I continued, "I can see the resemblance. He has your eyes and hair. You too share the same powers." He nodded again. "Why is it Dogan has never mentioned you? He told me his parents were killed, but he never told me that like his mother, his father possessed the same gift."

"My son still has a lot of anger running through him. He doesn't speak to me, and I cannot explain why because that is for him to tell ye.

Sometime in the future, he will tell ye why." He kissed my hands again. "I know my son can be rough at times, but someday, when he finds his mate, he will soften a bit. Then he will be more tolerable when it comes to ye, Sterling, and Rowan. Ye will see. Now I need to go because there is a storm coming. Remember, like yer mother and my wife, all ye need to do is call for me and I will be here."

"Wait." I held up my hand to him. "Can you at least tell me this," Looking down, trying to figure out how to ask him, but as he lifted my chin gently up, I asked, "Were you and Cici born and raised in Salvatoria?" He never answered my question with words but with a smile. The beautiful smile across his lips said it all...that my assumption was right...they were not originally from Salvatoria, and then everything went pitch-black.

Suddenly, I was awakened with a loud crack of thunder. The sound startled me so much that I instantly sat up. I looked over to Dogan, who was also jerked awake, as I tightened my cloak around me because of the cold. It was cool in the beginning of the night, but now, it was freezing. The wind was starting to pick up considerably. The sky was still black, but it had to be close to morning by the size of our fire.

"Why is it so cold? It's almost the beginning of summer, it should not be this cold," I yelled to him.

"I dinna ken why, but it doesn't sound good. Hurry! It's gonna hit here soon, we need to get going. There's no shelter, so the quicker we get to Hebridge, the better," he literally screamed over the wind.

Not arguing with him, I quickly got up and start putting on my weapons. After tying on my cloak, I put my bow on my back. Not bothering to eat once we had ourselves ready, we mounted our horses. As we weaved them through the trees, the flash of lightning helped light the way. Once we made it back to the road, we kicked our horses in high speed with no hesitation. It was not long after that light rain started to fall.

After an hour of running, the daylight started to light our way, and we got hit with the downpour. My cloak was soaking wet like the rest of me. My hood was stuck to my head. The rain was freezing, and my body was starting to stiffen due to the cold. My jaw hurt from all the chattering it was doing. I tried to clamp my jaw shut, but it did not help.

"Dogan! I am freezing," I yelled to him over the wind.

"I ken, but there's nowhere fer us to go," he yelled back. "We canna build a fire in this!"

"I do not know if I can go on much farther!" My stomach ached from my muscles being so tight. All I wanted was warmth…heat.

Dogan turned his head and glared at me. His hair was plastered against his forehead and around the side of his face. "If ye wanna to see the lieutenant…ye'll keep on going!" Closing my eyes to see Rowan in my mind, I tried to block out the cold rain. That did not last long though because another crack of lightning jolted me out of my vision of him. More chills raked through my body that was not caused by the freezing rain. I thought about the dream I woke up from and realized that it was not a dream. Dogan's father came and visited me. The more I thought about it, the more my body shook. Trying my best to push the thought to the back of my head, I decided to talk to Dogan about it once I was no longer cold and wet.

Chapter 20

No Rule Against Touching

J t was about late morning by the time we reached the edge of Hebridge. The storm still had not let up. I was hunched over in my saddle, and my whole body was shaking uncontrollably from the cold. Never slowing down the horses, we steered them toward the stables behind the barracks. Dogan flew off his horse and landed on the sloppy ground; he kicked up mud as he ran to pull open the stable doors. Once he had it open wide enough, I rode Ara in. The instant relief from the rain and wind was wonderful. Slowly, I slid myself off the saddle. The white hair on Ara's legs and belly were covered thick in mud. My whole body was cramping up from being so tense for that last few hours.

As Dogan pulled the stable doors shut, he froze once he really looked at me. Marching over, he took hold of my arm. I knew he could feel the tension in it. When his eyes widened, he pulled down my hood and pressed his warm tingling hand against the side of my neck.

"Good God, woman! Ye are ice-cold," he yelled angrily.

"I tr-ried t-telling you," I said, chattering.

"Get yer arse in the barracks," he ordered. "I'll take care o' yer horse."

Doing as I was told, I went out the side door and bolted across the yard to the back door of the barracks. Not bothering in to knock, I burst through the door. Startling only a few men that were in the living room, one of them ran over to me.

"My lady! Are you all right?" he asked me.

Shaking my head no, I said, "I am fre-e-ezing! I cannot s-s-stop s-shaking!"

Taking me by my shoulders, he guided me toward the hall, "Lieutenant, hurry," he yelled. There was a sound of a chair moving against the floor in his office. Just before we made it to the door, Rowan walked out.

"Lee," he gasped with a horrified look on his face. "I cannot believe you were out in this." He touched my face, and I pressed my cheek into his sizzling hand. "Bloody hell, you are freezing, love!" Before I could say anything, he took hold of my hand and pulled me toward his room. The heat in his room from the fireplace was welcoming.

"Where is Dogan?" he inquired.

"With…horses," was all I could manage out of my lips.

"Is he in the stables?"

I nodded yes to his question, and he walked back out to the hall. Rowan yelled out orders for someone to go out and give Dogan a hand. Walking back in, he shut the door behind him.

"Look at you! You have got a bloody armory on you!"

"Do not m-make me laugh," I said slowly and gave him a smirk.

"We need to get you out of these wet clothes before you get yourself sick. May I?" he asked as he laid a hand on the straps across my chest. I nodded yes to him. Rowan lifted my bow and arrows over my head. As he started to unbuckle the sword that was on my back, I tried to kick off one of my leather boots. Since they ran up just below my knee, I could not manage to take them off without using my hands. Looking down at my hands, I realized that they were still in the shape of holding the reins. It hurt as I tried to straighten my fingers out.

Once Rowan took off my cloak, he reached down for the boot I tried to take off. Laying a hand on his shoulder, I lifted my foot up.

He yanked the boot off and did the same to the other. While he was down there, he unstrapped the knives off my thighs. In doing so, he sent a different type of chill through my body. If I was not shaking already, he would have noticed it.

Standing back up, he gazed at me with loving eyes as he unbuckled my sword on my hip. He placed the sword with my other weapons. Never taking his eyes off mine, he pulled out my shirt from my trousers. Taking hold of that and the undershirt, he pulled them over my head. Heat started to rise up my neck into my face as I stared back at him. Instinctively, my arms went up and covered my bare breasts. No man has ever seen me naked before. Still looking at my face, he unbuttoned my trousers. He pulled them down and yanked them off my legs. Turning to his bed he pulled back the covers.

"Come, Lovalee, get in," he whispered. I wanted to quickly jump into bed so I could no longer be naked in front of him, but my body would not allow that action; so I tiptoed over, and I crawled into the bed. Lying on my right side and bringing up my legs to my chest, Rowan tucked the blankets tight around me. Burying my face into the pillow I prayed for the shaking to stop. I watched Rowan with half opened eyes at first as he laid my wet clothes on a rack in front of the fireplace. Closing them again, I tried to think of the hot summer sun in hopes it would stop the chills.

After a while, there was pressure on the other side of the bed. The blankets were lifted a little, and then I felt Rowan's hot tingling body against mine. On his side, he pulled me into his bare chest. When I straightened my legs down, he wrapped his legs around them. It was then that I realized that all he was wearing was his braies, which was a thin clothed undergarment.

With my face buried in his chest, I jerked my eyes open and said in my head, *"You are practically naked!"*

Rowan let out a soft laugh. *"Yes, love, I am! My body heat will help warm you up faster. I will try to behave."* Smiling, I pressed myself harder against him and took in his scent. God, I loved this man! Why could it not be him?

It was a good half hour by the time the shaking stopped and my muscles finally relaxed. Pulling my head from his chest, I looked at him. With his head on the pillow, he gazed back lovingly. Bringing my left hand up to the back of his head, I pulled my mouth to his. We both moaned instantly when we deepened the kiss. The man sent jolts through me that I had never experienced before. With our bodies pressed close together, I could feel him growing with excitement.

The next thing I knew, he rolled me on my back and was on top of me. As he worked his mouth on my jaw and neck, he slowly made his way down. I closed my eyes to savor the feeling his lips caused on my skin. When he covered his mouth on my breast, the sensation nearly took my breath away. All of a sudden, he stopped, and I found him looking at me with wide eyes.

"Holy hell, Lee! I am so sorry!" He rolled off me and onto his back beside me. "I lost control." He lifted his hands and covered his face as he cursed some more. Rolling onto my side, I pried his hands away from his face so he could look at me.

"Please, Row, do not be sorry! I want you to lose control!" I looked at him with pleading eyes.

"We can never have sex, Lee. You have to understand that." He looked at me with sympathy.

"I do understand, but…" Running my hand through the thick brown-reddish curls on his chest, I could feel the chills rake through his body. My hand traveled down his toned stomach and went under the blankets and inside his braies, where I took hold of him. A smile formed on my lips as his mouth slightly opened and his eyes widened. Bringing my mouth to his ear, I whispered, "Can we pleasure each other by touching? Or is there a rule against that too?"

He let out a moan and said in a husky voice, "No, there is no rule against touching." Rowan quickly pushed me onto my back and propped himself up on his elbow beside me. He had a beautiful smile as he touched my face and ran his fingertips down my neck. My whole body felt like it was on fire. "I have dreamt of touching you like this for years," he said so quietly that I barely heard him. Ever so lightly, he traced his fingers around my breasts and lingered there for a while before slowing moving down my stomach. His hand went down to my inner right thigh. His tingling touch was sending jolt after jolt throughout my whole body.

Never in my life had I experienced such feelings…such need. My whole body was aching for his touch; I never wanted him to stop. Rowan locked his blue-gray eyes to mine when he started to move his hand back up my thigh. Instinctively, I opened myself wider for him. Once his hand was where I wanted it to be, a light cry escaped my lips at the tingling sensation. My eyes widened as he slowly started to move his fingers, causing a new pleasure, and he covered my mouth with his to muffle the cry that started to escape. Instantly, I wrapped my arms around him, never wanting to let go.

For a short time, it felt like we were the only ones that existed in our world as we explored each other's body. We made love for the first time in the only way knew how, without having actual sex. Even though I still wanted to experience that, what just happened between the two of us was amazing. I would not trade that for the world.

While on my stomach and laying my head on his, he ran his fingertips up and down my spine. I would be happy to just stay here forever. Finally opening my eyes, I gazed out to him. The man had a relaxed smile on his face as he propped his other arm up behind his head. Reaching up, I touched the heart charm around his neck. There was a thought of wondering if he would always wear it even after he met the one he was destined to be with.

"I promise I will never take it off, Lovalee. Even after I find the one I am meant to be with." He spoke softly.

Smiling, I whispered, "Stay out of my head."

Feeling his fingers at the back of my neck, he lightly pulled at the chain. "This is new." The locket! There was so much I needed to tell him. Rolling on my back, I lay my head back down on his stomach. Looking down at the locket that was nestled between my bare breasts, I turned my head to the left and fixed my eyes on him. Then I had to close them when I felt his finger circling around one of my nipples. Swallowing a moan, I opened my eyes to find him gazing down at me in excitement.

Trying to block the thought of touching him for a moment, I said, "Take your thumb and press it on top of the locket." When he did so, the locket made a clicking sound, and Rowan lifted his hand. Slowly, it opened up, revealing the paper inside. He gave me a questionable look. Smiling, I said, "Since you opened it, the message is for you. Go ahead and take it." Gently, he took the paper and unfolded it. He was silent for a moment, and then I could feel a chill rake down his body. "What does it say?"

Rowan handed me the paper; his eyes were wide in shock. "How is that possible?" The tiny writing read,

> Cherish these moments you have with her because you know it can't last forever. Once she finds out who her soul mate is, then it will have to stop.

Sorrow filled my heart because I still wanted him as my soul mate. How could I ever love a man more than I love at this very moment? Not wanting to feel sad, I tried my best to push that feeling away. The time I got to spend with him, I wanted to be joyous and loving. Refolding the paper, I replaced it.

"Now, ask a question in your head and reopen the locket," I said to him.

Locking his eyes to mine, his beautiful voice filled my head. *"Please tell me that I will have other times to be with her instead of today?"*

Never taking my eyes off him, he reached and opened the locket. He brought up the paper, and a smile ran across his face as he handed me the note.

> You two have plenty more nights to come. Do not worry about that!

With the heat rising up to my face, Rowan laughed as he rubbed a hand down my cheek. "How is that locket possible, and where did it come from?"

"Rowan, I have learned so much in this last month that it's not even funny."

"Well, Lovalee"—he gave me a smile—"I am listening." After replacing the paper, I repositioned myself alongside him so I could lay my head on his shoulder. Rowan pulled up the blankets to cover up our bare skin. I told him everything. Starting with meeting my mother for the first time and how the locket used to belong to my grandmother. I also told him about the Fae and how their bloodlines run strong through us and who my grandmother was. There was also the story that Dogan told me about his life. I told him about that too and made him promise that he would keep it to himself for the time being. I ended by telling him what happened last night and how Dogan's energy expelled the dagger with such speed and accuracy.

"I cannot believe you are a princess of the Fae." He started to laugh in shock as he stared up at the beams on the ceiling. As we lay in each other's arms in silence, I could feel him pondering all I told him. He was still trying to register it all. That was when I remembered about the flowers I found in my room on my birthday. I turned my face to him and smiled.

"Pardon?" he smiled back.

"Thank you for the flowers and note I got on my birthday. I loved it!"

His smile broadened. "I take it that Dogan did well then by picking the flowers?"

Narrowing my eyes, but still smiling, I asked, "Are you telling me that you did not tell him what to get me?"

"I just said to pick a bouquet of different wildflowers." He paused. "Why? What did he get you?"

"Lilacs," I whispered. "How did he know?" I never told him that they were my favorite.

Rowan let out a hoot. "Nicely done, Dogan! I never even thought of your flower being in bloom right now. You must have really loved me, thinking that I remembered that. Do not get me wrong because I know it's your favorite. I just did not think of it at the time." He rolled to his side and buried his face in my neck and mumbled, "It's probably because you always smell of the flower. That's why he got those for you from me." There was a feeling of his smiling lips against my skin.

Laughing, I said, "You are tickling my neck!" As I tried to push away, he pulled me close and gave a throaty laugh as he buried his face into my neck again. My whole body had goose bumps now, and then my stomach started to rumble.

Rowan quickly lifted his head and looked at me. "When was the last time you ate?"

Giving him a small smile, I said, "Last night."

"Damn, Lee, it's got to be at least an hour past midday. I can bring you some food if you do not want to go and face some of the men that might be out there," he said.

"You know I do not give a damn what they think! I will go out there, but I do need some clothes first."

With a smile on his face, he traced a tingling finger down between my breasts. "I could just bring some food and you do not have worry about ever getting dressed." He sent a shiver throughout my body. Rowan let out a soft laugh and rolled to the other side of the bed. When he stood up, I had a clear view of his naked rear end as I yelled at him to stop. Freezing his body, he asked over his shoulder, "What is it?"

Crawling on my hands and knees, I went to him, taking two fingers and pressing them into the deep dimples above his bottom. Laughing out loud, I said, "You have dimples above your ass! I love it!"

Taking his hand, he rubbed them and my fingers. "Yes, I know. It's a Lythandas family trait. We all have it."

"It's adorable!" I said, looking up at him as he turned around. Taking his hands under my arms, he lifted me up to stand on my knees.

"Not as adorable as you," he said as he took my mouth with his. With his face close to mine, he said, "Your clothes still seem damp, so you will have to wear something of mine." As he went through his drawers for something for me to wear, I went over to my weapons. After sliding my sword off my belt, Rowan handed me trousers and a shirt. As I slipped into the pants, Rowan started to laugh at how big they were on me. Pulling them up high I wrapped the belt around the trousers so that they would stay up. Once I slipped on the over-sized shirt, I went over to him and looked at myself in the mirror.

"Oh my," I laughed. "My hair!" The braid was extremely loose, and hairs stuck out in all directions.

As I started to undo the braid so I could just wear my hair down, Rowan said as he watched me through the mirror, "You said that when you have energy released, no man or weapon can penetrate it unless they are like us."

"Yes," I said, looking at him through the mirror. "Why?"

"Do you think it can stop rain too and keep you dry?"

I looked at myself now with my loose hair over my shoulder. Curling my lip up with the thought of Dogan, I said, "There is only one way to find out." After yanking open the door, I marched up the hall in search of Dogan.

Dogan was not hard to find. He sat alone on the bench at the kitchen table eating. With Rowan right behind me as I walked into the gathering room, there was only one other guard in there sitting at the couch reading. The other men must have been doing their duties or sleeping. It was the same man I saw when I first got here.

He gave me a smile. "Are you all warmed up now, my lady?"

Giving him a shy smile, I replied, "Yes, I am." My face felt like it was on fire.

Once I got to him, I kneeled on the bench beside Dogan instead of sitting so I would not have to look up at him. Placing his utensil on the plate, he straightened his back before turning his head to glare at me.

Bringing my face close to his, I whispered, "With your core released, can rain penetrate it?"

Giving me a snide smile, he said, "Nay."

As I straightened, I smacked him hard across the back of the head, and he growled at me. "You damn fool," I hissed. "You could have saved us a lot of trouble by keeping us both dry."

"If ye ha' done like I asked last night, then I would ha'." Dogan glared his intense eyes at me.

My jaw dropped in shock. "You mean you did it out of spite?" To answer my question, he gave me an evil grin. My hands were balled up in fists and were ready to start hitting him, but Rowan interrupted my thoughts.

"If you do not mind me saying, I am rather glad that he did not use his energy." He smirked, standing on the other side of the table.

"Rowan," I said in shock.

Placing his hands in the middle of the table, he leaned forward to me and whispered while he smiled, "Then I would not have had the opportunity to warm you up, so to speak."

Quickly looking down while biting down on my lip, I sat on the bench beside Dogan. I could feel my whole face getting red with heat. Rowan laughed and touched my cheek before pushing away from the table. Still looking down, there was a feeling of Dogan's emerald eyes burning through me. Without looking at him, I quickly took hold of his wrist and filled my voice in his head.

"I can feel you judging me with your eyes, so stop it right now and return to your food. I am only a woman, and I do have needs!"

Dogan burst out a short hard laugh and said, "Smart arse!" He jerked his arm from my grip.

Rowan looked back from the counter and asked, "What hell is so funny? What did you say?"

"It's nothing. I just threw his words back at him, that's all," I explained and smiled sweetly at the man I loved.

Giving me an odd look, he went back to preparing us something to eat. "Is it always like this with you two, wanting to kill each other one moment and making each other laugh the next?"

Dogan and I fixed our eyes on each other, and just as I was about to answer his question, Dogan said, "Aye." He sounded grumpy because it was true.

I decided it was a good time to mention the dream I had earlier this morning. It should be interesting to see what kind of reaction I was going to get. "So, Dogan, when the storm hit this morning, it jolted me from a very interesting dream."

"So?" he said, uninterested and returned to eating his meal.

Giving him a snide grin, I said, "Are you not interested to hear what it was about?" He slowly turned his angry eyes on me, and when he did not say anything, I continued, "I met this wonderful man. Um, his name was Steaphan, I believe."

Dogan's eyes grew wide. Quickly, he grabbed hold of my arm and jerked me closer. He had fury in his eyes. *"What the hell did he say to ye?"* he demanded through his touch.

"Nothing much, he just wanted to introduce himself," I said privately back to him and then tilted my head slightly to the right and asked, *"How come you never mentioned your father was the same as us? And why are you angry with him?"*

He brought his angry face even closer to mine, *"That's none o' yer damn business! What else did he tell ye?"*

"Only that he is always around if I ever want to talk to him," I said through our touch and gave him a wicked grin.

"Dogan!" Rowan yelled in a warning tone, and the two of us jerked our heads to look at him, "I do not know what you two are talking about, but if you do not release her this instant, you and I are going to have problems."

Dogan let out a deep growl as he fixed his eyes back on me and then shoved me back. "Bloody fool," I mumbled as I scooted myself away from him to give us some space.

"Lee!" Rowan said my name in the same warning tone he did with Dogan, except not as loud. Raising my brows in question to his tone, he continued, "I heard what you mumbled. Here." He placed a bowl of mutton stew in front of me. "Now the three of us are going to sit here and have a pleasant conversation like *normal* adults."

"I would not call us normal," Dogan mumbled as he took another mouthful of his own food.

"Well, let's just pretend for the moment then," Rowan ordered and sat across from us and beamed me a soft smile.

For the next hour or so, the three of us sat at the table and softly talked about everything I learned over the last month. Even though Rowan already knew Dogan's story, he still asked him some questions about his past, and he answered them. As Dogan left to go have some tankards of ale at the pub down the road, we walked back down the hall to his room.

Since I was walking in front of him, I unbuckled my belt but held it tight until walking into the room. Once he closed the door behind him, I let my trousers fall to the floor and lifted my shirt over my head. Rowan let his beautiful eyes up and down my naked body. I could feel every inch of me start to flush. When I started to walk toward him, he lifted his shirt over his head. As I ran my hands up his chest, he closed his eyes at the touch. He held me under my arms and lifted me up; in doing so, I wrapped my legs around his waist. Rowan let out a moan as we kissed, and he wrapped his arms across my back.

When he sat down on the bed, he pushed back my hair behind my ears. "I thought before I was tortured with the thought of you, but now I think I may go crazy not seeing you." There was sadness in his eyes.

I looked away because I did not want to feel sadness of leaving, and I pressed my mouth against his ear. "Come home with me then, and you will not go crazy." As I kissed his neck and the top his shoulders, he suddenly grabbed hold of my hair with both hands and pulled my head back.

"I want to, believe me I do, but you know that would not be a good idea. The more we see each other, the harder it's going to be for us not to have sex. I am going to have to stay here, but I will come and see you as often as I can. I promise you that!" he said and kissed me as he stood back up. When he turned around, he plopped us hard onto the bed, causing us both to burst out in laughter.

Rowan gazed down with a face full of joy. As I ran my fingers along his smooth cheek, I thought about what Dogan said to me last night. Making sure not to look in his eyes I stared at his lips as I spoke, "Last night, Dogan made a comment on how he pitied the man I was destined to be with and that he would no sooner slit his own throat if he had to be stuck with a woman like me."

The reaction I got from Rowan surprised me. The man actually chuckled and quickly brought his face to my neck, where he kissed me and still continued to softly laugh. "Did he really say that to you?"

I began to get aggravated. "Yes," I snapped. "Do you agree with him? Do you think my soul mate will be miserable with me?"

Rowan lifted his head up and smiled down at me. Quickly, I turned my head away because I was upset that he thought this was funny. He took hold of my chin and made look at him. Rowan continued smiling as he shook his head. "Love, you are a rare breed of woman, and I admit most men would hate the thought of being married to a lass like yourself. But I can promise you one thing, your soul mate…" He tapped the tip of my nose with his finger. "He will love you unconditionally. He will know and understand you. The things you do or say that would scare off any normal man…it will be those things that he will love most about you."

The tears began to flow. "You really think so?"

Rowan chuckled and caught the tears that broke loose from my eyes. "Of course, Lovalee. I love you, do you really believe another man cannot?" I just shrugged my shoulders, and he leaned down and kissed me. "Do not listen to Dogan. He only says things like that to get you upset."

"Well, it worked," I cried.

He laughed. "Well, do not let it because then he wins. Just remember that."

Sniffling, I nodded and then added, "You can stop laughing at me now."

Rowan rolled over, taking me with him so that I was on top now. He had an enormous grin. "Sorry, love. It's just you're so precious even when you cry." His tingling hands ran the length of my spine and stopped when he had both of his hands on my bare bottom. Rowan's blue-gray eyes began to twinkle with excitement. "I am sure I can get your mind off of him and his words if you would like." I could not help but start to giggle as I leaned forward and took his mouth with mine.

For the rest of the day and evening, we stayed in his room and just enjoyed the feeling of each other. It still killed me to think that I will someday love another man. The mere thought of it did not seem possible, especially when my heart was swelling with love right now.

The next morning, I walked out on the front porch and stood next to Dogan. It was no longer windy and the rain died down to a light drizzle. Rowan came and stood on the other side of me, and I asked Dogan, "What are you thinking about?"

"I was thinking about staying another night, but it looks like the rain is finally starting to stop," he remarked. Even though I would love to stay another day with my love, I knew I needed to get back to Rosa.

"Maybe after we have some breakfast and get the horses ready, the rain will be finally done," I stated. Dogan nodded in agreement and walked back into the barracks. Rowan wrapped his arm around my shoulders as we followed him in.

Sure enough, as we walked our horses out of the stables, the clouds started to break up, and you could see some blue sky. It was warmer too, which made me happy. Looking at Rowan, I wrapped my arms around his neck in a hug, and he squeezed me tightly.

"I am going to miss you, Lovalee. I love you with all my heart," he whispered in my ear.

I closed my tear-filled eyes as I responded, "I know, and I love you too. I wish I could take you with me."

He let out a deep sigh. "Maybe in another lifetime, I will." Pulling my head back so I could look at him, he gave me a small smile as he wiped the tears away from my cheeks. When he took my mouth with his, I let out a light moan as he deepened the kiss.

"Goddamnit, ye two! Break apart now…ye'r making me sick," Dogan bellowed.

Instantly, we started to laugh. Rowan then took my face in his hands and whispered, "I love you."

"I love you too," I whispered back, smiling. A moment later, he gave me a boost into my saddle, and he went over to Dogan.

They took hold of each other's forearms. "I am sure I will be seeing you again soon. We do not know one another well yet, but we will. You are the same as me, brother, so we are already connected because of that."

Dogan nodded and gave him a half smile. "Aye, Lieutenant, we are. Next time ye are in the city, I'll buy ye an ale or two. There's a lot I'd like to talk to ye about."

"Well, I am sure I will be making a trip soon." He turned and gazed up at me with a smile. "May the trip go smoothly for you two today. It looks like you may have the sunshine on your side."

Dogan said his good-bye to Rowan and climbed into his saddle. We walked the horses slowly to the main road. Rowan walked beside me and laid a hand on my leg, and then I heard his voice. *"Tell Sterling I said hello and that I will be seeing him soon. Take care of yourself, Lee. Try not to lose your temper too much with Dogan, because I might have to kill him if he ever hurts you."*

Smiling and running my hand through his short hair, I said, "*I will let Sterling know, and I will try my best with Dogan. He just knows how to really get under my skin, but do not worry, I do not think he would ever hurt me severely.*"

"*He better not,*" he added and withdrew my hand from his head and kissed the inside of my palm. After I traced my finger down his cheek, I walked Ara out to the center of the road and stopped beside Dogan. Looking back one last time, I lipped the words *I love you*, and he did the same.

Turning, I fixed my eyes on Dogan. "Well, you bastard, are you ready to go?" I asked, and he just glared at me. "What's this, no comment?" Before he could respond, I gave Ara a swift kick to get running. Instantly, Dogan was back up beside me, and we were finally on the last stretch of our journey back home.

Chapter 21

Reunion

We ran the horses all day without talking to each other. Ever since we left Mastingham, Dogan had been very ornery. So when we stopped at midday to eat something and to let the horses drink, I just kept my mouth shut. He too never said a word to me. It was just a few hours before sundown when the trees finally cleared and opened up to the city ahead. There was clear view of Burreck Castle as we finally slowed the horses down to a trot.

"Well, we finally made it back home," I muttered to myself.

"Now it's back to reality," Dogan groaned.

"Is that what your problem has been?" I asked as he glared at me. "Did you like it that much at my family's home that you would rather be there instead of here?" I pointed to the city ahead.

"Fer the first time in my life I found something else that I'm good at instead o' being a soldier. So aye, I'd rather have stayed there. Hell, if I had known yer father paid that well sooner, I might ha' never left. But then there's that little girl somewhere here in the city. After I find her, I think I might go back to Mastingham and ask yer father fer a job," he said, sounding a little agitated.

Pulling back on the reins, I brought Ara to a complete stop. My legs were expanding in and out with Ara's still-heavy breaths. Dogan pulled back the reins also after he was a few horse lengths ahead of me. Turning around in the saddle, he yelled, "What the hell are ye doing?"

Finally, a smile came to my face when it dawned on me. "You love my family, and you consider them friends. That's why you did not want to leave."

"Goddamn it, woman! Nay, I just like the work, that's all!" He turned back around and kicked his horse to walk.

Giving Ara a few kicks, we ran up beside them. "I do not care what you say, Grump! I see how you acted around them, even with my Pa and Estelle. You like them, and you are going to miss them. It's all right if you do not admit to it because I know how you truly feel," I said, making sure to give him a big smile as he glared at me as usual.

"Can ye please shut the hell up?" he yelled. "I liked it better when ye were pissed off at me. 'Twas nice not to hear yer bloody voice all day!" He was right, I was still sort of mad at him for making us get wet yesterday, which was one of the reasons I did not talk to him today. The other was I just did not want to hear his grumpy voice.

"You should try being less grumpy and more happy. Like for that last month, you did a lot of laughing. Do not get back to your grumpy ass self because we are back to reality," I ordered.

Dogan stared straight ahead, but his lips did twitch a little. There was still hope for him yet. Without looking at me, he said, "Yer family is unlike any family I ha' met before. A person would ha' no soul if they could be around 'em without laughing."

"Thank you, Dogan. I will take that as a compliment."

As I looked ahead to the castle, my smile widened as he did his usual growl. The man exhausted me at times. I could kill him one moment, and with the snap of the fingers, I could hug him. As much as he aggravated me, the man was truly my friend. Even though he did not realize it yet, he will, and it most likely will piss him off too. I could not help but to start laughing to myself.

"What the hell is so funny?" he demanded.

"Nothing, Dogan. It's nothing."

Feeling him glaring at me for a moment, he said, "We'll ha' one o' the guards help ye carry yer stuff to yer room. If ye want, I'll wait and just bring Ara wit me to the stables."

He just called my horse by her name…that was a first! "I would appreciate that."

We walked both our horses up the huge stone steps as we went through the castle gates. Walking straight toward the massive double doors of the castle, there was a sweet aroma coming from the gardens to my right. It did feel good to back. I never realized how much I loved it here until now.

"I am glad to see you two made it this long without killing one another," said Caine Templeton, as we came to a stop.

"I know, it's a miracle in itself," I said jokingly and dismounted. "Would you mind helping me carry my stuff back to my room?"

"Of course not, Lady Lee. It will be my pleasure." He gave me a beautiful smile and started untying things off my saddle.

Once everything was off, I took Ara's reins up over her head so I was holding them in front of her. Rubbing my hand up and down the front of her face, I kissed her nose. "You did good, girl! You made me proud." Turning her around, I handed the reins up to Dogan. "If you see Wyck or Dylan, can you please ask them to give her a little extra grain." I patted the side of her sweaty neck. "She deserves it!"

"I suppose I can do that," he said.

"Also, if you see Sterling, tell him I will be over a little later after I am done visiting with the queen."

Dogan turned his horse around and brought Ara up beside him. "No worries! I'll make sure to tell yer other love interest that ye'll be over to see 'im."

Not being able to find anything to throw at him, I just yelled, "Oh, go to hell, Dogan!"

He threw back his head in a hard laugh. "Oh, 'tis great to be home," he said sarcastically.

After I thanked Templeton for giving me a hand, he left to go back to his duties. Resisting the urge to plop down on my bed, I started to take off all my weapons. After making room for the new weapons, I closed the wardrobe doors and headed back out to the hall. Not wanting to be completely weaponless, I left the ones in my boots. When I reached the bottom of the steps to the royal living quarters, Byron gave me massive smile.

"Well, look whose back!" Quickly, I went up the stairs and grabbed Byron's forearm in a shake. He said, still smiling, "It's good to have you back, Lee."

"It's good to be back." I nod toward the door. "Is she in?"

"She definitely is." Byron opened the door; I walked in and acknowledged the guards on the other side of the door. Slowly, I made my way down the hall where I made it to the first set of double doors on either side; I looked into the library first. She was not in there, so I looked into the dining room, and she was not in there either. There was a noise of a door opening up the hall. A maid walked out of the room, and I went straight for her. She stopped in her tracks when she saw me.

"My lady, you're back." The maid gave me a light smile as she slightly bowed her head.

"Yes." I smiled back at her. "Where can I find our queen?"

She pointed up the hall behind her. "She was out on the balcony a moment ago. I am sure she's still out there."

"Thank you," I said, walking past her up the hall. When I got to the end, to my right down the hall there was a fresh ocean breeze coming in from the open doors. As I reached the open doors, I came to a halt at the sight of her. Rosa's back was to me as she leaned against the stone railing with her face up in the wind. Her long strawberry hair blew lightly in the wind. As I stared at her beauty, I focused on her color. Slowly, her bright emerald aura pulsated from her body, and then there were these little white sparks bouncing out of it. I remembered Dogan telling me he saw them on her and that it meant that she was pregnant.

Rosa turned her face to the side and caught sight of me. "Lee," she screeched as she spun around. Instantly, she started to cry as she came toward me. I too started to cry when I noticed the beautiful little bump of a stomach.

"You are starting to show!" I said, crying tears of joy as I wrapped my arms around her. Instantly, I froze. Her whole body was vibrating with power, and quickly I pulled back and looked to her with shock. "You are a mage?"

Rosa gave me her famous smile. "Yes, and I can feel the power rolling off of you now too. You must have learned how to release your powers on your own then?"

"Most of it, but not completely yet. I cannot believe this." Taking her hands, I asked, "What is your gift?"

"I am a healer," she said, and Dogan told me that her color meant healer. "I have never used my powers on another person, but I have brought back to life a few animals when I was growing up."

"A healer?" I asked, and she nodded. "Is Bryce a Mage too?"

Rosa let out a light laugh. "No, Lee, he is not." Still staring at me with wide aqua eyes, she wrapped her arms around me again and gave me a light kiss on the cheek. "I am so glad you are home! I have missed my closest friend very much."

Wrapping my arms around her again, I responded, "I have missed you too, Rosa." I started to laugh at the thought of her having powers. "This is amazing! I never saw this coming…you being a mage, or should I say Fae?"

Rosa pulled back and gave me an odd look. "Fae?"

"Rosa, I have a lot to tell you."

"Well"—she wrapped her arm around mine—"that's good that we have all the time in the world." As we walked back into the hall, I started by telling her about Rowan.

It was dark out by the time I finished telling everything to Rosa. As we were finishing up our meal in the dining room, it dawned on me that I had not seen Bryce or Kaidan yet and I had been back for a few hours now.

"Where are Bryce and Kaidan? It's starting to get late," I asked with concern.

"Oh, they went to the duke's for dinner. Supposedly, Gavin is going to apologize for his actions, finally. I was invited too, but I was in no mood to see that weasel of a man." Cringing at the mere thought of him, she continued, "You must be tired from your journey."

"I am, but I have to go and see Sterling before I consider going to bed."

Rosa stood up. "Come, Lee." She reached for my hand, and I accepted it as I stood. "Go and see your friend then get some rest. You can see Bryce in the morning when you come and have breakfast with us."

"Thank you, Rosa." Giving her another hug, I said, "Have a good night."

"You have a good night too, and I will look for any books we may have on the Fae. I am interested to learn more about them now too."

"That would be terrific." Bending down a little and rubbing her belly lightly, I whispered, "Sweet dreams, little one!"

Rosa let out a loud bubbly laugh. "Bryce talks to the baby like that every day. He would have gotten a kick out of seeing you do that."

Laughing as I walked out to the hall, I said, "Good night, Rosa. I will see you in the morning." Rosa was still lightly laughing as the guard opened the door for me.

After stopping and grabbing my cloak from my room, I finally made it to the front doors of the castle. There were different guards outside now than when I arrived. Saying my good-evenings to them, I made my way across the courtyard to the castle gate. The city was quiet now, and the lanterns were lit. I passed a few people and said hello as they went by. I got startled when I heard someone yell from behind me.

"Angel!" Turning around, I caught sight of Dylan running toward me.

"Dylan!" Laughing with excitement in seeing him, I began running to meet him halfway. When I wrapped my arms around him, he squeezed me tight. Pulling back and smiling, I let his true color shine out. A dark murky pink formed around his body. I will have to remember to ask Dogan what that means.

"I have missed you." He smiled. "How is your family?"

"They are doing better. Thank you for asking. Did Dogan give you the message about giving Ara extra grain?"

"Was that the guard who brought her in?" he asked, and I nodded. "He gave Wyck the message, and I made sure she got it."

"Good, thanks! I am on my way to see someone, so I will come by the stables tomorrow to visit with you. Is everything going good for you still? Any memories yet?"

He laughed. "No, not yet, and everything is going great."

"Well, I am glad everything is great at least. I will see you tomorrow then?"

"Tomorrow." Dylan took my hand and kissed it. "Have a good night, angel."

"You too, Dylan." I smiled and continued down the cobblestone street toward the barracks. When I finally got to the door of the barracks, I knocked hard.

The door opened, and Captain Avery Coster was standing there with a smile. I did not see him much since he usually worked in the evenings. He was tall and lean with short sandy hair and beard. "Well, good evening, Lee. When are you going to stop knocking and just let yourself in?" he asked as he opened the door wider so I could walk in.

"Probably never, as I never know what I may walk into in here," I teased.

The captain laughed along with some other men at the kitchen table. "It is good to have you back."

"It feels good to be home, Captain." Looking around for Sterling, I caught sight of Dogan sitting on the couch with a book. "Is Sterling around?"

"Yes, he had a busy day, so he went to bed early," said the captain. "He said for you to wake him up when you got here because he wants to see you."

"Oh, that's all right. I will just wait until tomorrow," I said, sounding a little disappointed because I really wanted to see my friend.

"Ye better go and wake his arse up, woman," Dogan said from across the room. "If ye dinna, then we all will catch hell fer it."

The captain started to laugh. "He is right, Lee. Go and wake his ass up!"

"All right!" Laughing, I started for the hall and stuck my tongue out at Dogan as I passed.

"That's real mature," he muttered.

Smiling, I stopped at the third door on the right. Since he was a lieutenant, he shared a room with only one other man, unlike Dogan who had to share a room with several other men. I knew he would be alone in there right now, being it was Captain Coster that used the other bed. Pushing down slowly on the latch, I quietly opened the door. Even though the room was dark, I could see Sterling clearly in his deep-red glow. Shutting the door behind me, I eased myself toward him.

Sterling was lying shirtless with both his arms up behind his head. He was pure muscle and was gorgeous in his red glow. I froze at the side of the bed as I wondered if he was completely naked under that blanket. I said a quick prayer to myself in hopes that the man was wearing trousers at least. When I concentrated on his face, I notice the tightness of his lips. The fool was trying not smile!

"Hey, stop with the fake sleeping and give me a hug, you ass," I laughed at him.

Instantly, his eyes popped open as he sat up, taking hold of me and yanking me down on the bed with him. At first, he scared a scream out of me before I started laughing loud as he wrapped his arms around me in a hug. Practically sitting in his lap and tingling all over, I said, "Oh, I have missed you, Sterling."

Tightening his arms around me he, said softly, "It's good to have our Lee back home."

Taking his face in my hands, I gazed into his handsome face. "Red is a good color for you." I said, softly smiling.

"Dogan told me about you seeing the auras now." He smiled. "It's amazing! Is it not?"

Nodding as my eyes started to tear, I whispered, "Thank you!" I pressed my lips lightly to his. He gave a throaty laugh as he enjoyed the light tingling sensation against his lips.

Smiling, he asked, "What for, love?" He pushed a stray hair away from my face.

With tears rolling down my cheeks, I cried, "You know why." Sterling started to laugh. "Do not laugh at me you bloody fool!" I smacked him in the chest.

"Sorry, Lee," he said, still laughing and pulled me in a hug. "You are just so damn cute! How is he by the way?"

Laying my head on his shoulder, I sighed. "Rowan is wonderful. He wanted me to tell you that he says hello and that he will be seeing you soon."

Sterling leaned back against the wall and continued to smile at me. "Good. I cannot wait to see my brother again. So, love, tell me everything you learned this past month. Dogan gave me the gist of it, but he said that you would tell me everything." Positioning myself against the wall beside him, I began telling him all I had learned.

After I was done explaining everything to him, he took hold of my locket and examined it in the palm of his hand. "There is a question I would like to ask, but I would rather see these ladies in person and ask them myself. Would you introduce me?"

Smiling, "I would love to. Do you want to meet them now?"

"If you are up to it. Now, if you're too tired, we can wait and do it another day," he spoke gently. Most guards would not believe it if they heard him talk in such a soft tone. This was a side of him only a few people know about. Because of his bulky built and his rough attitudes during training, most men are intimidated by him.

"Now if you were Dogan, then I would be too tired," I replied, and he let out a loud laugh. "But lucky for you, you are not, so let's do this." We positioned ourselves so that we were facing each other on the bed. Once we took hold of our hands, we closed our eyes and began the breathing exercise.

After a while, Sterling's voice filled my head, *"Whenever you are ready, Lee."*

With the feeling of my core pushing at my ribs, I said, *"I am ready."*

Pushing hard, my energy released itself, and the whole room got encased with red light. Sterling was smiling before me and then he said, *"I just learned to release it myself about two weeks ago. Now, I am going to have to learn to do it with my eyes open."*

"Yes, me too," I groaned as I thought of Dogan, and then Sterling started to laugh at the memory I was thinking about. Shaking the thought from my head, I called, *"Ma? Cici? I have a gentleman here that would like to meet you.*

After the last word came out, the two of them walked through the closed door to my right. Instantly with excitement, I leaped off the bed. Never letting go of Sterling's hands, I pulled him up beside me. Quickly, he turned and looked behind on the bed. There the two of us still sat holding hands. Sterling turned and looked at me with wide eyes, "Bloody hell!"

Ma and Cici both let out an angelic laugh. I let go of Sterling's left hand and kept a tight grip on his right as I guided him toward the ladies.

"I would like you to meet Arabella Bayard and Cici Ramstien," I introduced, smiling at him.

Sterling laid a hand on his bare chest and bowed gracefully before them. "It is a pleasure to meet you, my ladies. I do apologize that I am not properly dressed. I was not thinking." The three of us started giggling at him. I did not think of that myself. At least he had trousers on.

Ma and Cici went to him, and they both wrapped their arms around him as they pressed their lips to his cheeks. Sterling let out a chuckle as he wrapped each arm around them and hugged.

"Why do I have a sudden feeling that Dogan is going to be very angry that I am meeting you both for the first time while he is not present?" he asked.

Cici laughed, "Because he is and he's about to burst through that door in three...two..." The bedroom door exploded open, and he gave us a look that could kill as he slammed the door behind him. The four of us were smiling hugely as he went over and sat on the bed. Instantly, his energy was released, and he jumped out of his body.

"Ye are really starting to piss me off, woman," he yelled. I swear I could almost see the steam coming out of his ears. He was boiling with anger.

"Oh, Dogan, I have been pissing you off ever since the day we met, so calm the hell down!" I shouted back at him, trying my best not to let his anger ruin my evening.

"Bloody hell, Sterling! Could ye at least put on a shirt before doing this? They're still ladies, fer God's sake," Dogan yelled at him.

Sterling laughed. "I was not thinking about that, besides, they do not seem to mind."

"Oh, we most certainly do not mind," Cici beamed, and Ma agreed while Dogan let out a growl.

"How about we try to ignore this *grump...*," I insisted, and Dogan curled his lip at me. "And get to the reason I called you here to meet Sterling."

"That's right! Ye have some questions for us," Cici said.

Then my mother added, "Like for instance, why I have never come to you like I did with Rowan?"

"That's one of them," Sterling agreed.

"Well, son..." Cici began. "Arabella and I have been watching and guiding the four of you for the last twenty-six years. Your time to meet us for the first time was not until now. Now that you have, you might get sick of us always popping in your dreams."

"Beautiful women like yourselves...I hardly doubt that," he said, giving them a huge smile.

"Watch yer words, Sterling," Dogan warned. "One o' 'em is my mother."

He laughed at him. "I know she is." Sterling fixed his eyes back on them. "Can you tell me if I am destined to be with someone like my friends are?"

"Oh, Sterling, you most certainly are." Ma laid a hand on his cheek. "Eventually, all four of you will be paired up with your soul mates, and then you will become a group of six. When that happens, all of you put together will become some of the strongest Fae Altecia has ever seen."

"Good Lord!" Sterling looked to Dogan and me. "Did you two know that?"

"Nay," Dogan added softly. He was just as shocked to hear this as Sterling.

"I knew about us being a group of six," I said, and Dogan gave me a questioning look. I winced instantly because that was something I forgot to tell him. It was something my mother said before he came to the river that day.

"I take it then that she will have the same powers as me?" Sterling asked, and they both nodded their heads. "How will I know who it is?"

"Just be patient, son. In time, we will give you visions dealing with her. Have no worries we will guide her to you." Cici smiled softly.

Sterling gave me an odd look and then said to our mothers, "Thank you, ladies, for coming and seeing me. Now that I know I can do this, do not be surprised if I ask for you again."

"And when you do…we will be here," Ma chimed. They both hug him individually.

When Ma wrapped her arms around me, I murmured, "Thank you."

"You are welcome, baby girl! I know you have some questions yourself, so just ask for me when you are ready for me to answer them," she said and kissed my lips lightly. As she went to Dogan, Cici took my face and kissed my lips lightly too.

"It's going to be tough now that you are back in the city, but can you please try to get my son to smile and laugh more?" she whispered.

"I do not know if I can, but I will try," I whispered back.

"That's all I ask," she said and went to Ma, who was standing by the door. I wanted to talk to her about her husband and decided to do that when I was alone. They both gave us huge smiles and then walked through the closed door. Sterling and I strolled past Dogan; as soon as we touched our physical bodies, our souls got sucked back into them. Once I opened my eyes for the first time, I turned to look at Dogan behind me. He opened his eyes, stood up, and marched out the room without saying a word. For the first time, it did not hurt when my core was sucked back in. Looking back to Sterling, he still had that odd look on his face.

"Sterling, what is wrong? Why do you keep looking at me like that?" I asked.

"Did you not hear what she said? After the four of us pair up with our soul mates, then we will be a group of six." He paused, and I just nodded in agreement of hearing that. "Lee! We already have three men, and so we need three women. You are not to be with Rowan, so that means you are destined to be with…Dogan…or me." All I could do was stare at him. This cannot be! No, no, no! There was instant tightness in my chest. I could not breathe! Trying to suck in air, it did not seem to be enough.

Sterling took my face and made me look to him again, "Easy, Lee." He gave me a beautiful smile and started to lightly laugh. "Relax, everything is going to be all right. Please tell me that it is the thought of Dogan that's making you hyperventilate and not me."

Unable to get the words out my mouth, I screamed in his head, *Dogan! I can never be with a man like him. Sterling, what am I supposed to do?"*

"You are going to keep on living. They said that they will give us visions when it comes the time to find our mates. The only fact that we have right now is that you are going to be with one of us. I have a strong feeling it's me." He lightly kissed my forehead. "You told me earlier that Dogan has a child, and it is her mother that he is destined to be with. Last time I checked, you did not have a kid." Finally, I smiled at him. That relieved me a little because he was right…I do not have a child. Sterling continued, "Speaking of that, two weeks ago I saw a young girl running in the street with a bunch other kids, and she had our color."

"Are you serious?" I practically crawled into his lap. "Who was she? It could be who Dogan is looking for. It would make sense why he is destined to be in her life if she's like us."

"I am not sure who she is. I tried to catch up with her, but they were too quick weaving through the crowds of people. Before I knew it, I lost sight of her completely. A day has not gone by since that I did not look for her."

Still sitting in the same positions we were in before we released our energies, I gazed at him with wonder. He was a hell of a good-looking man. With his muscular body, strong square jaw, and raven-colored hair, it is a wonder that no women have tried to scoop him up.

"You are one of my best friends, and for the first time, I am afraid of what the outcome may be," I said through our touch as I searched his face.

Everything softened: his eyes and even his smile. *"You are one of my best friends too. We will make it through this together, and no matter what happens…we all will still be together in the end."* Sterling squeezed my hands.

I laid my hand on the tattoo on his right arm that was similar to the band Rowan had. "Rowan said that he saw me with a man and that I was happy. He also said that he had a tattoo, but he did not know who the man was because he was paying attention to me."

"Let's just say that I am your one, and if he saw a tattoo like he said, then he lied on not knowing who he was. Rowan would know my tattoo if he saw it."

"Oh, Sterling, how are we going to handle this? I love you, believe me I do! It's just not the same love I have for Rowan," I whispered, laying my hand on his chest. My hand tingled against his skin.

"And I love you, but not in the way Rowan does. Maybe that will change over time, besides, we do not know for sure yet if it's me that you belong to," he said, laying his hand over mine.

"Oh, I sure hope it's you! God would not be that mean by sticking me with Dogan…would he?" I asked worryingly.

Laughingly, he said, "I do not know, love. How about for the time being we just continue being how we always have been with one another? Whoever you are meant to be with, it will happen whether we like it or not."

Moving forward, I wrapped my arms around his neck. In return Sterling squeezed me into his lap. At first, I did not speak as I just enjoyed the tingling feeling of our bodies touching. Finally, I said, "Thank you! You are a good man." I sighed. "I probably should head back to the castle and try to get some sleep."

With our arms still around each other, he said, "If you wait a moment, I will walk you back. It's late now, and I do not want you walking alone."

Pulling back, I gave him a smile. "Try to get some sleep, Sterling. I need to talk to Dogan anyway, and I am sure someone will walk with me after that."

Smiling, he nodded. "I do not know how much sleep I am going to get, but I will try." He paused. "Will you do something for me before you leave?"

"For you anything."

Sterling brushed his fingertips against my lips. His face suddenly grew serious, and then he shook his head. "Never mind."

A vision of us kissing by my bed chamber door appeared in my mind. I remember how terrific that kiss felt, especially when he deepened it. Also how we both exploded in laughter because we were kissing each other. But this scene was not from that night we kissed; it was different. We broke apart to find Rowan standing in the corridor. His face was filled with pain, as if it killed him to see us together. I realized then that this thought was coming from Sterling. Instantly, I squeezed his hand, "Sterling…"

"Lee…" He closed his eyes. "I will never kiss you like that again. As much as I want to experience that feeling again…" He took a deep breath and opened his eyes. The right corner of his mouth curled up slightly. "But if I get a vision that you are definitely my soul mate, then I will hunt you down. I will not care if you are with the king and queen…I will take my kiss then and the woman that comes with it."

I giggled softly and looked down when I suddenly felt shy. Sterling took hold of my chin and lifted my face back up. The man winked at me, and I bit on my bottom lip. I reached up and laid my right hand on his smooth cheek. We both smiled at each other.

"Good night, Sterling," I whispered.

"Good night and sweet dreams." He beamed as I got off the bed. I turned to look at him one more time as I went to the door. Sitting on the bed and smiling, his fair skin glistened in his red glow. I smiled back as I let his aura dissipate around him.

After shutting the door, I walked down the hall with no intention of talking to Dogan. I just told him that so he would not worry and go back to sleep. Out of the corner of my eye, I could see him sitting back on the couch with his legs stretched out and crossed at the ankles. He was back to his book, and I was not giving him a full glance as I walked toward the door.

"Good night, gentlemen," I said as I laid a hand on the door handle.

"Wait a moment, my lady. One of us will walk you back to the castle," responded a guard sitting at the table.

"I got it," Dogan announced, who was now directly behind me and made me almost jump out of my skin.

"Good Lord, Dogan," I yelled. "Do not do that!" I slapped him in the chest.

"And what's that?" he asked in all seriousness.

"You were just on the bloody couch a moment ago, and all of a sudden, you are behind me! I did not even sense your quick ass!"

"Well, if you would have tried—" he began to say, and I cut him off.

"Do not even say it," I hissed as I poked my finger at his thick chest. He was still livid that I did not try to release my core with my eyes open. Is he ever going to get over it? It's been days now. Mimicking his narrowing eyes. "Well, if you are walking with me then let's go. I have something to tell you." After saying my good-byes to the men, I stepped out the door, and the cool night air hit my face. As soon as he fell in step beside me, I told him about the girl. "Sterling said he saw a young girl running in the streets with the same color as us two weeks ago."

Dogan stopped in his tracks and spun me around to face him. "I beg your pardon? Where?" His eyes are no longer narrow but wide with excitement.

"I am not sure where. You will have to ask Sterling that." I paused for a moment. "Did you ever envision the girl with the same gift? How about the mother? Did you ever get to see her?" *Please say yes…then go on telling me how you still have not found her. There's no way in hell that I am the mother to this child. Right?*

After a few moments of silence, he spoke softly, "Aye and nay." His emerald eyes shined brightly from the lantern that was behind me. There could be so much emotion in them that it can surprise me at times.

"What kind of answer is that?" I asked a little annoyed.

"I never saw 'er face. Just the back o' her, and I dinna pay much attention to 'er because o' the look on the face o' the child she was holding. The poor thing looked back at me terrified and had been crying. My visions never showed me if they had the same gifts as us, but it makes sense if they do. That girl Sterling saw has to be my future daughter," Dogan said and started to walk again.

Standing still and staring at the spot where Dogan just stood, I thought about what he said. I laid my hand on my locket and was tempted to ask Ma which one of these men were to be my mate. All of a sudden, I decided that I was not ready to know just yet. Rowan just came back into my life, and I do not want to end what just started.

"Woman," Dogan snapped several steps ahead. Shaking the thoughts of soul mates out of my head, I went to him.

As I followed in step beside him, I figured I would ask him about Dylan, "What does a dark murky pink color mean?"

"Are ye talkin' about that lad who works at the stables?" he asked, and I nodded yes. Dogan continued, "It means a dishonest nature. He's not to be trusted, lass, and I rather ye not go to the stables by yerself anymore."

"He's not to be trusted? Dogan, you do not even know the man. He almost died, and he still has no memories of his past," I said, defending a man I call a friend.

"Oh, I ha' tried to talk to the man, but he avoids me like I'm some kind o' plague. Every time he catches sight o' me, he goes the other way. I ken men wit his color and none o' 'em were good. I'd not be surprised if he's lying about not havin' any memory. This Dylan is not yer friend. He may act and say nice things to ye, but that's how they work. They tell ye what ye want to hear then they'll turn on ye suddenly."

My body shook with an uncomfortable chill. "You are kind of scaring me, Dogan."

"Good," he snapped, and then he continued, "Dinna ever trust this man, and always ha' some type o' weapon on ye when he's around." The man did not even spare me a glance; he just kept his eyes straight ahead.

"What am I supposed to do? I told him that I would visit with him tomorrow."

"Just send 'im a message wit' some type o' excuse on why ye canna see him. The next time ye wanna go to the stables, let me ken. I'll show up a little bit after ye get there, and then ye can see first-hand what I mean," he ordered, and I nodded in agreement. I had met Dogan and Dylan on the same day, and I knew nothing of him, whereas with Dogan, I knew almost everything. Hell, I did not even know the man's true name. A feeling started to come over me that I needed to listen to him and just avoid Dylan for the time being. After a few moments in silence, Dogan broke it by saying, "There's Kimball up ahead."

Way up ahead, I could see the dark figure walking toward us, and I let his color shine out. Once I did that, a bright yellow light formed around his body, and I could see that it was for sure Kaidan.

"Kaidan," I screamed.

"Lee?" he yelled back.

"Thanks, Dogan, but I will be fine now. Go back to your book and have a good night." I gave him a smile and took off ahead toward Kaidan. I stopped after several steps and looked back at Dogan, who was still standing there. "What's it mean?"

"What are ye talking about?" he asked, looking puzzled.

"His color," I yelled because I was anxious to hug my brother.

"Easygoing, intelligent, and optimistic," he belted out, and his lips did that twitching thing he does when he's trying to fight a smile.

I gave him a huge smile as I turned, and Kaidan was already there, lifting me off the ground. Laughing, he spun me around as I rejoiced, "Brother, it's so good to see you! I have missed you."

Kaidan placed me back down on my feet and gave me a crooked grin. "And I have missed you. It looks like you two made it without killing each other." He looked behind me in the direction of Dogan. I turned myself around to catch sight of him walking away.

"Yes, we manage to get along for the most part, but we had our moments. So how is my best friend? Are you two doing well?" I asked.

"We are doing great. I take it that you have not seen her yet?" Kai had a small smile now as he gazed at me. He smelled of wine, which was not surprising since he just got back from the duke's.

"No, not yet. I figure I will see Mira tomorrow." I knew she was probably in bed already.

"I am sure she's sleeping by now, but she will be so happy to see you when she does." As we started to walk, he took his left arm and wrapped it around my neck and brought my head against his chest. "It's great to have you back, Lee. The castle is not the same without you around to rag on." While we both started laughing, I pinched him hard on his side, and he let go of my neck.

"It's good to be back," I said and meant it. This city was my home now, and the people I was close to were my second family. I did not know why yet, but for some reason, I was destined to be here.

"So tell me, Lee. How is your family and how's it going with your newfound powers? Did you learn anything new?"

Wrapping my right arm around his, I told him a shortened version of everything I learned the past month. We took a slow walk back to the castle, and when we reached our rooms, we said good-night.

It took me a while to finally fall into a deep sleep. The thoughts of the men in my life swirled around in my head. I loved Rowan with all my heart, and the thought of being with either Sterling or Dogan kind of scared me. They were both my friends, and I did love them in their own way, including Dogan. But if I was meant to be with Dogan, I really did not know how that would work out. The man knows actually how to piss me off, and he does it on purpose. Just as I do it to him. I guess the only thing to do was exactly what Sterling said: live my life the way I am, and someday, I will find out who that man was. When that happens, I will deal with it then.

Dawn finally came, and I was awakened with the weight of someone pouncing on my back, "Lee, I am so happy you are home! I have missed you so much," Mira screeched happily as she squeezed my shoulders. Laughing, I rolled over so I could wrap my arms around her in a hug.

"Good morning, Mira! I have missed you too," I sang in excitement on seeing my best friend.

The two of us caught up while I got ready for the day. I really did miss that. It was always our ritual to gossip in the morning. We did a lot of laughing. Mira could not believe about Rowan and the reasons for his leaving. Of course I told her about our last night together. It felt good to vent to her about men in general. I have been surrounded by men for the last month, and I think I would have gone crazy if I went a little longer. There was Estelle, but it was not the same as with Mira. She was more like a mother to me, and there are some things I just felt weird talking to her about.

Before leaving to have breakfast with the king and queen, I wrote a short letter to Dylan. I explained to him that I was going to be busy with the queen today and that I will see him soon. Mira took the letter when we left my room.

While walking up the corridor to the royal living quarters, I gazed down at the dress that I was wearing. The fabric felt funny as it hit my legs while walking. Wishing that I could continue wearing my trousers, I knew there was no way that would ever happen. Once the guards opened the door for me, the aroma of fresh food hit my nose. A smile spread across my face as I walked down the corridor towards the open doors to the dining room. Before I made it, Bryce walked into the hall, and his whole face lit up. As he came to me, a golden aura formed around his body. The color made him even more handsome.

"Our Lee finally made it back home," the king wrapped his arms around me and lifted me up in a tight squeeze.

Laughing, I said, "I sure did, and it's great to be back."

Bryce placed me back on my feet and stuck out his elbow for me to wrap my arm through. "So Rosa told me everything last night. You had quite the interesting month then." He continued as we walked to the dining room. "I am glad to hear your family is doing better."

"Yes, they are," I said, smiling as we walked in and caught sight of Rosa and Kaidan sitting at the table. "Your wife is literally glowing. I have this sudden urge to run over to her and rub that beautiful belly of hers," I murmured in his ear.

Bryce's smile widened ear to ear as he whispered, "I know what you mean, and please do! She would get a kick out of it."

I ran over and stood behind her as she sat. Wrapping my arm around her shoulder, I pressed my cheek to hers. With my right hand, I reached down and rubbed her belly, "Good morning you two!"

Rosa threw back her head as she let out a hearty laugh and wound up giving me a kiss on the cheek. "Good morning, Lee!" She patted the chair beside her, "Please sit. It's been too long since we had breakfast together."

As the four of us sat and enjoyed our food, we talked about the plans for the day. Some of the countrymen requested the king's audience today, and that would most likely take up his whole morning. Rosa said she found some books about the Fae last night, but there was still a lot more to find. That was her plan for the day, so it looked like that was going to be mine too. It would be fun and interesting to find information on the Fae, especially my royal bloodline.

Chapter 22

Soiree

Over the next few weeks, everything went back to normal. Every day, Rosa and I scanned the library for books on the Fae. We found a total of one hundred books so far, and we were not even halfway through the library yet. This was going to take a lot more time than I expected. Dogan and I went back to our normal training routines. We did train one day with real weapons. The man did not hold back, and I think he was fighting harder than he did before. The one thing I was proud of was he never cut me. It must be the fear of that happening because I had found myself being quicker to block his blows. Dogan bitched almost every training session about me wearing a dress. He complained that it was slowing me down and that I was quicker on my feet back in Mastingham. He also tried to talk to the general about it, but he would hear nothing of it. I was meant to be a lady, so I had to look the part.

Today was the annual soiree over at the barracks. They had one every year with music and a few kegs of ale. It started in the morning and went on late through the night. The party was an all-day festivity, so no matter what shift you worked, you could join in on the fun.

Once I got myself cleaned up after training with Dogan, I dabbed some perfume on my neck. Quickly running a brush through my hair, I decided that it would soon be time to get it cut. Standing to the side to see my reflection, my hair was now way past the middle of my back. There was a blue ribbon lying on the vanity, so I grabbed it and put in my pocket just in case I needed to pull my hair off my neck.

When I reached the steps that lead down to the main entrance, I could hear Kaidan's voice and then laughter…was that Dogan? Rounding the bend on the staircase, the two men come into view at the bottom. Dogan's smile faded when he saw me. So typical of him!

"Lee," Kaidan called. "Just the person I wanted to see."

"And why is that?" I asked, suspicious.

"I wanted to let you know that I just talked to Bryce, and he knows that neither of us will be here tonight."

"Pardon? Are ye two planning on staying at the barracks tonight?" Dogan asked like he was shocked that I would actually stay there.

"We always do. We just sleep wherever we pass out. Just ask Lee…" Kaidan beamed me a smile and continued. "She passed out on the floor of the back porch one year."

Groaning and covering my eyes with my hand, I asked, "Do you have to remind me of that?"

"Yes," he laughed and looked at Dogan. "She did not go last year because of that whole thing with Rowan leaving, so she's going to have to make up for it this year." He gave me a wink. "I will see you two there, I need to go and then get Mira."

As he headed back up the stairs, Dogan and I walked out the door together. Going down the front steps I stared up at the pink sky from the sinking summer sun. When we got halfway across the courtyard, I asked, "Why were you waiting for me, Dogan? I figured you would be at the barracks by now."

Still looking straight ahead with his hands clasped loosely behind him, he asked, "When was the last time ye saw yer horse?"

"Not since the day we got back…it's been weeks now. Why?" I truly did miss seeing her. There were some weeks that I would have been down to see her every day. It killed me, and I was sure she was missing me too.

"I want ye to go and see 'er. I'll stay hidden fer a while to see if this Dylan comes to ye."

I had been avoiding Dylan since what Dogan told me the night we arrived, "All right. Hopefully, she will be outside." A smile spread across my lips with the thoughts of seeing her.

We walked in silence, and when we reached the narrow street that led to the stables, Dogan stopped. "I'll wait here. I ha' a direct view o' the fence line. Just go to it. If that lad's around, he'll come to ye."

Nodding to him, I continued down the street. After a few strides, I came to a complete stop as the pain at the back of my head shot down my neck. That bastard! Repressing the urge to turn around and throw the sack back at him, I continued walking down the street. It might have been my imagination, but I swore I heard him chuckle as I rubbed the pain away.

My heart was pounding in my throat when I reached the fence; the pasture was full of a variety of colors and sizes of horses. The anxiety of seeing Dylan quickly faded away, and a smile spreads across my face with the sight of Ara running toward me. In excitement, I climbed up the wooden fence, sat down on the top railing, and swung my legs around as she reached me. Ara hit me in the chest with her head, and I had to grab hold of her mane so I did not fall backward off the fence.

I spoke in Salvie, "Hello, Ara girl! I know it's been too long since we saw each other." She rubbed her head against me and started to nibble on my leg. Laughter just bubbled out of me as I scratched the top of her head and snowy ears.

"Hello, stranger!" I jerked to my left to see Dylan walking out of the stables. That knot returned to my chest.

Trying to block it out, I gave him the best smile I could muster. "Hello, Dylan. How are you?"

"Better now that I am seeing you. I am surprised at how long it's been since you have been down here." He had a strange look in his eyes like he was trying to look through me. Maybe trying to figure out what had kept me away.

Staying seated on top of the fence, I just swung my legs around to the other side so I could face him. "I know...I have been busy with the queen," I lied. Inside, I wanted to drill him with questions, like what was it he's not telling me?

"How is she? I heard news of her being pregnant." Finally, he smiled up at me and laid a hand on the top railing of the fence. The man was awful close to me. A few months ago, I would have never thought anything of it, but now that I know what his true color means…well, the feeling I am getting from him now was not good.

"She's doing wonderfully." Quickly, I glanced in the direction Dogan was in, and I smiled in relief when I caught sight of him coming toward us. Waving my hand to him, I said to Dylan, "I would love for you to meet a friend of mine."

Dylan was looking in the direction I waved, and his face twitched slightly. It was like he was trying to control his expression. Quickly, he looked up to me soberly, "I am sorry, angel, but I need to go. I…ah, forgot to pick something up for Wyck today. He will kill me if he does not have it for tomorrow." He backed up a few steps and turned for the stables. "I will see you around!" Dylan yelled over his shoulder. My eyes were still locked in his direction even after he shut the stable doors. That was odd!

"D'ye believe me now?" Dogan asked as he stood beside me.

Giving him a puzzled look, I asked, "Once he saw you, he could not get away fast enough…why is that?"

"I ha' no idea," he muttered as he rubbed Ara's face. "He's not familiar to me. I will find out why, but not tonight."

As I started to climb down the fence, Dogan cupped his hand under my elbow and helped me down. Once on the ground, I stared up at him with wide eyes. "Well, that was very gentleman-like of you."

"I ha' a tendency to be one every now and then," he stated in a sober tone and started to walk in the direction he came from. I quickly ran up and fell into step beside him. I wanted to say thank-you to him but decided to just keep my mouth shut. It's just not worth it! We walked in a leisurely pace through the city toward the barracks. Even though earlier I wanted to hustle to the party, it was nice to just stroll through the city.

When we finally made it, the music and loud voices poured out the open windows and door. Once I followed Dogan in, the air was thick with scents of food and ale. He stopped abruptly, and I walk into him. *"Good Lord, this place is packed,"* he said as his voice filled my head.

Dogan was right, there were people everywhere, and I was sure there were more drinking out back too. Placing my hand on his shoulder to give me balance, I stood up on my toes and scanned the room. Catching sight of Sterling, he gestured to the both of us to come to him.

So I slapped Dogan on the side of the arm. "This way! Sterling wants both of us." Walking through the crowd of drunks, I pushed and slid my way through to Sterling.

"I never remember it being this crowded before," I reported, smiling at him.

"It was like this last year too, but you missed that one." When Dogan finally came up behind me, Sterling handed us both a tankard of ale. "I got something for you both and just consider them late birthday presents." He smiled as Dogan let out a low growl.

"Damn ye, woman," he yelled at me.

"I beg your pardon? I never said anything to him about that," I yelled back so he could hear me clearly over the music, and then smacked him in the chest. When his growl deepened because of the smack I gave him, I quickly pointed my finger up at him. "Don't ye dare growl at me!" I shouted back at him with my verison of a Salvie accent and narrowed my eyes like he always did to me.

A small smirk formed on his lips. I knew he wanted to laugh, but he kept it down. He bent his head down so his eyes were level with mine. When he purposely growled in his throat, I had to bite down on my lip to keep the laughter in. He said low and slowly, "Ye've got some nerve to tell *me* what to do."

Finally, Sterling cut in, and we both looked back at him. "I looked at your paperwork when you first joined, so I already knew about it. Besides, I really do not think you will turn my present down." His smile widened.

"It's been a while handsome," the woman purred out behind us. Turning, I saw the same woman with fiery hair that was all over Dogan at the pub so long ago. His whole face lit up, and those damn dimples popped out on either side of his face. The first time I saw this, it made me sick to think about it; but now after my night with Rowan…all I could do was smile at them. That night that felt so long ago now. Dogan told me he was a man, and he had needs—I understood that now. Oh, what I would give to have Rowan this instant. When Dogan walked away with his lady friend, I turned to Sterling.

"You know, Sterling, you did not have to get me anything." Then I started to sip on my drink.

"I know, but yours cost me a hell of a lot less than Dogan's, and it's sort of for me too." He took my hand, removed my drink, and kissed it. "Turn around, love."

Cocking my eyebrow up at him, I slowly began to turn around. Before I knew it, someone's arms were around me with their lips pressed hard against mine. Just as I was about to start swinging, I registered the tingling feeling and, I heard Rowan's throaty laugh.

"You were not just about to hit me now, Lovalee. Were you?" he asked in my head, and as I returned him a throaty laugh, I wrapped my arms tight around his neck and deepened the kiss.

"Never," I replied back to him.

When he pulled his face back, he gazed at me with smiling eyes and asked, "Did you find the one you are destined to be with yet?" Reaching up, I touched the reddish-brown stubble on his cheek. He was starting to grow out his beard again.

"No."

"Good!" He smiled, and when he let go of me, I turned to face Sterling. Walking over to him and taking his beautiful delighted face in my hands, I lightly pressed my lips to each of his cheeks.

"Thank you, Sterling. Even after what we learned a few weeks ago…I cannot believe you did this," I said to him through our touch. He wrapped his muscular arms loosely around my back and pressed his forehead to mine.

"You're welcome! We still do not know who for sure, and I figured you deserve to be happy with the man you love while you still have him. Besides, it's been too long since I have seen my brother.

"Well, is this not interesting…my two best friends are not becoming an item…are they?" asked Rowan, who had his arms wrapped around us both and pressed his forehead to ours.

Sterling threw his head back and laughed. "Well, someone had to take care of her after you broke her heart," he said sarcastically.

Rowan looked at him with sadness in his eyes. "Oh, brother, that was just wrong."

"Sorry, Row. I had to say it…you really did piss me off for what you did to the two of us. I know your reasoning behind it now, so I am over it. But on a serious note, Lee and I do have this secret love affair going on," he ended jokingly and gave me a wink.

"Well, save it for when I am not around," he said, smiling at me. "It's been a long time but can I have this dance?"

"I would love to, but only if I can dance with my secret lover later…he was always the better dancer," I remarked, giving Sterling a wink back. They both roared in laughter.

Rowan pulled me out of Sterling's arms and into his. Laughing still, he said, "I am glad to see the three of us can still be the same way with one another. I was afraid that it would be different when we were all together…I am happy it's not."

"Me too," I murmured.

"Me three! Now get your asses out there and have a good time because I will be coming soon for that dance." Smiling, he handed me my drink and went to start mingling with other people.

For hours, I ate, drank, and danced with whomever I could get my hands on. It had been too long since I had done this. I am not a heavy drinker, and I knew for sure that I would regret this in the morning. But the feeling in my head felt great at that moment.

When I walked back into the barracks after getting some fresh air, another song started to play, and I scanned the room for a dance partner. Not spotting anyone I know real well at first, and then I saw Dogan talking and laughing with a tankard in his hand. With my eyes glued to him, I stalked toward him on a mission. Dogan smiled down at me with drunken eyes as I took his ale from his hand and placed it on the table beside him.

"I ha' killed men fer less," he smirked as he stared down at his drink and then narrowed his emerald eyes at me.

"That's what I have been told, but I am not about to have you spill that on me while we dance." I beamed a smile up to him.

Dogan let out a hearty laugh, and I found myself liking the sound. It must be because I heard it so seldom. "There's no way in hell I'm dancing wit ye!" He scanned the room. "Where's that lieutenant o' yers?"

"I do not know, so that's why you are going to dance with me." Wrapping both my hands around his left arm, I started to pull him to the dance floor. Well, I tried to pull, but he did not budge. "Come on, you damn giant! Loosen up and have fun...like you did when you got drunk with my brothers." With another tug at his arm, he stepped forward, almost causing me to fall on my bottom, but he pulled me back up to my feet.

While I was laughing, he said, "Drink another one...it seems ye need it!"

When we got to the dance floor there was only a handful of couples dancing, and quickly he spun me around and pulled me to him. Instantly, I started to laugh in shock. The man was so smooth on his feet and did not miss a step. "Dogan! I did not know you had it in you. How did you learn to dance so well?" The man was so tall that I could not see over his shoulder.

"Mathair," he said as his right dimple showed.

"Well, your mother taught you well because I think you are a better dancer then Sterling." And that was amazing because Sterling was the best dance partner I have ever had.

He let out another laugh. "Ye think we're dancing well, but in reality, we're staggering back and forth."

I giggled at the mere thought of it. "I may be drunk, but I can tell you are a good dancer. Where is your lady friend? You should bring her out to dance...she would probably love that."

He rolled his eyes and let out a groan. "Oh, she's pissed off at me and left hours ago."

"Really? Oh my, I can never see how anyone can get pissed with you," I said sarcastically, and he laughed at me. "So tell me, Dogan, what the hell did you do to make her mad?"

As we were still dancing to the music, he muttered, "She told me she loves me."

"I beg your pardon?" I asked while trying to swallow the laugh that wanted to escape. "What did you say?"

"I told 'er that I'm sorry, but I dinna feel the same way. I do care fer the lass…she's a darling, but she's not my one."

"How do you know?" I asked. "She could be."

"First o' all, she doesn't ha' our gift, and second, she has a young son, not a daughter. And third, my woman doesn't ha' fiery hair," he announced. Dogan gazed down at me with a delighted expression, and it did look good on him. The man was constantly scowling; he needed to lighten up more often. Just as I was about to say that to him and ask him what color hair his woman had, he said. "I think I'm done dancing now."

"No, I am not," I protested.

He gave me his full-dimpled smile. "Wit me ye are." As he said that he turned me around and shoved me into Rowan's arms.

"Row," I yelled and pressed my lips hard to his. "Where have you been? I was looking for you."

"I was only out back." He gave me his beautiful crooked smile.

"Oh," I said and gave him another quick kiss, then we started to dance again.

Late that evening after the music stopped, I lay on the couch with my head on Rowan's lap. He ran his hand through my hair as I listened to the dozen or so men that were still up and talking. As I closed my drunken eyes, I said through our touch. *"I love you, Rowan, and I am happy you are here."*

"I love you too, Lovalee. Sweet dreams," he said, and I quickly fell asleep.

Slowly I opened my eyes and could see the sky through the window starting to lighten for the new day. Still in the same position

I fell asleep in, I looked down to see Rowan's hand loosely cupping my breast. A smile spread on my face as I rolled onto my back so I could look up at him. Quickly, I covered my mouth to hold back the laughter at the sight of him. His head was arched on the back of the couch with his mouth slightly open as he lightly snored. The poor man's neck was going to be all cramped up when he finally awakes. Moving his hand with caution so as not to wake him, I gradually sat up. I regretted that decision as my head instantly started to spin and pound. Letting out a quiet moan, I started to rub my temples. This was the reason why I did not drink often.

When I managed to stand up, I slowly made my way to the kitchen to try to make some tea. There was no one around, which was kind of odd. I had never heard this place this quiet. The other shifts must not have changed yet. After finally finding a teapot and filling it with water from outside, I set it on the woodstove. Throwing some more wood in, I stoked the fire as I stood there the whole time staring at the pot, wishing it would hurry and heat up. Then suddenly, there was the sound of someone coming down the steps.

Dogan came into view and instantly glared at me. He looked like hell! "Well, you are just a pleasant sight to see in the morning." He was barefooted, and his clothes from yesterday were wrinkled from sleep. His chestnut hair was sticking out every which way.

"Ye should talk, woman," he grumbled as he walked out the back door to the porch. Quickly, I touched my own hair and tried to brush it with my fingers. Rowan jerked up from a dead sleep and instantly moaned as he rubbed the back of his neck.

"Bloody hell," he groaned and leaned forward, resting his elbows on his knees. After a moment, he slowly turned his head, and a smile came when he saw me. "Good morning, love. How are you feeling?"

"Like hell." I laughed a little and turned to look at the pot of water again. After a moment, he was behind me wrapping his arms around my waist and pressing my back against him. I melted against his touch. Rowan turned my face to the side and took my mouth with his. Letting out a soft moan, I turned my body around without breaking my lips away from his. He lifted me up and placed me on the counter beside the woodstove. Laughing, I pulled my dress up a little and wrapped my legs around his waist. He took hold of my hair and angled my face up so my mouth was easier to access. When he deepened the kiss, he said in my head, *"I think my headache is starting to go away."*

"I may have to agree with you," I responded as he ran his other hand up my side and stopped just under my breast, *"Oh, what would I give to rip this fabric between us so that our skin can touch."* Rowan's response was a muffled noise that sounded like a moaning laugh.

"Goddamn it ye two! Get a room!" Dogan yelled. "It's too early to see that, and I'm hung over on top o' it!" Dogan stamped over and stood in front of the stove beside us. We both just smiled at him as he glared at us.

"I cannot help it, brother. She's too damn beautiful...do you not think?" Rowan asked him.

He narrowed his eyes then curled his lip. "I think she looks like hell."

Laughing at him, I said, "You should talk...bastard." And I punched him in the arm, which did not disturb him one bit. Dogan slipped out a vial from his pocket and poured a few drops of the liquid into the teapot. "What is that?" I asked.

"It's something to help wit the headache and nausea."

"Let me guess...another secret family recipe?" I asked sarcastically, and his tight lips twitched a bit to fight a smile. I do not understand why he had to fight it so. He might actually enjoy life more if he just loosened up and laughed more.

Once the tea was done, I sat next to Rowan at the table while Dogan sat across from us. We quietly talked about this and that as we sipped on our hot tea. There were sounds of someone walking up the hall, and Kaidan and Mira came into view. The sight of them brought a smile to my face because they were adorable.

"Good morning, you two. Where the hell did you sleep?" I asked and got up to grab two more cups for them.

Kaidan smiled. "Oh, I found some blankets and we slept on the floor in the general's office." Mira started to blush as she took a seat at the table.

Giving them both a huge smile, I placed the two cups of tea in front of them. When I returned to my seat, Rowan turned to me and asked, "How are you feeling now?"

Sitting there for a moment and thinking, I felt...great! My headache was completely gone, and the nausea was gone too. I answered his question with my Bayard smile. Rowan started to laugh and extented his arm across the table, Dogan took hold of it. "I do not know what the hell that was you put in there, but it worked. The pain in my neck is even gone." Rowan looked at me. "I think I just found my new best friend." Then he turned to Kaidan and Mira. "You two drink up! You will be happy you did. I do not know about all of you, but I am hungry." As he said that, he stood up and started preparing breakfast. A few more guards made their way downstairs and helped themselves to some tea. A majority of them either went back to their rooms or went and sat on one of the many chairs in the gathering room.

Rowan threw some eggs and side pork into a pan. "I give Sterling five minutes tops before he comes out here. It will depend if it's the sound of the food cooking or the smell that wakes him up first."

Sure enough, within minutes, Sterling staggered out shirtless and with a sleepy smile. "I thought I heard breakfast cooking." We all roared in laughter, including Dogan.

"You are so predictable, brother," Rowan laughed.

Sterling walked around and took a seat beside Dogan as I placed a cup of tea in front of him. "Thanks, love," he said with a wink.

"Could ye ha' least put on a shirt before comin' out here? There are ladies present," Dogan said in frustration. I was almost tempted to make comment of him referring me as a lady, but I bit down on my lip instead. He would most likely respond with something rude.

"You ladies do not mind, do you?" he asked Mira and me.

"I sure as hell do not mind. You are a fine specimen of a man, Sterling," I acknowledged and returned his wink he gave a moment ago.

"I would have to agree with Lee on that," Mira said, and I started to laugh at the shock on Kaidan's face.

"I beg your pardon?" Kaidan asked, sounding offended.

Mira laughed at her man and lightly patted his cheek. "Do not worry because you are an even finer-looking man."

Kaidan gave her a loving smile. "Good answer." He leaned in to give her a kiss.

"Bloody hell, ye all make me sick," Dogan said, annoyed.

It was nice to have breakfast with the five closest people in my life. As we finished our food, Rowan unconsciously wrapped his arm around my shoulder and started to rub my ear. I could not help but smile at the mere thoughtlessness of the action.

When I looked over to Dogan, his eyes moved back and forth between us, then he leaned forward a little, "What are ye gonna do when she finds her soul mate? I canna see ye not touching 'er anymore when she does, and I hope I'm around when he tries to kill ye fer that reason." He gave him a snide smile.

Rowan started to chuckle. "That's funny you should mention that because I had a vision of that happening. Since I know who it is…it will surely be a sight to see."

"Rowan," I yelled. "You said you did not know who it was."

"I lied. I am sorry, Lee." He presented me with a soft smile and lightly patted my leg under the table. That simple touch sent jolts throughout my body.

"I knew it," Sterling yelled and hit his fist on the table, causing some of the dishes to jump. "Just admit it so we can get this over with…It's me!"

Rowan's eyes widened. "I beg your pardon? Why do you think it's you?" he asked carefully.

"Yes, Sterling, why in the hell do you think it's ye? D'ye understand how many men are out in this world?" Dogan asked.

"I am surprised, Dogan, for how smart you are that you did not pick up on it either," Sterling stated, sounding annoyed. Dogan gave him an odd look, so he continued, "Your mothers said that the four of us will eventually be paired up, and we will make a group of six." He paused to see if it registered in Dogan's head. When it seemed it did not, he yelled, "Goddamn, Dogan! We already have three men." He pointed a finger at me. "Lee is not meant to be with Rowan, so that leaves her to be with you or me."

After he said the last part, Dogan's face got a little paler, and his eyes widened as his mouth dropped open a fraction. Quickly, his facial expression was back to its usual angry state, and he viciously glared at me. "Ye'r damn lucky that ye dinna ha' a child because I'd hang myself now just to put me out o' my misery."

Leaning forward and glaring back, I said, "The feeling is mutual, you ass!"

"Can you please just confirm that it's me?" Sterling pleaded.

"Aye, please do," Dogan added.

"Sorry, brothers, it's not my place to do that. Besides, I am not ready to give her up yet. It will be interesting to see how fate guides her to one of you." Rowan pulled me to his side and pressed his lips to the side of my face.

"Wait! We might be able to settle this right now." I looked to Dogan and asked, "Do you have a tattoo?"

"That's none o' yer damn business," he growled. Good Lord the man can be so stubborn.

"Yes, he has a tattoo," Sterling groaned, and Dogan balled his hand in a fist as he glared at him.

"Wow," Kaidan added. "All I can say is that you four have some major issues."

"You have no idea," I mumbled and rested my chin on my fist.

After we cleaned up, I said my good-byes to my men and left with Kaidan and Mira to go back to the castle. Just as I was about to walk out the door, Dogan hollered to me, "Bayard, meet me at dawn tomorrow for training." As I moaned in misery, Kaidan laughed in my face at my misfortune, and Dogan continued, "You too, Kimball!"

Kaidan gave him a serious look. "I beg your pardon?" Before Dogan could respond, I returned Kaidan's mocking laugh and shoved him out the door.

I spent the whole day with Rosa in the library. We did not do too much talking, just a lot reading. Even though I had books in front of me to occupy my mind, it still did not work. By the evening, I slowly made my way back to my room. The thoughts of the three men I shared powers with completely exhausted me. I just wanted to crawl into bed and fall in a dreamless sleep. If it was not for Rowan being somewhere in the city, I would do just that and not even bother going back out.

My room was dark with only the moonlight shining through my window. It had been so warm the last few days so there was no need for a fire even though it was still cool in the castle. As I walked blindly toward my nightstand to light the lamp, I froze at the shadowy sight of someone in my bed through the darkness. Instantly, I let their color shine, and Rowan's beautiful smile shined out. Half of his body was covered with blankets, leaving his bare chest in view. With his one arm propped behind his head, he whispered, "It's about time you made it back."

"Did anyone see you come in here?" I asked a little panicky.

He shook his head. "Nope. I was stealthy like feline."

Just like that, as quick as a snap of a finger, I was no longer exhausted. With the mere sight of his half-naked body, my whole body came alive. I could feel the passion burning all throughout me. I practically flew into my bed with excitement of feeling his loving arms around me. Eventually, I did fall asleep, but it was not until hours later.

Chapter 23

Behind Closed Doors

J was woken up with tingling lips pressed against my forehead. The feeling brought a sleepy smile to my face, and I tightened my arms around him. "Good morning, Lovalee," Rowan said in a light murmur. Oh, what would I give to wake up like this every morning!

"Good morning," I mumbled into his neck and then started kissing it.

He chuckled. "As much as I hate to say this, we need to get up. You need to meet with Dogan, and I need to see Bryce and Rosa before I head back to my post today."

"Do you really have to leave?" I asked as I heaved myself on top of his chest.

He ran his fingers featherlike down my bare spine, "I do, love, but I will be back. When? I do not know. Besides, you will not figure out who you're meant to be with if I am always around." I puckered my bottom lip at him, and he lightly smiled as he pulled my face down to him and kissed me.

After several moments of us trying to stop touching each other, Rowan finally left the bed and got dressed. He gave me several more kisses and promised that he would see me again soon and then slipped quietly out my door. Once dressed, I threw my hair up in a tight twist so it was off my neck and headed out to see if Kaidan was ready, praying that he would help get Rowan and the thoughts of him leaving out of my head.

Taking my fist, I pounded hard on Kaidan's door and got no answer. Pounding again on his door, I yelled, "Kai! Are you ready?" Still no answer. That's not like him. If he was up and out already, why did he not come knocking at my door? Did he not come because he knew Rowan was with me? Shrugging my shoulders to my own question, I headed down with my swords in my hand. I could not help but wonder how this session was going to be. He just found out yesterday that he might be destined to be with me. Dogan was pissed off about that, I knew. When he's pissed off, he lets out his frustrations on me during training. I let out a huge puff of air as I descend the stairs. There was no way this morning was going to be pleasant for me.

When finally reaching the hall that led to our training room, there was light streaming in from the open door. Before reaching the door, I took in another deep breath and tried to mentally prepare myself for what I was about to endure. Inside, Dogan was taking out several wooden swords out of the chest at the far end of the room. Looking down at my own swords in my hand, I asked, "We are not training with real weapons today?"

He closed the chest and looked back at me. "Where's Kimball?"

"I am not sure. When he never answered his door, I just figured he was already down here," I said to him. "Maybe the king needed him."

"Well, he could ha' sent word to one o' us if that's the case. Now get yer arse over here, woman." He cocked his head to the right a little.

After rolling my eyes, I slowly made my way toward him. When Dogan placed the wooden swords on the floor, I asked him again, "So why are we using the practice swords?"

"Because I want to try something," he said and took my swords out of my hand. After setting them on top of the chest, he pulled out a long piece of ivory cloth from his pants pocket and shook it out.

"What is that for?" I asked, feeling nervous of what his answer was going to be.

Dogan examined the cloth in his right hand and then gave me a devilish smile. "Turn around."

"If you think I am about to let you blindfold me, then you are *crazy*," I yelled and almost laughed at the mere thought of it.

"Oh, aye I am! Now turn around! Ye dinna need to make this any harder than it's already gonna be fer ye," he said with lifted eyebrows and signaled me to turn around with his hand. I knew that no matter how much I fought, that blindfold would end up on me. I sighed in defeat because there was no way around this.

When I turned my back to him, I asked, "Are you punishing me because of what you found out yesterday morning?"

As he laid the cloth over my eyes, he inquired, "Speaking o' that...how long did ye ken?"

"I found out the night we arrived back." Instantly, he tightened the blindfold so tight that I thought half of my head was about to pop off. "Ow! Is that necessary?"

"That was fer not telling me about it," he murmured with his lips only a whisper away from my ear and gave me a strong shove forward, making me take several steps so I did not fall on my face. After I turned myself around, I faced in the direction where he should be. I know he was doing this to try to make me force my powers out.

"You know what, Dogan? All you are is a big bully, and you cannot be pissed off at me for this. If it was the other way around, you would have done the same thing. Just admit it!" I yelled at him, well, I think I was yelling at him, but it could be the wall for all I knew. Wood suddenly hit the floor and slid to a stop at my feet.

"Pick 'em up," he ordered. There was the sound of someone walking in from the door behind me. "It's about damn time ye got here!" Bending down and reaching blindly for my weapons, and with a sword in both hands, I stood straight up.

"Well, that's just great," I said sarcastically. "You are making me fight Kaidan like this?" I pointed my thumb at my eyes.

"I want ye to concentrate, Lee. Ye can release yer energy when ye are sitting and quiet, now I want to try doing it standing. Once ye can, then we'll work on doing it wit yer eyes open," Dogan explained. I found it weird whenever Dogan said my first name. I was *woman* to him, and I found myself used to that name when it came to him. If I could, I would roll my eyes at him, but he had that awful blindfold so ungodly tight that it was starting to hurt my head. As I reached for my eyes, he yelled, "Don't ye dare touch that blind!"

"But you put it on too tight," I snapped back.

"'Tis fine, so stop complaining. Now concentrate and release yer light so ye can see," Dogan ordered. While standing there and trying not to get too angry with Dogan, I tried to focus on my core. That was short-lived when I suddenly got a sharp pain from a sword in the center of my back. The pain was so strong and unexpected that it took my breath away.

"Goddamn it, Dogan! I was not ready yet," I fiercely yelled.

"First o' all…," Dogan said a ways to my right, "that wasna me, and second, the enemy will not wait fer ye to be ready. So again, *concentrate*."

"How in the hell am I supposed to *concentrate* when I am getting wacked with a sword?" I screamed in frustration, and I start to spin in a slow circle with the sword in my right hand extended out. "And you, Kai," I sneered. "I see you are not holding back any. You just wait, you bastard! Better enjoy this while you can because I will get you back for this." After waiting a moment and getting no response, I asked, "What's this, no sarcastic remarks?"

"He was told not to talk, so ye need to use yer ears and yer power o' sight to fight 'im," Dogan explained.

"Have I ever told you that I despise you?" I asked.

When Dogan responded with, "Ye ha' told me a time or two." I had to smile because I never said his name, but he knew I was talking to him. Suddenly there, was a sense of someone coming up behind me, and I just let go and followed what my instincts were telling me to do. Quickly, I stepped to the side and spun around with my sword extended. I let out a cheer of excitement when the sword collided with another body, and I heard a grunt.

"Good again and try to use yer sight," Dogan commanded.

"I am trying!"

"Well, try harder!"

It was not as easy as he made it sound. Every time I tried concentrating on my energy, I got jolted from it whenever that damn sword of Kai's connected with my body. After several blows from Kaidan, I finally said a little prayer to myself. *Please, Lord, give me strength. Help me find my energy so I can be done with the pain they are causing me. I know I can do this! Just asking for a little help on how to do it...amen.*

It was like my prayer was answered as soon as I said *amen.* The pressure in my chest instantly appeared, and not hesitating a moment later, I pushed it out enough so I could see my surroundings. The sight in front of me was not what I expected, and I attacked at full force, catching my opponent off guard. With a sword in each of my hands, I used my right to block his blow and whack him hard in the shoulder with the left. As soon as my sword left his shoulder, I brought it around him and hit him in the back of his shins with as much power I could muster. The action caused him to lose his footing, and he fell flat on his back. Quickly, I hovered over him and pressed the point of my sword against his throat. Even though everything looked as if I was looking through a red-tinted glass, I stared down at the wide eyes before me. It was hard to distinguish what the true color was of his eyes, but I know they were a soft bluish gray.

"Rowan, my dear," I sneered with a curled lip.

"Lovalee," he said, forcing it out as he was still trying to catch the breath that left his lungs.

Cocking my head to the side, I gave him a snide smile. "I am not sure what pisses me off more...that it's been you this whole time inflicting pain on me or the fact that you lied to me about leaving."

"Yes...but you can see," he said with his beautiful smile. "Besides, you cannot hate me forever...you love me too much." Rowan gave me a wink.

Without knowing what else to say to him, I just bit down on my lip and shook my head at him. The man was too handsome for his own good. All of a sudden, there was a massive man coming up from behind me with his sword high above his head. Just as he started to bring his sword down on my back, I quickly stepped aside as Rowan rolled in the other direction. Dogan's sword collided with the white marble floor with a loud crack. I instantly cringed at the sound knowing that it could have been my back. Dogan turned his head to the left and gave me a genuine smile, which was rare for him. There was no helping it as I easily smiled back at him. I could not have been more proud of myself as I was now.

"Nicely done, woman! Nicely done indeed," Dogan praised me. It occurred to me that he was actually proud of what I just did. "I'm glad to see how ye just let yer light out just enough to see. The red is nicely encased around yer body. That's why I decided to use the lieutenant instead o' Kimball. I was afraid that ye'd expand the power out too far, and being that Kimball is not like us, ye could ha' hurt 'im. I see now that I was wrong, ye controlled it very well."

After standing there for a moment speechless, I finally said, "Wow, Dogan…Thank you." I know his compliments are few and far between, so I will not make a big deal out this even though inside I was all giddy with his approval.

"Now come get me, woman. Show me what ye got." He signaled me to him with his hand.

"As always, it will be my pleasure." I charged to him, and the sound of wood against wood echoed throughout the room. Once Dogan and I started fighting, Rowan joined in; but instead of attacking me, he attacked Dogan. Of course he dodged his blow.

"I think I told ye to fight wit' Lee here…remember?" He did not hide his annoyance but had a small smirk on his face.

"Of course I remember, but I have caused enough physical pain on her to last my lifetime. Besides, I would like to see what you got… see if you can take on the both of us." Rowan winked at me, and I returned it with a smile.

"Blindfolded," I said to Dogan.

Dogan rolled his eyes and reached into his pants pocket and pulled out more ivory cloth. With two pieces in hand, he handed one over to Rowan.

"Please tell me that you are jesting with me," Rowan said, sounding anxious.

"Rowan, you have not done it yet either?" I asked him. He just stared at me and did not say a word. Dogan let out a hearty laugh; the sound of it made me jump.

He gave me a devilish smile and said, "Well, woman, we still ha' some time…would ye like to pay 'im back fer *all* the pain he has caused ye?" I am not sure if he meant the physical pain I just endured or if he meant all the emotional pain he had caused when he broke my heart.

Either way, I was happy to do it. "Sorry, love, but it looks like it's your turn now." I grinned. Rowan let out a soft groan as he brought the cloth up to his face.

Needless to say, I got my payback, and Rowan learned how to release his light. After training was over, the three of us went our separate ways. Since Rowan was staying an extra night, I knew I would see him later. Rosa and I spent the day with Bryce and Kaidan. Some of the countrymen requested his audience, so he asked if Rosa was interested in being at his side. Of course, she jumped at the opportunity. It would be something different than just sitting around the castle or going for a walk in the garden. Doing things like this helped her feel like she had a purpose…like she was doing some good for our kingdom.

Later that evening, I made my way back to my bedchambers. My whole body ached, especially my back and arms. My priority was to get the hell out of this corset that Mira put on me after training. My back was burning in pain, and it started to affect my breathing. Upon opening my chamber door, I prayed that Mira was inside. If not, then I would have to send word for her and then that would take even longer. There was no Mira, but I did not walk into an empty room. Rowan was there sitting on my bed and was taking off his boots.

"I do not know about you, love, but I am hurting bad," Rowan muttered as he placed his elbows on his knees and gave me a half smile. Once locking the door behind me, I walked over to him and offered my hand.

"Well, shall we see?" I asked him, and he took my hand as we walked over to my full body mirror. As he lifted up his shirt, the bruises on his back came to view. While sucking in my breath, I very gently laid my hand on the bruises. I knew they were caused by me because that's where I hit him the majority of the time. "Oh, Row! I am so sorry." My eyes started to burn with tears when he finally spoke. There was no way to remove my eyes from the black-and-blue skin I caused.

"Well, Lovalee, my back may hurt, but it's not as painful as the front of my ribs. Dogan did not hold back at all...please tell me he never did this to you," Rowan said and slowly turned around to show me. Instantly, I brought my hands to my mouth to muffle the cry. In all the training sessions I have had with Dogan, never did I leave with bruised skin that extreme. Shaking my head no to his question, I reach out with a shaking hand toward his black-and-red skin. Rowan quickly stepped back, "Please do not, Lee. I think some of my ribs are broken and that's why the pain is so severe."

Trying to wipe the tears away, I walked over to my nightstand, "I have something that will help...with the bruising anyway. I am not sure if it will help with broken bones. Either way, you should feel somewhat better by tomorrow morning." I took out the jar of white paste that Dogan gave me so long ago now and the strips of cloth that Mira always kept with it. As I laid the items on the bed, Rowan was beside me.

"What is this?" Rowan asked as he picked up the jar and started opening it. When he brought the jar up to his nose, his whole face grimaced from the putrid smell. "You are not seriously thinking of putting this stuff on me...are you?" I nodded my head and gave him a sympathetic smile. "Have you smelt this stuff, and where did you get it anyway?" he inquired

Rowan practically rammed the jar at my nose, which caused me to laugh a little at his reaction to the smell. I swatted his hand away. "Yes, it smells horrible, but it works...trust me. I have used it plenty of times now, and Dogan was the one who gave it to me."

He curled his lip up at me when I mentioned his name. "I should have figured." He sounded disgusted as he walked back over to the mirror.

Softly as I could muster, I rubbed the paste on his back, rib cage, and both forearms that were lightly bruised compared to his back and chest. After the paste was applied, the areas were then covered with the cloths. Once it was all done, Rowan gazed at me. "I think it's your turn now, so why not turn around and I will unbutton the back of your dress?"

As he worked at the buttons that ran all the way down my spine, I stared at the both of us in the mirror. It still broke my heart that I could not be with him the way I wanted to. He was so handsome, and my heart still skipped a beat whenever he was near. *"Am I now... handsome?"* Rowan's voice filled my head as my cheeks reddened with heat.

Slowly, he lifted his head and gazed at me through the mirror. Giving him a smile, I said in my head back to him, *"Stay out of my head, Row! You were not supposed to hear that."*

Rowan chuckled and continued with the buttons. Finally, he pushed the dress off my shoulders and it fell to the floor. He let out a groan, "Why in hell are you wearing a corset? You hate these damn things," he said in frustration as he started to yank the string on my back.

I laughed at him. "As much as I hate to wear them, there are days when I have no choice in the matter."

Once he finished untying the corset, he let that too fall to the floor. After he lifted my shift over my head, he instantly laid his hands on my back as he fell to his knees. "Sweet mother of God, what have I done to you? I did hold back, Lee...I promise! I did not think I was hitting you that hard."

I turned my back away from him and toward the mirror so I could see for myself. I took in a sharp breath at the sight. It was bad, but not any worse then I received from Dogan. Looking back at Rowan, who was kneeling in front of me, I lifted his head and pressed my lips to his. "I will be fine, Row. Besides, I have seen worse."

"That crazy bastard has left marks on you worse than that?" he questioned angrily and pointed at me, indicating my back.

"Yes, and I was all healed the next day, so can you please help by rubbing that stuff on my back and arms?" I handed him the jar and turned around so he could rub the paste on my back. "We both have hurt each other's backs, so let's just say we are even now, and we both will stop feeling bad about doing it…deal?" Looking over my shoulder at him, I gave him a smile.

It took a moment, but he returned the smile and murmured, "Deal."

Once he was done bandaging me up, he helped me slip into a nightgown. We both climbed into bed and slowly lay down on our backs at the same time. Instantly, we started giggling at each other and how pathetic we must have look. He took my right hand and brought it up to his tingling lips.

"I am glad I decided to stay another night so we could beat the hell out of each other. To think that I could be sleeping in my own bed right now, pain free and…alone. This was the better choice." Rowan winked.

Laughing at him, I rolled to my side. "I am glad you stayed too." Laying my head on his shoulder, I placed my hand on his chest. With the instant comfort of him beside me, I let the exhaustion of the day take hold of me. Rowan kissed the top of my head and said in my mind, *"I love you."*

Smiling, I returned through our touch, *"And I love you."*

Rowan started to laugh as he stood in front of the mirror the next morning, "How is this possible? I think my ribs are healed too! There are no marks or pain at all!"

I grinned as I stared at his mark-free back as my eyes were glued to those adorable dimples above his ass. "I am not sure how it works. All I know is a mage, I mean a Fae, made it…it's magic!"

"Well, whatever it is…I feel terrific, like I could run all the way to Hebridge!" Rowan turned around to look at me. He all of a sudden had a mischievous look on his face. The man had me off my feet and on the bed before I could even think about letting out a screech. Laughter escaped my lips as he lay on top of me. While he moved the hair away from my face, I watched as his eyes looked at every inch of my face. "This is what I am going to miss," he said as he lightly traced my jawbone. "I will miss touching you…" Rowan leaned forward and kissed me. With lips a breath away, he continued, "And kissing you."

Breathless, I opened my eyes, "Let's just go, Rowan. We could jump on a ship right now and travel to another country and live our lives like we have always dreamed."

Rowan gave me a look like he was actually considering it. "That does sound tempting."

"We could easily do it. I know we would be happy," I said to him.

"You are being serious…right?" I nodded yes to his question, and he continued, "Nothing would make me happier at the moment than to run away with you, but…you know we cannot. You and I are meant for other people. They need us more than we need each other." I could feel the tears flowing down the side of my face and into my ears. "We are going to make it through this, Leelah. I promise you that. When you find out who you are destined to be with, you will be one step closer to freeing your heart of me."

"I do not want my heart to be free of you," I cried and brought my hands to his face.

His eyes started to glisten as he closed them and kissed the inside of my right palm. "I worded that wrong." He took hold of my hand and pressed it to my chest. "You will always hold me in your heart, but the pain of losing me will be gone." Then he pressed the same hand to his chest, and the tears fell from his eyes. "Just as I will always hold you in mine. The only difference is that the pain of losing you will last a lot longer for me than it will for you."

Instantly, we wrapped our arms around each other, and I buried my mouth in the side of his neck to help muffle the sobs. At that moment, it was the hardest I had cried in front of him. I think deep inside I already knew that this was the last time we would be alone behind closed doors. He was not going to come back until I figured out who my soul mate was. He never said it, but I just knew it. I did not want to let him go!

After we got our emotions to settle down, the two of us dressed for the day. I felt his eyes on me the whole time, like he was trying to see every inch of me so he would never forget what I looked like. When it was time for him to leave, I quietly opened my door and looked up and down the corridor. There was no one in sight, so I gestured him out to the hall. Since we were not married, if anyone had seen him leaving my chamber this early in the morning, they would look down on us and tell people how we were living in sin. I would rather people stay out of my business, so the less they knew, the better. Once we both were out in the hall, I shut my chamber door.

Rowan took my face in his hands and gazed in my eyes. "I do love you, and I do promise that I will write. Promise me that you will live your life like you always do, and please try to stay on Dogan's good side. The man is three times the size of you. He could kill you with the flick of his wrist."

I laughed a little at that. "I love you too, and do not worry about Dogan. You remember the story about me kneeing him in between the legs…right?"

"Yes, I forgot about that," he replied laughing. He softly touched my left cheek, and I closed my eyes for a moment to cherish the feeling.

"If the man would ever kill me, I think it would have happened right after that." I finally whispered, returning to the subject we were talking about.

"I guess you are right, but still be careful, for me."

Smirking, I said, "I will." He pressed his lips to mine and deepened the kiss before tightening his arms around me in a fierce hug. My whole body tingled from his touch. When he broke away, he lipped the words *I love you* one more time and turned his back to me as he started down the corridor. After several steps, he surprised me when he stopped, turned around, and came back to me. Rowan quickly pressed my body against the wall by my door and attacked my mouth one last time. When our lips parted, he looked at me with saddened eyes.

He said to me through our touch, *"I love you…never forget that!"*

"I will never forget," I said back to him, and Rowan backed away from me and hurried down the corridor. Just as he got to the bend in the hall, he stopped and looked back at me. He patted his chest with

his hand, and I returned the gesture. He would always be in my heart too. It was that gesture and the last kiss that answered the feeling I was experiencing earlier. The next time I saw his beautiful face, I will have knowledge of who my soul mate was.

Chapter 24

The Child

For the next month, I received one letter from Rowan, which was great. I was afraid he would not write me at all. Sterling and I made a point of us meeting at least once a week for dinner and dancing. Some weeks, we would get together more than once, which I could not complain about that. The man was always a joy to be around. Dogan, on the other hand, there was never joy when you were around him. I found it easier to just stay pissed off at him all the time. It took to much energy to be happy with him one moment and want to kill him the next. So, being angry seemed to work for me.

We had been working a lot with the bow and arrows he made me. I was quite accurate with the bow too. Just like throwing the knives, Dogan thought the bow should be one of my specialties too. Last week, for training, Dogan had me tag along with him and a few other guards when they went hunting. He knew I could shoot at a still target while standing; he wanted to see how I would do on horseback and shoot at a living thing. Needless to say, I ended up wounding the deer, and the men had to track it down to kill it. I could tell Dogan was a bit irritated that I did not kill it, but he was pleased that I at least hit the damn thing. That evening, I ended up enjoying fresh venison back at the barracks.

"I know you are anxious about seeing this weasel, so please talk to me," Mira stated as she worked on tightening my corset. We were having brunch at the duke and duchess's today. I had not seen them or Gavin since the night I broke his nose, which had been months now. I was almost tempted to pretend that I was sick but decided that I could not avoid this situation any longer. Kaidan, on the other hand, was truly sick and was not coming with us. Bryce said the day before that he was going to grab one of the guards to attend with us.

"I am not looking forward to it, Mira, but the king said Gavin wants to apologize for his actions. I have no choice in the matter anyway, I have to go." To change the subject, I said, "How is Kaidan feeling? I peeked in on him yesterday, and he was really hot with fever."

Mira let out a hard breath. "He seems to be feeling better today. The treatment the medical aides have been giving him seems to be working. We expect he will back to his normal self after a few days."

"Good, I am glad to hear that." I smiled, and she continued pulling and tugging at my back.

As I walked up the steps to the royal living quarters, Byron beamed a smile down to me. There was no helping but to return the smile back at him. "Good morning, Lee," he said as he opened the door for me, and then whispered, "Good luck today, and if he tries anything, just break his nose again."

I laughed and patted his shoulder. "Thank you, Bryon. I will try to remember that." As I made my way down the corridor, I could hear talking coming from the library. A smile formed on my lips when I heard the distinctive voice of one my best friends. Sure enough, when I walked into the room, there stood Sterling dressed in fine clothing, with his sword strapped to his hip.

"Now, Your Highness, you did not tell me that a beautiful woman was accompanying us today," he said with a massive smile and looked back at the King.

"I did forget to tell you that…where are my manners?" Bryce placed his hand on Sterling's back and gestured him forward, "My lady…," he said to me as I tried my best to keep the laughter deep inside that wanted so badly to escape. "I would like you to meet, Lieutenant Sterling Fenwick. Lieutenant, this is Lady Leelah Bayard." It was not until Sterling took my hand and brought it to his lips that the laughter finally escaped me.

Since he was still holding my hand, I spoke to him through our touch. *"Does this mean I have to suffer most of my day with you by my side?"*

Sterling's chocolate eyes twinkled. *"It seems so. It's going to be horrible being in your presence all day."*

"Ha-ha, I know it's going to be terrible!" It was not until I hit him in the chest that I realized I said that out loud. I looked shyly at Bryce, who was smiling with raised eyebrows.

"Were you two just talking...mentally?" he asked. I looked up at Sterling shyly, and I was severely embarrassed because we should not have done that in front of the king. That was not very respectful toward him.

Sterling spoke before I could, "Yes, Your Majesty. I apologize for that. We are just so used to doing it, and we did not mean any disrespect towards you."

"First of all, Sterling, when we are in here, you can call me Bryce, and second I am not angry at all that you two talked that way. I am most fascinated really, and I wish I had the abilities to do the same." Bryce then looked at me. "Besides, I know you are nervous about today, and since Kaidan cannot be with us, I thought having one of your closest friends would help."

Smiling at Bryce, I said, "Thank you." And I turned to Sterling, who was still grinning. "It will help a great deal."

"Good, now if you will excuse me, I need to see what's holding up my pregnant wife," Bryce said and then left the room.

"I have been dreading this day for a long time now, but with you here, my dread is gone...Thank you," I whispered.

"That's what I am here for." He wrapped his arm around my shoulders and squeezed me to his side, "I will make sure certain individuals will not come near you." I nodded my head, knowing he would do just that.

On the long carriage ride to the duke's residence, the four of us had light conversations about the weather and the city. Bryce even asked us how it was going with our newfound powers. Unlike me, Sterling could express his energy with his eyes open. I have been working on that every day, but it still has not happened for me. Just before we arrived, I told Sterling privately how Kaidan always jumped out and unfolded the steps before the driver could. I said that Rosa and Bryce would get a kick out of it.

Sure enough, when the carriage stopped in front of the door, Sterling got out and then unfolded the steps. He held his hand out. "My lady."

"Why thank you, Lieutenant," I said magically without laughing.

Bryce walked out of the carriage, laughing, "Please tell me that you told him to do that?"

"Me?" I lay a hand on my chest as I acted innocent. "I never said a word about it."

"Out loud you may not have," he said as he helped his still laughing wife out of the carriage. She was more than halfway through her pregnancy now, and she was filling out beautifully. I cringed a little when I heard the door behind me open. Sterling touched my wrist as I turned to see Marvin Thelas walking toward us.

Marvin wrapped his arms around Bryce in a bear hug and then went to Rosa. "Rosa, you are growing more beautiful every time I see you." He brought her hand to his lips.

"Thank you, Marvin."

When Marvin looked to me, his eyes saddened, and he came over and took both of my hands, "Lady Leelah, I do not have enough words to express how sorry I am for what my son did to you. I was hoping you would come back and pleasure us with your presence here. I would have understood though if you never wanted to see us again."

"Thank you, Marvin. The duchess and you have always been a pleasure to be around...I could not stay away from the two of you forever." After giving him a genuine smile, I looked at Bryce as Marvin kissed my hands. He lipped the words *thank you*, and I nodded to him.

"I am glad to hear that." Marvin smiled back and then looked at Sterling and then back to Bryce. "Where is Kaidan?"

"Sorry, Uncle, but Kaidan was unable to join us today." He came over and stood next to his uncle. "This is one of my lieutenants, Sterling Fenwick. You have met him before, it's just been a while."

"I remember, Bryce! I am not that old," he said as he winked at me and stuck his hand out to Sterling. "Lieutenant Fenwick, it's a pleasure to see you again."

Sterling took hold of his forearm. "The feeling is likewise, Duke Thelas."

"Please, while you are in my home, call me Marvin," he said to him and Sterling nodded in acknowledgement. "Now everyone please come on in. Brunch is about to be served."

As Bryce and Rosa walked in, Sterling stuck out his elbow, and I slipped my hand through and placed it on his forearm while he escorted me in.

"Everything is going to be fine, Lee. Just breathe. I am here," Sterling said privately.

"If the bastard tries anything again I might do more than break his nose!" I took in a deep breath. *"I am breathing...thank you,"* I said while I squeezed his hand that he laid over mine.

Of course, Gavin was late as usual. Brunch was over and the men left to do what they do while we waited for dessert to be served. I was enjoying the conversation with the duchess and Rosa when Gavin walked in.

"Gavin," the duchess screeched. "Where have you been? You knew they were coming today."

He gave her a smile that only a mother could love and bent down to kiss her cheek. "I know, Mother, and I am sorry that I am late. I got held up. I got here as fast as I could."

His mother's face softened immediately. "It's all right. I am just glad that you are here."

Gavin strolled over to Rosa, who was beside me, and kissed her hand. "Rosa, you are as beautiful as ever. How are you feeling?"

"Great, thank you for asking," she said with a lovely ring to her voice then his eyes lock on mine. As I looked away, he walked behind me and lightly traced his fingers across my shoulder. My whole body tightened and my hands on my lap rolled up in fists. If he even laid a finger on my leg, I was going to punch him. He then took a seat in the chair beside me...Sterling's seat.

"Lady Leelah, there is an apology in order for the way I treated you so many months back." Gavin took my hand, and I relaxed my hand out of a fist as he kissed it. "It was wrong and uncalled for. Could you find it in yourself to ever forgive me?" Gavin's nose had a slight curve to it now. I smiled softly because I was the one who caused that curve.

No was the true answer I wanted to say, but instead I replied, "Thank you, Gavin, and in time I will learn to forgive you." There was suddenly loud laughter as the men were returning to the room.

It was then when Rosa and the duchess were placing their attention to the other men that he whispered in my ear, "I will never forgive you for humiliating me like that. I will pay you back for that and continue where I left off."

It took everything in me to not look at him and to keep a straight face. As soon as Sterling walked in, Gavin sat straight. Even though my face was expressionless, I knew Sterling would see right through that and I was right. As Sterling came walking toward us, the duke said with annoyance in his voice, "Gavin, how lovely for you to finally join us."

"I got a little preoccupied, but I finally made it," he said to his father.

Sterling was standing behind me when he addressed Gavin, "I am sorry, my lord, but you are in my seat." I could tell by the tone in his voice that he was trying his best to keep calm.

Gavin slowly looked up behind him. "Lieutenant Fenwick, am I correct?" Sterling nodded his head. "Well, there are plenty of other seats, so sit somewhere else."

While taking in a sharp breath, Sterling pressed his hand against my back. *"This bastard has no clue how easily I could break his neck!"*

"Easy, Sterling, please try to stay calm."

"I am never calm when it comes to this worthless piece of trash!"

Just as I was about to respond to Sterling, Bryce retorted, "Gavin, Lieutenant Fenwick did not just come as my guard but as

Lady Leelah's escort too. Now you better find a different seat, or I will make my lieutenant move you."

Inside my head, I was jumping up and down and cheering at the king. If he was any other person, I would probably have given him a big kiss. Gavin shoved his chair back and glared up at Sterling. I do not know who he was kidding. Sterling easily outweighed him by seventy-five stones in pure muscle. As Gavin yanked back a chair on the other side of the table, Sterling did the opposite by sitting down calm and collected. He instantly took hold of my hand under the table.

"I am sorry I was not here when he first showed up."

Gazing at him, I said, *"It's fine. You are here now, and that's all that matters."*

"What did he say to you when I walked in? Your face might have been expressionless, but it spoke a thousand words to me."

I gave him a small smile. *"You know me too well!"* He raised his eyebrows, waiting for me to tell him so I did. *"He said he would never forgive me for humiliating him and that I will pay for it and that he will continue where he left off."*

Sterling started to squeeze my hand, and I could feel the anger rolling off him. He jerked his head and started glaring at Gavin. In return, Gavin stared back at us with wide eyes like he knew that I just told Sterling what he said to me.

Taking my other hand, I laid it over our combined hands. *"Sterling! Please look at me. Keep your anger in. This is not the place or time."*

Sterling gazed back at me, and his eyes started to soften. *"That man better pray he never meets me in an alleyway. I will make that curve in his nose the least of his worries."* I could not help it as a soft laugh escaped my lips, and I bit down on them when it happened.

"Lady Leelah, I could not help but notice…were you and the lieutenant having a conversation together telepathically?" The duke asked sounding genuinely curious and amazed. Nervously, I looked at Sterling and then to Bryce.

Instead of me answering the duke, Bryce did. "Well, Uncle, our lovely Lee has recently came across some newfound power, and

Lieutenant Fenwick is blessed with the same. They can speak to each other without saying it out loud but only when they touch." The king actually sounded proud of us.

"So, is Bryce saying that you two are mages?" he asked.

"Yes," Sterling and I said in unison. It still surprised me when I really pondered about it, me as a mage, or the correct term, *Fae*. Sometimes, I felt like I was living in a dream. I could feel Gavin's angry gaze burning through me, but I tried to ignore him and kept my eyes on the duke.

"That's truly amazing. Is there anything else you can do beside talk to one another?" he asked.

We looked to the king to get a sign that it was all right to talk about it. When he nodded yes, Sterling said, "Everyone's soul forms an aura that surrounds their body, and we can see that. We can also push our aura out away from our bodies, which can give us extra protection if we need it."

The duchess grabbed her husband's hand, and they shared a quick glance. "Let me guess…Is my aura gold?" he asked, and since I already had his color showing for me, I almost fell off my chair because he was right. He and his wife were the same color as the king. Gavin, on the other hand, was the same as Dylan…a dark murky pink. Ha, imagine that.

Both of us were speechless, and finally I asked softly, "How do you know that?"

"Can you two speak to the dead also?"

"Yes, how do you know that?" Sterling pressed the question again.

"Six years ago, we lost my wife's nephew Hector in a horseriding accident. He too possessed the same powers. He was a wonderful lad and is still greatly missed. You see, he was in love with a commoner. None of us ever got to officially meet her. She supposedly was pregnant, and he was planning to marry her. She too had the same gift. That's how he found out he could talk like you two can. My wife's sister and husband did not agree with the marriage because she was without a title, and it would put shame on the family. When the pregnant lass showed up to the funeral, my sister-in-law told her that she was not welcomed there." Marvin looked to his wife, who had tears now rolling down her face.

The duchess continued where her husband stopped. "She told the poor woman to take her soon-to-be bastard child and to never show her face here again. I have not talked much with my sister since that day. She said the woman was only there for the money, but I knew that was not true. The woman was truly grieving the loss of the one she loved. We never found out what her name was, but we always look for her whenever we go to the city."

I looked to Sterling and said, *"How old was that child you saw running in the city?"*

"I would say about five or six. It's a good possibility Hector's lover and child might be the ones Dogan has been looking for." Still holding my hand, he squeezed it because he knew what was going through my head. Was it him then that I am truly destined to be with?

On the way back to the castle, the four of us rode in silence. Bryce and Rosa knew some about our destinies, but I never told them everything. They probably knew that we needed to digest the information that we just found out. They also knew that we have been looking for a young girl who possessed the same gifts, so I am sure they were thinking the same thing we were. Was that girl Hector's child?

When the four of us made it back to the royal living quarters, it was past suppertime. We stayed at the Thelas's estate talking hours past brunch and ended up having dinner there too. Bryce turned to us. "It's been a long day," he said, "and I am going to stay here and enjoy the rest of the evening with my wife. You two are free to do whatever you like."

Sterling and I said our thank-yous and wished them a good night. As we walked down the corridor, Sterling stopped me just before my chamber door. He looked down at my locket and took it in his hands. Since he was lightly touching me with his arm, I heard what he asked.

"Is the girl that I saw Hector's child, and is it the same girl Dogan has been searching for?"

I found myself holding my breath as he opened the locket. He unfolded the paper so we both could read it at the same time. It read,

Yes

My heart started to pound. I could feel it and hear it in my ears. Sterling and I just stood there in the corridor, just staring at one another. Thinking the same thing. It had to mean that it was us who were destined to be together. He slipped the paper back into the locket and asked another question without taking his eyes off mine.

"Is Lee my soul mate?"

Sterling hesitated for a moment then opened the locket again. I held my breath as he unfolded the paper, I could tell that his hands were shaking a little. I knew why because what we were about to read could change everything. The two of us stared down at the paper and read the small print before us.

> *I am sorry, but it's not the time for you two to know the truth. Be patient. I will be giving you both visions soon, and then you can start moving ahead in your lives.*

"What the hell is that supposed to mean?" Sterling bellowed. "And be patient? How the hell am I supposed to be patient? I need to know, Lee! I cannot stand not knowing! Everything to me seems to be pointing to you. Why are they dragging this out so long? Why cannot they just confirm my hunches and tell me that it's you?" he ended calmly and took my hand.

A piece of raven hair came loose and fell in front of his face. Taking my hand, I pushed the hair back in place. "All we can do is go with our hunches right now, and hopefully, soon those hunches will be confirmed." As he placed the paper back in the locket, his eyes that were still staring into mine changed.

They softened, almost lovingly maybe. "Do you want it to be me?" he asked so quietly that with my still-pounding heart, I almost did not hear him.

"Since I am meant to be with one of you…I would rather be with my best friend and not with a man who does everything in his power to make my life miserable." Sterling laughed a little at that, which was good because I could feel tears coming soon, and I did not want to cry. "We will make it through this, and we will be happy with the outcome...hopefully."

Sterling took my face in his hands and tilted it up as he brought his face closer to mine. Closing my eyes for a moment, I concentrated on the tingling feeling of his touch. His face was so close to mine that we were barely touching, and he murmured, "Never in my life have I ever considered us in that way, but I do agree with you. If I am meant to be with anyone, I would rather it be my best friend too." After he said that, there was no stopping it as the tears lightly fell down my cheeks. Ever so lightly, he pressed his lips to mine and lingered there for a moment before pulling away. He gave me his beautiful smile and wiped the tears from my cheeks. "At least we did not burst out in laughter this time." I started laughing at that as I wiped my eyes dry. That was true, we did not laugh. Maybe because we finally came to accepting the fact the two of us are meant to be together.

A servant came into view at the end of the corridor and was walking toward us. "I am going to search for Dogan and tell him about the information we have learned." He stuck out his arm and asked, "Would you like to come, my lady?"

Giggling at his beautiful expression, I wrapped my arm around his. "I would love to, Lieutenant." We headed the rest of the way down the corridor in search of Dogan.

Chapter 25

Mixed Emotions

When we walked into the barracks, the men in the gathering room went quiet when they saw us. One of the guards broke the silence by saying, "Now look at the two of you." I smiled at his comment. We both were dressed in fine clothing. Even though I was always wearing a gown, the one I wore today was more elegant being we went to Duke Thelas's today. My hair, which was usually worn down or in a tail, was pinned up off my neck with locks of curls hanging down. If they did not know us, they would have assumed we were some type of nobility. The guard continued, "My lady, you look ravishing as ever!"

I bowed my head to him and said, "Thank you."

"Is Ramstien still here?" Sterling asked.

"Yes, Lieutenant, I believe he's still upstairs getting ready for his shift," another guard replied.

He nodded to him and looked at me. "Wait in my room while I go and get him."

As he went up the stairs I went down the hall toward his room. Just as I was about to open his door, it opened before me. There stood Captain Coster with wide eyes, "Leelah! If I did not know better, I would have thought you as a noblewoman."

Laughing I said, "Thank you, Captain. Sorry, I was just about to walk in. I did not think about knocking first."

"It's fine, I was just about to leave anyway," he said while opening the door wider. "Is there anything I can help you with, or are you waiting for Sterling?"

"Sterling, and I need to talk with Dogan, so he told me to wait here."

The captain looked around their room that was lightly lit by an oil lamp. "Well, come on in and make yourself comfortable. Is there anything I can get you?"

"No, thank you, Captain. I am fine."

"Very well. Have a good night, my lady." He gave me a mocking bow as he walked out of the room, leaving the door open behind him.

Instead of sitting on the only chair in the room, I went and sat on Sterling's bed while I waited for my men to come. While listening to other men talking, I heard the captain yell, "You better hurry up, Lieutenant! It's not every day that you have beautiful nobility waiting in your room."

As the other men started to laugh, I groaned and covered my face in embarrassment. Then I yelled at the top of my lungs so they could hear me over their laughter, "Laugh it up, you bastards!" The embarrassment faded away when they all roared even louder, which caused me to laugh also.

After a few minutes, Sterling finally came to view in the doorway, and he looked irritated, "You have no idea how stubborn this man can be sometimes. It's like pulling teeth."

"Oh, you do not have to tell me," I said to him.

Dogan started talking before he reached the doorway in his normal arrogant tone. "If I dinna hear 'er loud bloody mouth a few moments ago, I'd ha' thought I was coming to see someone o' importance." He came to view and stared at me with his intense eyes.

"She is of importance, you damn fool! Now get your ass in the room," as he said that he shoved Dogan forward. He staggered into the room and glared at me while a growl started to form in his throat.

Just as I was about to tell him, do not growl at me, he spoke to Sterling.

"I'm only warning ye once…never shove me again," Dogan practically hissed to him.

Even though Sterling was several inches shorter than Dogan, he still managed to get himself up in his face, "Last time I checked, I am your superior, so I am warning you once…never talk to me like that again!" Sterling grabbed the chair and slammed it to the floor beside him, "Now take a seat!"

"I'm good, *Lieutenant*. I'll stand," Dogan said tightly and then continue to glare at me.

"That's an order," Sterling said in a demanding tone.

Dogan started rolling his head and clenching his fists, but he finally forced himself in the chair. I finally burst when Sterling sat beside me on the bed, "Good Lord, Dogan! What the hell is your problem? Did you not sleep well or something?"

"I slept fine," he snapped with a curled lip.

"Then stop being a grumpy ass for just a few minutes then you can go and do what you need to do," I said to him in frustration. "As a matter of fact, what is really the problem because lately, you have been more irritable than usual. Did I do something to piss you off?" I needed to know because he has been rougher with me lately, and I do not understand why.

"What haven't ye done?" he grumbled.

"Well, that does not explain anything to me, so please do tell," I said, agitated. I just wanted to get to the bottom of this.

"Ye want to ken what's bothering me," he yelled. "A bitch like yerself even existing! That's what is bothering me!"

With my teeth and fists clenched, I finally let out a scream in disgust and lunged myself at him. Just as my fist was a breath away from his face, I was abrubtly pulled back and slammed back on the bed with Sterling on top of me. As he pinned me down, he yelled as his hair fell loose into his face, "Bloody stop fighting me and control yourself! That's an order!" My breath was heaving in and out of my lungs when I finally stopped fighting against Sterling's grip. He slowly turned his face to Dogan, and his voice was deep with anger, "What you said was uncalled for, and I know that you did not mean it."

"Oh, I meant what I said," Dogan said with his voice low. "And don't say that I dinna mean it because ye don't ken me."

Sterling, who was still holding me down, started to laugh at him, "Dogan you have been here for several months now. So I can say that I do know you and that you did not mean what you said because you care for this lass more than you would like to think. As a matter of fact, I think that's why you said it because you do care for her and that just plain pisses you off."

Dogan's whole face was tight with anger and spoke through his clamped teeth, "What did ye need to talk to me about?"

Sterling looked down at me. "If I let you go, will you sit beside me like a proper lady and not go after him again?" He gave me a smile. "I know how much you want to gouge his eyes out, but you have to refrain yourself."

I fixed my eyes on Dogan and mumbled, "I want to do more than just gouge out his eyes." I let out a puff of air and looked back to Sterling, "I will promise to behave."

Once the two of us got ourselves situated side by side, Sterling began to tell Dogan why he was asked to talk with us. "You are here because we learned some new information today." Dogan gave him a puzzled look and he continued. "It's about your daughter." His still-angry emerald eyes widened instantly.

Dogan took a deep breath and asked, "What did you find out?" Sterling told him the whole story about Hector, his lover, and their unborn child. I was going to add in some things but thought it would be better if I just kept my mouth shut.

"So ye think that the girl I'm looking fer is Hector's child?" he asked.

"We know for a fact it is," Sterling said and looked at me for a moment before he continued, "When we left the king and queen, I took Lee's locket and asked it two questions. I asked, 'Is the girl I saw in the city Hector's child and is she the one that you have been searching for?' There was a single word on the paper, and it read *yes*." Dogan started rubbing his face as he let it all sink in.

Finally, he spoke, "Well, that should relieve ye a little bit then," he said, addressing me. "She's got a mother wit the same powers, so that means I dinna ha' to kill myself because I'll not be getting stuck wit ye." My mouth dropped in disgust. What a bastard!

"We still do not know that for sure. None of us have had visions yet," Sterling said.

"Put the pieces together, Sterling. They fit perfectly for me. Now if there's nothing else…can I be excused?" Sterling nodded yes to his question. Quickly, he was up on his feet and out slamming the door.

Staring at the empty chair, Sterling said sarcastically, "That went well!"

Suddenly, there was tightness in my chest. I tried to take a deep breath to settle the feeling but could not with my corset on. Taking hold of my dress at my chest, I tried to grab my corset to pull it forward, but it would not give. My short breathing started to quicken and the panic set in.

Sterling touched my shoulder. "Lee what's wrong?"

Without taking my eyes off the chair, I forced out, "I need to know! Why will she not tell us? I cannot be with him, Sterling! I'm afraid there is a reason why she will not say yes about the two of us." I looked to him with panic as the tears started to come. "I do not want to be with him. You see how he treats me. What if in the end it is him…I do not think I will be able to handle that."

Sterling started to rub my back to try to settle me down. "Everything is going to be fine. I know how arrogant the man is toward you, but I know he only does that to cover the fact that he actually cares for you."

"Please do not say that!" Quickly, I stood up to see if it would help me breath better, but it did not. The tightness worsened, and I kept pulling at the front of my dress. Sterling was instantly at my side.

"Breathe, Lee! You are starting to hyperventilate," he said in concern.

"This damn corset!" The tears streamed down my cheeks as I panicked. "I cannot breathe!"

"All right, do not faint on me," Sterling ordered as he started working at the buttons on my back. "They are too bloody small for my fingers, it will take me forever to get them all undone. Give me one of your knives!" He held his hand out, and I gave him a questioning look. "If you want to breathe, you will give me a knife." Quickly, I handed him the one off my right thigh. "Now try to keep still." I held my breath for a second as he laid the blade flat against my lower back. With one quick move, he ran the blade up my spine. The noise of tiny buttons littered the floor, and my dress loosened forward on me. "Now seriously, stay still because the blade could easily cut you." After taking several more short breaths, I held it again with my back straight as a board. Even though I was wearing an undershirt under the corset, I could still feel the coolness of the blade through the thin fabric. In two slices, the corset snapped forward, and my lungs fully expand as I fell to my knees. Sterling was right there with his arms around my shoulders, "There you go. Not so quick…slower. Good, you are going to be all right."

"Thank you," I said breathlessly. Instead of talking, I felt his tingling touch through my undershirt as he rubbed up and down my back. As my breath came back to normal, I started to feel like an idiot. What the hell is going on with me? I never used to get panic attacks like this, and I have had at least two, all because of Dogan. Reaching behind me and taking hold of the end of the corset, I pulled it the rest of the way off.

Sterling started laughing, so I asked, "What is so funny?"

"It was only a little while ago that it was you who was calming me down," he whispered, blessing me with his contagious smile.

Covering my face in my hands, I spoke. "I know. I am an emotional mess. One moment I am strong and collected, the next…well you just saw." After a long while of sitting on the floor brooding, Sterling stood up. Turning my head, I watched him as he started to unbuckle his sword. I asked, "What are you doing?"

"I am getting ready for bed. It's getting late and Bryce wants me at the castle in the morning." He sat on his bed and started taking off his boots.

Standing up myself, I asked, "Well, do you have a cloak I can borrow? I really do not want to walk all the way to the castle with the back of my dress open."

Sterling placed his boots under the bed and beamed a smile at me. "Oh you can borrow my cloak…in the morning. It's too far of a walk to be going to the castle alone at this hour."

"I can handle myself, Sterling," I said with my hands on my hips. "I am the guardian of the queen, for God's sake!"

"I know you can just as I know you would have done some damage to Dogan earlier if I allowed your fists to connect with him. But I am still not allowing you to leave. Now you can sleep in the captain's bed." He gestured with his head to the other bed against the right wall.

I started laughing at him as he pulled down the covers. "You have got to be jesting with me!"

He laughed at me as he got into the bed. "I am not jesting, so go make yourself comfortable."

Walking up to the bed, I asked, "Are you crazy?" Then continued while pointing at his door, "Do you know what the other men would think if they saw me leave your room in the morning? They would think of me as a whore. The majority of them know of my relationship with Rowan, and then they will see me leaving his best friend's room. No, I am sorry, but I cannot do that."

"Leelah…" He began laughing while shaking his head. "You are no whore and the majority of the men know of our relationship… friendship. Besides the old Lee would not give a damn of what other people think. Now take off your shoes, your knives, and go to bed."

I was almost tempted to take off for his door, but it was not worth the energy. Sterling would have a hold of me before I could reach the handle. With a groan, I plopped on the other bed in defeat. This was not how I planned to end my evening. While taking off the knives on my thighs, Sterling said, "I promise we will be out of here before anyone gets up to start the next shift."

"I am holding you to that." After placing my knives and shoes under the bed, I got myself as comfortable as I could get. With a sigh, I murmured, "Good night."

"Sweet dreams, love," he whispered back.

It was still dark when I woke up. Letting Sterling's aura show, I could tell his eyes were still closed. Ever so slowly, I lifted my legs and brought them over the edge of the bed. When I bent down to retrieve my boots from under the bed, I cringed when he spoke, "And where may I ask do you think you're going?"

"Back to the castle," I whispered. "It's got to be getting close to dawn."

"Not without me you are," he stated as he sat up and swung his legs over the edge. "I meant to talk to you about Rowan last night," he said as he leaned over, and the room was filled with new light. "How are you doing with all of that anyway? We have not talked about it in a while."

"The best I can do I guess. He never said it, but I do not think I will see him again until I know who the man I am meant to be with is." Looking back at him, I continued, "It's just a hunch."

With his eyes locked on me, he asked, "And how do you feel about that?"

Gazing at him, I was surprised at my own answer, "A little bit disappointed but…mostly relieved."

"Relieved?" he asked in astonishment.

"Yes, I believe so. I have been an emotional mess as of late, and if I saw his face all the time, it would only make matters worse." I cannot believe it, but it was truly how I felt.

Sterling's eyes opened wider and gazed at me lovingly. "You are just realizing this now." I nodded instead of speaking. He got up and came over to me. After giving me a light kiss to my forehead, he said, "I am going to go to the bathing room to wash up. I will not be long, so promise me you will not leave." He walked over to his wardrobe to grab his uniform.

"I promise."

With his uniform in hand, he bent down and picked up something off the floor. He came over and placed it in my hand. "Here, while you are waiting you can pick these up." A small white button from my dress. After he left the room, I got on my hands and knees and searched for all the buttons that scattered in all directions. Once confident that I found them all, I placed them in a pile on the bed. Then I slowly removed all the pins in my hair as some had started to cause me pain. With my hair pin-free, I took my hands and shook out the locks that were still up.

When Sterling returned wearing his normal guard attire, he helped me put on his cloak. Since he was taller than me, the fabric lightly dragged on the floor. He brought up the hood and pulled it down over my face.

"There, no one will ever know that it's you under that hood," he said and handed me my corset, which I tucked under my arm. He then took the pile of pins and buttons and stuffed them in his pocket.

While holding the cloak closed in front of me, Sterling walked out to see if there was anyone in the gathering room. I watched him from the doorway, and when he waved me to him, I hurried down the hall. It was instant relief when we stepped outside to greet the cool early morning air. Once we were a block away from the barracks he whispered, "I told you that I would have you out of there before the shifts switched."

"Thank you," I said, staring at the ground smiling and bumped myself into him. In return, he wrapped his arm around my shoulders. "We do not have to be with Bryce and Rosa for a few hours yet. What are you going to do?"

"The castle is huge. I will find something to keep me busy until then." He beamed a smile down to me.

By the time we actually made it to the castle walls, the sky was starting to lighten and the stars were disappearing one by one. As we walked up the stairs of the walls gate, my heart started to pound at the sight of the men at the front door of the castle. It was not all the men I was nervous of seeing, it was just one in particular. With his arm no longer around my shoulders I took hold of his hand, "Did you know that Dogan was at guard at the front door?"

"No," he groaned. "Just walk straight up the steps and do not say anything to him. If he tries to start something…let me handle it, all right?"

Nodding my head yes, I kept walking forward with my head down. *Please, Lord, do not let him be his normal arrogant self. I do not want to make a scene in front of the half-dozen or so other men. I* took a deep breath as we reached the first steps toward the door. The majority of the men said good morning to the lieutenant and did not acknowledge me. As I was about to pass Dogan, I was only four steps from the top when he took hold of my arm with a fierce grip. He yanked down my hood, and the two of us glared at one another.

"Ye are unbelievable." He gave me a look of disgust.

"It's not what it looks like, and you know it," Sterling retorted with his hand grabbing the arm that Dogan had a hold of me with.

"It's exactly what it looks like," he stated to Sterling and narrowed his angry eyes back at me. "Ye just canna help yerself, can ye?"

"What hell is that supposed to mean?" I asked angrily and stood on my toes while I pushed myself to him so that I was closer to his face.

"You better release her now...so help me God," Sterling warned. Dogan and I glared at each other as I tried to search his head for what he was thinking and then he shoved me away from him.

"Go ahead up, Lee. I will see you at breakfast," Sterling said without taking his eyes off Dogan. Taking hold of my dress I made the rest of the way up the stairs.

Just as I reached the platform Dogan hollered to me, so I turned to glare at him. "Just to let ye know, that corset there"—he pointed at it which was now visibly in my hand—"works better on!" He bared a wicked grin. I looked over at the other men as the heat rose in my cheeks and fixed my eyes on Dogan.

"Like I said before, and I will say it again...go rot in hell!"

"I look forward to the opportunity!" He gave me a mocking smile as I stormed through the door. Once inside, I bent over as I tried to catch my breath that I just realized I have been holding.

As the door shuts, I heard Sterling bellowed, "You and I need to talk so let's go!"

The guards stood in front of the closed door with raised eyebrows at me. "Do not even ask," I mumbled as I headed for the staircase to go to my room.

"Lee?" I turned to find Mira walking toward me. "What are you doing up and about this early?" She stood at the foot of the stairs with me, waiting for me to answer her, and then she really looked at me. She opened the cloak a little more and gazed at my dress, "Are you just arriving?" Letting out another deep breath, I placed the torn corset in her hands and ascended the stairs. A moment later, she was at my side still looking at the corset, "Well, by the looks of this, I would say one of us had a very exciting evening. Please do tell!"

"Believe me it was not exciting, and I will explain everything once we are behind my closed door," I whispered to her, and she nodded, but her smile never faded.

Once dressed for the day, I sat at my vanity while Mira braided my hair, "Mira, you have no idea how all of this feels. You are lucky that you can be with the man that you love. For me, it's like I am being forced into an arranged marriage."

"Think of it this way...at least you know of and are friends with these men. It could be like the king and queen's. They never met till they were married, and look at them now. It took some time, but they learned to love each other. You are already a step ahead by knowing Sterling and Dogan. I am just saying, it could be worse." She smiled at me as she finished my braid.

"The worst-case scenario is if I have to be with Dogan," I whined to her.

Mira wrapped her arms around me and rested her chin on my shoulders. "And by the sounds of it, Sterling is probably the man for you, so try to let go of the what-ifs."

She made me smirk because she was right. "Thank you."

Mira kissed my cheek and said, "That's what friends are for." A knock came at my door, and she went to answer it. "Lieutenant, how lovely to see you!" I swiveled in my seat to see the door, but I still could not see him.

"Good morning, Mira. May I come in?" Sterling asked. She opened the door wider, and he strolled in. "You can stay, Mira, but can you please shut the door."

"Most certainly, Lieutenant." After the door was shut, Sterling turned to Mira.

"I assume Lee told you what happened?" he asked.

She nodded. "Yes, she told me."

"Good." He reached into his pocket and poured all my buttons and hairpins into her hands, "Hopefully, I did not ruin the dress too bad."

Mira laughed at him as she brought the items to the vanity. "The buttons can easily be sewn on and the corset can be restrung."

I forced a smile, and he finally spoke to me. "I am sorry for earlier."

Shaking my head, I said, "Please do not apologize. It happened, and I am fine." I smiled at Mira. "She helped me settle down."

Finally, his lovely smile showed, and he said, "Good. Thank you, Mira, for that." She bowed to him, and he continued, "I had a talk with him, and he promises to try to be less agitated when it comes to us."

I laughed at that. It's hard to picture Dogan promising anything. "What did he say to you?"

"Let me just say that he and I have an understanding now."

"An understanding, about what?" I asked, wanting to know more.

"I will see you at breakfast, Lee." He looked at Mira and bowed. "Ladies." Quickly, he walked out the door, and I yelled after him.

"Sterling!" But I got no response. Damn men…What the hell?

I looked at Mira, who was smiling at me from my wardrobe. "I love Kaidan do not get me wrong, but if I were you, I would not be upset about being with a man like Sterling. The man is beautiful in every way possible."

My mouth dropped in shock. "Mira," I screeched, taking hold of the brush on the vanity and chucked it at her. She laughed as she dodged the flying weapon.

The corridor was brightly lit as I made my way to the king and queen. When I first arrived this morning, only a few candles were lit so there was just enough light to see. The guards let me in, and I came to a stop before the dining room when I heard laughter. Sterling had a beautiful laugh, and it made me smile as I walked into the room, but that smile was short-lived when I saw who he was talking to by the fireplace.

"Oh, sweet Lord," I yelled at the ceiling. Could this day get any worse? "What the hell are you doing here?"

As I marched toward them, Dogan turned around and faced me. "I was invited."

I asked Sterling, "Why was he invited, and what the hell is going on here?" I pointed at the both of them. "What are you two, the best of friends now?"

"Oh, it seems so!" Dogan gave me a sarcastic grin as he wrapped his arm around Sterling's shoulders. Giving them both a dirty look I turned on my heels to find Rosa. I froze when I found Bryce standing behind me.

"Good morning, Leelah!"

"Good morning." I forced him a smile then asked, "Why was Dogan invited for breakfast?"

"You will find out soon enough."

Wanting to scream, I bit down on my lip then finally said, "If you will excuse me, Your Highness, I am going to go and search for your wife." I glared at the men behind me. "There are too many men in this room for me to handle at the moment." Looking back at Bryce, he stepped aside so I could go.

When I made it to the hallway, I heard the king say, "You two come join me in the library while we wait for the women to join us for breakfast."

After several steps down the hall, my whole body froze with a touch of a hand on my face. I could not see anyone, but I could feel it. My body shook with a chill. "It's all right, Lee. Ye know I will not hurt ye." Dogan's mother's voice was beside my ear. Again, another chill raked through my body.

"Cici?" I asked barely with a breath. "How?"

"I am capable of doing a lot of things. Now the reason I am here is because of my son. You remember you told me that you will try your best at making my son laugh and smile," she whispered in my ear.

"How can I?" I asked. "You see how treats me."

"Do you think you are the only one that has to deal with this? The only way Dogan knows how to handle his emotions is with anger. You are strong, Leelah! You can be the better person here. If you keep being the exact opposite of him, then he will eventually stop being an ass with you. I promise." I closed my eyes when it felt like her lips were on my cheek.

"Lee!" All of a sudden, my whole body was shaking. "Lee, what's wrong? Look at me, damn it!" Finally, it registered in my head that it was Sterling who was shaking me. I looked up to him with wide eyes as I let sink in what just happened to me. "What happened? Your body is freezing, and it was like you could not hear me."

"It was Cici," I whispered to him.

"Dogan's mother?" he asked, looking behind me; and in return, I did the same. Dogan, who was standing beside Bryce, had a blank expression.

"Could you hear her?" I asked Sterling.

"No, what did she say?"

"I cannot right now. Please let go of me." He did without hesitation, and I continued down the hall quickly. With the sounds of heavy footsteps, I whirled around to yell at Sterling only to find Dogan only a breath away from me.

Looking up at him, he asked, "What did she say?"

Shaking my head, I said, "I cannot, Dogan." As I turned to continue down the hall, he took hold of my arm. After rolling my eyes, I pleaded to him, "Dogan, please!"

Instantly, his whole face softened. "I'm sorry fer earlier and fer what I said last night. It was uncalled for, and I was wrong." He released my arm, and I took a few steps backward without taking my eyes off his. Without saying a word, I turned my back to him and continued in search of Rosa. Dogan never apologizes. Why is he now? What would I give to have my old life back at the farm right now? Life was so much simpler then.

When the five of us finally sat at the table for breakfast, Bryce waited until our plates were full before he started speaking, "I am sure you all know that I will be leaving for Claratina within the next few weeks to sign that peace treaty." The three of us nodded in agreement. Claratina was a country to the east of here. We have been at peace with that country for the last twenty years, but the king of

Claratina wanted to make it official. Bryce wanted as many allies as he could get, so of course, he was going to go. Our countries are separated by the Celtic Sea. Needless to say, our king is going to be gone for quite a while to just sign a paper. He continued, "I am going to be taking about a hundred men with me. I know I usually have you come with me, Sterling, but I am going to have you stay here."

Sterling nodded. "All right."

"For the first time, I have knowledge of at least four of my guards who possess special powers. Three of them are before me now." He took his wife's hand and smiled at her. "Because Rosa is in her last half of the pregnancy, I cannot bring her along with me. Since I know what the three of you are capable of, I would sleep better knowing that you are here. One of you can take Kaidan's room while we are away, and there is another room across from Lee's that you can use."

"You want Dogan and I to actually sleep here when you are away?" Sterling asked.

"Yes. Will that be a problem?" Bryce asked.

"Nay, Your Highness," Dogan answered.

"It will not be a problem," Sterling finished. I looked across to Dogan for the first time since I sat at the table. When his eyes fixed on mine, I quickly looked away.

"Good, it's settled then, now please eat and enjoy." He picked up his fork and dove in. Looking to Sterling, he gave a look of concern and lipped the words, "You all right?" After taking a deep breath and realizing that I was truly all right, I gave him a smile and nodded yes. To reinforce that I was all right, I grabbed his hand under the table, *"Yes, I am just fine."*

"Good." He smiled as he rubbed his thump across the top of my hand. I can feel Dogan's stare burning through from across the table. Clearing my throat, I looked at him quickly before returning to my plate.

Chapter 26

Salvatorian

It was three weeks later when the king and his entourage left for Claratina. That was an emotional day for Rosa. She kept to herself most of the day with fear and sadness of her husband not being able to be there when their child was born. He reassured her that he would be back in plenty of time before the birth.

Sterling ended up taking Kaidan's room and Dogan was across the hall. The king had been gone just over a month and a half now, and I had to admit I liked having the two of them so close. Dogan was still a mean fool, but I had been doing what Cici told me to do. It does seem to help a little. I found him having to turn away from me more now because he's fighting a smile. Sterling and I sneak through the hidden doors of our wardrobe almost every night. Just to talk mostly, and he's been helping me access my core with my eyes open. I still have not done it by myself yet, but I know I will. Patience and time. That's what the two of them keep ramming into my head.

If we were not enjoying the queen's company, then the three of us would be down enjoying Varon's cooking firsthand. I was getting used to my little pack of three. Both men were the exact opposite of each other, yet at the same time they were similar. One was sweet, loving, and always was there when you needed him. The other was mean, grumpy, and loved to make your life a living nightmare, but he has showed signs of charm to other woman, so there is hope for the man. Our pack was still short a member…Rowan. I know some day in the future, all of us will be together as a unit, but I did not know how far into the future that would be.

"I am quite tired, Lee so I think I am going to head to bed," Rosa said to me while we sat on one of the lounging chairs in the library. She looked exhausted as she rubbed her *growing bigger every day* belly. I knew the baby kept her up late last night with a lot of kicking.

"You have not eaten dinner yet. Do you want me go and get you something?" I asked her.

"No, thank you. I am not hungry at the moment." Then her face lit up, "Lee, hurry feel!" Quickly, she snatched my hand and laid it on her belly. "Right there! Do you feel it?"

There was pressure like something was trying to poke through. Scooting closer to her, I laid my other hand on her belly. Laughter bubbled in my throat in pure amazement, "Rosa, how beautiful! I can actually feel it moving around in there." Never in my life had I ever experienced anything like it before.

"I told you that it's in the evenings when he or she is most active." She laid her hands over mine. "I am glad this happened before you left. I know you have been wanting to see what it was like."

"Me too." There was no way my grin was going to fade. I continued to lightly laugh as I rubbed her belly and felt the baby kick.

When finally leaving Rosa, I started to rub my own belly when it growled. It was time for dinner and to find my men to see if they would like to join me. As I got closer to my room, there was a guard knocking at my door so I hollered to him, "Can I help you?"

"My lady," he said and walked over to me. "I just want to let you know that one of the stable hands came by. The lad wanted us to tell you that there is something wrong with your horse. I guess she's not acting her normal self and was wondering if you could go down and take a look."

My heart dropped. "She's sick?"

"I suppose so, my lady. I am just telling you what I was told."

"Thank you, I do appreciate it." I bowed my head to him and hurried to my room so I could grab my cloak.

I ran so fast down the corridor that I almost fell flat on my face when I reached the stairs. Luckily for the railing, that did not happen. As I rounded the bend in the staircase, I yelled to the guards when they came into view, "Open the damn doors!" By the time I reached them, it was open just enough for me to squeeze through. While running across the courtyard, Sterling was coming toward me.

"I cannot talk right now," I yelled at him as I was about to pass him, but he took hold of my arm and spun me around.

"Whoa, Lee! Why in such a hurry? What's wrong?" he asked in concern when he saw the panic in my face.

"Something is wrong with Ara! Please let go of me so I can check on her."

"Do you want me to come?"

"No, Sterling! I will be fine. Go see Varon and order me something delicious for dinner. I will be back by the time it's done." I forced a grin.

"All right." He let go of me, and I took off again.

He hollered behind me, "Be careful!"

"I will!" I yelled back. The crisp fall evening air helped cool my heated cheeks. It was going to be snowing before we knew it. When the stables came into view, I pushed my now-burning legs to run faster. *Almost there! Please let her be all right!*

After sliding the door open and practically falling in, I hurried to her stall. Ara threw her head back in excitement and came over to nibble on my shoulder.

"Are you all right, Ara girl?" I rubbed my hands up and down her massive neck and then stepped back so I could get a good look at her face. I did not notice it when I first walked in, and I do not know how I missed it. She was wearing a riding bridle with a bit in her mouth. Looking around at her back, she was wearing my saddle too. Taking hold of her reins, I brought her head down to my level. She was not sick, she was just fine. "Why are you saddled?"

"Because I saddled her." I jumped to his voice. Dylan, who was standing a few stalls up, started to make his way toward me. My heart was pounding so hard that I was afraid he might hear it. I stopped coming here altogether a few months back. If I needed my horse, someone else would get her for me. After everything I learned from Dogan and what the color dark murky pink meant, I lost all trust for the man. For the first time, I was afraid of him; this did not feel right, and he did not look right. He had not shaved in several days by the looks of it and who knows when he had a haircut last? "Why have you been avoiding me, angel? Ever since you came back from your family's, you have changed. Is it because of that bastard Ramstien?"

There was a twist in my heart, and I wanted to say, *as a matter a fact, yes*! Instead I asked, "How do you know Ramstien? And do not lie to me because I see how you act whenever the man comes near you. Do you have your memories back?"

"Look, Lee, I do not have time to explain everything right now, but I will eventually. I need you to come with me. We do not have much time." He took firm hold of me.

"What the hell are you talking about? I cannot go anywhere! As a matter of fact, I need to go back to the queen now, so I would appreciate it if you would let go of me!" After trying to push him away, he pressed me against the stall beside Ara's. She was whinnying and kicking the stall walls. Ara knew the trouble I was in. With his body pressed against mine, he traced my face with his left hand, and I jerked away from his touch.

"I am crazy about you, angel…I love you! I cannot let you go back to the castle. Something is about to happen, and I can ensure your safety." Just as I felt like I was about to get sick, the man pressed his lips to mine. Quickly, I move my mouth to the side and struggled against his body.

"What's about to happen? And please, Dylan, do not kiss me again because I do not feel the same!"

"Goddamn it," he yelled and slammed his fist against the wood beside my head. It was not the action that sent a chill down my spine but that he spoke with the Salvie accent. "I lied to ye, Leelah, but I had too. Ye did save my life that day, and I woke up wit my memories, it just made everything easier if they thought I lost it. My name is Lars Kellen." As he spoke, I slowly retrieved the knife off my right thigh. Dogan was right! The man was never to be trusted. He fooled us all. How did he keep our accent for so long and never slip, until now?

With my hand tight around the hilt of the blade, I stated with disgust, "You are a spy for King Alistair." Narrowing my eyes, I continued, "Ramstien was right...you are dishonest. You are probably lying right now about your true feelings for me."

He let out a wicked laugh. "And ye think Ramstien is honest? Sorry to break it to ye, love, but Ramstien is working fer the same side as me."

"You are lying," I screamed. Pushing him back just enough to bring my knife up, I dug it into the top of his left shoulder. The man let out a horrific scream. Once he let go of me, I yanked out the knife and ran like hell. Not looking back, I never stopped even when I reached the castle gates and practically ran into Dogan and Sterling.

"Good Lord, Lee. You are shaking...what happened?" Sterling said as he laid a hand on my left shoulder. Looking at Dogan with terrified eyes, he gazed down at my right hand and lifted it up. "Is that blood?" Sterling asked. Even in the dark, you could see the crimson still wet on my blade.

Dogan wrapped his hands around the hand that was holding the knife. "Whose blood is this?" he asked calmly.

"Dylan," I whispered. The two of them shared looks, and Sterling took off in the direction I came in.

"Go to yer chamber. Sterling and I'll be there as soon as we can." I nodded and hurried toward the castle. Dogan yelled to one of the guards, "Calus, search for Mira. Tell her Lee needs her." The guard ran in ahead of me, and I kept my vision straight ahead, never giving anyone the slightest glance.

After the blood was cleaned off my knife I put it back against my thigh. I started pacing my room back and forth. Mira tried her best to settle me down, but it just was not working. I was not waiting long before I got a knock on my door. Mira quickly opened it, and my two men walked in with three other guards who stood out in the corridor. The both of them came and stood in front of me and used their eyes to search for any blood on me.

"We found blood in the stables, but it looks like he got away by horse." Sterling asked, "What happened? Did he hurt you?"

"Ara?" I asked. My heart sank with the thought of him taking my horse.

"Ara, is fine and still in her stall," Sterling said.

Looking down, I took a deep breath to try to help settle me before I started talking. Suddenly, there was tingling fingers on my chin as Dogan lifted my head so I would look at them. "What did the man do, Leelah?" he asked softly, saying my name with a ring in his accent, which was both rare for him.

"He's been a spy this whole time. He has never suffered any type of memory loss. Something bad is about to happen. That's why he tricked me to go down there. He said he loved me and he wanted me to go with him because it was the only way to ensure my safety. He ended by saying that you were fighting for the same side as him... King Alistair." Dogan's face got hard when I said his ex-king's name.

"D'ye believe 'im?" he asked angrily. "D'ye think I'm still working fer Alistair?"

Quickly, I shook my head no, and Sterling slapped him on the shoulder. "Lee and I personally know for a fact that you are no longer apart of the Salvie army."

Dogan's shoulders instantly started to ease, and he took a step closer to me so that we were barely touching, "Are you sure that you are not hurt anywhere?" I nodded yes, and he continued, "Did he say anything else? Like his true name?"

Widening my eyes, I cried, "Yes, he did, I almost forgot! He knows you, Dogan. He said his name was...Lars...Kellen."

Instantly, Dogan's face went lax and paled. "Oh my God," he whispered out in Salvie before he turned on his heels for the door. He started barking orders. Even though they were all higher ranks than him, they all listened and scattered. "Get the general and tell him to meet us in the war room, it's an emergency!" He gestured Sterling to him. "Let's go, brother! We need to prepare for an attack." The two of them took off down the corridor.

Standing there, unable to move or speak, I stared out the empty door. Mira stood in front of me and placed her hands on my shoulders. While gazing into her terrified eyes, she said, "Lee, look at me. Please do not freeze up on me now! I am scared! What should we do?"

Shaking my head and trying to bring my mind back to the now, I swallowed what fear I had down, "We need to get to Rosa, but I need to find out what's going on." Running over to my wardrobe and opening the compartment on the bottom, I took one of the knives and handed over to Mira. I said as she stared down at it, "Put that in your pocket." When she did, I continued, "I am going to bring you to Rosa. She'll probably be in her room. Find her and stay with her until I return...all right?" She nodded as she looked like she was about to cry. With my arm around her, we hurried out the door toward the royal living quarters. Once we reached the doors, I said, "Please let Mira in. Something is happening, we might become under attack. I need to find out the details so I am having my maid stay with the queen until I come back...please!"

Quickly, the men opened the door and let her in for me. As they shut the door, I took off down the steps and yelled over my shoulder, "Do not open that door for anyone?" Stopping at the bottom, I looked at the men, wishing Byron was working. "Do you understand?" They nodded, and I said, "Only for me...no one else!" Then I continued down the corridor.

When I reached the front entrance of the castle, there were guards running every which way. It was chaos. Dodging out of a guard's way, I finally made it to the corridor that ran along the far end of the castle. The war room was packed full of uniformed men. There was a layout of the city on the table. The general looked down at it with Dogan and Sterling on either side of him. He was yelling out orders for where men should go. Behind the general and my two men was a huge window that looked out to the ocean. Something inside me was pulling me toward it. I weaved my way through the crowd and stopped when I was behind the general. Staring out into the darkness for a while, I started to turn around to listen to the general. Suddenly there was a crack of lighting so loud that everyone in the room went quiet. The whole sky lit up showing a horrific view. "Oh my God!" I barely whispered out. Hundreds, and I mean hundreds, of ships came to view on the ocean. I have lived near the ocean all my life, and I have never seen so many ships at once. I took hold of Dogan's arm, who was now standing beside me.

"It's too late! They are already here," someone yelled, and then the bell tower high above the castle sent out the alarm of the attack. The men flooded out of the room. The general, I, and my little pack continued silently staring out the window in disbelief. Suddenly, there were sounds coming from the hall of horrific screaming and steel against steel.

"They are in the castle already? How?" Sterling roared.

"Alistair must have had some ships hit shore above the city," Dogan yelled as he withdrew swords from his hip and back. The swords I made him.

"Rosa," I screamed in panic. As I was running with them toward the door, Dogan yelled my name.

I stopped to look at him and he said, "Here, you are going to need one of these." He handed me one of his swords. It's heavier than mine, but I could control it if I use both hands. Taking hold of my face with one hand, he squeezed my cheeks. "Remember everything I taught ye. This is the real thing now. They are ruthless, and they'll not care that ye'r a woman. Stay sharp!" Out the door we went.

Dogan and I were side by side as we ran behind the general and Sterling. He pushed out his aura so it encased the both of us. "If ye stay close to me, this will protect ye, but ye still can fight." I nodded in acknowledgement.

When we reached the main entrance of the castle, it was still in complete chaos. The only difference was now the floor was littered with bodies of both kingdoms and blood. Lots and lots of blood. The four of us scattered, and I kept close to Dogan. Men charged us, and I kept my back toward Dogan as I prepared for my opponents' blow. The Salvie was bigger than Dogan, and as he swung the sword for my head, I instinctually ducked down. Dogan's aura served its purpose and expelled the sword as soon as it tried to enter, causing the man to jerk back a step. Taking that as my opportunity, I jammed my sword into his gut. Using all my strength, I jerked it up before pulling out. The aura prevented the blood from landing on me. The man fell to his knees and stared at me with what looked like amazement.

As we made our way through the lobby, I killed three men, and then I saw men of the Salvie army running up the stairs that would eventually lead them to the queen. There was a sudden opening to the staircase, so I took it and left behind Dogan's protective aura. I heard him yell my name and curse as I ran. Halfway to the stairs, a soldier stepped in my path. He had a wicked grin and attired in animal fur and leather. Rosa was my top priority, and I needed to get to her. There was no way in hell I was about to let this man get in my way of doing that. Screaming, I ran toward him as I lifted my sword.

The man had more power and took my sword down instantly. He might have been more powerful than me, but I was quicker on my feet. Spinning around, I wacked my blade across the back of his legs. He let out a bloodcurdling scream as he fell to his knees. Blood poured out the cuts and soaked the back of his legs. I am not sure if the redness I saw was from anger or if it was my aura trying to push its way out. Either way, what I did next still took me by surprise. While standing behind him and bringing up my sword, I instantly swung it around in front of me. As it connected with the side of his neck, I screamed as I let the momentum of the blade cut him completely through until his head detached from his body. I felt his warm blood hit my face as it sprayed down the front of me.

All the screaming around me faded away. Sucking in the breath that I was holding, I stared down horrified at the decapitated body before me as the blood continued to pulsate out where the head used to be. Then the body suddenly collapsed forward. I looked ahead to find Dogan charging toward me. It took a moment then all the noise returned to my ears.

"Goddamn it, woman! Behind ye! Run," Dogan screamed.

Without thinking, I jammed my sword behind me, and it stuck into something. The low monstrous growl made the hair stand on the back of my neck. Slowly, I turned around. There was my sword stuck in a massive thigh covered in nothing but thick chestnut fur. Slowly my eyes scanned up the beast; he had to be at least a foot taller than Dogan's height. Not in my wildest dreams had I ever seen anything like it. The whole body was covered in fur with hands like mine but enormous...deadlier.

The head on the other hand was not a man's at all either. It resembled a wolf but again enormous and terrifying. The fear inside me locked my body up. There was no way for me to run even if I tried. The beast curled his lips up on his long snout as he growled, bringing to view the massive canines. The teeth were three times the size of a normal wolf. Saliva began to drip from his mouth like he was hungry...hungry for me.

The creature was quick and had his hand around my throat before I even realized that he moved. As he lifted me off the ground with ease, he yanked out the sword from his thigh and dropped it to the ground. Wrapping my arms around his, I tried to relieve some pressure around my neck, but it did not help. My breathing was cut off completely, and the more I tried to move, the tighter he squeezed.

When the beast brought me closer to his face, I looked away with my eyes. I did not want those monstrous teeth to be the last thing I saw in my life. Out of the corner of my eye, I gained sight of Dogan, who was still trying to get to me. As I felt the warm drool and hot breath on my neck, Dogan froze and screamed, "No!" as he let his aura shrink back into his core.

"Dogan!" I tried to scream to warn him, but I only heard it in my head. A man came up behind him and jammed the hilt of his sword to the back of his head. I watched in horror as Dogan's eyes rolled to the back of his head as he collapsed to the ground. Closing my eyes, I said a quick prayer that I die from the suffocation and not by this beast ripping me into pieces. Just on the verge of passing out, I heard someone yell in Salvie, "We have orders not to kill any of the women in the castle. Now take her and any guards that are alive to the cells along the cliffs."

I cringed as the creature pressed his nose against my face while he growled. Instantly, I was flying through the air and came to an abrupt stop. As my head smacked hard against the stone wall, I swore I heard Sterling yelling for me as everything finally went silent.

As I started to wake up, there was a tingling sensation all around my body. If it was not for the pounding headache, I would have thought everything I just endured was a nightmare. All I saw was pitch-black when I opened my eyes. With my back against a hard chest and strong arms wrapped around my stomach, I knew by the touch it was Sterling. We were sitting on a damp stone floor. Since I was sitting between his legs, he also had them wrapped around my legs. Moaning, I gently lifted my hand to my left temple. I winced instantly when I touched the huge knot and felt the dried blood all around it. Slowly looking up at him over my left shoulder, I let his red light show so I could see his face.

"Welcome back, beautiful," he whispered with a soft smile, and he touched my cheek as he kissed my forehead.

"Oh, Sterling," I said, turning onto my hip, and as I wrapped my arms around him in a hug, I scratched my hands on the stone wall he was leaning against.

"You gave me quite a scare. You hit that wall hard, and you have been unconscious for a few hours now." He rubbed my back and continued to hug me as I felt his lips against my neck. "Your head was bleeding terribly, I thought I was never going to get it to stop."

The memory of Dogan being hit in the back of the head flooded back in my mind. Quickly pulling back to look at Sterling, I cried, "Dogan!"

"I'm right here, woman," he mumbled. Looking behind me, I saw him resting his forehead against his arms that were on his bent knees. "And aye, I'm fine too."

Returning me to the position I woke up in, Sterling wrapped his arms back around my waist. I noticed then all the blood on both of Sterling's arms. "Are you hurt?" I touched his one arm to feel the blood was dry like that on my face.

"I'm fine, love," Sterling whispered. "Some of the blood is from men I had killed, but most of it came from you." I looked down at myself then and saw the whole front of my dress was red. I felt my neck, and that too was caked with dried blood. A moan escaped my lips as I leaned my head back against Sterling. I lightly sighed then when I felt his lips lightly on the side of my face. The three of us are still alive...now what do we do?

Finally, I stared across to Dogan; he continued to sit there with his head down. There was another guard sitting next to him. He had a bright yellow light around him. I think that color meant easygoing and optimistic, but I was not completely sure. There are too many colors to remember them all. With my eyes adjusted to the darkness, I looked to my left at the cell door. The sound of the ocean below came blowing in through the steel bars. My body shook as the cold damp breeze followed. A cell this size was meant to hold two adults, and there were four of us stuffed in here. As Sterling tightened his arms around me, I thought of Rosa. Taking hold of my locket, I asked it a question.

"Is Queen Rosa all right...and Mira?" Sterling laid his chin on my shoulder as I opened it. In the *soft* red glow of our auras, I was able to read what it said.

Queen Rosa and Mira are both alive and together.

"Oh, thank God," Sterling and I said in unison. After replacing the paper in the locket, I looked to Dogan, who still had not lifted his head from his knees.

"What is wrong with Dogan? Did he get hurt?" I asked Sterling in my head.

"You did not just give me quite a scare, Lee. I was the first one of us to wake up in here. Dogan was next, and he completely lost it when he saw you bleeding and me frantically trying to stop it. He thought you were dead because of the last thing he remembered before getting hit in the head. I think he's just pissed off at himself for losing it like that, and now he's trying to pull himself back together," Sterling said as I fixed my eyes across at Dogan. Slowly, he lifted his head and glared at us. His scar over his right eye looked more pronounced in his glare all of a sudden.

"I'd greatly appreciate it if ye two would shut the hell up," Dogan roared in our heads, and I smiled as Sterling started to bounce in silent laughter.

"Ah, there's the Dogan we all know and love. Welcome back," Sterling said, and Dogan pulled his feet away that were touching us.

The other guard with us was sitting closest to the cell door, and he finally spoke softly, "There's someone coming."

"Pretend ye'r still knocked out," Dogan whispered harshly, and when I just gave him a look wondering why, he continued, "Dinna look at me like that and just do it!" He took hold of my feet and straightened my legs, and Sterling wrapped his legs over the top of them like they were when I first woke up. Laying my head to the left, I closed my eyes. I released my energy just enough so I could see through my closed eyes as a Salvie soldier stopped at the cell door with a lantern in hand.

"That woman is still out?" he asked in Salvie, sounding frustrated.

"It seems so," Dogan replied in his native tongue. "You better hope she doesn't die because that's going to piss off Alistair's pet, and he will make sure you all pay for that."

"You would like to think that, you traitorous bastard," the soldier said, and Dogan jumped to his feet. As he walked up to the cell door the soldier back up to the railing that prevented one from falling to the beach below.

Dogan let out an evil laugh. "Still afraid of me even with a cell door between us?"

The man forced him a sneer. "I am going to be in the front row tomorrow when they behead you!"

"I bet you would love to see that," Dogan stated. The man glared at him and looked at me one last time before returning in the direction he came from. When Dogan turned and looked down at me, I opened my eyes, and my energy instantly sucked back into my chest.

"Now if only ye could do that wit yer damn eyes open," he lightly growled and kicked my foot as he returned to the floor beside the other guard. The other man was giving me a confused look but did the smart thing and just kept his mouth shut. The guard was probably afraid if he asked about it, Dogan would hit him. Bending my knees up, I leaned them against Sterling's inner left thigh.

As he pushed my legs off his thigh, he said, "Lee, you got something jamming into my thigh...bloody hell! Do you still have your knives?" Quickly, I felt my thighs and my knives were still in place. Instantly Dogan throws up my dress to see my boots and quickly grabbed the knives that were in them. The man had a grin so huge that his dimples came to view.

Sterling said, "Thank God those damn fools just assumed you were just an average lady and never searched you for weapons."

Still smiling with the knives in hand, Dogan said, "Fer the first time since I ha' met ye, I ha' the sudden urge to kiss ye!"

"Oh, good God," I said a little scared of seeing him come at me to do that. "Please do not!"

Dogan took in a deep breath. "Dinna worry, the feeling left as quickly as it came."

"Thank the Lord because I would hate to stab you for that," I said as Sterling lightly bounced behind me. As Dogan handed the other guard a knife, I retrieved the ones off my thighs and handed one to Sterling.

"The only chance we're going to get is when they come in here to take 'er to Lars Kellen." An awful chill raked through my body when he said his name. Dogan continued, "They ken that we're not gonna let 'em just walk in here and take 'er without a fight. I ken fer a fact that they're going to come in here wit a soldier on each o' us as they try to take 'er away. That's when these are going to come in handy." He held his knife up by the tip of the blade and threw it up in the air and then caught it by the hilt. "When I say the word, do whatever ye got to do, but just make sure ye kill 'em."

"Once we are out of here, I will head north to Hebridge and see if word of the attack reached there yet," Sterling said and pointed to the other guard. "I want you to head south and spread the word to the first post you get to, and the other men will spread out from there." Then he pointed to Dogan, "I want you and Lee to get the queen and head west. Keep heading west until you reach the king. Once the word is spread of the attack...well, you all know of the meeting point west of the city." I nodded my head. There was a plan if this should ever happen. Once a post knows of the attack, the guards will head to the meeting point that was west of the city with all the weapons and armor they have and prepare for battle.

"Any ideas on how we can get into the castle?" Dogan asked me.

"A ways from the north wall, there is a hidden door in the center of a patch of evergreens. It will bring us underground that leads to secret corridors that run throughout the castle walls."

He replied, "Ha' ye been to this hidden door before?"

"Only once when I first moved here, but I remember where it is."

"Ramstien," the other guard whispered harshly. "That same soldier is coming back and he has a few men with him."

"It looks like this might be our chance...when I say 'Now', kill the bastard in front o' ye," he whispered to all of us as we hid our knives.

"Ah, Lady Leelah Bayard, you are finally awake. Thank you for that because I was thinking I would have to carry you all the way to that asshole Kellen," said the same soldier from earlier, but he spoke in his Salvie tongue. "Oh, I'm sorry! You probably don't understand me, you crazy little cunt." He tilted his head to the right and gave me a mocking smile.

Before I could even give the man my reaction, my two men roared in laughter. At first, I thought they were laughing at me, but then I realized that it was the soldier they were laughing at. Dogan knew firsthand how I felt about that word, and that's why they thought it was hilarious that he called me that, thinking I did not understand. As I tried to get on my feet, Dogan quickly stood up while still laughing and pulled me up to my feet.

"Are ye going to give 'im a swift kick in the balls fer that one?" Dogan teased, giving me a devilish grin.

"I would love to, but I will try to refrain myself," I said to him and then looked back at the soldier, who was smiling at me. He probably thought Sterling and Dogan were laughing at me, but in reality, it was him they were laughing at.

"What do you think I am...prudent?" I asked him in Salvie. "Now, I would like to see you come in here and call me that to my face!" The grin quickly faded from the soldier's face. I looked over at Sterling, who was standing to the left of me. He had the look of approval written all over his face.

As the soldier started to unlock the cell door, he said, "If any of you try to stop me from taking her, you will be killed instantly." The four of us had our backs pressed against the walls as the soldiers came in with swords drawn. As the Salvatorians kept my men pressed against the wall, the cell suddenly got engulfed with a rancid smell like these men had not bathed in months. The odor was so strong and revolting that my stomach actually started to turn. The one who called me *that word I despise* came to me with an evil grin, showing that he was missing his one front tooth. All four soldiers were just as tall and built like Dogan. Before I thought it was cramped with the four of us stuffed in here, now it was practically suffocating.

Once on me, he took his dagger and lightly traced my jaw with the tip of it. "I can see now why Kellen wants you so badly," he said in Salvie. "You and I will have to find a private place to go before I bring you to him." I looked over to Dogan on the far wall. I know what he looks like when he's angry, but there were no words to explain the look I saw right then. All I knew was it was not good.

"Now," Dogan snapped just loud enough for us to hear. Before the man could react, I brought my right hand up and pierced my blade into the side of his neck. As the other three soldiers collapsed to the floor, I yanked my knife back. With a horrified look, the soldier covered the side of his neck with his hand. Thick crimson pumped out between his fingers as he fell to the floor. The four soldiers lay in a large heap before us.

I stood there and watched as my men unbuckled the dead soldiers' swords and put them on themselves. Slipping my knife back on my thigh, I did the same as the other men and took the belt off. After I unsheathed the sword, I handed the belt over to Dogan. "Here put this one on too. When we get in the castle, I will be able to retrieve my swords, and then you can have this one too." I held up my sword. He did not argue and took the belt out of my hands. After I picked up the dagger, the soldier dropped. Sterling peeked out the door.

"Since we are in the first cell, it should not be too difficult to get out of here," Sterling said and then pulled me to him. "Be careful and stay sharp, love!" He pressed his lips hard to my forehead.

"You do the same," I said to him, praying God's white light of protection over all of us.

Sterling and the other guard exited the cell first then Dogan shut the cell door after we came out. The beach was littered with small fires and hundreds of men. As we all ran along the narrow path on the sandstone cliff, I prayed for no soldiers to see us. If they did, it would be difficult to fight when you could easily fall down to the beach and ocean below. Once we were off the cliffs, the four of us walked cautiously down an alley as we emerged into the city. At the end of the alley, Sterling checked up and down the street, and staying close to the building, he headed north toward the castle. The other man headed south toward the port.

"We're going to head straight. I figure we can loop around and grab two horses before heading past the north wall," Dogan said when he took hold of my arm. *"And like Sterling said, 'stay sharp.' If ye sense someone behind ye, dinna hesitate."*

"All right! Is it clear enough for us to run across?" I asked. My heart was pounding, and all I wanted to do was get to Rosa.

He let go of my arm and made a dash across the street with me right on his heels. Staying close to the building, we made our way to the end, and Dogan peered around the corner. After a moment, he turned left down the other street. As we made our way down the street, dashing across small alleyways when they came, there were sounds of talking coming up behind us. We turned left into the next alley we came to. Pressing our backs against the building, we hoped the darkness would help conceal us as the soldiers past.

Taking my back off the building, I stood behind Dogan as he watched and waited for it to be clear enough for us to continue down. A chill went down my spine when I sensed someone behind me. With the dagger tight in my right and the sword in my left, I cleared my head as I spun around. Catching the massive soldier off guard, I jammed my sword into his gut. While at the same time I thrust my dagger at his throat to prevent him from screaming and revealing us. Quickly, I pulled both blades out at the same time. Fresh blood showered my face and arms again as the man collapsed to the ground while grabbing his throat. Dogan stood beside me, looked down at the soldier, and then to me with raised eyebrows. A slow grin formed on his face. The man had a long reddish beard with streaks of gray running through. He was about the size of Dogan but years older. Like most of the soldiers, he too was dressed in animal fur and leather.

"I did like you said, I did not hesitate," I whispered to him.

His grin widened as he took both his hands and wiped the fresh blood from my face. The gentle touch startled me, but I could not get my feet to move, and then he whispered, "Nay, ye dinna hesitate, and that's good because ye ha' no idea who ye just killed." He started to laugh lightly like he was in shock. "Woman, I'd like ye to meet General Leland Tybalt."

I gazed down in shock at the dead man before me, "General Tybalt?" Dogan nodded, and I continued, "The same general who ordered the murder of your parents? The same general you lived with until you were eighteen?"

"Aye, the one and only, so thank ye! 'Tis one last person I dinna ha' to kill because ye already did." Dogan patted my shoulders in approval and went back to the edge of the building. It hit me right then of all the men I had killed so far; I killed those men without thinking twice. All of a sudden, Dogan was in front of me, taking hold of my face and squeezed my cheeks; all the gentleness was gone as he glared down at me.

"Dinna even think about letting yer emotions take hold o' ye. D'ye hear me? Because if ye do, ye'll end up getting yerself killed!" When he was done yelling in my head, I nodded that I understood. He jerked his hand away from me and signaled me to follow him, which I did. After running along buildings for several blocks, I stopped at an alleyway when I heard a soft cry from a child. Dogan stopped and signaled me to keep following him.

"It's a child, Dogan! I have to see," I whispered as I took off down the alley. Dogan swore behind me. When I got to the other end of the building, I peered around to the back of it. There huddled in a ball, whimpering, was a little girl with her deep-red aura pushed out from her body to protect her. Not even caring to look for any soldiers, I ran toward the girl who was surely the child Dogan had been searching for. I placed my sword and dagger down before I slid down into her expressed light. Laying my hand on her tingling shoulder, I whispered, "It's all right darling. I am not going to hurt you." When she lifted her head and looked at me with tear-filled eyes, my heart dropped. "Oh my God, Cora!"

"Lee," she cried and was up with her arms tight around my neck instantly. When I stood up, she wrapped her legs tight around my waist. I have not seen her since I learned of my powers.

"I cannot believe it…you are like me! Where is Nana, sweetie?"

"A scary monster killed her. She told me to hide so I did," she cried in my head.

Chapter 27

Dogan

"**G**oddamn it, woman!" I let out in a harsh whisper as she took off down the alley. I swear to God the woman was gonna push me to the brink o' insanity. As I head after 'er, she dashed behind the building without taking the time to make sure 'twas clear first. Wait till I get my hands on her! I'm gonna kill 'er!

When I rounded the back o' the building, my whole body froze at the sight before me. There, Lee stood wit' her back to me and wit' *our* daughter wrapped around her. This was exactly what my mother showed me so long ago. Fer the first time in my life, I felt the panic start to form in my chest. I canna believe after all these months, the woman I ha' been looking fer has been right under my nose this whole damn time.

I ha' to admit that the woman affected me in a way that no lass has ever before, which was the reason I'd been more snappy at 'er in the last few months. But…no! It canna be 'er! I dinna want it to be 'er…right? The woman drives me absolutely crazy! That poor bairn doesn't even ha' a chance if 'tis us that has to raise 'er because we'll end up killing one another.

The girl lifted 'er head as she gazed at me wit the same terrified eyes I had invisioned. "Papa?" she whispered out o' 'er tiny lips. At that very moment, I fell deeply and unconditionally in love wit the bairn I hardly knew.

Chapter 28

Rescue

J turned around when Cora said the word *Papa* to find Dogan staring at us with a blank look. "You know?" I asked her quietly.

She nodded her head as she rubbed her eyes, "Cici and Arabella comes and sees me all the time."

Muffling my cry as Dogan and I walked toward each other, "I know her, Dogan," I whispered, trying to keep the tears at bay. "I have known her for years, but I have not seen her since I learned of my powers. It's her, Dogan! Your daughter's name is Cora." Cora reached out for him, and slowly he took her out of my arms. She looked so petite against him, and something changed in his eyes as he looked at me…was it tears? He drew her head back so he could look at her. Dogan laid his massive hand on the side of her face. I knew they were probably talking to each other, but I refrained myself from touching him to hear what was being said. Without taking his eyes off her, he said, "Grab yer weapons, woman! We need to continue on."

With weapons in my hands, we continued west as we ran along the back of buildings. We hid whenever soldiers came near. It started to dawn on me how eerily quiet it was. There were no sights or sounds of regular civilians and of our guards. Only Salvatorian soldiers, and that too were not a lot. Most of the soldiers I did see were back at the beach. There were not even any dead bodies that I noticed, only darkness. When we reached another edge of a building, I touched Dogan's arm that was holding Cora. I felt his whole arm tense up from my touch, which was odd to me.

"Why is it so quiet? Where is everyone?"

"I'm assuming most o' the soldiers are at and around the castle. That's why I want to keep heading west, and once we reach the outskirts, we'll head north and loop around to grab a pair o' horses before we go to the hidden door," he said and then continued forward.

As I kept pace behind him, my mind drifted toward Cora. It still did not seem possible that it was her that Dogan had been searching for. I know her mother; the one who abandoned her over two years ago also possessed the same gift. How am I going to break it to him that she left a long time ago? Now that he has Cora, he's going to have to still search for her mother. I am sure that he's going to be frustrated that he still has not found them both, but at least he did find Cora, so that puts him a step closer to his destiny.

When we reached the end of the city, we continued to stay close to the buildings as we started north. It felt like we had been running forever and that we were never going to reach the queen. After several blocks, we finally reached the main street that led up to the castle. Dogan peered up the street and then returned, pressing his back against the building.

"We found where everyone is at. Take a look," he whispered. With Dogan moving out of the way, I slowly looked up the street. Several blocks up was where the first of the lit torches were located, casting an orange glow all the way up to the castle that was also brightly lit. The street was packed full of hundreds of Salvie soldiers. I knew at the sight that the castle too was filled with them. They were all uniformed in animal fur and leather. It was the normal attire for the Salvatorians. An enormous man on horseback came into view and was heading right toward us.

"There's someone coming on a horse. If we can get that, then we could ride into the pasture, and then I could grab Ara from the stables. She should be still saddled up. Since there's no moonlight we should not be spotted running in the pasture," I whispered to Dogan as he looked to see the man coming toward us. He placed Cora in my arms and took my sword and sheathed it then stuffed my dagger in the side of his belt.

"Cora, I want ye to close yer eyes," Dogan whispered, and she nodded her little head as she tightened her grip around my neck and buried her face. "Woman, I want ye to act terrified. I ha' an idea." I nodded, a little scared of what his idea was. Taking hold of my braid, he thrust me out to the street, but at the same time kept himself hidden in the shadows.

Dogan spoke in his native tongue, "Look at what I found! A mother and daughter…would you like to have some fun?" The massive man gave me a wicked grin, showing some missing teeth. My eyes widened as if in terror. Dogan yanked my braid down, causing me to let out a soft cry in pain as he pulled me back toward him.

"Was that necessary?" I growled.

"Oh aye," he yelled in my head.

The man rode his horse around the building toward us. His grin was still wicked. "A mother and a daughter, eh?"

Once the soldier was in the shadow with us, Dogan was swift. I made sure Cora's face was in the opposite direction as he yanked the man down and slit his throat. Quickly he mounted the horse and I handed Cora up to him. Once she was secure in front of him, he took hold of my arm as I yanked up my dress. Instantly, I was up and swung my leg around the horse behind him. We were already moving as I wrapped my arms around his waist. We rode west a little bit farther before cutting across toward the pasture.

"Hang on," Dogan said as he kept jamming his heels into the dark Hybrid to go faster. A moment later, the bouncing stopped as the horse flew through the air and over the pasture fence. As the hooves hit ground on the other side, I loosened my tight grip around Dogan.

The horses scattered as we flew up the pasture, and we made it to the sables in no time. There were soldiers all around the front of it. He pulled back on the reins, bringing the Hybrid to a sudden stop a hundred yards away. When he jumped down, I asked, "What are you doing?"

"I canna take the chance o' ye going in there and getting caught. Ye ken how to reach the queen, I don't. If I'm not back quickly, then continue without me." He handed me back the dagger.

Quietly, I hissed his name as he took off toward the stables. With my pounding heart, I moved up into the saddle and tried to put my feet into the stirrups, but they were too long for me to reach. When I wrapped my arm around Cora, I took hold of the reins with the hand that was still holding the dagger. I said a quick prayer that Dogan could make it out without being detected because this was the only weapon I had beside my one knife on my right thigh. He took my sword.

"I am scared, Lee," Cora whimpered.

"I know, sweetie," I whispered and kissed the top of her head as I watched Dogan's red light disappear into the stables from the pasture door. My eyes never tore away from that exact point. *Please hurry!* Someone had to have noticed our escape by now. Our time was getting crucial.

Dogan's bright light suddenly reappeared as he burst out the door on Ara's back. Her snowy coat now had a red tint to it from his aura. I never realized it before but Ara had an aura around her too; it was the same as her coat, a snowy white. He stopped alongside me.

"Let's go! Ye lead," he ordered. Not being able to reach the stirrups, I tightened my thighs and kicked the Hybrid into a run. Before we reached the fence line, I loosened the reins down in my right hand as I held tight to Cora. Dogan and Ara were beside us and we all were flying through the air at the same time. I veered my horse like we were heading to Hebridge. Thoughts of Sterling and Rowan came to mind, wondering if Sterling was going to make it there.

Slowing the horse to a walk, I turned into the woods. With Dogan behind me, I cringed at the sound of crunching leaves as we weave through the fall foliage. Once we reached the patch of Evergreens, I dismounted and took Cora down into my arms. Taking hold of the reins in front of the horse, I pushed my way through the thick branches. It opened up to a bare center. I walked my horse to the other side to give Dogan enough room as he appeared with Ara behind him. He pushed his aura a little more from his body to help light the area.

"Where's the door?" he asked. I handed Cora back to him and walked to the center of the clearing. The whole ground was littered with dead evergreen branches. Reaching down, I grabbed hold of the screen that was camouflaged with dead evergreen. Once I lifted the screen and placed it to the side, the old wooden door came to view.

Dogan shifted Cora to his left hip as he reached down for the handle. After several pulls, the door finally dislodged itself and creaked as he opened it. The sandstone steps came to view and disappeared into the pitch of night below.

The two of us glanced at each other before I descended the steps. It was cool, damp, and the smell of decaying soil attacked my nose. Dogan's aura helped light the way. I was able to walk the narrow corridor with ease, but Dogan on the other hand had more difficulty. This corridor was made with no intention of having men of his size coming through. While he walked hunched over behind me, he let out a deep growl, but it was short-lived when Cora spoke.

"You have to watch your head, Papa," she said with her sweet innocent voice.

I had to smile because she was so cute, and I was still not sure if I would ever get used to hearing her call him that. "Yeah, *Papa*...you big beast," I said, jesting with him. The bastard then gave me a rough shove forward. I bit down on my bottom lip so I would not laugh.

When we finally reached the end, the ceiling lifted as we entered the corridor that ran the inside of the castle's walls. I pointed to my left, "My room is not far from here. I can retrieve all my weapons." Dogan nodded, and then we headed in that direction.

When we stopped at the spiral staircase that led to my wardrobe Dogan whispered as he looked at the door to his left, "So this is how ye got to the gardens at night without going through the front entrance." I did not say anything to him and felt my way up the steps. When I reached the top, I sat on my knees and strained my ears to hear if there was anyone in my room. Dogan sat on the steps behind me. Taking a deep breath, I unlocked the hidden latch. Slowly, I pushed the door open all the way. There was no light flowing in the crack of the wardrobe doors, so I opened up the hidden compartment underneath. I quickly grabbed my swords, bow, and arrows and all my knives I had left, all the while passing them back to Dogan. After closing the compartment, I snatched my cloak inside.

Once I had the hidden door shut, I opened the one leading to Kaidan's room, and that too seemed to be dark inside. I felt along his clothes, hoping he had an extra cloak inside and to my delight he did. After everything was closed up, I went down the stairs and handed Dogan the cloak. "It might be small for you, but at least it's something," I said to him, and he nodded as he tied it on. At least his arms and back would be protected from the cold fall air. As I strapped my swords to my back and waist, Dogan took the dagger I had and stuffed it in the side of his belt and then placed the bow and arrows across his shoulders. I put my knives in their proper places and tied on my cloak. "All right, let's find Rosa."

We headed up the way we came and then passed the corridor that led back outside. I had only been down this way once, so I hoped I remembered which stairs led to where. When we stopped at the fourth staircase, I whispered, "I think this one will lead us to the master suite. Being how late it is, maybe they will have her in there."

"Ye think? Ye dinna know fer sure?" he whispered in a harsh tone.

"I have only been down here once, so my memory might be a little foggy, but I am almost certain," I whispered forcefully back at him.

Dogan shook his head in disapproval and then placed Cora down on the bottom step. "I want ye to stay here while we go see if the queen's up there. Release yer light so ye dinna ha' to be afraid o' the dark." Instantly, with her eyes still open, Cora pushed her light out around her. I kind of envied her at that moment because there she was, at five years old, and was able to do that with her eyes open. Then there was me at twenty-six, still struggling about how to do it. Dogan smiled pleasantly at her before he made his way up the spiral stairs with me on his heels. When we reached the top, he laid a hand on my shoulder, *"How d'ye open this?"*

Leaning over him, running my hand over the smooth wood, I stopped at the slight indention. As I pushed it in; the little handle popped out and I unlocked the door. Dogan slowly pushed the door open into the wardrobe. He then pushed the clothing as quietly as he could to each end of it. A soft light poured in through the slight gap of the two doors. While he peered through the gap I laid my hand on his tingling back.

"What do you see?" I asked.

"Straight ahead, I can see the queen and Mira both lying on the bed. They're still awake, but I canna tell what's to the left. There's most likely a soldier in there wit' 'em."

While still on his hands and knees, he slowly opened one of the doors. Over his shoulder, I could see Rosa, who was lying on her side and was facing in our direction. Mira was directly behind her with her arm around the queen. Rosa's eyes widened and laid a finger over her lips to remain quiet and then pointed at the direction toward the room door. As Dogan peered around the wardrobe door, I felt his whole body tense up. He closed the wardrobe, turned to me, and took hold of my face. I was really getting sick of him grabbing me like this. *"There's a soldier sleeping on a chair next to the door. Ye and I are going into that room without making a sound...d'ye understand?"* I nodded with his hand still pinching my cheeks. *"I want ye to walk behind 'im and yank his arms back...I'll take care o' the rest."*

Dogan abruptly let go of my face and slowly pushed the door open. As he crawled out onto the area with plush rug and got to his feet, he grabbed hold of me under my arms and helped me to my feet. Mira and Rosa both stared at me with terrified eyes that were puffy from crying. I looked over to the left to see the man sleeping in the chair, with his head hanging down, his shoulder-length auburn hair hung close to his face. His chest was just as broad as Dogan's, and his arms just as massive. How the hell did he possibly think I could hold his arms back?

Dogan took out his dagger and then touched my shoulder, *"Ye can do this! I'll be quick!"*

Nodding, I started my way toward the man. Luckily, the rug helped conceal our footing. When I stood behind him, I fixed my eyes on Dogan and waited for his signal. The nod came, and quickly I slid my hands under his arms, yanked them back, and locked my own hands together behind the chair. Just as I did that, Dogan covered the man's mouth with his hand and practically sat on his lap. The man jerked, causing my chest to hit the back of the chair. As the soldier struggled to break free from my grip, Dogan, who was practically nose to nose with me, fixed his eyes on mine as he whispered Salvie so quietly in the soldier's ear that I barely heard him. "Hello, brother! When you get to hell, make sure to tell your father *hello* for me." He took his dagger and jammed it into his throat. His intense emerald eyes stayed locked on to mine as the body convoluted, trying to break free from us. Within seconds, the arms that I held went limp. Was this man he just killed General Tybalt's son? I will have to ask him about that later.

I walked around the front of the motionless body and stared at him. His head hung to the side now with lifeless eyes still wide with fear. The blood pulsated out from his neck, covering the whole front of him in the thick crimson. I turned away from him to find Dogan who had blood all over the front of him, handing Rosa and Mira cloaks from the wardrobe. Going to them, he gestured me to lead them in, so I did. Rosa held to the back of my cloak as we walk down the narrow staircase. I could see Cora's red glow at the bottom, but I knew Rosa and Mira could not see that, so I tried to keep my pace slow. When we reached the bottom, Cora jumped up into my arms.

"It's dark down here, but with our auras, it lights it up enough for Dogan and me to see. Just hold on to each other, and we will guide you out," I whispered to Rosa and Mira.

"I cannot believe you are here, Lee. Are you hurt badly? Because there's so much blood on you. I thought you were dead," Rosa cried, and when she wrapped her arms around me, she pulled back and started feeling at Cora who was in my arms. "Who is this?"

"It's Cora. We found her in an alley," I said.

"Oh, Cora!" Through her emerald-green aura, I can see tears fall as she touched Cora's face. "Where's Vi?" she asked me.

"She did not make it," I murmured, and Rosa just bit down her lip as she nodded that she understood.

"Lee, we need to keep moving. Ye lead and everyone else hang on to one another. Stay in a single line," Dogan ordered and I started walking using Cora's light for my vision. It felt like it took too long when we finally reached the steps that led outside. Once we were all outside, he shut the door and recovered it with the camouflage screen.

"All right, we're going to walk the horses out o' the evergreens and then we're heading west," Dogan said and then pointed to me. "You and the queen are going on Ara. Mira and Cora will ride with me."

Taking Ara's reins, I pushed our way through the evergreens. Once we cleared them, I ordered her to bow down. Even though Ara was down on the ground, Rosa still needed help onto her. I sat in front of her so that I could have better control. She wrapped her arms around me as I commanded Ara to stand. When we were all ready, we slowly walked the horses out of the woods. As we exited the woods, we got a clear view to the right of the castle. It looked to be on fire with all the torches lit, and there was a lot of shouting echoing through the sky. Without hesitating a moment longer, we kicked our Hybrids into a run and ran along the fence line of the pasture as we started west.

Before I knew it, we were reaching the end of the pasture and only a little ways to go until we would reach the road that would lead us farther from the city. Through the darkness, two figures on horseback started to come to view. The royal-blue light forming on both of them showed that they had their backs to us. Quickly, I looked over to Dogan, and he nodded. We both pulled back on the reins to slow our rides to a stop. We were about fifty yards away, and I could tell that they were Salvatorian soldiers. They were the only souls I could see.

Dogan pulled the bow off his shoulder and grabbed an arrow. He whispered something to Mira and Cora and then stood up in his stirrups. With the arrow in place, Dogan pulled back the bowstring with pure perfection. His shoulders were down as he let the string roll off his fingertips. Once the arrow was released, I quickly looked over to the men. As the one hunched over in his saddle, the second arrow was already in the air. The second man fell completely off his horse. I was awestruck. Never in my life did I see such quick accuracy with a bow. When I looked back at him, he was already sitting back in his saddle, and the bow was returned to his back.

Never looking back at me, he kicked his horse, and I did the same. As we passed the dead men, I noticed Dogan covering Cora's eyes with his hand. The one still hunched over on his horse had an arrow in his neck while the other soldier lay on the ground with an arrow in his chest. The other two horses took off into the woods as we ran by. The tension in my shoulders started to relax the farther we got. If I looked behind me now, there would be no more view of the city. We never slowed down and kept our horses at a full run.

After hours of never slowing down, the sky started to lighten for the new day. Rosa rested her head against my back. Taking hold of her hands that were around my stomach I looked back to her. "Rosa, how are you feeling?"

"Just a little weak. I have not eaten anything since late yesterday morning," she responded with a small voice.

Looking over to Dogan, I yelled, "We need to stop at the next place and see if they could spare us some food for her."

"All right," he said and then gazed at the queen with a look of concern.

We rode for another hour, it seemed like, when we finally saw a cottage several yards back from the road. I rode Ara practically to the front door and ordered her to bow down. As I was helping Rosa off the horse, the front door opened. A woman with radiant red hair pulled back into bun wore a beautiful smile as she stood in the doorway. Her aura was a bright indigo, and it pulsated around her body. "It's about time you five have gotten here. I have been up all night waiting," she said as Dogan, who was standing closest to the door, looked back at me.

"Do either o' ye ken this woman?" he asked us, and we shook our heads no.

The woman continued, "Please come in because we do not have much time."

Dogan placed Cora in Mira's arms and walked into the house with his hand on the hilt of his sword. We walked in behind him, and the smell of herbs danced around in my nose. It was a cozy country cottage with a small kitchen to the left. In the living room before us stood a man with arms around two young boys not much older than Cora.

She gestured Rosa to the kitchen table where one lone plate sat filled with eggs, side pork, and biscuits. The woman said to her, "Please sit and eat, Your Highness. You and your unborn child need all the strength you can get."

"Who are ye and how did ye ken we stopped here so she could eat?" Dogan demanded.

"Well, Dogan, I received a vision of this day about a week ago." She walked up to him and held out her hand. "My name is Donelle, and this is my husband, Oren, and our sons."

Instead of taking her hand, he asked as his face heated with anger, "Are ye telling me, ye ken o' the attack and never told anyone?"

"No, I did not know with the first vision that it was the attack that brought you five to us. I woke up early last night with a vision of the attack and realized that it was happening that very moment. If I knew ahead of time, I would surely have sent word to someone," she stated and continued to stand there with her hand out to him. Finally, he took it, and then he froze.

After a moment, he asked cautiously, "What's yer power?"

"I am blessed with visions of the future and can see someone's life in the past, present, and future as soon as I touch them," Donelle replied, and he quickly yanked his hand from her. With Cora and Mira on the other side of me, I peered over to Rosa as she quietly ate the food before her.

Donelle lifted up a sack from the chair beside the queen and walked over to me. "Leelah," she said with a smile in which I returned in awe that she knew my name. "Please take this. There is enough food for the three of you to eat for several days." I took the sack that was surprisingly heavy and laid it over my shoulder.

"Three of us?" I asked. There were five. Why did she say three?

"You all have a long road ahead of you, and you need less delay as possible. My family and I can keep Mira and Cora safe here," she answered.

"Nay," Dogan yelled than looked to me urgently. "There's no way in hell I'm leaving 'em here."

Donelle never let Dogan's anger get to her. She looked to him smiling and continued talking in a calm and easy tone. "I know you just found her, but what you're about to endure is going to be too dangerous for them both. We can keep them safe and warm. I would keep you all here if I could, but King Alistair has a powerful mage and will know if the queen was here. Even if we could hide her very well."

"What makes 'em not stop here after we leave?" Dogan asked.

"They are not interested in them. You are a traitor, so they want you," she said, pointing to him and looked over at Rosa. "King Alistair is obsessed with the queen and wants her for himself." Then she looked at me. "And one man in particular is never going to stop until he has you. No matter the consequences." The hair stood at the back of my neck with the thought of Lars Kellen. "If you will excuse me for a moment, there is one more thing I need to grab." As she walked down the hall at the right of the room, I watched Cora as she slid out of Mira's arms. She ran past me to Dogan with her arms raised up. He lifted her with ease.

"There's no way I'm leaving ye here," he quietly said to her.

Cora lifted her hand, and when she touched his short beard on his jaw, she started to giggle. Dogan's brilliant smile came to view. She rubbed her petite hand across the rough stubble. I do not think she's been around many men in her short life. It's only been her and her Nana. As she traced a finger down his long scar, she asked, "Did it hurt?"

"Just a wee bit. 'Twas nothing I couldna handle," he whispered to her.

When she went back to touching his beard, she said, "I will be all right, Papa. I had a dream about this place. Those boy's names are Bernard and Braydon. I am going to have a lot of fun with them." Dogan and I looked over to Oren and his sons. Donelle never said the names of her boys.

"The child is correct. That's the names of my boys," Oren was amazed.

"Oh my God. Cora is the child you have been looking for?" asked Rosa, who was now sitting sideways in her chair and looking up at Dogan.

"Aye, Yer Majesty," Dogan said to her.

I walked over to the speechless Rosa and saw her plate was practically empty. I laid a hand on her shoulder. "How are you feeling now?"

"Better. Stronger." She gave me a small smile and patted my hand on her shoulder and then really looked at me. "Good Lord, Lee! You are really covered all in blood. Are you sure you are all right?"

I softly smiled and touch the tender knot on my temple. "Yes, I am fine."

Donelle walked back into the living room with what appeared to be a black cloak with silver thread in a crisscrossing pattern. She went straight to Rosa as she stood up.

"Your Majesty, I would like you to wear this during your journey." Donelle put it on over the cloak Rosa was already wearing. "It will help keep you warm and safe." As she tied it around her neck, Donelle whispered something in her ear. After it was tied, she backed away from Rosa and stood by me.

When Rosa lifted the hood, she gave us all a beautiful smile, and then she was gone. Panic set in, and I screamed Rosa's name as I withdrew my sword off my hip. As I held my blade at Donelle, Dogan too had his out and the tip of the blade against her throat.

"Settle you two," Rosa said, and then she appeared back where she was. She started laughing. "That was amazing. I felt so light, like I was floating, but I could still see and hear you all."

"What is this?" Dogan demanded as he grabbed at the cloak.

"It's been passed down in my family for generations. Any mage can use it, including you two," she said, pointing to Dogan and me. "All she has to do is think about being invisible, and she will be."

We both sheathed our swords, and Dogan said, "Please do it again." Instantly, Rosa was gone again, and Dogan waved his hand through the area she was standing. "I canna even feel her. How's that possible?"

"I am not sure how it's possible, it just is. That's why she feels so light because her whole body disappears. It's like only her soul remains," Donelle explained, and Rosa reappeared next to Dogan, laughing in amazement.

Donelle's smile quickly faded. "There are four soldiers that are going to be here any second. You two need to kill them." Dogan placed Cora down beside Mira and checked out the window. I stood by his side. Sure enough, four Salvie soldiers came to view. It had lightened considerably since we arrived here. He withdrew his sword, and out the door he went.

I fixed my eyes on Mira as I withdrew my knives off my boots, "Please keep Cora away from the windows."

"I will," she replied as she held Cora close to her side. "Be careful, Lee."

Running for the door, I slammed it behind me. There stood Dogan in the middle of the yard with a sword in each hand as the four riders came toward him. As I bolted toward him, I put my knives into motion, and as they cut through the air, I retrieved the other two off my thighs. By the time I reached Dogan, all four knives were gone and were stuck to the forehead of each soldier as they collapsed off their horses.

I stared down at the scene before me in disbelief. I actually did it! After all those times practicing on the wooden dummies and never landing all four knives to their heads, when the time came for me to do it…I actually did!

Feeling Dogan's gaze on me, I turned to shyly look at him beside me. His eyebrows were lifted, and he had a look of pure amazement. "Where in the *hell* did that come from?"

I shrugged my shoulders and whispered, because I was still in shock that I actually did it, "I do not know. I just locked my eyes on them, ran, and threw without thinking about it."

Dogan laughed as he walked up to me and poked his finger against my forehead. He brought his face down so his adorable dimple smile was close to me. "I always kent my teachings were absorbing into that thick skull o' yers. There had been times when ye ha' made me proud, but those times will never exceed the proudness I ha' right now."

Left speechless, I started to feel a little uncomfortable, but then Oren walked out the front door. He spoke to Dogan, "Would you give me a hand with these bodies before you leave? My wife made me dig a hole last night out back for them when she had her vision."

As Dogan walked over to the bodies, I said, "Dogan, can you make sure to—"

"I'll grab yer knives," he said finishing what I was going to ask. I was going to say, thank you, but decided not to and walked back to the house.

Donelle was standing by the doorway when I walked in, greeting me with a smile. "Just like I envisioned. You are truly a rare woman…a warrior."

"Are you saying that you knew that I would kill them all?" I asked, and she nodded. "But you said that the two of us need to kill them."

"If I told you that it was you that would kill them all, then you would not have been so accurate. You would have thought too much about it." She arched a brow, and when I agreed, she asked, "May I take your hand?" I hesitated for a moment then I held out my right hand to her. When she clasped her warm hands around mine, I felt what Dogan must have felt. She vibrated with power, and then her smile returned to her face. "Like I saw with Dogan, you too are going to be a great service for this country someday. You are quite strong, and I do not mean in the physical strength."

I laughed at that. "Oh, I would not say that. I have been an emotional mess as of late."

Donelle's smile widened. "Yes, I can see that. I also see who your heart aches for…Rowan, is it?" I nodded and was surprised with myself when I felt no tears coming with the thought of him. She continued, "I am sorry you cannot be with him, but I do promise that your heart will learn to love another man. When that happens, it will be a love unlike you have ever experienced."

"You know who it is? Can you confirm who I think it is?" I asked, thinking of Sterling.

"I am sorry, Leelah, but I cannot do that. What I can tell you is that you will gain knowledge of who it is within a few days' time."

I felt instant relief when she said that. I will know soon, and I said, "Thank you." It was then that I realized that we were alone, and I panicked, "Where is the queen?"

Donelle laid a hand on my shoulder, "They are all fine. I just had them go into my bedroom so they did not see any of the bodies." She walked over to the hall and called, "You all can come out now."

Rosa walked out first with Mira and Cora right behind her. She looked to me and stated, "That was quick."

"Your Majesty, your guard is quite swift when it comes to her knives," Donelle said to her.

Rosa was shocked and asked me, "You killed them...all of them?" I just gave her a small smile as she came and wrapped her arms around me. "I am truly blessed to have you by my side."

"My queen?" Donelle asked, and Rosa looked to her. "There is something I need to tell you before you go."

Rosa broke away from me and went to her, "What is it, Donelle?"

"Something will happen during your journey, and your powers will be needed. Do not be afraid about your unborn child's safety because of all the power you will need to generate. Your child is blessed with your same gift, so no harm will come to him," she said, and Rosa quickly covered her mouth and looked back at me with tears in her eyes.

Rosa then lay her hand on her round belly. "Him? I am having a boy?"

Still beaming a smile, she answered, "Yes, Your Majesty."

Rosa started to laugh and cry as she rubbed her belly. "I am having a boy," she said to me as I laid my arm over her shoulder. The thought of how excited the king would be brought tears to my eyes.

"What's wrong?" Dogan asked urgently when he walked in and saw the queen rubbing her belly.

Wiping my eyes, I smiled at him, "She just found out that she's having a son."

Donelle said, "I would love to keep you all here, but I cannot. There is a larger group of soldiers leaving the city in search of you all. You need to leave now so you can keep several hours ahead of them."

Dogan nodded and handed me my knives that were clean of blood and then went over, taking Cora out of Mira's arms and said to her, "Mira is in charge, so ye better listen to whatever she says...do I make myself clear?"

"Yes, Papa. I will be good. Can you make me a promise?" she asked as she laid her hand on his cheek.

"What's that?" he asked and the two of them stared at each other and talked privately. When he squeezed her to him in a hug, he had that look again in his eyes. They were glistening when he locked on to mine, and he whispered, "I promise."

"Papa," Cora strained out. "I cannot breathe!"

Horrified, he quickly held her out in front of him. With his hands extended out under her arms, he said, "Sorry...are ye all right?" Cora started giggling and was reaching for him.

When he slowly brought her back against him, she kissed his cheek and said, "Yes." She turned around in his arms and reached her arm out to me. "Lee." When I reached her, she practically climbed on to me. While I gazed into her emerald eyes, she touched my cheek.

"Can you protect Papa for me?" she asked.

"I think Papa can take care of himself, but I will do my best," I said privately back to her and then looked at Dogan as he narrowed his eyes.

"I love you, Lee," she cried and then gave me a fierce hug.

Squeezing her back, I pressed my lips to the side of her face. *"Oh, I love you too, Cora. Make sure you do what Papa said and be a good girl for Mira."* Pulling her face back so she could see my smile, and I said, *"Believe me...you do not want to see Papa angry."*

She smiled back and turned in my arms to look at Dogan, *"I am not afraid of him, but I promise to be a good girl."* I gave her one last squeeze before setting her down, and I turned to Mira. With tears, we embraced.

"I know you can take care of yourself, but still be careful," she whispered.

"I will. Please watch over Cora," I whispered back.

"I will. When you see Kaidan, tell him that I love him."

Pulling back, I smiled at her. "I will tell him."

When we all walked outside, Oren was tying bedrolls and water sacks to our saddles. Rosa turned to Donelle. "You all have done too much."

"In my eyes, it is not enough," she said to her.

"Thank you for everything, and in time I will reward you for all your generosity."

"Helping you was enough reward for me."

I watched as Dogan commanded Ara down, and she did with no hesitation. He helped Rosa into the saddle and then ordered her up.

He looked to me. "She'll be more comfortable riding alone so ye are riding wit me."

Just great! And then I said to him, "You should have grabbed one of the soldiers' horses, then we all could have our own."

As he mounted his silky ebony Hybrid, he remarked, "If they dinna get spooked after ye killed all the riders, I would ha'." He held his hand down to me, and I rolled my eyes as I took it. Instantly, I was up in the air and sitting behind him. Dogan pointed down at Cora, who was clinging next to Mira.

"Remember what I told ye," he demanded with his normal rough voice.

"I will be good, Papa."

While we were walking the horses away from the cottage, Dogan asked Rosa, "D'ye think ye can handle running at full speed?"

"Yes, I can handle it," she said and kicked Ara with her heels. After a few minutes of running, Dogan's voice filled my head.

"What did Cora say to ye?"

"Are you going to tell me what she said to you? When I got no response, I added, *"I did not think so!"*

Chapter 29

Black as Death

It was less than a half hour into our run when we came to a crossroads. All that was there was a guard's post. It is here where everyone is supposed to meet if the castle should ever get seized. There were two guards standing on the porch when we brought our horses to a halt. Instantly, they dropped down on a knee when they saw Rosa.

"Ha' ye heard about the attack?" Dogan asked.

The guards lifted their heads and quickly stood. "What attack?" one asked.

"King Alistair attacked last night and seized the castle. We're going to keep heading west in search o' the king and to spread the word. Ye ken what ye need to do." They nodded to us, and we continued running west.

A little past midday, we made a short stop so Rosa could stretch her legs, and we could have a quick bite to eat. I washed off most of the blood as I could at the stream we found. I was still filthy, but at least my face and hands were no longer sticky and crusted with blood.

After Dogan lifted me back onto the horse, I touched my bow that was across his back. "Here, why not take these off and I will hold them," I said as I tried the lift the bow over his head.

"Why? Ye already ha' a sword and sack o' food on yer back," he argued as I struggled to take the things off him.

"I have to lean forward while we are riding, and leaning into a bow and arrows is not very comfortable."

"Then dinna lean into me," he grumbled.

I smacked him hard in the arm. "You know very well if I lean back there's a good possibility I would fall off! Now stop being such a bloody fool and take them off!"

Quickly, he spun around in the saddle, took hold of my face, and pinched my cheeks. He glared as he brought my face close to his, "If ye ever hit me again I'll throw ye off this horse myself."

With my cheeks still pinched together, I said, "You know what? I would appreciate it if you would stop grabbing my face like this." Then I forced myself to smile. Rosa, who was on Ara, was watching us and started giggling. I could only imagine how funny my face looked. As I continued to smile, I watched as the corners of Dogan's mouth struggled to stay still. Quickly, he let go of my face and returned facing forward in the saddle. He lifted the bow and arrows over his head and handed them back to me. As I slipped them on, I said to him sarcastically, "Why will you not look at me, Dogan? I know you want to smile."

As we took off again I pressed myself tight to his back, and he said through our touch, *"Ye might ha' yer funny moments, but that still doesn't change the fact that ye'r a bitch most o' the time!"* As I laughed at him, I squeezed him tighter while burying my face in the center of his back, and he let out a low growl.

It was a few hours before sundown when I mentioned Cora's mother. I figured since we will be stopping soon for the night, I will ask him now since I was touching him.

"Dogan?"

"What is it now?"

"It's about Cora's mother." I felt his whole body tense, and when he did not respond, I continued, *"She abandoned Cora years ago. Vi said she never knew where she went."*

"Listen, dinna ever mention Cora's mother to me again. Do I make myself clear?" he yelled in my head.

Instead of taking his tone in offense, I spoke calmly back to him. *"There's no reason to bite my head off, Dogan. I just wanted to let you know."*

I felt his lungs expand as he took in air. *"I ha' Cora, which means it will not be long before 'er mother finds me."*

"Do you know what she looks like?" I asked.

"Oh, I ha' a clear vision of 'er," he said, and I thought of Sterling. If Dogan has seen what she looks like, then that only means…No, I am not going to think about destinies or soul mates. Donelle said I would know in a few days' time, and I will handle it then.

After we ate, the three of us huddled around the fire to keep warm. With Rosa and me lying on our sides facing the fire, Dogan faced us as he leaned back against a tree. He decided to keep watch for the first half of the night, and I would watch the second half.

As I lay there trying to let the noise of the fire put me to sleep, the thoughts of Lars Kellen came to mind. I asked him quietly, "Tell me what you know of Lars Kellen."

He let out a deep breath. I know it irritated him whenever I asked questions. Finally, he spoke, "A lot o' us like to call 'im Alistair's pet. Ye could never trust the man because he'd stab ye in the back the first chance he got. But fer the king, on the other hand, he'd grovel before him. If Alistair said jump, he would jump. It makes me sick that I dinna recognize him. Not only did he hide his accent, but his whole look had changed. As long as I had known him, he had hair past his shoulders and a full beard. I never saw 'im different."

I cut in. "Why is he so small? He's about as tall as I am. When I think of Salvies, I think of men like you."

"His parents are originally from here but came over to Salvatoria when he was still in the womb." He paused. "Donelle was right, ye now. Kellen will not stop until he has ye. I pray he has the balls to come after ye himself. It'd do me great pleasure to break his neck."

Speaking of necks, I thought of the man he killed in the queen's bedchamber. "In the royal bedchamber, was that man you killed General Tybalt's son?" The man who caused the wicked scar over his eye.

"Aye." Once he confirmed what I already knew, I closed my eyes and pictured Dogan smiling as he snapped Lars Kellen's neck. The vision brought a smile to my lips as I slowly fell asleep.

I got jolted with a swift kick at me feet. My eyes snapped open and got the sight of Dogan standing over me, "Get up, it's yer turn." After I pushed myself into the sitting position, I stretched my arms out to help smooth out the kinks in my back. When Dogan sat on his bedroll, he whispered, "If I'm not awake by the time the sky starts to lighten, then wake me up."

"So you are giving me permission to kick you then?" I asked, thinking of how he just woke me up. He just curled his lip at me and covered his face with his hood as he lay down.

While sitting there for the last few hours of the night, I would jerk my head to any noise that I heard. I never saw anyone though. The one good thing with my powers was I could see people's auras. So no one would be able to sneak up on us in the dark.

As much as I did not want to, my mind kept drifting toward Sterling. Was it terrible of me that I did not want to be with him in that way? He's my best friend, and that's how I still see him. Just trying to picture the man naked makes me want to laugh.

Now there's Cora. I still cannot believe that it's been her this whole time. That little girl means so much to me, she always has. I looked over to the big mass hiding under the cloak. I never wanted it to be him either. He said he saw what she looked like. He would tell me if it was me that he saw…would he not? No! If the man knew for sure that it was me, then he sure as hell would not let me know about it. I could not blame him in this case because I would probably do the same thing. Great! Here I am, thinking about the things I did not want to think about. Just when I started to convince myself that it was Sterling, I started to second-guess myself.

As the sky started to lighten, I smiled to myself as I slowly stood up. Walking quietly, I stood over Dogan, Just as I was about to kick him, he mumbled, "I'm up so dinna even think about it." So I kicked him anyway.

We ran at full speed all morning, never stopping as we went through small villages or other people we passed on the road. We did come upon another post and spread the word of the attack. It was a few hours past midday when a group of men on horseback came to view ahead of us. Five of them had the aura like Kellen and Gavin, a dark murky pink. There was one different from the others, and the color made my muscles tighten in fear. Black as death is what came to me. There was no other way to describe it.

"I have a bad feeling about the men up ahead," I muttered privately to Dogan.

"I ha' the same feeling," he said, and then addressed Rosa. "Dinna slow down fer anything and pull yer hood down so those men canna see yer face." She did as she was told.

Dogan kept us close to Rosa as we grew closer to the men. Our two horses were practically touching as we raced past them. The one with the black light had a bald head and gave me a toothless grin. Once we passed, I could feel all six of them staring at our wake. After a few minutes, I still could not let go of the feeling in my chest. Even after looking behind to find those men were long gone.

"Why can I not let go of this bad feeling?" I asked him through our touch.

"Because there was nothing good about that man we saw...just pure evil. How far is it to the next guard post?" he asked.

"At least another half day's ride. Why?" I asked and looked to the sky. It will be dark in a few hours.

"Damn it! I'd rather not sleep outside wit a man like that close by."

"If it was just us two, I would say let's keep riding, but we have Rosa to think about."

"I know! Tonight, when we make camp, we need to stay vigilant. It might be paranoia talking, but I dinna want to be caught in an ambush," he said, and I nodded in agreement.

We found a small clearing among hemlocks about a hundred yards from the road. It was down a short ridge with a narrow stream nearby. Dogan felt confident that we could not be seen from the road. I slept the first half, which took me forever to actually fall asleep, but exhaustion finally took hold of me.

I got awakened again by a kick from Dogan, "Remember, stay vigilant," he whispered. He lay down with his head closest to me. We never told Rosa about how we felt about the men we saw. We did not want to frighten her.

Reaching into the sack of food, I pulled out a stale biscuit. I was starting to get fidgety, and I needed to hold on to something. The biscuit seemed to help a bit. I kept moving it about in each hand and took a bite into it every now and then. Why was I so anxious? Those men would not show up here at this time of night. They have to sleep themselves. With the thought of that, it finally settled me down, and I finished off my biscuit.

It was about an hour later when I thought I caught sight of something. Straining my eyes as I gazed out over the fire before me, I saw it again. The pink light was bright against the night. As quickly as I saw it, it was gone again. My heart started to pound, then farther to the left I caught a glimmer of pink again. Damn it, they actually did come looking for us! Pretending to stretch, I pressed my leg against Dogan's head.

"We have company," I yelled to him in my head.

"How many do ye see?" he asked calmly. I was surprised on how fast he responded. Was he even sleeping? Scanning the woods before me, I caught a glimmer to my right.

"Three so far. As quickly as I see them, they disappear behind the trees."

"All right," he spoke calmly still. *"I'm going to sit up. Tell Rosa to hide herself."* Slowly, he started to sit up.

Since Rosa's head was by me, I lightly touched her face and whispered her name. Her eyes slowly opened, and I brought my face close to her, "We have men trying to sneak up on us. We need you to hide yourself and do not reappear until its safe…all right?"

"All right…please be careful," she murmured with a frightened look and gave me a kiss on the cheek. Once I backed away from her, she disappeared.

Dogan instantly jumped to his feet and held his hand down to me, and I took it. Once I was on my feet, he spoke to me. *"It's that same damn group o' men. They're all around us. The one in black is to the right. It still has a glow against the night,"* he announced, and sure enough I could see it, and it made a chill go down the length of my spine. What did they want from us? Why were they doing this? The one in black gave me such an awful feeling that I was afraid that if he actually did touch me…it would kill me. Like I said before, black as death. I think he could easily kill me.

He never let go of my left hand as he hollered out into the trees, "We ken ye'r out there. We can see ye…all six o' ye. If any o' ye ha' brains, then ye'll leave right now because ye picked the wrong people to mess wit."

Laughter came in all direction, and then the man in black spoke while still keeping himself concealed by the trees. "Well, listen to you, Salvie. I would have to say that you are far from home and you have no idea who you are messing with. By the looks of it, you are the ones that are outnumbered."

Dogan let go of my hand and pushed his cloak past his shoulders, revealing the king's coat of arms on his chest. Even though the whole front of his shirt was covered in dry blood, you could clearly still see the design. "I'm not that far from my home, only a few days away actually."

"You think because you are a part of the royal guard that it should scare me?" the black one inquired.

"It should make ye think twice," Dogan warned.

"Where is the other woman? She was there a few moments ago?" he asked.

"She's none o' yer concern," Dogan bellowed. I have been watching one of the pink men to my far right. He had been inching closer and closer since Dogan started talking. Slipping my right hand into the slit of my dress, I wrapped my hand around the hilt of the blade on my thigh. Even though I was staring straight ahead, I was still watching the man who was now behind the tree by our camp.

The man charged at me with his sword raised high. I never moved my body, only my arm. As soon as he appeared, my knife was cutting through the air. It lodged itself directly in the center of the man's throat, making him fly back with the impact. Then Dogan yelled out to the other men, "Like I said, ye'r messing wit the wrong people."

All hell broke loose! The men charged out of the woods with swords, maces, and war hammers. With noise coming from behind me, I quickly turned around with my other knife in my left hand. Again, my knife was in the air and struck the man right between the eyes. As he collapsed, I withdrew my swords and ducked when I sensed someone behind me. I could feel the breeze as the mace that was covered in spikes at the end swung around where my head use to be.

Quickly, I turned around and faced my opponent. He gave me a wicked grin to show me a few missing teeth. I reflected the next blow he thrust down on me and jabbed my left sword into his gut. As he screamed in pain, he tried for one last swing at me. I sliced my sword down his left arm. I did not cut all the way through, just enough to hang open and to reveal the bone. The man dropped his mace and collapsed to the ground. His eyes were wide while his face was tight with agony. I felt like I was in a trance watching the man's life slowly slip away, and then lifeless eyes looked back at me.

Finally, I pulled myself away from him and saw two other men dead by our campfire, but no Dogan. I scanned the woods before me; there was still one man left…the one in black. There was no sight of Dogan either, so I decided to turn around and check behind me.

The pain was so excruciating that I screamed at the top of my lungs as I heard Rosa and Dogan scream my name. I looked down in horror at the blade that was protruding out of my stomach. As it was yanked up and out, I hunched over, pressing my hands to my stomach. There were instant tears as I looked down at my hands that were covered in the deep red of my blood. It felt like a horrible dream, and I was praying for me to wake up.

Instantly, I was floating in the air and in Dogan's arms. "I failed you," I cried.

"No. Nay. Ye dinna fail me," he laid me down by the fire and screamed. "Rosa!"

"I am here," she yelled and appeared on her knees on the other side of me.

"Hurry! Heal her, goddamn it," Dogan yelled, and Rosa removed my hands that were still pressing to my stomach. When I started coughing I could feel and taste the blood in my mouth.

Dogan took my hand and touched my face. He was pale, and his face was close to mine. "Hang in there, Lee. Everything's going to be fine." I shook my head no because I did not feel fine. This was bad!

I coughed some more, and blood filled my throat. *I am going to die.* Turning my head, I spat out what I could of the blood and sobbed, "I was supposed to live a life. I do not want to die now!" My body felt like it was getting colder and colder, suddenly, feeling like I would never feel warm again.

"Shh, ye'r not gonna die on me now," he ordered with his face still close to mine. "Ye hear me? That's an order!"

As my breathing started to become difficult, I noticed a beautiful white light start to stream through the trees. The longer I watched it, the brighter it got; and before I knew it, the trees were gone, and there was nothing but white. I had to squint my eyes shut. "The light is so bright!"

"Nay! Damn it, Lee! Dinna go to that light…d'ye hear me?" he yelled, forcing me to look at him. I felt, instantly, warm and loved. The pain was starting to subside.

This was it. It was time for me to leave this world to meet my Maker and face my judgment. Amazingly, I was not scared. Joy flowed through me as I gave him a soft smile, "I am sorry. Make sure you get her to the king."

"Nay! It's not supposed to be this way! I need ye. I canna raise 'er on my own," he screamed.

There was a figure walking toward us. With the bright light, it was difficult to make it out until she stood before us. She was in a white gown with her long wavy brunette hair over her left shoulder. With her beautiful smile, she held her hand down to me, "Mama?" I whispered.

Dogan roared, "Arabella, dinna take 'er from me! She doesna even ken!"

Chapter 30

Vision of the Future

Not being able to tear my eyes away from my mother, I lifted my hand, and she pulled me up swiftly. Instantly, I wrapped my arms around her in a fierce hug. She was so warm, and all the pain and coldness I was feeling was completely gone. I looked down at my lifeless body; Rosa had her hands against my stomach. Emerald light shined bright against my wound. Dogan tried to make me look at him, but he knew that I was already gone. After he closed my eyes, he pressed his forehead to mine and then slowly looked out angrily in our direction. Even though his intense eyes were angry, that did not stop the tears that ran down his cheeks, which made me take a step back. I never saw him this distraught before. I have felt sadness from him and seen his eyes glisten with joy with Cora, but never like this. It surprised me that the man was even capable of expressing that type of feeling.

"I'll never forgive ye fer this, Arabella, or my mother fer that matter. Ye tease me wit' these visions, and then ye allow this to happen," he yelled and then looked down at me and lightly traced my jaw with his hand. I touched my own jaw, suddenly wishing I could feel his gentle touch.

My mother walked up to him and touched his cheek. His whole face went lax, and his jaw dropped. I knew he could feel her, and she said to him, "Don't worry, Dogan. I promise to bring her back to you. I just need a little time with her first." Ma came back to stand next to me, and as the sight of them and my body started to fade, I saw Dogan start to break down.

My mother took both my hands and stood before me, and I stated, "I am dead."

"Just for the time being. Rosa will have you back shortly." She smiled and looked down at my stomach. "How do you feel?"

Looking down to find no blood and my dress was not torn, I looked back at her and smiled. "I feel great." I looked around me, and everything was just white, nothing else. "Is this heaven then?"

"The beginning stages of it, yes."

I was instantly in love with the feeling that wrapped around me. "I am not sure if I want to go back. It feels good here…like I am home."

Ma took my face in her hands, "That's because this was your first home, but you still have a long life to live in the physical world. You will return *home* someday, but not for a very, very long time."

"What's in store for me in my life, Mama? Can you at least show me something? Because I am tired of the wondering. I need to know," I said. In the beginning, I did not want to know because I did not want to lose Rowan again. But now, the wondering of which man was my soul mate was really starting to eat at my insides. I know now that I will never lose Rowan; he will always be in my life, just not in the way I dreamt it to be.

"I am going to give you a vision of the future. The sights, sounds, and feelings you'll experience are exactly how it will be for you at that time," she said.

"All right," I replied, surprised with myself that I was not even nervous to see my future.

One moment I was staring at my mother, and the next I was back in my bedchamber at the castle. I was kneeling on my bed, and I was naked. There was a man before me sitting on the edge with his back to me. His bare back was broad, strong, and littered with scars. As I walked on my knees toward him, I lay my fingertips on his tattoo and smiled at the tingling sensation. It was in lines that weave in and out, forming a knot of some sort. It covered his whole right shoulder blade, continued up over his shoulder, and I knew his right bicep would be covered in it too. The tattoo also traveled down covering half of his right arm. It was massive, and I enjoyed tracing my tingling fingertips along the lines.

My heart was swelling with him so near. He was my husband, and the thoughts of him having to leave me soon for war brought tears to my eyes. I started to kiss his shoulder and made my way to the beginning of his neck trying to savor his clove spiced scent, which I loved. Then he grabbed my arm, and I screeched, laughing as he pulled me around into his lap.

Next thing I knew, I was staring at my mother again, "No! Take me back. I never got to see his face." I wrapped my arms around myself and whispered, "I did not want to leave that love I was feeling, and I knew he felt the same for me."

"You don't need to see his face," she murmured and laid a hand on my heart. "Because in your heart, you know exactly who it is."

"Dogan." I started to weep. "Why him, Mama? You know we will just end up killing each other."

She laughed. "In that vision you just experienced, you didn't want to kill him…you wanted to do something a whole lot different."

I was a little embarrassed at what she said because she was right. I wanted him. "Then how many cuts and bruises do we have to go through before we make it to that point?" I asked.

She let out another angelic laugh. "There will be some cuts and bruises, but the two of you will stop fighting it, as you just saw."

"What about Cora's mother? She is the same as us, right?" I asked.

My mother nodded. "Yes, but she lost faith a long time ago. She was lost after Hector died, and she could not bear the sight of her own daughter because she looks too much like him. That's why she abandoned her." She pointed to me. "You are her mother now." I grabbed hold of my dress at my chest as a tight pressure started to form.

"It's time for you to return to them now," my mother said.

"No, I am not ready to leave yet. I still have questions." I winced as my heart tried to beat and the action almost brought me to my knees.

"And I'll answer them all in time." She kissed my lips. "I love you, baby girl, and everything is going to happen like it's supposed too." I tried to speak as I was being pulled away from her, but I could not, and then everything went dark.

Slowly, my eyes started to open. I was still in the woods, and it was morning. How could it be morning already? I was not with my mother that long. Rosa was beside me. She was godawful pale, and she gave me a soft smile, "Thank God, Lee. I thought we lost you forever."

Sitting up a little, balancing myself on my elbows, I looked down at my stomach. The dress was torn and covered in dry blood. Once touching it and confirming that the wound was healed, I looked back at Rosa, "You healed me." When she nodded, I continued, "How are you feeling? You are very pale."

"I am weak, but I will be fine," she said with a weak smile. Rosa touched my temple. "I healed that knot you had too. All there's left is a scar." I reached up, and sure enough, the knot was gone and the throbbing pain too.

"What happened? What happened to the man who stabbed me through the back?" I asked.

"Dogan practically beheaded the man as soon as he jammed his sword through you." She laid a hand on mine. "The man has been distraught, Lee. He has been by your side most of the time until just recently. He went and took care of all the bodies."

As I looked around, there was no sight of him. "Where is he now?" I tried to stand up but could not by myself. Rosa took hold of my arm and helped me up.

"He's down by the stream filling the water sacks. Do you think you can walk?" she asked, and I took a shaky step and then another.

"Yes, I think I can."

"Go to him then. He needs to know that you are going to be all right," she whispered.

I touched her hand that was still holding my arm and said, "Thank you."

Rosa took my face in her hands. "You are my closest friend, and it would kill me if anything happened to you. Now go to him before I drag you over myself." She lightly pressed her lips to mine. She made me smile as I turned for the stream. It was not until I rounded a huge hemlock that I finally saw him. His back was toward me as he was squatted by the stream. The morning sun had beams hitting the water, making it sparkle. My heart was tight in my throat, and I was having difficulty swallowing. I grew more nervous with every shaky step I took. What should I say to him?

I stopped several feet away from him, and he slowly stood up. Trying to block out my pounding heart, I finally whispered, "I am sorry."

"Stop saying that," he ordered without turning to look at me.

"But I am! After all those months of training, I did not even realize that man was behind me, and I should have. Now the queen is extremely weak because of me and my failure to you." A lump formed in my throat as my eyes started to sting with tears.

Slowly, he turned around and fixed his eyes on me, "Ye are not a failure, lass. Think o' all those men ye ha' killed in the last few days. A normal woman would ha' not been able to handle that physically, let alone emotionally. If anyone failed, 'twas me for not getting to 'im fast enough."

Before I knew it, he was inches away from me, and I closed my eyes as he lifted my face up to him. "My mother showed me things," I practically blurted out. Finally, I opened my eyes to find his intense stare. "I know, Dogan, and I know you know too."

As his jaw tightened he said, "I dinna ken what ye are talking about."

Anger suddenly boiled in my chest. "You are lying! I heard what you said, 'I cannot raise her on my own.' How long have you known?"

"Ye were dying and not hearing correctly. I dinna ken anything," he yelled in my face. There was a noise of a branch snapping, and the two of us jerked our heads to the left to find Ara coming around a tree.

"We need to pack up and get back on the road. We already lost an hour o' daylight." He marched away angrily, and Ara came, gently pressing her head against my arm.

Laying a shaky hand against her face, I asked, "What are we going to do about him?"

Once everything was packed up, Dogan lifted and placed me on the horse before he mounted himself. As we continued our journey on the road, I clung tight to him and rested my face on his back. I was extremely weak and was afraid of falling off. We never spoke to each other again since the stream, and I preferred that at the moment.

It was before midday when we reached the town of Morningstar. Dogan finally spoke as we slowed the horses down to a trot. "We're gonna stay here fer the night."

After I jerked my head up, I said, "Why? We still have at least a half a day of daylight."

"Look at 'er," he whispered with concern, and I looked over to Rosa. She was extremely pale with dark bags under her eyes. "She needs a full meal and a bed to rest. We'll stay at the barracks here and head back out at first light."

"What about those men Donelle said were searching for us?" Rosa asked.

"We'll worry about that if it happens. We'll keep our horses saddled just in case," Dogan explained as we stopped in front of the guard's post. He dismounted and looked up at me as he pulled me down to him, "Ye look just as bad." When he commanded Ara down, he took the queen's hand, "We're staying here, and dinna try to argue wit' me because ye'll not win."

Rosa lightly laughed. "All right, I will not argue with you."

A guard walked out the front door as we came to the steps. "Your Majesty!" He fell down on one knee.

Dogan spoke as he helped Rosa up the steps. "The castle has been seized by King Alistair. We need a full meal and somewhere to sleep. Ye ken what ye need to do, so hurry and send men out so they continue spreading the word." The guard ran back in and started barking orders. Four men bolted out the door, and the guard we spoke to came back out and took a good look at me. I recognized his face, but I could not remember his name.

"Good Lord, my lady." He came to me and stared down in horror at the front of my dress. "Do we need to get you a doctor?"

"No, sir, I am healed, just weak." He wrapped him arm around my waist and helped me into the barracks.

After we ate lunch, Rosa and I went to the bathing room to wash up. After I got Rosa stripped down, I helped her into the steel tub. She moaned as she sunk down into the water. Just as I was about to undress myself, a knock come from the door. Before I opened it, I checked behind to make sure the queen could not be seen from the privacy screen.

"Yes," I said and found Dogan on the other side. He had a pile of clothes in his hand and handed them to me.

"I collected money from all the guards and bought some clothing fer the both o' ye. Hopefully, they fit."

I looked down at the clothing in shock and then added, "Thank you." He never said anything else, just turned around and continued back down the hall.

As I shut the door, Rosa asked, "Did Dogan say he bought us clothes?" I rounded the screen and showed her the pile in my hands. She clapped her hands together as she laughed. "How wonderful! Hold them out so we can see what he picked out!"

Laying the pile on the chair, I lifted the top dress. It was a beautiful aqua color, but the material was heavy and would surely keep her warm. By the looks of the size, I knew it had to be for her. I held it up against me. "I think this one might be for you."

"It's absolutely beautiful." She reached out and grabbed the fabric. "And it should be a lot warmer than the dress I was wearing." She let go of it and said, "All right, let's see what he got you." As I lay the dress down on the other chair, I gazed down at the pile, and a smile spread on my face. Laughing, I picked up the two pieces of clothing and pressed them against me as I turned to face Rosa. She instantly started giggling. "The man knows you too well."

I held out the clothes before me so I could closely inspect them. In my right hand, I held a cream-colored long-sleeved wool shirt, and in my left chestnut-colored trousers. They looked like they should fit...I hope.

Instead of striping out of my ruined dress, I decided to help Rosa finish bathing so I could get her to bed. As I touched her bare stomach, the baby kicked my hand in response. I began to giggle. "He seems as strong as ever." I could feel the power radiating off her belly.

Rosa gave me a tired smile as she rubbed her belly. "I think he's going to be very powerful as he grows up. I truly believe if it was not for him, I might have not been able to save you." She laid her hand over mine. "I may have been drained, but think you are right...he seems stronger."

Once I was washed, I dressed in my new clean clothes. I ran my fingertips over the new scar on my belly before pulling my shirt down over it. The top fit perfect, the trousers were a size too big, but nothing a belt could not fix. With my hair cleaned, Rosa braided it for me, and I did the same for her. The lieutenant here let us use his room, so once I was confident that Rosa was finally asleep, I left the room to search out Dogan.

It still was not quite suppertime when I walked in the gathering room. Guards huddled around the table discussing the attack when one of them noticed me, "My lady, can I help you with anything?"

"No, I am fine. I was just looking for Ramstien," I reported.

"I saw him walk down the hall just a moment ago. He's probably in one of the rooms," another guard said.

"Thank you." I turned and went back down the hall. Just as I was about to pass an open door, I froze when I saw him. He was standing by a bed and had his back to me as he threw another uniform top on the bed, "Dogan?"

Without turning around, he asked, "Did the clothes fit?"

"They were good, thank you." As I said that, he lifted his old uniform top up over his head. I sucked in my breath at the sight of his back. The same scarred back I envisioned me touching and kissing. My eyes locked on his tattoo. "The tattoo," I murmured.

"Aye, woman," he said with annoyance. "Have ye not seen one before?"

I could not stop myself even if I tried as I walked slowly toward him. "That exact tattoo...yes, I have." I noticed his whole back tighten. As I reached my hand up toward it, I said, "It cannot be...you?"

Just before my fingertips touched his ink, the man spun around and took hold of my throat with his right hand. As he lifted me up on my toes, he brought his face down to me, and we both glared at each other. My left hand was wrapped around his wrist, and I had the sudden urge to touch his face.

"I'm afraid so," he murmured, and then his lips were pressed hard against mine. You would have thought I would have smacked him or pushed him away, but I did not. Instead, I ran my hands up his arms to his wide muscular shoulders. With no clothing to grab on to, I grabbed hold of his hair so I could try to be lifted up to his level. I felt his tense body start to relax with the sensation as he wrapped his left arm around my back to pull me closer to him.

My head was spinning, and all I wanted was more. *"Bloody hell,"* Dogan spoke softly through our touch. With his right hand still around my throat, he brought his left down to my bottom and then lifted me up to his height. As he deepened the kiss, I wrapped my legs tight around his waist as he slammed my back against the wall. I felt like he was sucking the life out of me. Rowan's kisses were never like this. It was so demanding, with so much need. His hair was cool and damp as my fingers ran through it, and then I held on tight. After a moment, he broke his mouth from mine and started running kisses along my right jawline. When he brought his lips to my ear, he pressed them there softly.

I stared out over his shoulder, breathless and in shock. As he rubbed my chin with his rough thumb, he spoke with his lips still against my ear. "If ye ever—And. I. Mean. Ever—get yerself killed on me again, I'll kill myself, hunt yer soul down, and kill ye again. Do I make myself clear?" I nodded as the tears started to come. Then his grip around my throat began to tighten as his chest vibrated in a low deep growl. "I wanna hear ye say it…do I make myself clear?"

"Aye," I lightly cried out. Instantly, he placed me back on my feet. He snatched his clean shirt off the bed and stormed out of the room. My knees gave out, and I slid my back, which was still against the wall, all the way down to the floor. After burying my face into my knees, I silently sobbed to myself.

After some time, I finally got control of myself and slowly stood up. As I crept to doorway, I peeked around to make sure no one was in the hallway. With no one in sight, I made my way back up the hall to the lieutenant's room. My hand was on the handle of the door when I heard Dogan's voice flowing from the gathering room; quickly, I went in.

Once my boots were off, I pulled the blankets down beside Rosa. As I crawled in, she rolled over to face me. She opened her sleepy eyes and gazed at me. While lying on my side facing her, she took my hand. "Oh Lee, what's wrong? Did Dogan say something to you?"

As the tears started to pour out again, I smiled because she knew the man could really get to me at times. "It's not what he said but what he did."

"Do you want to talk about it?" she asked and I shook my head no as I buried my face into the pillow. I am not sure if I ever want to talk to her about it. What would I say? That he kissed me and that I liked it? That I did not want him to stop? I instantly wished that Mira was here. She's the only one that I confided in about everything. She would know exactly what to say to calm me down. "Well, when you are ready, I am here to listen," Rosa said and then kissed my hand.

Removing my face from the pillow, I gazed at her through my blurred vision and sobbed, "Thank you." It was not long, but I finally cried myself to sleep.

Chapter 31

Dogan

Suddenly, I went quiet when I heard the sound o' a door behind me. When I looked, I caught sight o' Leelah quickly slipping in. My heart that was still pounding went even faster. What the hell was I thinking in kissing 'er like that? Wit' fists clenched at my side, I was growing even more irritated wit' myself.

"Ramstien," the lieutenant asked behind me. "Are you all right, lad?"

Quickly, I locked my eyes to him and cleared my throat, "I'm fine, Lieutenant. I'm gonna get some fresh air and check on our horses." Before he could say anything else, I quickly walked out o' the room and out the front door.

There was extreme tightness in my chest, and the cold night air was a relief. If I stayed in there fer a moment longer, I might ha' started hyperventilating. *Goddamn ye, woman! No woman in my life has ever affected me like ye do!* I felt like screaming and cursing God fer causing these emotions that were going through me. Since we arrived back from Mastingham, I couldna go through a day without seeing 'er. Even if we werena scheduled fer training, I'd still find a way to at least get a glimpse o' 'er.

Oh. I ha' been so pissed off at myself fer that even though when I would catch 'er strolling through the city, I would chuck one my sacks full o' sand at 'er. She was better at sensing 'em now, and sometimes when she'd duck, the sack would accidently hit someone else and then that person would think 'twas 'er that threw it. There were times though when I'd catch 'er off guard and nail 'er hard in the back o' the head. I ken it hurt like hell, but it did my heart good that she was in pain because she had no idea the pain she caused me. I kent she wasna my one, but deep inside, I always hoped she was. Now that I ken 'tis 'er fer sure, I'm scared to death, causing me to be pissed off all over again because I never get scared. Bloody hell! When the lass died in my arms…that was the most frightening day o' my life since the day my parents died.

My mind kept drifting back to the kiss we just shared. I ha' never experienced anything like that, and I ha' kissed my fair share o' women in my life. She caused my whole head to spin, and wit' 'er body tightly wrapped around me, I could tell she dinna want to stop either.

As I reached the stables, I punched the wall by the door in frustration. My knuckles burned in pain as I opened the door. I canna be doing this or feeling like this. This is what makes a man weak and could get him killed.

Our horses were loose in the center aisle so they could be easily grabbed if the need came. Ara slowly strolled toward me. I couldna help but smile as she pressed 'er forehead against my chest. The Hybrid was amazing. She's too intelligent fer a cuddy. As I rubbed my hands up and down the sides o' 'er face I spoke in Salvie, "What am I to do? The woman is just as stubborn as me. The two of us are going to fight against this…do you know that?" I looked into her one eye, and she let out a snort like she understood. "I canna picture the two o' us falling into each other's arms and deeply in love. Nay, we're gonna keep snapping, punching, and scratching until there's nothing left. 'Tis only then I can see us finally accepting it, and I don't ken how far away that is, but this I ken…it's not gonna be anytime soon."

Chapter 32

Breathe and Concentrate

When I woke up, it was still dark outside, and my stomach started growling. Slowly, I dragged myself out of bed without waking Rosa. Scooping up my boots, knives, and swords, I left the room.

The gathering room and kitchen were nicely lit with lanterns and a massive fire in the fireplace. There were some men in the kitchen preparing food, and the lieutenant was sitting at the table with what looked like a map before him. I went and took a seat next to him.

"Good morning, Lady Lee. You are up early. There are still a few hours before sunrise," he said as I laid my weapons on the table. The man was older than me, possibly older than Dogan. He wore his sandy hair short, but his beard was longer.

Slipping on my boots, I said, "I have slept enough, and it will be pointless for me to lie in there if all I am doing is tossing and turning."

He smiled. "That's exactly what Ramstien said."

Instantly, I sat straight. "He's awake?" I said trying to conceal the panic. I was still not ready to face him yet.

"Yes, he got up not too long ago. He's out checking on your horses." He nodded toward the front door.

Once my knives were strapped to my thighs, I stood up and started to put on my swords. The lieutenant cast me a smile and then remarked, "I remember when I first met you a few years ago. I thought the king was crazy hiring a woman to protect the queen. It was not till yesterday that I changed my thoughts about you. Ramstien told us about your fighting and all the men you have killed. I do have to say that it left me speechless. For the first time, my lady, I am honored and proud to have you as part of the royal guard." He stuck his hand out to me. Instead of taking it, I took hold of his forearm. His smile widened as he took hold of mine.

"Thank you, Lieutenant." I smiled and then looked down at the map of our country. "What do we have here?"

"This is a map showing where all the guard posts are located," he said, pointing at the map and then he looked back at me. "I tried talking to Ramstien about having you three stay here. The king will be passing through when he arrives back to the country. I am sure he's already back by now, and it's just a matter of time before he gets here. I can have most of my men stay here with you until the king arrives, then we can all head to the emergency meeting point together."

"Let me guess, Dogan said no," I stated, and personally, I liked the lieutenant's idea. At least Rosa will have comfort, and there was close to a hundred men here.

"He's dead set to continue on your journey to the king. He does not want to get caught in fight with the Salvie soldiers that are looking for you all. He's afraid what will happen if we get overpowered. I got just shy of one hundred men still here, so maybe you can talk to him and convince him it's better to stay," he said.

"She can talk all she wants, Lieutenant. We're leaving at first light, and I'll not be content until we reach the king," Dogan announced from the front door. He glared at me and asked, "Why the hell are ye up so early?"

My heart went instantly in my throat when his eyes locked on to mine. Trying to swallow it down, I said softly, "I could not sleep."

"Ye and I both," he grumbled and walked over to see what the men were making to eat. I heard a noise of a door to the left by the hall and looked to see Rosa shutting it behind her. She was wearing her aqua dress Dogan got her, and she looked radiant. It flowed beautifully down off her belly.

"Well, I guess I am not the only one who could not sleep," she said, beaming everyone her famous smile. She looked refreshed, and the bags under her eyes were gone. The lieutenant stood up and bowed.

"Good morning, Your Majesty," he chimed.

"Good morning, Lieutenant." She lifted her nose in the air. "What's cooking because it smells delicious." She lightly touched my shoulders as she took a seat beside me.

"It looks to be crepes and eggs," Dogan said. "Would ye like some?"

"That would be wonderful. Thank you, Dogan," she said to him, and he gave her his infamous dimpled smile, which he does so freely with her or any other woman for that matter. As soon as his eyes shifted away from her to me, his whole face tightened, and the dimples disappeared. Why does he have to be so angry with me? Does he not realize he's only making this whole situation worse by acting like that? The fool did not even ask if I wanted anything to eat, which I did!

Dogan gave her another smile as he gently placed the plate of food in front of her, "Enjoy, Your Highness." She smiled back at him and said thank-you.

As I stared down at her crepes that had canned berries over it, my stomach growled viciously. I was just about to get up to make myself a plate when Dogan slammed a plate in front of me. The food itself actually jumped on the plate with the force he threw it down. I yelled at him as he took a seat across from me with his own plate, "Really?"

As he stabbed his eggs with his utensil, he said, "If ye are not hungry, I'm sure someone else would gladly take it."

Anger started to boil in me again. "Of course I am, you damn fool! It must get real exhausting to be angry with me all the time," I retorted as I jammed my fork into the crepe.

He shook his head and swallowed his food before he spoke. "Nay, I get a lot o' enjoyment actually." He stuffed more eggs in his mouth and then gave me a mocking grin. Oh, I so had the urge to chuck my plate at him, but I refrained myself because I was too hungry to waste food like that.

"Your Highness?" the lieutenant asked and then pointed at Dogan and me. "Have these two been like this the whole ride from Burreck City?"

Rosa laughed. "They had their moments. These two have a...a love-hate relationship." When she said the word *love*, I nearly choked on the eggs in my mouth. By the sounds of it, so did Dogan. Rosa then pointed at the both of us and spoke to the lieutenant. "See what I mean? They just do not like to admit to it." Dogan glared and then curled his lip up at me. Glaring back at him, I gave him a mocking lip curl.

When we finished eating our breakfast, Dogan finally spoke again, "Since we're up and about early this morning, any o' ye against riding in the dark? The sky is clear, so the moonlight will help light the way."

I looked to Rosa because it was up to her, and she said, "Well, I feel great, and all I want to do is see my husband. So leaving a few hours before sunrise will only bring me that much closer to him."

"Good, then let's grab our belongings and head out," he ordered and stood up.

When he came back in after bringing our horses around to the front, Rosa and I were saying our good-byes to the lieutenant. With our cloaks on, I held my bow and arrows in my hand. As I slipped the arrows over my head and secured them against my back, Rosa said, "Thank you again for everything, Lieutenant. You helped us out a great deal."

"I wish I could do more, Your Majesty," he said to her. "Are you sure you do not want me to send any of my men with you?"

Rosa looked at Dogan and me and smiled. "My two guards are more powerful then you may think. They will not let anything happen to me, and I have my own tricks that will help protect me. So do not worry about us, Lieutenant. You and your men should start heading to the meeting point and begin preparing for war."

The front door burst open, and a guard stood before us breathless. "A group of Salvatorian soldiers just entered the town. There are more than fifty of them."

"Why have they been riding through the night? Do they not sleep?" I asked Dogan in panic.

"Donelle said they ha' a powerful mage. Maybe he saw us here, so they continued through the night. Probably hoping we'd be still sleeping. We need to leave *now*!" he shouted, going to Rosa and taking her by the arm. When I followed them out the door, there was screaming and chaos going on the other side of the town. As Dogan and Rosa ran down the steps, I stayed on the porch with my eyes locked on the mob. A soldier on a horse charged out of it and headed straight toward us. With my bow still in hand, I quickly withdrew an arrow off my back.

Once I placed the knock of the arrow onto the bowstring, I pulled back. Taking a deep breath, I slowly let it out as I locked on to my target. As the bowstring rolled off my fingertips, the arrow cut through the air. Just as it lodged itself into the soldier's chest, three more on horseback made it past the guards.

"We need to go, Lee," Dogan hollered up to me. Rosa was already on Ara, when I got to Dogan. With my bow in my other hand, I held up my right so he could lift me up behind him. Except he did not put me behind, he brought me up facing him.

"What the hell are you doing?" I yelled in his face as we were already on the move.

He yelled to Rosa, "Get in front o' us and push 'er to run as fast as ye can." As Rosa rounded to the front of us, he fixed his eyes on me as he expelled his light all around us, "I need ye to slip yer feet into the stirrups, stand up, and kill those bastards behind us."

"Dogan, I cannot reach them," I screamed, "I tried the night we escaped from Burreck City."

"I raised 'em up a few days ago just in case ye ever needed to ride without me, so slip yer damn feet in," he yelled in frustration.

While hanging on the front of him, I watched as he removed his feet, and I slipped mine into the stirrups. They were raised just enough that I was able to place the balls of my feet into them. Locking my legs, I straightened my torso. Dogan instantly placed his strong right hand against my lower back and pressed me tight against him. As I tried to block out the tingling sensation of his touch, I reached over my shoulder and retrieved an arrow.

The three men started to gain on us. Bringing the bow up behind him, I placed the arrow on the string again as I pulled back. Through his red light, I could still see the men's auras before me. As I released the arrow, it shot like lightning as Dogan's light expelled it. It lodged itself in the ground just before one of the men.

"Damn it, Dogan! I cannot do this! You are the marksmen, you should be the one shooting," I yelled out as I grabbed his shoulders to help steady myself.

"Ye can and will do this. Ye are a marksman too. Ye always hit yer target with complete accuracy when we trained wit the bow. Ye never did when we trained using yer knives, and look how well ye done wit' 'em in the last few days. Ye can do this! Feel the rhythm o' the horse's run. Flow wit it, breathe, and concentrate on the men behind me," he yelled over the noise of our horse. If the man had this much confidence in me, then there's no doubt I could do this.

Taking a deep breath, I retrieved another arrow. With it drawn back, I concentrated on the man in the middle. As I followed the rhythm of the horse's gait, I aimed my arrow just a bit higher. The air in my lungs slowly expressed when I let go of the string. The arrow exploded out again, but this time, it hit my target. The man was knocked off his horse with the momentum of the arrow as it entered his chest.

"Terrific! Two more…ye got this!" Dogan praised as I retrieved another arrow. Again, when my arrow left my fingertips, it penetrated the man to the left. When I had the other arrow in the air, the third man dodged his head to the left just in time, and the arrow flew past him.

"Damn it," I screamed as I reached behind me for another arrow. When I reached for it, I realized I only had three left. I said a quick prayer as I locked my eyes on the man and released the arrow. That time, he was not able to dodge it as it went through his chest. As the man collapsed forward on his horse, my legs finally gave out, and I sat down in front of Dogan.

He took my bow from me and slipped it over his shoulder. When he kicked my feet out of the stirrups I brought them up and wrapped them around his waist. As I enveloped my arms around him, I squeezed myself tight to his chest.

"Must ye really hold on to me like this?" he grumbled in my head. *"I'd feel more comfortable if ye'd at least turn yerself around."*

"Shut the hell up, Dogan! And yes, I do. Your touch will help anchor me, so just deal with it," I yelled back at him as I pressed the side of my face against hard his chest. I noticed that in the last few days, whenever he touched me, his tingling touch had grown more intense. It was stronger and more vibrant than Rowan's had ever been.

Using the sensation to soothe me, Rosa came to view as Dogan rode up beside her. She was absolutely radiant with her bright emerald light and with the white sparks shooting out from it. Her eyes were alert and looked to have determination. As I watched her, Dogan wrapped his arm around my back and tightened it as he rested his chin on top of my head. He finally stopped fighting against the sensation of our touch and accepted it. With my ear against his chest, I could hear his heart, and the pounding had softened considerably since I first laid my head there.

"Ye did good, woman. Ye show potential o' being a great warrior someday. Wit' God as my witness, I'm gonna make sure that happens," he said gently, and I did not respond. I just kept my eyes on Rosa and enjoyed the comfort of his embrace. I know he feels the same as me and was not pleased that he's destined to be with me. We are *soul mates*. The word made me laugh. Then my mind drifted to the vision my mother showed me. I was head over heels in love. Even though I did not see it, I know when he playfully snatched my arm and dragged me into his lap, he would be smiling at me. His infamous dimpled smile. How long are we going to fight with each other until that happens? It did not even seem possible. *"Just fer yer information,"*

he stated in my head, *"it won't be my infamous smile ye'll see but most likely a curled angry lip."*

I clamped my eyes shut in embarrassment and was horrified that he was reading my thoughts. *"Please stay the hell out of my head. You were not supposed to see that. And you know what? I know you would be smiling because at that moment, you loved me with all your heart, unlike right now."* My whole face felt like it was on fire. As he tightened his arm around me even more, I tried to see if I could read his toughts as well as he did mine, but I was getting nothing. He was blocking me somehow or maybe I was still not strong enough with my powers to read his thoughts.

After a few hours, the sky had finally lightened for the new day. I lifted my head, placed my chin on his shoulder, and gazed out behind us. The trees had lost most of their leaves. Still a few reds, orange, and browns clung to the branches, not yet ready to leave their home. I had a question that has been bugging me, so I bit my lip and finally asked him privately, hoping he would not bite my head off.

"I have only one question, and please do not bite my head off because I need to know. How long have you known it was me?" I asked and then held my breath for his response. As his massive chest released the air in his lungs, he rested his chin on my shoulder. His warm breath sent chills throughout my body as it blew against the side of my neck. Dogan must have thought I was cold because he tightened his left arm around me.

"When I first rounded that building and saw ye wit yer back to me holding Cora. That was what my mother showed me years ago. And believe me it pissed me off right then…and it still does. When I first arrived here and met ye fer the first time, I thought 'twas ye. Once I found out that ye dinna ha' a daughter I threw the idea out o' my head. Then I met Sterling and Rowan and the word destiny *kept getting thrown all over the place, and everything started getting more complicating. And believe me,"* he growled, *"when I see Rowan, I'm gonna kill him. He kent 'twas me the first time he laid eyes on me in Hebridge. He and our mothers ha' been playing wit' our heads this whole goddamn time!"*

The man can really surprise me at times. I figured he was going to argue with me and tell me to drop it. Instead, he blurted all that out.

"You are not going to kill, Rowan. Because like it or not, you do like the man. You might not know him as well as you do Sterling, but you will. You see Sterling as a friend, and in time, you will see Rowan the same way. Besides, if you even try to start something with Rowan when you see him, which is probably going to be soon, then you will have to deal with my wrath," I said to him, and then I could feel the bubbling laughter in his chest.

"Please, woman! I could snap ye in half wit' a flick o' the wrist," he responded with a hint of amusement.

"Have you forgotten that I have a great trainer...I can take you!"

"In yer dreams, my wee lass," he laughed. I just smiled as I continued gazing at the view behind us, wishing that we would reach the king soon. Like Dogan, I would not be content until Rosa was in his arms.

"Since I answered yer question...will ye answer mine?" he asked, and after a moment he continued, *"What did Cora say to ye at the cottage before we left?"*

Smiling I said, *"She wanted me to protect you...keep you safe."*

He let out a light throaty laugh and brought his lips a whisper away from my ear. His breath was hot against the cold exposed skin, and then he murmured, "She said something similar to me. I ha' a feeling that she kens a lot more than us." He was sending jolts throughout my body again with his lips so close to my skin. Quickly, I turned my head and laid it on his shoulder and began to watch Rosa again while we ran.

It was almost midday when we came to an enormous group of royal guards. There were a couple hundred of them, and all of them were wearing combat armor. They told us that they got word and were heading to the meeting point. Still no word if the king arrived back in the country yet. We continued on.

After a short break, we were back on the road at full speed. I was back in my normal position behind Dogan. It was not long before two royal guards emerged on top of the hill we were running up. My heart pounded with excitement when I saw the flag one of the guards was carrying.

"They are with the king!" I announced, and Rosa yelled at Ara as she flicked her reins and gave her several more kicks to make her go faster. The other guard took off back in the other direction once they got a good look at us. We came to a sliding stop at the top of the hill by the guard with the flag. My eyes widened in shock at the scene before me. For as far as I could see, there was nothing but the blue-and-gray of royal guards. At least a thousand, possibly more.

The guard spoke to us, "As soon as we reached shore, the word of the attack just reached the city. Word was also said about you two going to get the queen and then heading west," he said and looked at Rosa. "Our king has been sick with worry over you, Your Majesty."

"Please take me to him," Rosa cried to him urgently.

He led the way; Rosa followed with us riding right behind her. All men on horseback and on foot bowed as we passed. We finally caught sight of two carriages ahead. One would be for the king to sleep in at night while the other held supplies. It was then I saw him charging toward us on horseback. He yanked back on the reins and was off the horse before it stopped.

"Rosa!" he yelled as he reached up to her.

"Bryce!" she cried as she reached for him, and he pulled her down into his arms. Her whole body shook as the sobs she's been holding in this whole time finally escaped. When he looked up at Dogan and me, it was then I noticed how pale his skin was against his dark beard.

"Thank you," he whispered, and we both nodded. Bryce wrapped his arm around her waist and guided her toward one of the carriages and then ordered, "We keep moving and do not stop until sundown." As I watched the two of them walk away, I caught a glimps of Templeton. He had a worried look on this face, and I granted him a small smile and nodded. He returned my smile and nod, but it did not change the worried expression he had.

Just as I was about to climb off Dogan's horse so I could get on Ara, I heard my name being yelled, "Lee!" Kaidan pulled back the reins beside us.

"Kai," I cried and reached over to him. He grabbed a hold under my arms and pulled me off Dogan's horse and into his lap. My brother squeezed me half to death in a hug.

"Oh, thank God, Lee! I have not been able to sleep since we arrived. My mind has been flooded with thoughts of Rosa, you, and…Mira." He spoke her name quietly.

I pulled back and took hold of his face. "She is safe, Kai. We found Cora too, so we left the both of them with a good family that's several hours west of the city. You will see her in a few days, and she wanted me to tell you that she loves you."

"Thank you for that. I have been thinking of the worst!" He was squeezing me tight in another hug when Ara came beside us. Dogan, who was still on his horse, was holding her reins on the other side. Taking hold of my saddle, I pulled myself over on top of her and took the reins from Dogan's hands.

Kaidan looked over to Dogan and said, "Is that my cloak?"

I looked to him and smiled. "Yes, he needed something. It's a bit small."

"A bit?" Kaidan laughed. "He looks like a Hybrid trying to fit into a regular horse's skin."

Laughter burst out of me as I fixed my eyes on Dogan. "That's a great analogy, Kai!"

He shook his head at us and lightly smiled as he addressed Kaidan. "It's good to see ye too, Kimball…ye asshole!" He then lightly kicked his horse as he rode up ahead of us. I was about to make a comment on how he pronounced the *asshole* correctly but decided to leave it be.

Kaidan laughed and then said, "How was it riding with him all this way?"

"Oh, you do not want to know," I groaned, shaking my head.

"That bad?"

"Bad cannot even begin to explain it."

"Well, by the looks of it, we have time, so why not start from the beginning, like when the castle came under attack?" he asked. I told him everything that happened, even my death. I left out the words like *destiny* and *soul mates* because I was not sure how much he knew about that and what Mira might have told him.

Chapter 33

Lieutenants

We were just a few hours from Morningstar when we finally made camp. Campfires littered both sides of the woods, and the night air sparkled in a rainbow of colors from the guards' auras. I sat with Kaidan and a few other men that were closest to the carriage that held the king and queen. Dogan sat at the next fire over. The two of us had been avoiding each other since we reached the king, which I was happy about. When the back door to the carriage opened, Bryce's gold aura emerged from the darkness. As he made his way over to our camp, the men started to rise, and he held his hand out.

"No, please stay seated." And he walked over to me and asked, "Do you know where Ramstien is?"

Turning to look behind me, I was about to yell his name, but he heard the king ask and he was already jumping to his feet. As he walked over to us, Bryce held his hand down to me, "Will you take a walk with me, my lady?" He gave me his charming smile, and I took his hand.

When I was up at his side, he said to Dogan, "Walk with me." The two of us followed in step on either side of him. We walked in silence for a few moments, and once we were leaving the encampment, he started to speak. "Rosa told me everything you three have endured in the last several days, and Kaidan told me how the two of you reached her. I do not know how I could ever repay either of you."

"Having her here with you is a reward enough," I responded softly.

"She's right, Yer Majesty. It's our duty," Dogan agreed.

The king stopped walking and turned to face us. "I do not care what you two think because I have never been more proud of two guards as I am right now." He looked directly at me. "She told me about how well you fought. When we first came ashore, there was word spreading about your fighting and how you decapitated a man when the castle first came under attack. Is that true?" I just nodded and he smiled. "Good God, Lee. I knew you were good, but I never realized how exceptional you have become. Rosa also told me about how she healed you. I know once you learn to use your powers at full strength, then I can see you becoming unstoppable."

He looked to Dogan. "You need to keep working with her on that. Once we win back the castle anyway. I know you have only been with us just shy of seven months, but you have gone well above your calling to serve for me. I have never done this before, but I want you to be one of my top men." My mouth dropped when he pulled out the royal blue band with the gold insignia that indicated lieutenant out of his pocket. If a guard was exceptional, it would take at least ten years to make top ranks. And that is if he's good; most men never actually make it to that point. Bryce took the band and tied it around his right arm. Once it was on, Bryce took hold of Dogan's forearm, and he took the king's. "Thank you again for all that you did, and I hope you will serve for me for years to come."

"There's no other place I'd rather be, Yer Majesty," Dogan bowed his head, and Bryce came and stood before me.

"My dear Leelah, you are a rare breed of woman. I know we have kept your true purpose hidden for the last several years, but that's all going to change. Once we win back the castle, you will have royal guard uniforms made to fit you. So you will not have to bother wearing a dress anymore, which will give you better mobility anyway. Except of course for special occasion, you will have to grit your teeth and bear it. You are still a lady, so you will have to look the part every now and then." I looked down as I laughed, and he lifted my chin back up. He cast me his charming smile again. "I am proud to name you the first woman in the royal guard, the first in Altecia's history. What makes me even prouder is adding a lieutenant to the beginning of it." As he pulled out the royal blue band out of his pocket, it took all of me to not cover my face and cry. I just stood there straight as a board and in shock. As he tied the band around my right arm, I swallowed the lump down in my throat.

"Your Majesty, you have left me speechless," I whispered as I could feel the tears coming.

"You do not need to say a word, but what you do need to do is…" He held his hands out to the sides and smiled. "I still have not received a hug from my friend."

Laughing and crying, I went to him and wrapped my arms around his neck. He squeezed me tight and lifted me off the ground. "Thank you again for everything," he whispered in my ear and placed me back on my feet. I looked up to Dogan, and he gazed down with proudness written all over his face.

Bryce wrapped an arm over each of our shoulders and said, "Let's head back to camp so I can make an announcement of my two new lieutenants."

When we reached the center of the encampment, he hollered so all the men around us could hear, "I am sure by now all of you have heard the story of what these two did to keep the queen safe. So none of you should not be surprised that I have honored them with the rank of lieutenants. If I hear any of you address Leelah here by lady or anything less than lieutenant, then you will have to answer to me. Do you all understand?"

The voices echoed for miles it seemed like as they all yelled, "Yes, sir!"

"Now you two, go back to your fires and get some rest, I want to be moving again before dawn," he said, and three of us separated after saying good-night.

"Congratulations, Lieutenant," the men at my fire said as I took a seat beside Kaidan.

I beamed them all a smile and said, "Thank you."

"You are such a bitch!" Kaidan yelled smiling.

"Kimball!" Sergeant Sumner boomed, which caused me to laugh.

"It's all right, Sumner. Kaidan is one of the few people that can get away with calling me that." I looked to my brother, laughing. "So why am I a bitch?"

"Because I have been here more than half as long as you and now you are a higher rank than me," he explained, still smiling and shook his head in disbelief.

Puckering my lips out as I patted his cheek, I teased, "Poor laddie!" The other four men roared in laughter. Quickly, he grabbed my hand; and as he pulled me toward him, he wrapped his left arm around my neck.

"Just because you are higher rank than me does not change the fact that I can still and will beat your ass!" he joked as he rubbed his knuckles on the top of my head and then started playfully slapping my face. Kaidan had me laughing so hard that it took a moment to get out of his grip. I finally got myself angled enough to give him a good elbow to the gut. Once I sat back up, I laughed at him as I flattened the hair he just messed up.

"I have missed you, Kai." I smiled and reached down to grab hold of his hand.

"I have missed you too, and I am proud of you, Lieutenant." He took my hand and then kissed it.

Later that night I woke up suddenly with my head pounding. It was so painful my ears were ringing, and I felt like I was about to throw up. When I sat up, it just got worse, and I pressed my palms to my head. All the men around my fire were sleeping, including Kaidan. As I scanned around the encampment trying to look at the other men's auras to see if anyone was awake, it just amplified the pain.

Looking behind me, I could see Dogan's massive form lying down so I forced myself up. I had to squint with my eyes as I made my way to him and continued holding my hands against my head. When I fell to my knees beside him, I lightly touched his shoulder.

Dogan jerked at my touch and had his dagger against my throat the instant I touched him. He looked at me with shock. "Good Lord, woman!" he said in a harsh whisper. "What the hell d'ye think ye'r doing?"

Closing my eyes, I whispered, "Make it stop, Dogan. Please make the pain stop!"

There was the feeling of him sitting up to face me, "Damn it! I was afraid this was gonna to happen. Ye ha' been using yer sight a lot the last several days. I started getting a headache myself before I went to sleep, but I found some tea that helped relieve it. Let me go and see if I can find some more."

"I did not have this when I went to sleep," I cried as I hunched over. "I just woke up with it!"

He laid a hand on my head. "Try to relax and dinna move. I'll be back as quick as I can."

I curled up on his bedroll while I waited for him, which felt like forever. His scent still lingered on the bedding, and I tried to concentrate on that, but it did not help. When he returned, he knelt down beside me and helped me sit up. "Drink all o' this." He handed me a cup. "It'll help." I did not smell it or care if it was hot. Once the liquid touched my lip, I let it flow down my throat and did not stop until the cup was empty.

Keeping my eyes shut, I placed the cup on the ground and grabbed hold of my head again. "How long till the pain stops?" I whispered.

"It's gonna to take a wee while," he whispered, and I let out a moan because I just want it to stop now. Never in my life have I experience a headache this intense. "Oh, bloody hell!" he said, sounding annoyed. "Get yer arse over here, lass!" Opening my eyes just enough to see him leaning his back against a tree, he was holding his hand out to me. Laying my hand in his, he roughly pulled me to him. There I was on my side lying between his legs with my head against his chest.

"What the hell do you think you are doing?" I mumbled and found myself not pushing away but burying my face into his chest, wishing for the pain to stop.

"We both need to rest, and there's no way I'd be able to sleep wit' ye lying there in pain. Wit' ye close to me, it'll reassure me that ye'r all right, so ye are just gonna to ha' to deal wit' this," he grumbled. For the time being, I would deal with him because his touch was comforting, and I was too tired and in too much pain to move. Maneuvering both of our cloaks, he managed to cover us equally. I realized that even if we did not have them, I would still be warm. The heat from his body was wrapping around me.

Some hours later, I woke up headache free. I did not open my eyes, only felt the touch around me. I was still in the same position I fell asleep in. My head slowly rose up and down with his breathing. It felt like he must have had his head resting on top of mine. His massive arms were around me even though I could not see them, yet I knew his hands were locked together to keep them there.

I found myself not wanting to move, I could stay like this forever. I knew if I did, he would probably turn into his old arrogant self again. Suddenly, there was a feeling like someone was staring. Since my eyes were already closed, I searched out my core and then was able to release my light so I could see.

There stood Kaidan with a crooked grin and his arms crossed against his chest. It was still dark out, and I finally whispered, "Good morning, Kai." Once I spoke, Dogan's breathing instantly changed, and I knew he was waking up.

Kaidan widened his grin. "That's right, I forgot! Our new lieutenant has these newfound powers of sight, even with her eyes closed," he teased and continued. "I do have to say, though, this is one sight I did not expect to see."

With his head still leaning against mine, Dogan's voice filled my head. *"If he doesn't shut the hell up right now...I'll make him!"*

"Easy, Dogan," I said back to him. When I brought back in my light, I opened my eyes and turned my head to the right a little so I could look at Kaidan. "Kai, I woke up sick with a headache last night. Dogan just helped me out."

Kaidan laughed at me. "I would say! You two do make a cute couple all cuddled up like that." I wanted to slap him and laugh at him at the same time.

"I'm warning ye once, Kimball," Dogan grumbled out as lifted his head. "If ye dinna shut the hell up, I'll make yer face look ten times worse than what I did last time."

Kaidan, the ass that he was, laughed at him and said, "I would like to see you try, *big boy!*"

I just had a split second, but I was able to grab Dogan's dagger off his belt as he tried to push me away so he could go after him. My eyebrows raised as I laid the flat of his blade against his cheek. "Do not move, Dogan!" I had my chest against his. "Kaidan is a good man who sometimes does not know when to shut up. If you go after him it will only anger Bryce. Do not make him regret making you lieutenant. Kaidan is not worth it!" If Dogan could kill me with his eyes, I would so be dead right now.

"Thanks a lot, Lee! What am I worth then?" Kaidan asked angrily.

Without removing my eyes off, Dogan I yelled, "Kai! Can you go please? You and I will talk in a moment."

Once he marched off, Dogan growled, "Ye better remove that goddamn blade from my face, or else."

"He's my friend...my brother! You're twice his size and did a good number on his face last time." When I placed his dagger back, he grabbed a hold of my face. Quickly, I grabbed his face too like he always grabbed mine. I might not have the strength like him, but I have nails that I can dig into the skin.

"I never want ye to do that to me again. D'ye understand me?" he asked, bringing my face closer to him.

As I dug my nails into his cheeks, I said, "If you promise me that you will never lay a hand on any of my friends, and you know who they are, then I promise to never do that again." Our faces were only a few inches apart, and then I noticed Dogan's eyes shift down to my lips. I got instant butterflies in my stomach. I wanted to experience it again...that amazing feeling. Before I knew it, our lips were a breath away from each other, and I do not know which one of us moved; maybe we both did. There were too many men around; we could not do this here, so I quickly said in my head, *"No, Dogan! We cannot do this here. I am sorry for pulling your dagger on you, now please let go of me."*

He instantly let me free, and as I stood up, I noticed the other men around the fire were up and staring at us. As I started to walk away, Dogan said quietly, "I promise." I stopped and looked back at him, and he added, "I promise not to lay a hand on any o' them."

"I promise to never do that to you again," I stated quickly then continued off in search of Kaidan.

Kaidan was talking to Bryce outside his carriage. "Good morning, Lieutenant," the king greeted with a smile.

Forcing a smile back, I said, "Good morning, Bryce. Can I speak to Kaidan for a moment?"

"Of course. I need to check on something anyway before we start going again," he said and then he walked away.

"Kaidan," I sighed. "I am sorry for earlier." I took his face so he would look at me.

"No, you were right. I do not know when to shut up sometimes. I will try to keep my mouth shut from now on," he groaned, looking disgusted with himself.

Smiling at him, I replied, "Please do not do that! That's what I love most about you. My brothers always treated me like you do, and it helps me miss them less with you around being an ass!" He laughed a little, and I continued, "You're worth a hell of a lot, and please never change."

He pulled me in a hug and murmured, "I am sorry though. I just could not help myself when I saw your small form leaning against that monster of a man. It was pretty comical looking." When I pinched him on the side, he said, "Are we good then?"

Looking at him and smiling, I said, "Yes, we are good."

Later that morning just before entering Morningstar, the men really slowed down and stared at the three Salvie soldiers hanging from the trees by the road.

"Are those the men you killed? Are those your arrows?" Kaidan asked.

"Yes," I whispered, not tearing my eyes off them. "Who do you think hung them up like that?"

"'Twas probably that large group of guards we passed before reaching the king," Dogan stated, who was to the left of me and was staring up too as we passed.

It took five whole days for us to reach the outskirts of the meeting point. We had to travel slowly because of the men that were on foot. In those five days, Dogan and I barely said two words to each other. It felt better to avoid each other, but at the same time, the man was always near. Whether we were riding or at camp in the evening, I always saw him close by and with his intense eyes locked on me.

There was fear inside of me of what might happen if we were too close to each other. After what happened the morning I pulled his dagger on him, I wanted to kiss him again. When it came to Dogan now, my feelings were really starting to mix. He still knows how to make my anger boil, but now, there was something new forming. I do not think it was love, but maybe lust. I do not have feelings for him like I did for Rowan. And there was the kicker...the word *did*.

Ever since my death a week ago, I have not thought of Rowan, not even once. I think after he left the last time, my heart was and still is trying not to hurt for him. I still love him, do not get me wrong; but something is changing in me, and I am still not sure if I like it.

We were just a few minutes' ride from the intersection, and there where guards everywhere. Trees were cut down on either side of the road to make room for everyone. Tents were pitched and small campfires littered the forest floor. There were assault ladders propped against trees. A battering ram and several catapults lined the side of the road. It made me cringe with thoughts of them using those things on our castle. After everything was said and done, it's going to take us a long time to repair after this.

When we finally reached the intersection, I looked up and down the road. It was an ocean of blue and gray for as far as the eye could see. There's tens of thousands of men, all ready to win back our kingdom. Men were cheering as we rode by because the king has finally arrived, and in a few days' time, they will be heading out for Burreck City.

Kaidan, who was riding beside me, asked, "How much longer until we reach Mira?"

Smiling, I reached over and patted his shoulder. "Not too much longer, brother." He took a deep breath while smiling. The man was nervous and anxious to see the woman he loved.

My heart jumped when I heard someone scream my name. As I turned to look behind, I caught sight of Rowan pushing men out of his way as he tried to get to me. With the sunlight, the highlights of red in his hair were shining bright, and the beard was considerably thicker since the last time I saw him. Even though things were changing inside of me, it still did not change the fact that my heart still skipped at beat at the mere sight of him. I pulled back on the reins when he finally reached me. He moved my foot from the stirrup, grabbed hold of my saddle, and pulled himself up behind me.

Rowan squeezed my back tight to his chest. "Thank God you are all right. Sterling had to practically knock me out when he told us about the attack. I was worried sick!" I stared out straight ahead, afraid to look at him and start crying. *I know who it is now*, how was I going to tell him that? He took hold of my face and forced it to the side as he brought his head around and lightly pressed his lips to mine. His whole body tightened as he slowly pulled away from my lips. Rowan's beautiful blue-gray eyes were saddened. "You know," he slowly whispered, saying it in a statement and not in a question. I still could not speak, only kept my eyes locked to his as my vision started to blur. "Does Dogan know yet?" he whispered, and before I could nod yes, Dogan was beside us with his hand tight around his arm.

"Ye kent 'twas me the instant ye laid eyes on me in Hebridge!" Dogan growled as he pulled at Rowan's arm.

Rowan narrowed his eyes and spoke with a tight voice. "I knew it was you a good year before we actually met."

"Ye are a dead man, Lieutenant!" he said in a harsh whisper. "What's stopping me in not killing ye right now?"

"Well," I noticed him looking at the band on Dogan's arm, and he continued, "*Lieutenant,* I would have to say that's because of this woman right here." He yanked his arm from Dogan's grip and wrapped it around me. "Personally, I do not see why you are so pissed off. You should be pleased to be destined to a woman as beautiful as her."

Dogan glared and then gave me a wicked grin. "In my lifetime I have had my fair share of more radiant women than her."

My jaw dropped, and as my body started to shake with anger, I asked, "Is that so? Like that whore with the fiery hair that you so fancy?"

His grin widened. "Exactly," he slowly pronounced the word. I could not take it anymore. I just wanted to kill him. I screamed in disgust and threw myself at him. Using Ara for momentum, I pushed off the side of her. When I collided with him, the two of us went over the other side of his horse, slamming hard to the ground. The horses reared up at the sudden commotion, but I did not care at that moment if I got trampled by them. All I cared about was inflicting pain on him.

Lying above him, I watched as he tried to regain the air that left his lungs. Not waiting a moment longer, I pushed up and slapped my right hand hard across his face. His jaw tightened, and he closed his eyes as a growl rumbled in his throat. My hand burned viciously in pain. Finally, he sneered with his angry eyes fixed on me. "Ye call that a slap? I know fer a fact ye can hit a hell o' lot harder than that!"

Gritting my teeth, I closed my hand in a tight fist, and as I lifted my arm up to punch him, I was instantly in the air and off him. Rowan had his arms tight around me, and I did everything I could to break free. As I tried elbowing him and swinging, he finally got hold of my arms and pinned them at my side, "Damn it, Row! Let go of me!"

"Get control of yourself, Lee! Or should I say Lieutenant by the band I just noticed? I have never seen you act this crazy before," Rowan yelled.

"Dogan here tends to draw out the crazy side of her," Kaidan stated casually, who was standing next to us, shaking his head.

"Let go o' 'er, Rowan," Dogan demanded as he stood up. "This is between me and 'er."

"I would have to say that this is more than just between the two of you," he said.

Dogan marched right up to us, and just before he reached us, Kaidan stepped between and laid a hand on his chest as I looked up at him. "Do not do this, Dogan, not here, not with the king in that carriage behind us."

He never acknowledged him and only easily glared at me from over Kaidan's head. "Ye ha' no room to be pissed at my comment to ye when 'twas a moment ago that yer lips were locked wit his," he retorted without beckoning to Rowan. My heart sank because he was right.

"First of all, I made her kiss me, and she never kissed me back." I felt his whole body freeze up behind me, and then he whispered in shock, "Oh my God…you never kissed me back." I fought back the tears that wanted to come as I stared back at Dogan.

As he pushed against Kaidan, he said, whispering angrily because we had an audience of men staring at us, "Just admit, it's 'im ye'll be happier wit'. Ye never want to be wit' a man like myself. Ye ken some o' my history…the men I ha' killed, the families I ha' hurt. Why'd ye ever want to be wit' a man wit' a history like that?" I did not answer him because that was not how I felt anymore. Yes, I know what he has done, but that was his past and a past that he regrets. He was not that same man. If he would have asked me that question over a week ago, I would have said, yes, I would be happier with Rowan. After my vision of my future, I realized that I would be happier with him. "What, are ye speechless now? Damn it, woman I just want to hear ye say it! Admit it!" he said in an angry whisper again. No! I wanted to say, it's you that will make me my happiest you stubborn ass, but I continued keeping my mouth shut.

Kaidan looked back at me in shock and then back to Dogan, "Oh my God! Are you two…"

"No!" the both of us yelled at him in unison.

"Wow, whatever the issue may be between the two of you, it needs to stop this instant. Bryce is going to wonder what the holdup is, so let's get going!" he ordered and took hold of Dogan's arm as he glared down at him. "Do not look at me like that, Lieutenant! I have a woman waiting to see me, and from what I hear, you have a little girl waiting too, so let's go!" He finally tore his eyes from me as he walked over and mounted his horse.

Rowan mounted Ara and held his hand down to me. "I want you to ride sitting sideways so I can look at you while we talk."

We spoke privately through our touch as we headed closer to the home of Donelle and Oren. I did not want the men to hear me since they already heard enough. I told him everything that had happened. He was devastated when he heard about my death, but I told him about my mother and how wonderful it felt in heaven. Rowan lightly traced the scar on my left temple as I talked. I even told him about the vision I received from her. He simply smiled and told me to keep a tight hold on that vision because someday, it would come to be.

"How am I ever going to love a man like that?" I asked, staring into his gorgeous eyes.

"By everything I just witnessed, I would say you are heading in that direction." he said, and I gave him a questioning look as he continued. *"You never responded to him when he wanted you to admit it was me you would rather be with, and when I kissed you...I received a kiss from a woman whose heart is slowly starting to change."*

"I do not want it to change," I cried in my head.

He touched my face. *"As much as it's killing me...this is how it's supposed to be. And God as my witness, I do not care how many cuts and bruises I will receive from that man. It's never going to stop me from doing this."* He brought his face to me and pressed his lips to mine. This time, I did kiss him back. When we broke apart I laid my head on his shoulder.

"He promised me that he would never lay a hand on you or any of my friends," I said.

Rowan started laughing. *"Sorry to break it to you, love, but Dogan and I will have a time when the two of us would like nothing but to kill each other."* He continued laughing when I jerked my head up and gave him a concerned look. *"Do not worry though, we will only beat each other to a bloody pulp and then come out as the best of friends. Have no concern because this is not going to happen for quite a while yet."*

"My feelings are all messed up now because of him," I trembled.

"Because you are fighting with the feelings that want to love him. By the anger he expressed earlier, I expect he's going through the same thing," he reported, and after a moment, he started lightly pouncing in laughter. Before I knew it, he was laughing so hard he had tears coming from his eyes.

The laughter made me smile at the sight of him. He was so damn handsome, and I asked, "What is so funny?"

As he rubbed the tears from his eyes, he said, "The vision of you throwing yourself at him and the both of you flying off that horse. That was the funniest damn thing I have ever seen. You should have seen the shock in his eyes!" As he threw his head back in laughter I thought back to that incident and could not stop the laughter that came up from my belly. It had to have been a sight to see. A woman like myself taking out a man that's three times my size. Before I knew it, I was laughing as hard as him and had to wipe the tears from my own eyes.

Chapter 34

The Cottage

hen we made it to Donelle's cottage, Kaidan and Dogan were already there with their arms wrapped around their loved ones. I pulled back on the reins a good thirty yards from the house. As I dismounted, Rowan jumped down beside me and said quietly as he looked over to Dogan and Cora, "That's the exact girl I envisioned you two with."

Looking back at him, I asked, "What did you envision? Can you tell me?"

He took my hand and gave me a soft smile. "It was before dawn, you and Cora were sleeping in the same bed together. He just arrived and I got a sense he was gone for a long time. He stood in the room watching you both lovingly, and he had a wiggly puppy in his hand. As he reached the bed, he placed the puppy onto it, and it pounced right to you both. The puppy first attacked your face with kisses until you swatted it away, and then it started kissing Cora as she woke up. Just as you were about to roll on you back, Dogan pounced on you. You screamed in excitement, but that was short-lived as he pressed his lips to your mouth. Without lifting himself off you he grabbed Cora and brought her to you both. The way you looked at him...in all the years we have known each other, you have never looked at me like that."

Still holding his hands, I bowed my head and whispered, "I am sorry you had to see that."

Rowan shook his head and lightly touched my face so I would look at him again. "Do not be because I am not. It does my heart good to know that you will be happy, and he truly does love you, or he will anyway."

"Lee!" Someone hollered, and I knew who it was before I looked around Rowan's shoulder to see Sterling galloping toward us. As soon as he was off his horse, he had me up in the air in a tight hug. "Oh, thank God!" he mumbled into my neck, causing me to laugh because it tickled. "As soon as I got word that you all arrived, I hurried as best as I could." He placed me back on my feet.

Reaching up, I touched his cheek that had dark stubble and gave him a light smile. "I had a vision, Sterling," I said to him softly. He needed to know.

He forced a smile. "So have I, love. Half of me is relieved it's not you, and the other half feels like I have lost you before I ever had you." I knew what he meant by that because we were both convinced it was us who were meant to be together.

Laying a hand over his heart, I said, "You will always have me, but just as friends, like it always has been."

While looking down at my arm, he moved the cloak out of the way and touched the lieutenant insignia. When he looked back at me, he asked, "What have you been through to be honored such a high rank?"

Rowan slapped his brother on the shoulders. "That, my brother, is a long story, and I will tell you all of it later because right now, there seems to be a little girl who wants to see her."

When I turned around, I watched as Cora wiggled her way out of Dogan's grip. "That's her," Sterling stated behind me.

Cora ran to me as fast as her legs allowed her to, and I prayed that the skirt of her dress would not trip her. Her long chestnut locks blew behind her, and I fell down to my knees as she reached me. With her arms tight around my neck, I felt her tiny body shake as she cried. Squeezing her tighter, I said, "Shhh, easy, darling. Why are you crying?"

She pulled back to look at me with her eyes full of tears. "I have missed you, Lee."

Pressing my forehead to hers, I said, "Oh, sweetie, I have missed you too." I took her face and gave her a loud kiss on the lips, hoping to make her laugh, and it did. As I wiped the tears from her cheeks, I caught her looking behind me, and she smiled. Standing up with her still tight against my chest, I turned around to face my men.

"Cora, I would like you to meet two of my best friends. Lieutenants…"

"Row and Sterling," Cora finished for me. As I looked at my men in shock, they both smiled hugely.

"How do you know our names?" Rowan asked.

"I have had lots of dreams about you two. And you are just like me, and we are going to be the best of friends too," she reported, all excited.

Sterling started laughing. "Is that so?"

She nodded and added as she pointed to him, "And you always like to play tricks on me!"

Sterling leaned forward with a grin ear to ear. "And do any of them ever work?"

She started laughing and shaking her head. "Nope because I am too smart!" She had the two of them roaring with laughter with her cuteness.

Sterling then said, "We will have to see about that because I have a lot of tricks up my sleeve."

Rowan finally added, "Cora, I can easily see us becoming the best of friends." He took her tiny hand and brought it up to his lips. I noticed a change in his eyes, but it only lasted a brief second. The gesture caused her to giggle as she buried her face in my neck in embarrassment.

As Rowan winked at me, I asked Cora through our touch, *"Do you know about me?"*

She lifted her head and gazed at me for a moment. *"You know now?"* she asked, and I nodded yes. *"I have known you as my mama ever since the beginning."*

My mouth dropped as the tears flooded my eyes. I thought back to the day when I first met her. This girl ran right to me and gave me a fierce hug. Then she pulled back, told me her name, and she looked at me like she already knew who I was. *"Why didn't you ever say anything to me?"*

She was crying again herself. *"Because Cici said it had to be our little secret. She said you had to change before you could ever know about me. You have changed! I can feel it! Can I call you Mama now?"*

When a whimper escaped my lips, I squeezed her in a hug again, and as my legs gave out, I fell to my knees. *"I have changed and I am never allowing you out of my sight again. Dogan…I mean Papa and I are not officially together yet. So for the time being, can you continue calling me Lee, and when we are finally made into a family, then you can call me Mama. There are only a few people that know about all of this, and I would rather keep it like that. Other people just would not understand."*

"That's fine because we will be a family," she said, looking back at me. *"I am good at keeping secrets. I will call you Lee, but when I touch you, can I call you Mama?"* I nodded, laughing and crying at the same time.

Rowan knelt down beside us. "Are you all right?"

I looked at him, smiling, as I wiped the tears from my cheeks, "Yes, Row. I am going to be all right." I smiled back at Cora. "Everything is going to be just fine." For the first time since I found out that it was Dogan, I felt at peace. I am not alone…I have her! After all these years of knowing her, she knew that someday I would be her mother.

Mira fell down to the ground beside us and kissed my cheek as she wrapped her arms around in a hug. When she pulled, back I said, "It's so good to see you."

"It's good to see you too," she murmured then she looked at Cora. Mira then looked behind her to Dogan, who was slowly making his way to us. She gave me a soft smile. "It's him."

I nodded. "There's a lot I need to talk to you about, but that can wait." Smiling back at Cora, I asked Mira, "Was she good?"

"Oh, she was a pleasure. She always picked up after herself," she said and then looked up to Dogan, who came up behind her. "She's a tough little thing. Cora handled herself quite well when it came to roughhousing with those two young boys." He had a proud look as Cora left me and went to him.

For the next four days, the men prepared for battle. Mira and I still had not had enough time by ourselves to talk. I figured after they left, we could talk. Bryce asked Donelle and her husband if they would mind us staying with them until it was safe for us to go home. Of course, Donelle and Oren were pleased to have all of us stay there.

In the evenings, Rosa stayed with Bryce in their carriage and Mira slept somewhere in the woods with Kaidan. Cora and I slept together in one of the boys' beds at the cottage. Dogan never talked to me. Whenever he showed up, it was to see Cora only. I found him not even glancing at me. Rowan and Sterling, on the other hand, were over to see me at different times each day. I still had them at least.

On the morning of our men's departure Bryce, Kaidan, and Dogan came to the cottage to say their good-byes. As Dogan was talking to Cora, I looked out to the guards in the road. When I spotted Sterling and Rowan, I smiled and laid a hand over my heart. The two of them instantly took their fists to their chests. They both said their own good-byes to Cora and I last night. They had hoped if they were not there when Dogan was saying good-bye to Cora that he would actually talk to me.

After hugging Kaidan, Bryce came beside us. The breastplate of his armor made his chest look broader, more powerful. "Keep a good eye on her, Lieutenant. Make sure my wife does not do anything too strenuous. The baby will be coming soon, and I do not want any harm brought to either of them."

"I promise, Bryce. I will not let any harm come upon her," I said to him with confidence.

"I know you will protect her," he murmured, and after giving me a hug, he walked back to his wife to kiss her one last time.

As Dogan mounted his horse, I walked over to him. The chain-mail he wore over his head stretched down his neck and connected to the hauberk. That and the rest of the silver armor made him seem unstoppable. A warrior of sorts. He was holding a burgonet in his left hand, which was an open-faced helm.

Looking up at him, I laid my hand on his leg, "Dogan," I whispered but stopped as he started to reach down.

As he lightly slapped my face with a little more force than I appreciated, he murmured, "Dinna worry, woman. Ye canna get rid o' me this easily."

My mouth dropped in disgust and murmured back harshly, "You have not talked to me in three days and now you are about to leave for battle and that's all you have to say to me?"

The man just gave a smirk as he placed his helm on and pulled the reins to the left so the horse would turn around. I wanted to yell at him. Ask him why he had to be the way he was. I know there was a soft side somewhere in that massive body, but how much fighting and searching do I have to do before I find it?

As I watched him start to ride away, he stopped and gazed back at me. It felt like forever that his intense gaze was locked on to mine, and then he hollered, "I want ye to hold on to something for me. Make sure ye dinna lose it because I'm gonna want it back." After he said that, he tossed something over his shoulder. It arched up in the air and came down straight to me.

Cupping my hands as it came down, I caught it before me. I looked down in wonder at the small oval stone in my hand. Why the hell does he have a stone on him, and why would he want it back? As I started moving it around and rubbing my thumb on the smooth surface, it finally hit me. I have seen this exact stone before. Quickly, I looked up. Dogan was already beside my two other men and was moving down the road toward Burreck City.

As I stared out in disbelief. Mira came beside me and wrapped an arm around my waist. With her chin resting on my shoulder, she looked down at the object in my hand, "Why is that man carrying around a rock?"

I gazed back down at it and rubbed it against my hand, "It's a small cobblestone. The same exact one I chucked at his head so many months ago." I was in shock, and I did not think I could ever believe it. He's had this the whole time? Did he carry it with him when we went to Mastingham together?

Mira whispered in my ear, "Well, it looks like this man cares for you more than you ever imagined." I looked at her with wide eyes, and she lightly laughed. "Now that all the men are leaving, I think it's time you and I talked."

A large gust of cold fall air swept through, causing me to close my cloak in front of me. Donelle said behind us, "Your Highness... Cora, you two should come in out of the cold." As Rosa walked back toward the door, lightly crying, Cora stopped and looked back at me.

"Are you coming?" she asked.

"I will be in in a moment," I told her, and Donelle smiled at me as she laid her hand on Cora's shoulder and guided her in.

Mira took hold of my hand, and we walked over to the bench that was beside the front door. With my hand still holding hers, I looked out ahead and watched the guards slowly pass and continued to rub Dogan's stone in my other hand. It was still warm from his body. "So I take it my friend is going through an extreme mix of emotions that she does not know how to handle."

I lightly smiled and muttered without looking at her, "I guess so."

"Kaidan told me about how you died and that you said that you saw your mother. He told me that you did not remember much of it, only that you saw her. Now since I know a lot more about all of this than him, I would say that was a lie." I looked at her then because she knows me all too well, and she continued, "Please tell me what you did not tell him."

Keeping my voice down, I told her everything I saw and what my mother had told me. I also told her how Dogan was before and after I died and then I ended by telling her about the intense kiss we shared in Morningstar.

"I know you are afraid and not sure if you could ever love him because he's the exact opposite of Rowan. But I think that's the exact reason you will fall deeply and unconditionally for him." As I stared at her, she continued, "I know how the man treats you, but I think that's all going to change soon. I have seen him out and about in the city the last several months. Any Altecian woman would melt in the arms of a man like him."

"Mira," I quietly screeched.

She laughed, "I am serious. We just do not grow men like him here. I have seen how he acts around other women, like at the markets. All he has to do is smile, and when he does, his whole face lights up, revealing those beautiful dimples. One night I was at the pub with Kaidan having dinner, and he was there. Several different women went to him to see if he would dance with them. Surprisingly, he accepted and danced for most of the night. He had the women laughing and blushing the whole time."

"Why are you telling me this?" I asked, finding myself getting a little jealous because that's the side I rarely saw.

"Because somewhere within him is a tender and charming side. A side that he hides from you for some reason. I think now that you two know that you are soul mates and now you have Cora, you will find him starting to change. Like your mother said, 'Everything is going to happen like it's supposed too.' Both of you are the same... you are both bullheaded!" As I laughed, she added, "Live your life, Lee, and before you know it, you will find each other locked in an embrace that neither of you will ever want to let go of."

"Thank you, Mira. I have needed you since the morning I woke up from my death." I wrapped my arms around her in a hug.

"I am sorry I was not there for you then, but I am here now. I always will be," she murmured as she squeezed me back.

It's been a week now since our men left for Burreck City and still no word. I found myself getting a little anxious not knowing what was going on. What if we could not gain control again? What would happen to all of us then?

I was sitting with Rosa in the living room reading while she was crocheting something for her unborn son. Mira walked in from the hall, and she had a look of concern on her face, so I asked, "Mira, is everything all right?"

"Something is wrong with Cora." I quickly stood up, and she said. "She's crying and I cannot touch her."

I practically ran past her and down the hall. Cora was lying on one of the boys' beds in the shape of a ball with her deep-red light expanded out from her body. As I went to her, I entered the light and sat beside her on the bed. When I touched her, she opened her eyes, but kept her light expanded out.

"How can you touch me?" she quietly cried.

"Because you and I are the same. Why are you crying?" I asked softly as I moved the stray brown locks from her face.

She clamped her eyes shut as she buried her face into the pillow. *"I am scared that Papa is going to go be with the angels like Nana,"* she cried through our touch.

"Oh, Cora," I said out loud and lay beside her and brought her to my chest. "Your Papa is a strong warrior, and have you forgotten that he is like us? His light will protect him, and before you know it, he's going to be here to see you again."

"You promise?" she asked, sniffling as she looked back at me.

Deep in my heart, I knew we were not going to lose him, so I replied, "I promise." She smiled as she rubbed her little fists against her eyes, and when she reopened them she continued to have her aura stretched out before her. "How do you do that?" I asked in amazement, "How do you release your light from your body with your eyes open?"

"It's easy," she chimed and continued staring at me as she brought it back in and then pushed it back out again. "You cannot do it?"

Shaking my head, I said, "No, I can only do it with my eyes closed. If I try with my eyes open, I feel like my eyes are going to pop out." I quickly widen my eyes big, and she started giggling.

"Your eyes cannot pop out," she laughed and then sat up. "I can help you."

As I sat up, I crossed my legs in front of me while I faced her. "How can you help me?"

She laid her tiny hand in between my breasts. "Let's pretend that I am pulling it out."

Smiling, I said, "All right." As I looked down at her hand, I could feel my energy in my chest. I could feel it trying to break free, but I was afraid to push it out. My eyes locked on to her hand and concentrated as she slowly started to pull away. I stared down in amazement as it looked like she really had a hold of it. Before I knew it, I was staring at her in shock as my light stretched out before us.

"See, your eyes did not pop out!" She smiled.

Laughter exploded at the top of my lungs as I could see all over the room without turning my head. Quickly, I pulled her into my arms and squeezed her, "Thank you, Cora! I cannot believe I have actually done it." I found myself thinking of Dogan and how proud he's going to be when he finds out what I have been able to do.

For the next two weeks, the three of us did whatever we could to help the time pass by. I even found myself going out and helping Oren split wood. He protested at first then finally gave up when he realized that I was not taking no for an answer. I needed to do some kind of hard physical labor. It felt wonderful to swing that ax and feel the pressure as it went through the log.

All four of us slept in the boys' room. Cora slept with Rosa since she needed more room, and Mira and I shared the other small bed. Every night, I held Dogan's stone close to my chest and said a prayer of protection over our men. Donelle tried to give up her bed for all of us, but the queen would not hear of it. One morning, the four of us woke up early; it was before dawn. It was like none of us could sleep, like it was the day we could finally go home. We still had not heard any word yet even though it had been over three weeks, and we were getting really anxious.

As the four of us were up and preparing breakfast, Donelle emerged from the hallway with sleepy eyes. The smile she beamed at us was not so sleepy looking. "The king is coming and should be here before midday. We won back the castle, and the Salvatorians have retreated!" We all cheered in excitement and formed a group hug. Maybe that's why we could not sleep because somehow, we all sensed he was coming.

Once we had all our personal items together in the living room, it was still early morning. I needed to do something to help pass the time or I would go insane waiting. I called Cora over to me, "Have you ever ridden a horse by yourself?" When she shook her head no I said, "I need to saddle up Ara. If you want, I can show you how to do that and teach you how to ride while we wait for them to get here."

She did not say anything and only smiled hugely as she ran and retrieved her cloak that Donelle had given her. When we went outside to head over to the small barn I noticed it was the coldest morning so far. As I looked up to the gray sky, it felt like it could snow.

Inside the barn, I explained everything to Cora about how the bridle works and how to put on a saddle. She watched attentively, never allowing her eyes to stray away. Once we walked her outside, I guided her toward the house. Laying my hand on Ara's face I commanded, "Sios." She instantly bent her legs and went down to the ground.

"Sios?" Cora asked.

"Yes, it's the Salvie word for *down*. All the commands Ara knows are in the Salvatorian language."

"You know how to speak it?" she asked in amazement.

"I sure can. It's Papa's native tongue too. You will learn it because we will teach you." I smiled a little when I said the word *we*. It came out so smoothly.

As she laid a hand on Ara's side she asked, "Do all horses do this?"

I lifted her up and placed her on the saddle. "No, Ara is very special and the only one that I know of that can do it."

"If I ever get my own horse, I want one like Ara," she said, smiling as she reached for her tan mane. Placing my foot in the stirrup, I swung up my other leg and sat behind her in the saddle. As I ordered her to stand, Cora grabbed hold of my hands as we started to move up.

Ara slowly walked around the front yard. Holding the reins in my right hand out in front of her, I explained the proper way of using them. After watching me for a while, how to turn right to left and how to stop, I handed her the reins. She gave me a nervous smile. Ara was excellent. Even though Cora only tugged the reins lightly to the left and right, Ara still turned. Cora got giddy with excitement.

As I sat there behind her and let her maneuver Ara around the yard, it started to lightly snow. Cora whipped her head around. "It's snowing!" she screeched as her face was completely lit up. I laughed as I stretched my arms out and watched as the tiny flakes landed on my dark-blue cloak. They melted instantly. When Cora did the same as me, she let go of the reins. The two separate straps fell across Ara's massive neck and went to the ground.

"Uh-oh," Cora whispered as she gave a small smile, and I just laughed at her as I jumped down. Taking the reins, I whipped them both up across either side of her neck. As I handed them back up to her, I froze when I first heard the noise.

As I gestured Cora to be quiet, the sound grew louder. I started to smile as I pulled her off the saddle. The sound was familiar to me because I was raised around it…the sounds of horses running. I ran to the house, yelling, "Rosa! He's coming! I can hear them!"

As Rosa burst from the doorway, the riders emerged from the road. Bryce and Dogan were in front with three other guards behind. The men came to a sliding stop and jumped off their horses. As Bryce ran to Rosa, Dogan slowly came to us. He was smiling at Cora, who was in my arms, and for a brief moment, his eyes locked on to me, and the smile never faded. When he stood before us, Cora stretched her arms out to him, and he scooped her up.

My heart was pounding at the sight of him. I was nervous for some reason, and I hated that. The two of them spoke privately, and then he gave her a questioning look. He quickly gave me the same look and said, "She said that ye learned something new?" While smiling at them, I pushed out my aura, and Dogan's dimpled smile came to view. "How did ye finally learn to do it?"

"I had a wee lass help me out." I grinned, and he gazed at his daughter.

"Ye helped 'er?" he asked, and she nodded her head, smiling ear to ear. As I brought back in my light, I reach into my pocket for his stone, which had been on me every day since he left. Taking his left hand, I placed the stone in his palm and closed his fingers over it.

With my hands still holding on to his, I said, "I cannot believe you have been carrying this around the whole time."

His smile softened. "It not every day a woman throws a stone at me wit' full intentions o' hitting me in the head." I shifted my eyes downward as I started to laugh.

"Lee?" Mira asked quietly as she touched my shoulder. Instantly, my heart sank, and I quickly looked at the other men. Kaidan was not with them. I was so wrapped up in seeing Dogan and how he was with Cora that I did not even notice.

"Where's Kaidan?" I asked in panic to Dogan. His face came instantly somber, and I looked over to Bryce and asked the same question, "Where's Kaidan?" I yelled. As Bryce walked over to us, his face was also somber, and I grabbed hold of Mira as a light whimper slipped from her lips. Oh, God, please…do not tell me he is dead!

"He was severely wounded and lost an extreme amount of blood." As Mira and I both let out a cry in shock, he held up his hand. "He is still alive though. He's been in and out of consciousness for the last couple of days."

Mira became hysterical and ran over to Ara and pulled at her reins, trying to get her to bow down. I quickly looked back at the king; he nodded. "Go and take her to him. That's why I brought extra guards so you could leave ahead of us. We will be fine."

"Thank you," I said and as I turned to go to Ara, Dogan was lifting Mira up and placing her behind my saddle. When I ran to them, he turned around and weaved his hands together. Placing my foot in his hands, he boosted me up into my saddle. The two of us just gazed at each other for a moment as his tingling hand squeezed my leg, and then I kicked and yanked Ara's reins to the right.

I leaned forward as I made Ara run at her top speed. Mira held tight around my waist and had her face pressed into my back. I could feel her crying, and my heart broke for her. It's times like this that I wished I could magically appear to the place I wanted to go.

Chapter 35

The Return

After an hour in the run to Burreck City, it started to snow harder and was actually starting to stick to the ground. Without any gloves, my hands started to get numb from the cold. I realized then that I left all my weapons at Donelle's, except for my knives that were on me. I did not worry about it though because I knew Dogan would see them in the living room, and he would grab them.

It was late afternoon by the time we reached the city. As the city came to view, I had to pull back the reins as I examined the sight before me. "Holy mother of God," Mira whispered behind me. It seemed like half of the buildings were gone and still smoking. From my spot at the edge of the city, I could tell the castle wall was badly damaged. I could not imagine how bad it was going to look close up. "Our beautiful city! Half of it is gone," Mira lightly cried as it was true. If I know Bryce as well as I thought I did, he's going to rebuild, and the city would be bigger and better.

I gave Ara a kick so we could enter the city. We took it slow, weaving out of men's way. It was filthy and had a smell of death and smoke. My eyes scanned for anyone I knew, but the men I saw were covered in soot and were unrecognizable to me. I was afraid of what the death toll was going to be. How many men did we lose? How many innocents? We passed wagons that were filled with dead bodies piled on top of each other. The smell was revolting.

After a half hour of making our slow passage through the city, our hearts sank when we reached the castle. The walls' gate was completely destroyed and the wall left of it was demolished. As Ara walked up the steps to enter the courtyard of the castle, I heard both of our names being called. When I caught sight of Rowan, I sped my horse up. At the center of the courtyard, I pulled Ara to a stop.

He helped Mira off my horse, and she clung to him as the sobs came out. After I dismounted, I stood next to them and rubbed her back. Rowan took hold of me with his right arm and brought me to him so he could hug us both. "Please take me to him," Mira mumbled into his shoulder. As he looked at me with his saddened eyes, he wrapped his arm around her shoulders and guided her toward the medical ward's door. I followed in step behind them.

The medical ward's corridor always gave me an eerie feeling, but at that moment, the feeling was heightened. Cries and moans of pain came from men as we passed closed doors. The sounds sent chills down my spine. The smells of death and blood mixed with a musty scent. It was starting to make me nauseous.

Rowan finally came to a stop at a door and looked at both of us as he laid his hand on the handle. "Were you told of what happened to him?" We did not speak only shook our heads no. "All right, it's going to be a shock for you both, and he's extremely pale." He pushed down on the latch and then slowly pushed the door open.

Mira went into the small room first and instantly collapsed to her knees at the side of his bed. There was a single candle to light the room. He was as white as Ara's coat, and as I made it closer to him, I saw what brought Mira to her knees. After holding back the tears this whole time, they finally flowed out at the sight before me.

Kaidan's left arm was missing from the elbow down. It was bandaged up, but there was still blood trying to leak through. Slowly, I knelt down trembling beside her and laid a hand on my brother's chest as I bowed my head and prayed.

Dear Heavenly Father...please do not take Kaidan from us. He is too young and should be able to live a long life here. Please...please give him strength to pull through this...Amen.

Crying myself, I turned to Mira, wrapping my arms around her and then pressed my lips hard against her cheek. "Pray, Mira! Pray hard! Kaidan is strong, he can pull through this...I just know it." When she folded her hands and bowed her head, I looked up at Rowan. Reaching my hand up to him, he pulled me up to my feet and into his arms.

As he squeezed me, he pressed his lips against my neck. He pulled back then to look at me. "You are right. Kaidan is strong, and he will make it through this." He paused. "I need to get back out there. Once I see Sterling, I will let him know you are here because he's going to want to see you." Rowan placed his fingers on my chin and lifted my face up. He leaned in and pressed his lips against mine. "I will talk to you later," he whispered and left the room.

The two of us stayed with him for hours. He never woke up in that time. Aides came in at different times to check on him. They changed his bandage once, and I had to look away. The sight put a knot in my stomach. I could not imagine the pain he went through when it happened, and I thought of the blade that pierced my back and went through my stomach. Never mind, I did know the pain he must have endured. I sat in the only chair in the room beside his bed. My knees were up to my chest, and I rested my head on them as I continued to keep my eyes on him. Mira was lying on the opposite side of him with her back against the stone wall. She lightly touched his face as she continued to whisper things in his ear.

When I heard the door opening, I lifted my head and gave my friend a small smile. Sterling walked in with a tray in hand and spoke softly, "Have either of you left since you got here?"

"No, why?" I asked.

He placed the tray on the stand beside me. "I did not think so. I brought some food for us."

"I am not hungry," Mira said to him.

"You need to eat something, Mira. Kaidan will not be pleased when he wakes up to find out that you would not eat," he insisted.

She sat up, keeping her back against the wall and placed her legs over Kaidan's. Sterling handed her a bowl of stew and a biscuit. Since he was in front of me passing the food to her, I got a good look at the insignia on his arm. "Sterling?" I whispered and looked up at him with wide eyes as he stood before me. "Why are you wearing the general's mark?"

Sterling sighed and knelt down before me. "General Wolfe was part of the group of men that were hung after we escaped," he said quietly.

Staring at him in disbelief, I asked, "And Captain Coster?" The captain was second in command, and if anything ever happened to the general, they would automatically be promoted to that position.

"He too was hung," he said with his face full of anguish.

I looked away in shame because we escaped without trying to help anyone else that was in the cells after us. "We should have freed them before we escaped," I whispered.

As he stood up, he quickly grabbed my face and made me look up at him, "We cannot blame ourselves for their deaths. I was pissed off at myself at first because I was thinking the same thing. A few days ago, I meditated and asked for Arabella to come to me, and when she did, she brought the general with her."

I was shocked. "She did? What did he say?"

"That he was proud of how we escaped and rescued the queen. He said if we tried to save everyone, then the rescue would not have been as successful. So what we did was right, and we cannot think about the what-ifs. Do you understand me, Lieutenant? Do not be upset thinking what we did was selfish, it was right."

When I nodded and fought back the tears, he let go of my face. As he handed me a bowl of stew, he grabbed the last for himself and leaned against the closed door.

"Do we have a count yet on the men we lost?" I asked and then took my first bite of the now-warm stew.

"We have lost well over three thousand guards. We expect the count of innocent civilians to be close or even higher," he explained, and I tried to swallow what food I had in my mouth.

"How are we going to come back from this?" I asked. This has left our city with a terrible scar…like the one over Dogan's right eye.

"We are going to rebuild. There are already men showing up from all over of the country that want to enlist in the royal guard. A lot of them are angry because they have lost family members, and they want revenge. We have tried to tell them that it's going to be a long time before we ever consider paying Alistair back for all of this, but most do not seem to care. They just want to be a part of the guard and help bring our city back," he stated and then took another bite of his dinner.

The three of us finished our stew in silence. When Mira was done, she handed me her bowl and went back to lying beside her love. I placed our bowls on the tray at the same time as Sterling. I looked up at him as he stood before me, and then he knelt down before me again. He took my hands while taking in a deep breath, like he was preparing himself. A knot began to form in my chest with fear and he said softly, "There is another reason I came down here… there's something I need to ask you."

I took a deep breath myself before responding, "All right, what is it?"

"I wanted to make sure it was all right with you and that you could handle it before I asked him. I would like to ask Rowan to be my captain. I understand all that you are going through at the moment, and if you think it will be too difficult for you to have Rowan living back in the city, then I will find someone else to ask." He rubbed his thumbs over the top of my hands.

Giving him a light smile, I removed my right hand and touched the rough stubble on his cheek. "How am I blessed to have such a wonderful friend?" He just gave me a crooked smile as he leaned into my hand, and I continued, "Of course you can ask him, and he would be great at the job. As much as it breaks my heart to admit, my feelings are already starting to change. Now that I know it's Dogan, those nights I have spent with Rowan are over. As for Dogan, I am not sure how he's going to feel about it."

"Do not worry about him. I can handle Dogan just fine. He is just going to have to deal with it because I believe this is just the first step toward our destinies," he said and looked over at Kaidan. Looking over myself, I was wishing he would wake so we could talk to him.

"When he wakes up and builds back his strength, do you think he will still be able to protect the king?" I asked.

"No, he is done as a royal guard," he whispered; when Mira started crying again, he continued as he reached over and touched her shoulder. "He will not be able to protect him anymore, but the king wants him to be one of his top advisors. Kaidan has learned a lot over years as he stood by our king. Everything is going to be all right." He looked back at me. "Everything is going to happen like it's supposed to."

A chill ran down the length of my spine when he spoke the words my mother said, "Why did you just say that?"

"Because what I am about to tell you might push you over the edge a little." He took hold of both of my hands again and squeezed. "I am only doing this so you do not hit me when you find out."

My heart started pounding, and he was making me nervous. "What's going on, Sterling?"

With a small smile, he whispered, "Bryce has named Dogan as his new personal guard."

My mouth dropped open for a moment, and then I snapped it shut. "Please tell me that you are jesting with me!" He lightly laughed at my expression and shook his head no. "Sterling!" I screeched. "Why him? Out of all his guards, why him?"

"He's got his reasons." He looked back at Kaidan. "When Kaidan got wounded, Dogan appeared out of nowhere and attended to him. He expressed his light to put a protective barrier around him and the king." He paused. "If it was not for Dogan, we *would* have lost Kaidan and Bryce."

There was proudness in me for his swift thinking and protecting them, but at the same time there was anxiety on having to see him every day. "No," I murmured. "It was already bad enough that we saw each other for an hour or two every few days for training. I do not know what will happen if we are in each other's presence every single day." Then I thought about how Sterling and Dogan stayed in the castle for that month and a half before the castle came under attack. We managed all right I guess.

"Like I said, everything is happening like it's supposed too." He stood up and pulled me off the chair. "Why not come with me. It's getting late, and I will walk you to your room."

I looked back at Mira and my brother, not ready to leave. Mira said, "I will be fine, Lee. Sterling is right, you cannot sleep in the chair all night." I went to her and leaned across Kaidan and kissed her cheek.

"I will be back in the morning then." I then pressed my lips lightly to Kaidan's warm damp brow. When I turned around, Sterling opened the door for me. He followed me out into the corridor and stuck out his elbow to me.

"Will you walk with me, Lieutenant?" he asked with his crooked smile.

"I would love to, *General.*" When I slipped my hand through his arm, I began to think about him being the head person of the royal guard, "General! I cannot believe it. Does this mean I have to listen to any order you give me?"

"Yes, it does." He smiled and then gave me a wink.

I laughed and held tighter to his arm as I thought of Dogan and Cora. "Did the Majesties make it back yet?"

"If that's your way of asking if Dogan and Cora arrived yet, then the answer in no." I elbowed him in the side, and he continued. "They will be taking a slow ride back because of the queen, but I expect them to be here soon."

When I looked at him, I found him smiling at me. God, the man was handsome; whoever was his soul mate was going to be a very lucky woman. After thinking that, I said, "So you never told me what your vision was. Did you get to see her?"

He took a deep breath with a content smile on his face. "She was beautiful, Lee. Her hair is the color of the sun with tight ringlets of curls."

"Did she look familiar to you?" I asked.

He shook his head. "No, she's not from our country."

"Really? How do you know that?"

"The woman is taller than me. I would say she's about Dogan's height."

I laughed. "I beg your pardon?"

He shook his own head laughing. "I am serious. She's not a Salvatorian because she is too elegant to be one of them. She was royalty though because she was wearing a crown…a princess maybe. I remember how the pearly skin of her face looked so soft, and as I reached up to touch her, your mother ended the dream. Oh, was I pissed at her!"

I laughed at his last comment and rubbed my hand up and down his arm. "I understand, she did the same thing to me." I pause. "Did she tell you how long it's going to be until you find each other."

"Well, I am going to be like Rowan. It's not going to happen for another twenty years at least. She told me once Rowan is united with his soul mate, then it will not be long before she arrives to the city."

"Holy hell, Sterling! You will be like…fifty-three years old," I said in shock, and he chuckled at the expression on my face. "I am sorry you have to wait that long."

"I think I will survive, and your mother has promised to keep giving me visions of her until then," he stated, and as we emerged into the main hall by the front doors, I looked in amazement at how spotless it was. The last time I was in here, there was blood all over the floor and walls, and bodies lay everywhere. At the looks of it now, you would have never known unless you were there. As we made it to the staircase, I noticed the fuchsia rug that ran all the way up the steps and down the corridors of the castle was gone. "I cannot believe how cleaned up it is in here."

"The king did not want any signs of blood when the queen returned. They had to tear up all the runners because it was stained even all the way up to your room and the royal living quarters. We will get that replaced in time." As we made our way up the stairs, he continued speaking to me, but through our touch, *"How are you handling this whole thing with Dogan?"*

I laughed. *"This whole thing is a mess. The man really drives me crazy and you know that. If he could only be a little bit more tender and less of an ass, we might be able to make this work."*

He laughed in my head. *"That's highly doubtful. I am still mad that I missed you tackling him off his horse. You know, men are still laughing about that. That's like the third incident now I have missed with you attacking him besides the time you tried to attack him in my room but I stopped you. Now I am wishing I never had."* He beamed me a beautiful smile. *"If I ever hear of another one that I missed, then you will have to deal with me."*

"Is that a threat, General?"

He brought his face close to mine and crinkled his nose. "Yes!"

Playfully, I hit him in the chest, and before I knew it we were standing before my door. Sterling opened it for me, and the aroma of lilacs filled my nose. It's been over a month since I smelt that scent. When I walked in, my room looked the way I left it. There was a fire burning, and I noticed a basin sitting by it with cloths beside it. Sterling came up behind me. "I found a servant and told her to make sure your room was ready for you and to set out some water with the scent of lilacs for you to wash up with."

I turned around and wrapped my arms around his waist. The whole gesture made me get a lump in my throat. "Thank you," I whispered as I looked at him.

He pressed his tingling lips to the scar on my left temple and said, "You're welcome. Try not to think too much tonight and sleep. Everything is going to happen as it's supposed to, all right?" When I nodded yes, he added, "Sweet dreams, Leelah. I am sure I will see you sometime tomorrow."

I said good night as he shut the door behind him. Once I undressed and washed up with the lovely lilac water, I slipped into a nightgown and crawled into my own bed. I moaned in pleasure as I burrowed myself in.

Sometime during the night, I was woken up by my door opening. Through my sleepy half-slit eyes, I noticed an enormous man walk in. I was not concerned because I knew that body anywhere. As Dogan placed my weapons I forgot on my desk, he came toward me. Now if I had been fully awake, my heart would probably be pounding; instead, it did not because I was still half asleep.

Since I was lying on my side facing in his direction, he laid his hand lightly on the right side of my face. The sensation from his warm touch made me close my eyes the rest of the way. It was soothing and was helping me to drift back into a deep sleep. Then I felt him lean down, and he whispered in my ear, "'Tis a real shame that ye'r not as peaceful and innocent as ye look right now."

With my eyes still closed, I mumbled, "Oh, go to hell, Dogan."

"Ah, never mind, ye are still a wench even in yer sleep," he teased with a light, laugh and I felt the corners of my mouth start to curve up.

My eyes were still closed when I heard him open the door, "Woman?" he asked quietly.

"Hmm," I managed to get out and still did not open my eyes to look at him.

"I'm starting to think that I'll not like it in hell. If that meant leaving ye here alone…wit' Cora then no, I dinna want to go there." The man said it in such a low whisper that I was not sure if I heard him right. When I heard the latch of the door as it closed, my eyes sprung open. Instantly, I sat up looking at the door.

Did I just dream that or did that really just happen? His clove spiced scent still lingered in the room, and I looked over to my weapons on the desk. "Oh, bloody hell," I moaned and fell back onto my pillow. With visions of Dogan in my head, I quickly fell back to sleep.

Chapter 36

Dogan

A sigh slipped from my lips as I quietly closed the door behind me. I gazed down at the tiny person before me…m'daughter. She stood in the middle o' the corridor staring up at me wit' sleepy eyes. The slow ride back to the city was exhausting fer the both o' us.

"Come on, lassie," I whispered to 'er. "Let's get ye to bed."

Crossing the hall, I opened the door to 'er new room. The fire was already lit, and I walked over to the nightstand and lit the oil lamp. When the new light filled the room, Cora cried, "My dolly!" She flew 'erself onto the bed and crawled over, snatching the doll off the pillow. "Where did you find it?" Cora gazed up wit' tear-filled eyes as she clung the doll close to 'er chest.

Swallowing the lump in my throat, I said, "I found yer dolly and some other toys at yer ole house." With directions from the king, Rowan and I went there a few days ago. We found 'er Nana Vi dead in the kitchen. Well, what was left o' 'er body anyway. It was definitely a wolf that got 'er, there was no denying that. The doll I placed on the bed was the one I found on the ground by the open back door o' the house. I had a strong feeling 'twas important to 'er and thought she might ha' dropped it when she ran away.

"Thank you," she whispered and kissed the doll as tears rolled down 'er round little cheeks. "Nana made me this dolly when I first came to live with her. It's my favorite."

I began to feel awkward because I ha' not been around many bairns in my life, and suddenly I wished Lee was here. She'd ken what to do. I was just about to turn to wake 'er up when coolness fell upon my cheek.

"Ye can do this, my son. Just go and console your daughter," said the voice o' my mother in my ear. I jerked my head to the left, but she wasna there. *"She doesn't bite. I promise."*

"Stay out o' my business, Mathair," I growled in my head. I ha' not talked 'er or Arabella since the attack on the castle. I was tired o' their head games. Why couldna they just said, oh, by the way, ye ken that woman who drives ye absolutely mad and is always on yer mind…well, aye she is yer soul mate. But no, they dinna, they just dragged it out and then had me watch in horror as she died in my arms. It's going to be a while before I can allow myself to forgive 'em fer that. I added, *"Don't ye dare speak to me again. When I'm ready to talk or even see ye, I'll call fer ye."*

When my mother dinna respond, I walked to the bed and pulled back the blankets. "Take yer shoes off, darling, and get under the covers." I thought about having 'er get into a nightgown, but I wasna sure if there was one in the clothes we brought back from 'er house. Lee can figure that out tomorrow; fer now, she'll just sleep in 'er dress.

As I sat on the bed and leaned back against the headboard, I laughed at the way she chucked 'er shoes off the bed. I was actually quite impressed at the velocity they flew at. When she got 'erself under the covers, I pulled the blankets over the both o' us as she curled tight to the right side o' my chest. Slowly, I laid my right arm down over 'er tiny form. My whole right side was tingling from 'er touch.

Cora was slightly sniffling from 'er tears. Still not sure what I should say or do, I began to lightly pat 'er wit my hand, "Dinna cry, m'sweet wee lassie. Everything is going to be all right," I whispered as I began to feel awkward again. Why was this lassie meant to be raised by me? I ha' no experience with children…the thought o' asking Lee fer help made me cringe. I ken though if I did, no matter how much she'd hate it, she would because she loved this lassie and wants the best fer 'er.

"You promise?" she asked with a slight whimper.

"Oh aye," I assured 'er. "I promise."

I sat there fer a while wit' 'er tight against me as I stared across at the fire. My mind wondered wit' thoughts o' the woman across the hall. She looked stunning when I went into 'er room earlier. I've seen 'er sleep countless times before, but there was something different in seeing 'er in a nightgown and in 'er own bed. She was absolutely breathtaking.

I literally began to shake the thoughts o' 'er out o' my head and then stopped at Cora's voice. "Papa?" I thought she was already sleeping.

"Aye?" I gazed down at 'er.

Cora opened 'er mouth wide in a yawn and then said wit 'er eyes closed, "When are you and Lee going to get married so we can be a family?"

My jaw dropped, and then I laughed sort of in shock to 'er question. "I dinna ha' an answer to that question yet, Cora."

"Do you love her?" she asked sleepily.

Bloody hell! How the hell was I supposed to answer that question? The same way I answered the last? This bairn was killing me. Do I love 'er? Lee has been in my thoughts practically every day fer the last few months. The damn woman even invades my dreams at night. I must say I hate that by the way. I ha' lost count on how many times I woke up sweating and finding myself hard because of 'er. Damn it! That wasna love…that was bloody lust!

"She loves you," Cora whispered so quietly that I wasna sure if I heard 'er correctly.

"Pardon?"

"Every night, Lee…Mama slept with your stone in her hand," she said and yawned again.

"Did she now?" Cora nodded 'er tiny head. "And how d'ye know she loves me because o' that?" I asked, curious to what she would say.

"Because if she did not, then she would not sleep with it," she stated. "Mama loves you, Papa. Just like how you love her...you two just do not know it yet."

Lightly laughing at 'er and shaking my head, I asked, "How old are ye?"

"Five," she mumbled.

Five. I continued shaking my head. If she's talking like this now at five years old, then what's she going to be like at ten or fifteen.

"I love you, Papa," she whispered.

Smiling, I leaned forward and kissed the top o' 'er head, "I love ye too, my wee lassie."

After sitting there for a good fifteen minutes in silence, I noticed 'er breathing slowed and kent that she was finally asleep. Cautiously, I slipped off the bed. Once I had the blankets tucked tight around 'er I stood there staring down at the sleeping bairn. I still dinna really know 'er yet, but I was already completely in love wit 'er. How's that even possible? Shaking my head in disbelief, I turned out the oil lamp and went fer the door.

Closing 'er door quietly behind me, I looked up and down the dim corridor. There was still one thing I had to do before I even considered sleeping. The clicking o' my boots echoed off the walls as I walked down the corridor. 'Twas gonna be a few days yet before they got new runners on the corridor floors.

As I descended the stairs toward the main entrance, I noticed the guards beginning to open one o' the doors, thinking that I was leaving.

"Dinna bother," I hollered down to 'em. "I'm heading over to the medical ward."

"All right, Lieutenant," the one man said, and they pushed the door shut again.

Keeping to myself, I just nodded to other men I passed as I made my way through the castle to the medical ward. 'Twas late, but the castle was still busy wit' men and women cleaning and trying their best to get the castle in order again. I could hear the cries and moans from the men inside before I even opened the bloody door. It sent an eerie chill down my spine and caused the memory o' the fighting earlier this week to flood back into my mind.

The visibility was horrible wit the smoke o' the burning buildings all around us. King Bryce ordered the catapults set and had debris flying through the air, some on fire hence the fiery building before us now. He didna care what got destroyed because everything could be rebuilt later. All he cared about was getting his kingdom back and the bloody Salvies the hell out o' his country.

I've killed two dozen men upon entering the city, and I kent everyone o' 'em by name. I'll admit that bothered me. 'Tis bad enough to kill a man, but to ken their name and face made it even worse. At one time, I called these men my brothers, and a majority o' 'em was good-hearted people. 'Twas their commander…their king who was the evil son o' bitch!

I caught glimpses o' Rowan and Sterling's red light through the haze. I've been trying my best to reach up to 'em. Somewhere up there, King Bryce and Kaidan Kimball were fighting, and I had this urgent feeling I needed to get up there by 'em.

King Alistair never fought alongside his men. He always stayed hidden and had other men do the dirty work. King Bryce was the exact opposite. He said that this was his country and he was damn well gonna fight fer it. I admired him fer that, and at the same time I thought he was a bloody imbecile. If he gets himself killed, what'll happen to the kingdom then?

The castle gates and wall finally started to appear before me through the haze. My heart stopped fer a moment at the sight ahead o' me. I screamed, "Kimball!" But I kent my voice was lost over the roar o' screaming men. I watched in horror as the sword came down on the small gap o' his armor and taking half o' Kaidan's arm in its wake.

My sword drove through the gut o' the man before me and pushed him to the ground as I took off in their direction. The king was covered in blood and was kneeling down beside his guard, his friend. My lungs hurt as my eyes burned from the smoke, but I could still see the man who was about to drive his sword in the back o' my new king.

Practically flying myself upon the king and Kimball, I laid my hands on 'em and expressed my light around us. The man who was about to make the killing blow flew backwards from the sudden barrier I formed around us.

Kaidan was on his back, and the screaming coming out o' 'im felt like a thousand knives piercing my skin. My hand was on his chest as I watched the blood pulsate out o' his half arm.

"Dogan!" the king yelled, and I jerked my attention to him. The spots o' blood were bright against his paled face.

"Grab hold o' my shoulder, and fer the love o' God don't let go," I yelled to him. "D'ye understands? Because if ye do, then ye'll be thrown outta the protective barrier I ha' formed."

The king nodded and grabbed hold o' my shoulder, and then I let go o' him so I could attend to Kaidan. Instantly, I pulled his helm off.

"Leave me, Dogan!" Kaidan screamed. "Get Bryce the hell out of here!"

I grabbed the armor plate on his shoulder and upper arm and screamed myself as I ripped it off o' him, "The only way I'm leaving is wit' ye wit' us!" I reached fer his belt and started to undo it as Kaidan grabbed my forearm wit' his only hand.

"Why?" he asked as tears ran down the side o' his face. The poor lad was shaking terribly. "I am going to die, Dogan. Don't waste your time with me!"

"Because o' Mira, that's why," I yelled at him. "And because o' Lee! Yer not gonna die, brother. I'm going to see to that!"

As I unbuckled his belt, I pulled it out from underneath o' 'im. When I pulled the sword's sheath off the belt, I watched as Kaidan's eyes rolled to the back o' his head, and his screaming in pain stopped.

"Damn it, Dogan," the king screamed. "Is he dead?"

I wrapped the belt around the end o' Kaidan's arm and pulled tight. As I worked to tie it off, I yelled, "Nay! He's most likely passed out from the pain." I looked to the king then. "I'm gonna stand up. Dinna let go o' me!" And he nodded.

Once on my feet, I bent over and took hold o' the dead weight o' Kaidan. The man was a good nine or ten inches shorter than me, but that dinna change the fact that he was a heavy bastard.

Wit' Kaidan over my shoulder, I looked around, realizing we were completely surrounded wit' Salvie soldiers trying to enter my light to reach us. I found myself not being able to move as they all pushed hard against my barrier. A smile formed on my lips as I watched two men wit' deep-red auras fighting their ways toward us.

It took several minutes, but Rowan and Sterling entered my protective barrier wit' bloodstained armor. My light stretched out in a ten-foot diameter. I tried to push it out farther to give us more room, but wit' the enemy surrounding us, I dinna ha' the strength alone.

"Damn it," Sterling yelled. "Is he dead?"

I adjusted the weight o' Kaidan on my shoulder, "Nay, but he's close. I did manage to stop the bleeding."

They nodded, and Rowan turned to the king, "We saw King Alistair retreating. We tried to get to him, but there were too many soldiers around him. It looks to be that we won, but we need to kill these bastards around us before attempting to get into the castle."

"The three o' us together might be able to wipe out all these men in one shot," I shouted to 'em.

"What about my men who are on the other side of these soldiers fighting?" Bryce asked.

"You are our king, Bryce," Sterling yelled. "You are the main factor here. If some of our men should die to protect you, then so be it."

"The king and Kaidan are connected to me, so when ye express yer light, it shouldna affect 'em," I explained to my brothers. "Lay yer hands upon me, and on the count o' three, push out yer light as hard and fast as ye can."

Nodding, they both laid their hands on my left shoulder where the king was holding on too. "One...two...three!" It was like an explosion o' red. Never in my life ha' I ever experienced anything like it. Men were catapulted into the air, landing killing blows as they slammed into stone walls or what was left o' buildings around us.

My brothers and I stared at one another wide-eyed before looking around. Between the three o' us, we made a dome o' deep-red light in a seventy-five-plus-feet diameter. I realized then that my mother was right, we were stronger together. If this was what we could do wit' three o' us, imagine what we could do wit six.

Standing in the narrow cool corridor o' the medical ward, I stared upon the closed door that concealed Sergeant Kaidan Kimball. Inhaling a deep breath, I knocked on the wood. Not getting a response, I slowly opened the door. The single candle on the stand flickered upon my entering. Kaidan lay motionless and alone on the bed. I was surprised at that. I figured Mira would ha' been in here wit 'im.

Sitting down on the only chair in the room, I reached out and laid my hand across his forehead. He was burning hot and sweating something terrible. Sighing, I folded my hands together, bent my head down, and said a short prayer fer his soul.

Reaching out, I took hold o' his right hand that was lying over his stomach. "Ye better pull through, ye bloody bastard! I went through hell carrying ye to safety and to find ye a doctor. So ye better come back to us and make all my effort worth my while. Can ye hear me? Damn it, move or something so I know ye are listening!" I yelled at 'im.

I'm not sure if 'twas just coincidence or if he truly did hear me, but his finger twitched along my palm. I liked to think that finger moved because he did hear me and that made me smile. Quickly, I let go o' his hand when the door opened behind me. Mira walked in, and 'er brows arched up at the sight o' me.

Jumping to my feet, I bowed before 'er. "Evening, m'lady. I was just leaving."

Mira smiled softly up at me and then looked down at Kaidan, "Please do not leave on my account, Dogan." She took the cloth from the basin on the stand and wringed out the water. As she started to rub his sweaty face wit' it she said, "I went outside for a bit to get some fresh air and to get away from the horrible distressing sounds in here. I saw Rowan while I was out there." She sat in the chair and looked up to me then. "He told me what you did. My love would be dead right now if it was not for you." She held up 'er hand to me.

Hesitating at first, I finally took it in my own. "Thank you." Tears rolled down 'er cheeks. Oh, bloody hell!

I rubbed my thumb across the top o' 'er hand. "No need to thank me, Mira. Just keep talking to 'im. I believe he can hear us. If he knows ye are here, it'll make 'im more determined to pull through." I bent down and pressed my lips lightly to 'er knuckles.

She blushed slightly while nodding 'er head. I released 'er hand and went fer the door. "Dogan?"

Wit' my hand on the latch, I looked back at 'er, "Aye?"

"Deep down I think I hoped it was you," she said.

"Pardon?" I narrowed my eyes at 'er.

Mira smiled genuinely. "Lee is my best friend, and I know her like the back of my hand. She's got the stubbornness and the quick temper to match yours."

I actually chuckled at 'er, "That, m'lady, may be the destruction o' us. I could see Lee and me always butting heads fer that reason."

The smile on 'er lips widen, "Right now…yes. But once you two have an understanding of each other, I believe you two will be a perfect match."

I lightly laughed, shaking my head. "We'll just see about that." I opened the door and bowed to 'er one last time. "Good night, Mira."

"Good night and thank you again," she whispered as I shut the door. Slowly I made my way back to my new room. I was not in a real hurry because I kent the woman sleeping in the room next to mine would haunt me in my dreams. Well, I hated 'er at that very moment, because I kent there was nothing I could do about it.

Chapter 37

The Arrival

J woke up the next morning lying in bed thinking about what Dogan said. I still do not know if I just dreamt it or if it really happened. Dragging myself out of my warm comfort, I searched out a clean pair of trousers and top. Once my knives were strapped around my thighs, I slipped on my boots and went over to my vanity so I could do something with my hair.

It was then that I noticed it. I never stood before my vanity last night, so I never saw it. Lying beside my brush was a note. The name engraved on top made my body go instantly cold. *Angel*, it read.

Shaking, I picked up the note and broke the waxed seal on the back. While holding my breath, I opened it; it read,

> I imagine you do not believe me when I tell you this, but I do truly love you. I promise someday I will find a way for us to be together.

Oh my God, he was in my room! Even though I knew he was not in here now, I still checked everywhere including under the bed and my wardrobe. Once I was convinced that I was alone, I looked back down at the note in my hand. It made me sick to know that Lars Kellen was in here at some point. Folding the note up, I stuffed it in my pocket and quickly brushed my hair up to a tail. When I walked out of my room, I turned left to head down to Kaidan before going to see Bryce and Rosa.

Briskly, I made my way down the medical ward's narrow corridors. Instead of knocking, I slowly opened the door; Mira was sitting in the chair beside him. She was in a different dress, so she must have left sometime during the night to change.

"How is he doing?" I asked her. She looked tired.

"He's been the same all night, except just recently, he started to mumble a little, and he's moving his head back and forth," she explained.

I took a seat at the edge of the small bed and laid a hand on his chest. As I looked to her, I asked, "How are you doing?"

"I am all right. I was up and down all night with all the moaning and cries down here, so I am just a little tired," she said, giving me a small smile and then reached over to touch Kaidan's pale face. The door suddenly burst open, making us both jump. Dogan filled the doorway, glaring as he was huffing out air; he was obviously running.

"Why can ye never be where ye'r supposed to be?" he growled.

Quickly, I stood up. "What's wrong?"

"She's gone into labor, and she needs ye!"

"Pardon?" I panicked. "It's too early, and she still has a month left at least!"

"Well, the baby doesna agree! Let's go!" The man was too fast for me. Before I knew it, I was up in the air and over his shoulder.

As he ran out the door, I screamed at him while punching his back, "Dogan Ramstien, put me down this instant! I have two feet that can perfectly run!"

"That may be, but that doesna change the fact that I'm still faster than ye," he said, and as he ran through the medical ward's corridors, I saw aides flatten themselves against the walls as we passed.

"I am not jesting with you! I am serious, Dogan. This is ridiculous!" I screamed and continued wiggling and punching him in the lower back.

"I'm not jesting wit' ye either," he yelled. "And quit hittin' me!"

As we stormed out of the ward, I looked down at his dagger on his hip. Biting down on my lip, I quickly wrapped my hand around the hilt of the blade. I hesitated then because I did promise not to pull his dagger on him again. Just as I was about to remove my hand from the hilt, a sharp pain came across my ass. I let go of the blade as I jerked my head up in shock. "You did not just do that!"

"If yer referring to the slap I just did to yer arse, then aye, I did. Dinna try to reach fer my dagger again!" he warned, and even though I could not see his face, I knew he had a smirk.

"You bastard!" I yelled and slapped him hard on the ass. "You have no right to touch me there!"

He started to laugh roughly due to the running and said privately by our touch, *"That's funny ye should say that because several weeks ago, ye didna seem to mind my hand against yer arse!"*

I felt the heat rise in my cheeks as I thought about the kiss we shared and how he scooped my up by my bottom so I would be up at his level. I yelled angrily, "That was different! You did not have me over your shoulder like a sack of grain!"

He laughed as he ran up the staircase, skipping four steps at a time. When we reached the top, I finally stopped fighting and pressed my elbows hard into his back as I rested my chin in my hands. My hair that was in a tail kept swinging forward and tickling my face.

Dogan said, "When was the last time ye bathed because ye kind o' smell."

My jaw dropped, and I quickly smelt the sleeves and the front of my shirt. All I could smell was lilacs. I was so mad that I hysterically started laughing. "I do not smell, you bastard! You can never have anything nice to say, can you?" He did not respond, but I got a sense of him smiling. *Oh God, why have you destined me with this man? Is this some kind of joke to you?*

As Dogan ran up the steps to the royal living quarters and through the open door, I watched Byron follow our wake as he tilted his head, smiling, and gave me a small wave. I just stuck my tongue out at him. I was glad to see him to know that he was still alive. When Dogan placed me back down on my feet, I quickly slapped both my hands against his chest. Then I had to grab hold of his shirt when the dizziness kicked in from being placed back on my feet so fast.

"Lee, are you all right?" Bryce asked beside me.

It took only a few seconds for the lightheadedness to stop, and then I glared back up at Dogan. "Do not ever do that to me again!"

"Which part?" he asked with a wicked grin.

"All of it," I growled at him and then jerked my head to Bryce. "Where is she?" I asked it a little too harshly than I should have, but I was still riled up from Dogan.

He pointed nervously at the door. "In our room." I suddenly heard Rosa scream, and I quickly knocked on the door. As I waited for the door to open I unstrapped my knives off my thighs. Wrapping the small belts around them, I tossed them to Dogan as the door opened a crack. Once the servant noticed it was me, she opened it wide enough for me to slip in.

There were several women in the room. The drapes on the windows were opened wide to allow the light of the morning to stream in. Even the dark-burgundy drapes on the canopy bed were removed. Rosa was on the bed, half sitting up. She was drenched in sweat and was wearing a long ivory nightgown that was pulled up past her knees. She locked her glaring eyes on me. "Lee, where the hell have you been?" she yelled, sounding angry.

Quickly, I kicked off my boots and said, "I am sorry! I was down checking on Kaidan." As I made it to the side of the bed, her eyes softened, and she grabbed my hand.

"I am sorry I snapped. You are here now, and that's all that matters." As she lay back down against the pillows, I sat on the bed beside her. "I never expected the pain to be this intense, and I cannot get comfortable." She hit the pillows. "I want to be sitting up a little more, but these damn pillows are not enough support."

"Can you sit and lean forward for a moment? I want to try something," I said to her and she sat up. Maneuvering myself on the bed, I sat directly behind her. Once I had all the pillows up against my back, I placed my hand on her shoulder and pulled her back against my chest. With my knees up on either side of her, she placed her hands on them. "How is that? Any better?"

She exhaled a huge puff of air. "This is much better. Thank you, Lee."

Her hair was still down and was sticking to the back of her neck. Without saying anything, I pulled the tie from my own hair and started pulling Rosa's light-strawberry curls up off her neck. I ended up tying it all up in a nest on top of her head. Once I was done, she leaned her head back on my right shoulder and smiled up at me, "Why am I so blessed to have you?"

I laughed at her. "I would not say blessed."

Her face suddenly tightened. "The pain is coming again." She leaned up a little off my chest as she dug her nails into my knees. She screamed like she did before I came into the room. With the screaming, it sounded like she was crying too. A servant tried to press a cool cloth against her forehead, and Rosa swatted her away.

Sticking my hand out to the woman, I ordered, "Give it to me." She quickly placed the damp cloth in my hand. As the pain started to subside, she slowly leaned back against me. Taking the cloth, I ran it around her face, neck, and chest. She did not speak, only breathed heavily. Another woman sat on her knees before Rosa, watching every time the pain started and she had to push.

I was in there with Rosa against me for over an hour, and she leaned forward as she started to push again. She was not making any noise, and I could see the side of her face was turning purple from holding her breath. "Breathe, Rosa…breathe!" I yelled at her, and she let out a loud cry as she collapsed against my chest.

My eyes widened when I heard screaming coming from a tiny voice. The woman took the baby up to her chest as another servant handed her a small blanket. The baby was covered in a substance that looked to be blood maybe, and I had to look away, afraid that I might get sick. After witnessing everything Rosa just went through and the baby coming out looking all slimy, it is definitely making me wonder if I ever want to have one myself. Rosa was the first woman I have ever been around during the whole pregnancy. I never knew giving birth was so intense and so painful. Another woman started massaging Rosa's stomach then to help pass the placenta, and of course, I had to look away again.

Still leaning all her weight into me, she held out her hand. "Please let me see him," she said, sounding exhausted. It took a few moments, but they got the baby cleaned up and wrapped in a fresh blanket.

"Here is your little prince, Your Majesty," the midwife said as she laid him in her arms, and the baby instantly stopped crying. The baby had a bright emerald aura around him just like his mother. I rested my chin on her left shoulder as I looked down at him. Tears started to roll out at the sight of him. His eyes were ocean blue as he gazed up at his mother. She was lightly crying as she touched his face.

Leaning my head against hers, I whispered, "He's beautiful, Rosa."

"I know," she cried out, smiling.

"Have you two picked out a name yet?" I asked her.

Rosa shook her head. "No we have not decided yet. I never even told Bryce that I knew we were having a boy."

"Would you like me to go get him?" She nodded and leaned forward so I could move away. Once I was off the bed, I propped the pillows back up as she scooted back to them. Leaning forward, I kissed the side of her face. "Congratulations, Mama."

She looked to me, laughing and crying. "Thank you, Lee, for everything."

I bowed to her and scooped up my boots as I walked to the door. When I opened it, I found Bryce and Dogan leaning against the wall across from me. As I shut the door behind me, Bryce came to me with a look of concern. "Is she all right? And the baby? I heard crying."

I smiled up to him. "They are both fine. Your beautiful wife is waiting patiently to introduce you to your precious little prince."

His whole face instantly lit up. "We have a boy?" He started laughing. "I have a son!" He quickly wrapped his arms around Dogan in a hug, which I could tell made him a little uncomfortable. Then just as quick, he had me up spinning in the air. "I have a son!" he yelled and placed me back on my feet. I have not seen him this excited since the day he found out they were having a baby. He quickly gave me a kiss on the lips, and then grinning ear to ear, he said to both of us, "You two are free to do what you like because I am not planning on leaving my wife's side today." We both bowed in understanding, and he quickly went into the room.

Still smiling myself, I looked at Dogan. If he was Kaidan I would be hugging him right now, but he's not. He too had a light smile on his face as I slipped on my boots. He handed me back my knives, and slowly, the two of us made our way down the corridor of the quarters. I figured since I had him alone I would ask him, "Did you see or hear of anything from Lars Kellen when you got to the city?"

"No, the weasel must ha' escaped wit Alistair." He looked to me. "Why?" I stuffed my hand in my pocket and grabbed the note I found this morning. Knowing he would be furious if I did not tell him about it, I handed it to him.

As he took it I said, "I found this on my vanity this morning."

"Who's Angel?" he asked, giving me an odd look.

"It's what Kellen used to call me," I mumbled and his face instantly got tight with anger. He stopped and opened the note.

The note crumbled into a ball in his hand. "Over my dead body," he growled and stuffed the ball in his pocket. As he marched ahead of me, I scurried up beside him again, and we walked out of the royal living quarters together.

While we were walking down the steps to the corridor, I asked, "Do you know where Cora is?"

"She should be in 'er room, which is directly across from ours," he explained, and my heart went in my throat, and I froze in the corridor at the word *ours*.

"I beg your pardon?" I forced out. Dogan stopped and gave me a puzzled look.

"She's just across the hall...why the hell are ye looking at me like that?" he asked in frustration.

"Why did you say," I muttered nervously. "Ours?"

After staring at me for a moment, his eyebrows slowly lifted, and his whole face lit up with laughter. "Bloody hell, lass!" He came to me, shaking his head. "Our *rooms!* I'm staying in Kaidan's old room now. Good Lord!" Still laughing, he shoved me forward so I would start walking again and then while beside me, he bent down so his lips were a breath away from my ear. "Just because we just found out we're soul mates doesna mean I'm about to consummate the relationship…not now at least." His hot breath sent a chill down the back of my neck.

I could not even look at him as heat rose in my face in embarrassment. I am such an idiot! I should have known he would be staying in Kaidan's room. As I stopped at Cora's door, Dogan slapped me in the back of the head as he continued down the corridor.

I glared at his back. "What the hell was that for?"

"That was for actually thinking ye and I were gonna share a room," he laughed over his shoulder.

Clenching my fists and wanting to kill him, I turned to the door, "Bloody fool," I mumbled to myself and knocked on the door.

"I heard that, woman," he yelled from down the hall. Of course, he did! I was rolling my eyes as a maid opened the door. Cora, who was sitting on the bed playing with a doll, lit up when she saw me. As she scurried to get off the bed, I knelt down by the doorway. She wrapped her arms tight around my neck.

"*Hello, Mama,*" she said through our touch, and I smiled.

"Cora, I have some exciting news," I said to her.

She pulled back so she could see me. "What is it?"

"Queen Rosa's baby was just born, and she had a little prince."

She started jumping around and clapping in excitement, "Can we go so I can see him?"

"Not today, but tomorrow you can, all right?" She nodded her head, but I could tell she was disappointed. "Have you eaten lunch yet?"

She shook her head no, and she looked down the corridor and smiled when she noticed who was walking away from us. "Can Papa come have lunch with us?" I wanted to say no, but instead, I nodded my head yes.

As she took off down the hall toward him, I stood up and spoke to the maid, "I will have her with me for the rest of the day, so if you have other things, you do not need to worry about her."

She bowed her head. "Thank you, my lady…I mean Lieutenant." I just smiled at her and then looked back down the corridor.